The Northeast Corner

The Northeast Corner

COLBY HALLORAN

FIFTH
AVENUE
PRESS

Fifth Avenue Press is a locally focused and publicly owned publishing imprint of the Ann Arbor District Library. It is dedicated to supporting the local writing community by promoting the production of original fiction, nonfiction, and poetry written for children, teens, and adults.

First Printing 2024

Layout and design: Amy Arendts, Ann Arbor District Library
Cover photo: Samuel Schneider
Editor: Emily Murphy, Ann Arbor District Library

ISBN: 978-1-956697-37-7 (Paperback); 978-1-956697-38-4 (Ebook)

Fifth Avenue Press
343 S Fifth Ave.
Ann Arbor, MI 48104

fifthavenue.press

For John who said, "Yes, you can."

Author's Note

I started writing about Ann Arbor twenty-five years ago while living in Brooklyn, New York. Writing about home (while away from home) was a distraction from writing about the sudden death in 1981 of my theatre partner in Tribeca. The Tribeca work was grim. The Ann Arbor fragments provided relief. I named these fragments so whimsically I often couldn't find them on my computer the next day.

Slowly, the Ann Arbor work gained weight. I started by describing when my family was cheerful and healthy at the dinner table. Eventually, I could describe how they struggled.

When I returned to Ann Arbor in 2006, I faced the real streets and the real houses. I visited Forest Hill Cemetery, scattering peanuts to lure squirrels to my parents' graves. I visited my sister in Ohio until she died in 2015.

About 95% of this book is based on events I know happened, and 5% is based on what could have happened. When I lost my nerve, I could hear my father saying, "Just tell it straight."

I have changed the names of a few people and streets, but not the names of my family.

"If you love them, they are yours to write about."

—Alice S. Morris, New York City (1903-1993)

Part I

––––––

1957–1963
1015 Ferdon Road, Ann Arbor

Rules and More Rules

Governments have rules. Schools have rules. Churches have rules. Families have rules.

The rules in my family are:

When the pocket doors to the living room are closed, it means the grown-ups are not to be disturbed. If you have an emergency, knock before you open the pocket doors. An emergency is not baked potatoes exploding in the oven. An emergency is Marky getting hit by a car or the pressure cooker lid flying off.

Two bites are required of every item on your plate. A bite is not one pea or one carrot; a bite is a forkful or a spoonful. If you must wash your bite down with a gulp of milk, reach slowly for your glass.

Do not play with the candles. Let the wax drip.

Do not play with your napkin ring.

Never take the food on your plate for granted. Somebody worked hard to grow the food, and somebody worked hard to pay for the food, and somebody worked hard to prepare the food. There is not an endless supply of food all over this world.

Do not give Marky scraps at the dinner table. Later, he can lick our plates, in the pantry.

If you must go to the lavatory during dinner, quietly excuse yourself. Nobody needs to know where you are going.

Sit up straight. At Mother's boarding school, there were nails in the back of the dining room chairs. Be grateful your chair does not have nails.

The hand not holding the fork stays in your lap.

When you've finished eating, put your knife and fork in the four o'clock position, and don't push your plate forward like a convict.

The student on the third floor pays rent; don't invade his privacy.

Don't interrupt.

Don't talk with your mouth full.

Don't ask too many questions.

If you have a story to tell, tell it briefly.

When an older person enters the room, stand up and shake their hand firmly when you are introduced. If their hand is shaking, do not giggle; they could have Parkinson's.

Writing a thank-you note is not sufficient. You must address the envelope, put a stamp on it, write your name and address on the back, and take it to the nearest mailbox.

Respect absolutely every single person on this earth.

Homework

"It's high time you joined in the grown-up dinner conversation," says Mother. "What with your sister gone to college and your father's new denture," she says, "I can't be the only one talking."

"But I haven't been spoken—"

"That rule was for children," she smiles, "and you crossed that line a long time ago."

"What line?"

"You're being literal again. Sam? What's wrong?"

My father has both thumbs in his mouth. He better not take out his new denture. When he did that last night, he looked a hundred years old.

"Shall I call Dr. Gilmore?"

No answer.

"Have a soft roll."

No answer.

"No to Dr. Gilmore or no to the rolls?"

"No to *both*," he says, stabbing lima beans until there are four on his fork. His new denture is not why he eats so fast. He eats fast because there wasn't enough food at the orphanage.

"Yes, darling?" Mother turns to me.

"Did Uncle Walter know Marie Curie?"

"Next time he comes for dinner, we'll ask him."

"He won't answer. He never answers."

Eyebrows up.

I continue, "When you ask him a question, he always says, 'You'd best consult my Goddaughter.'"

"Well, you *are* his Goddaughter, darling."

"How's Walter doing?" asks my father.

She's been to see Uncle Walter every day since he got home.

"Darling," she turns to me, "Can you please make sure I turned off the oven?"

Ever since the accident, she refuses to talk about Uncle Walter in front of me. I don't get it! I leave quietly.

"*. . . cleaned out her closet,*" says Mother, smiling at me when I return, as if I asked her to clean out my godmother's closet and she has finished her chore. Okay. So, she cleaned out Aunt Martha's closet, which explains that suitcase in the back seat.

The sorority girls across Washtenaw are singing. It's not pledge week, so something else must be going on. I don't want a roll. I want to hear how Uncle Walter is *now* that he's back home, not about the accident. I will throw up if I hear her tell one more person "Martha and Walter were in an automobile accident. Their taxi swerved to avoid hitting a mountain goat and went off the road. Aunt Martha and the driver died instantly. Uncle Walter climbed back up the mountain without a scratch. Oh my, and he'll be seventy in June."

"Darling?" she asks me, "Is your mind on higher things?"

"Where was their accident?"

"Greece."

Greece! I did not expect to hear that!

"So, Toots," my father asks me, "what's going on in science class?"

"We're studying weather patterns. This week—tornados."

"What's new about tornados?"

"Well, when a tornado comes, you proceed without delay to the southwest corner of your basement."

"Why the southwest corner?"

"If you live in the northern hemisphere, tornados come from the southwest. In Michigan, they peak in June. When you hear the siren, go immediately to the southwest corner of your basement and crouch down. When the tornado hits, you will just feel a thud. But if you're in the northeast corner, you could die from all the flying debris. If you're at school, where you go depends on what floor you're on. If your classroom is on the second or third floor, you go down to the first floor; if your class is on the first floor, you go out to the hallway and welcome the students coming from upstairs, kneel down and put your hands over your head in a cross position, and look at the linoleum and wait for further instructions. If you're outdoors, you lie down flat in a ditch or sunken area. Tornados form when four conditions are present."

"Which are—?"

"The time of year—mostly June, but also July and August. Sickly, dark, gray-green sky. Not a leaf moving. Sound of a train."

"Darling, Ann Arbor is surrounded by seven hills, off which a tornado will surely bounce."

"Mr. Leinbach's never heard of the seven hills."

"Mr. Leinbach, your teacher?"

"Yes! He doesn't see any hills on the map."

"Was he looking at a *contour* map?"

"When we drove out to visit Mrs. Wollner at the mental hospital, I did not see one hill. That road was flat. And last week driving to the egg lady—no hills there."

"Farmers need flat land to grow their crops."

"So where *are* the seven hills?"

"Not far."

"*Where!?*"

"In my fifty-four years as a resident of Ann Arbor, not *once* has a tornado touched down."

My father winks.

Mother puts her fork down and grips the edge of the table. "I wonder how your teachers tolerate you asking so many questions."

I try not to yell. "Scientists ask, 'Why?' That's who they are!"

"You are not a scientist."

"Not yet," says my father, wiggling his denture.

She's forgotten my birthday presents—the biography of Marie Curie and the Bausch & Lomb microscope. Marky whimpers. His paws are twitching.

"Just dreaming," says my father. "Chasing a rabbit."

"I couldn't get Marky to come down to the basement today," I say.

"What business does Marky have in the basement?" Mother asks.

"He needed to cool off. He was panting. I pulled him to the top of the basement stairs, but when I went down, he wouldn't follow me. I called, 'Marky come,' but he just stood at the top panting."

"Dogs don't like steep stairs," says my father.

"He goes up and down the front stairs."

"They're not as steep. And he can rest on the landing."

"But what about when a tornado . . ."

"You just told us what to do." Mother laughs. "We go to the southwest corner of the basement and say our prayers."

"But Marky won't go down to the basement!"

"All this tornado talk—you'll be up all night."

"We can't leave Marky *up here*."

"Sam?"

He yawns. His denture drops down. Marky rolls over. The circles under Mother's eyes just get darker.

"If a tornado comes, your father will *carry* Marky down to the basement."

She takes her plate and the meatloaf out to the kitchen.

"But what if there's a tornado *when Daddy's at work!?* What if a tornado comes at four o'clock? He doesn't get home from work until five-thirty!"

She calls from the kitchen. "Finish clearing, please."

"What if nobody's home?!"

I pick up his plate and my plate. Mother comes back with lemon pie.

"I beg your pardon?"

"What if Daddy's at work and you're at the Farmer's Market, and what if I'm at the park and Marky is here all alone? Tornados don't just come when all the family members are home. What if the tornado comes at one o'clock in the afternoon and Daddy's driving home from work and his car gets sucked up in the funnel?"

"Don't worry, Toots. I'll find a ditch."

"Dessert plates, please."

Marky follows me out to the kitchen. As the door swings shut, Mother says something about all the questions I ask. When I come back, I don't say what I'm thinking, which is that we should take Marky back to obedience school. He knows "Stay," "Come," "Sit," "Lie Down," and "Release." Plus I taught him "Roll Over" and "Rub the Belly."

"I'm sure Marky will find a safe place," says my father.

"Under the sideboard? That isn't very safe."

The look on Mother's face means no more questions. Marky scratches on the pantry door. Mother gets up to open it. Marky goes back to his place by the sideboard. He sighs when he lies down. A great big sigh.

"Darling, what is tonight's English assignment?"

"Compare two things. Milly is comparing her violin to a clarinet so I thought I would compare our grand piano to a flute."

My father frowns. "Was musical instruments Milly's idea?"

I had forgotten the rule about copying: if you have to draw a horse, it helps to look through the National Geographic, but you cannot copy another person's idea. If you have an original idea, you can get a patent.

"I *was* going to compare me to Kate."

"*Myself* to Kate," Mother says.

"But Kate's at college now. I don't know what she's wearing or doing."

"Well, she's seven years older," says Mother. "And she's taller, but you have the same parents, and you both have brown hair. Remember your matching candy cane dresses?"

"Those don't fit anymore."

"No, sadly, those days are over."

"Why is that sad?"

"Why? Why? Why?"

"Marie Curie asked 'Why?' She won the Nobel Prize."

"She did?"

"She discovered radium. She won twice."

"A French woman. Imagine."

"She wasn't French. She was Polish. Her husband was French. Her room was so cold that ice covered the windows, and she had to wear her coat to bed, and when it was very, very cold, she piled all her clothes on top of her blanket, and got under the covers, and pulled her chair toward the bed. Then she lifted the chair onto the bed on top, to hold the clothes in place. She died in 1937."

"That's a very compelling story," says Mother. "Very well told."

Leo

They are out on the porch when I bring down my homework. Usually, I have to look for Mother's glasses, but she has them in her pocket.

"I compared my parents."

"My sainted aunt!"

Mother turns on the standing lamp and begins to read.

"*Comparison: My Parents.* Sam?"

"I'm listening."

"*Similarities: Both born in 1907. Both Episcopalian. Both hate tinsel. Both not afraid of tornados. Both help Mrs. Wollner next door. Both don't snore.* Actually, your father snores," she sighs.

Not true. When I have my tornado dream, I go to his room, but sometimes, to be fair, I go to her room. Nobody snores.

She continues to read, "*Differences: She is a woman; he is a man. She is tall; he is short.*"

"Five nine isn't short," says my father.

"Indeed, it is not," says Mother.

"*She listens to trumpet music; he listens to South Pacific. Her favorite food is a tongue sandwich; his favorite food is lima beans. She smokes Salems; he smokes Viceroys. She is afraid of heights; he climbed a smokestack. She doesn't talk to strangers; he talks to hobos. Her swear words are 'My sainted aunt,' 'Hell's bells,' and 'Go fry ice'; his swear words are 'Damn,' 'Goddamn,' 'Hell,' 'Son-of-a-bitch,' 'Jesus Christ,' and probably a few more. She is afraid of rusty needles; he is afraid of a bad wiring job. She drinks martinis; he drinks VO on the rocks. She likes antique; he likes modern.* That's quite a list. What is 'Gray Area'?"

"When two things are similar *and* different."

"I see. *Gray Area: Both worked in New York City (Difference: He was born there; she was born in Ann Arbor). Both kneel in church (Difference: She bows her head and closes her eyes; he never bows his head or closes his eyes). Both play the piano (Difference: She plays hymns; he plays 'Hello Georgie.')* Well," she takes off her glasses, "that's very thorough. Sam?" She hands him my paper.

While he inspects for neatness, she looks at the garden.

I can't stop comparing them. She has thick hair. He has practically no hair. He is a slow reader; she is a fast reader.

"Here and here." He touches two places where I didn't thoroughly erase.

Headlights from the cars on Washtenaw Avenue flicker across Mother's forehead. Her hankie falls on the floor. She picks it up. I feel a breeze. My father lights his cigarette, cupping both hands around the flame. Smoke goes through the screen. Mother says the standing lamp by the fireplace isn't working. He says he'll take a look at it.

Marky comes in. He's been drinking from his water bowl. My father pats the side of his chair. Marky comes over for a head rub. When you rub his head, he holds his tail down, then when you finish rubbing, his tail goes up. Marky lies down by the wall. Then he stretches. One back leg sticks straight out, quivers, then drops. There is nothing we can do about his arthritis.

Marky is a black standard poodle. Standard poodles have long legs. Marky has short legs. That made him cheaper. His full name is Marcus Aurelius Fortunatis Tidd Schneider. Marky was born a year before me, so Marky was home when they brought me home from

Christmas 1952

the hospital. I have known Marky as long as I've known my parents and my older sister, Kate. When people ask if we have any pets, of course I say Marky. When they ask if Marky is a cat or a dog or a bird, I say Marky is my brother, and everybody tries to smile. Nobody understands, and I don't care.

"Ten more days until the longest day of the year," says Mother. She points to the sky. "I see a bat."

Mother loves bats and chameleons, spiders and centipedes, even mice. My father loves dogs and fish. We still haven't figured out how Marky will get down to the basement if there's a tornado and nobody is home. I hope Mr. Leinbach is right. He says every living creature has a primal instinct to survive.

Christmas 1955

Not Sure About the Train

My father walks in the back door scowling. He says he left his bifocals at the office. His wire-rims are in his sock drawer next to his handkerchiefs. I take them downstairs. They're on the porch having cocktails.

"I like your wire-rims better."

"I'm not a professor, sweetheart."

"But bifocals make you look like a gangster."

"I prefer gangster."

"Those bifocals are famous," says Mother. Eyebrows up.

I'm about to ask why, but she shakes her head. Not now. Mother hands him the sports section of *The Ann Arbor News*. There is a nice breeze on the porch. I pet Marky.

"Oh my. Cecil Pearl. Uncle Walter knew Dr. Pearl." She reads aloud, "*Born in Midland, Michigan, and graduated from Princeton, became full professor of Physics in 1939. Burial Saturday, July 15, at Forest Hill after a funeral at the Congregational Church.*"

"Just put me in a pine box" my father says.

Every time she reads aloud the obituaries, he says, "When you're dead you're dead," and "Put me in a pine box."

"Good Lord," says Mother. "There's been a shooting on the west side! *On July 12th, shortly after one a.m., Bert Wilson was shot and killed by his wife at 202 Chapin Street.* Shades of Tizabel." My father looks up.

"Tizabel?"

"Oh, Sam. You loved Tizzy's rhubarb pie."

"Tizzy made those pies?"

"She did indeed, and she had a gentle nature, which is why it came as such a shock."

"What came as a shock?"

"When she shot Charlie."

"You never told us this!"

Mother sips her martini. Here comes a story.

"Tizzy lived in Ypsilanti with two aunts and a sister. She came to help Nanny after Bapa died and was a great comfort. She slept in the nursery upstairs."

Another sip.

"Tizzy was being courted by a gentleman named Charlie, who came on Friday afternoons to take her back to Ypsilanti in time for her meetings. Tizzy was a member of several lodges and social clubs. Charlie would park on the street then walk up the driveway and walk over by the pricker bush so he could see Tizzy through the window. Tizzy liked to roll out her pie crust in the icebox room on the long counter under the window. Charlie would shout, 'Is Tizzy very busy?' That was their little joke because Tizzy was very active in her organizations. Perhaps Charlie wanted Tizzy to spend her evenings with him."

Another sip.

"Well, one Friday Charlie didn't come. And he didn't come the next Friday. Weeks went by—no Charlie. Then, one day, there stands Charlie by the pricker bush shouting, 'Is Tizzy very busy?' Tizzy put down her rolling pin, walked out the back door, reached into her apron pocket, and shot him."

"Tizzy had a gun in her apron?!!"

"She'd had enough."

"She shot Charlie by the pricker bush?"

My father drops his newspaper. "Did she hit him?"

"In the shoulder," says Mother. "Nanny was distraught at the thought of Tizzy spending the night at the jailhouse which, in those days, was particularly unsavory. Nanny took Tizzy chicken salad sandwiches and fresh clothes every day until she was let out."

"Was Tizzy from Germany?" I've always wanted to know.

"Tizzy was from Ypsilanti. I told you, Darling."

"You said Nanny's servants were German."

"When I was a little girl, they were German. That was long before Tizzy."

"Did Vee Vee know Tizzy?"

"Vee Vee was Tizzy's cousin. When Tizzy married Charlie, Vee Vee started—"

"Charlie married the woman who shot him?!" says my father.

"They were in love," Mother smiles.

"Mother, what was Vee Vee's real name?"

"Vearlor."

My father sneezes. Once my father starts sneezing, he can't stop. That's three in a row.

"Do we have a gun?" I ask.

"There are no guns in this house," he sneezes. That's four.

"Did you ever shoot a gun?"

"At Hope Farm there was a rifle in the barn."

"Why would an orphanage have a rifle?"

"Hope Farm was a working farm. Farms have guns."

Another sneeze. Five.

"Did you ever shoot that gun?"

"Once. I missed a squirrel."

Usually, he won't talk about Hope Farm, but sneezing has loosened him up. Mother goes to get him a glass of water.

"Did you like Hope Farm?"

"Best years of my life." Sneeze.

"Before Hope Farm where did you live?"

"New York City," another sneeze.

"What happened to the rock?"

"What rock?"

"The rock the boy threw."

He's not going to tell the rock story, but I know it by heart.

The Schneiders lived in Germantown in New York City. At the bottom of the hill, there was a railroad bridge where one day, under that bridge, my father got into a fight with a gang of older boys. Uncle Grover, who is three years older than my father, didn't break up the fight. He wanted to teach his little brother a lesson: don't pick fights with older boys. When an older boy threw a rock and hit my father in the forehead, blood poured out. Uncle Grover picked up the rock and dragged my father all bloody, up the hill. Their parents were dead, and their grandmother had gone to deliver the choir robes she ironed for the church around the corner, so a neighbor lady got out her sewing basket and sewed up his forehead. You can see the scar over his right eyebrow. His grandmother kept the rock in the icebox. The scar is red. When he gets a sunburn, you can't see the scar as much.

Uncle Grover and Aunt Emma live in New York City, in the Bronx. You say *the* Bronx. You don't say *the* Manhattan or *the* Brooklyn. Mother says we sorely (which means truly) wish Uncle Grover and Aunt Emma didn't live so far away. My father has a New York City accent, but it's not as strong as Uncle Grover's.

Each year, after we all talk to Uncle Grover and Aunt Emma on Christmas night, my father goes into the living room and sits in the dark. We are not to disturb him, even if the pocket doors are open. Uncle Grover is a repairman for Otis Elevator Company which is why every time Mother takes the elevator to the girdle department at Goodyear's, she looks at the OTIS brass plaque in the elevator floor and tells the story about how Uncle Grover was working at the bottom of an elevator shaft when a cable broke and the elevator car dropped in the shaft. Uncle Grover thought he would die, but the elevator car stopped four inches from his head. There were sparks and a big bang. Uncle Grover lost the sight in one eye and the hearing in one ear, and Aunt Emma had a stroke—not on the same day—which is why,

Mother says, my father sits in the dark after our Christmas phone call. I can't bear to think about Uncle Grover's calamities.

Mother comes back with a glass of water. He takes a sip, puts down his cigarette. Sneezes. I've lost count. She takes the newspaper away from him. We think he is allergic to printing ink.

"What were your parents' names?" I ask my father.

"Sophie and Frederick."

I have never asked this question, but today I have to: "How did they die?"

"Mother had a stroke. Father was hit by a train . . . not sure about the train."

Not sure about the train?! I can't believe he just said that. *Not sure about the train.* The train *killed* his father. How can he not be sure? We don't have any pictures of his parents. We only have pictures of Mother's parents.

"How old were you, Daddy?"

"Not sure about that, either." Another sneeze.

Mother says, "You were seven."

"Do you miss your parents?"

"Hard to miss people you don't remember."

"Were you scared?"

No answer. He doesn't look the least bit sad or scared.

"Where was your house?"

"Tenement on 102nd Street. East side."

"What is a tenement?"

"An apartment house with families on every floor."

"What floor were you?"

"Pretty high floor."

"How do you know?"

"I remember a lot of stairs."

Cigarette ash falls on his knee. He brushes it off and sneezes again.

"So where is the rock now?"

"What rock?"

"The rock your grandmother put in the icebox?"

"Toots, that rock is long gone."

"So, nothing is left?"

"*I'm* left."

You would think he would cry thinking about his dead parents, but no—not a twitch or a sad look. Another sneeze. And another. His record is nineteen.

Mother's parents, Mabel and Morris Tilley

My father at Hope Farm

Uncle Grover and my father

Vee Vee at her church, 1957

Crossing the State Line

Our final English assignment is to describe a ritual in precise detail. When I tell Mother I am going to write about Daddy leaving for work, she says I will have no trouble with this assignment. When I tell him the title—*My Father Every Morning*—he says, "Not much to tell."

He's wrong. There is a lot to tell.

When I get down to the kitchen in the morning, my father is standing next to the stove, stirring sugar into his coffee and wearing a white shirt. He never wears striped shirts or colored shirts.

How he chooses which bow tie is a pot shot. A pot shot is a mystery. Some bow ties are flecked, some are polka dot, and some are striped. He doesn't know why the stripes are diagonal. You adjust the bow tie by sliding the little pickaxe into the slit next to your size. My father is 15 ½. He tried wearing a long tie until Mother told him, "Sam, you're a bow-tie man."

His suit jacket is on the back of his chair in the breakfast room, a monogrammed white handkerchief in the pocket. His handkerchiefs come from Van Boven's. "SFS" is for Samuel Frank Schneider, the two "S's" are black and the "F" is gray.

He has three summer suits: khaki, blue seersucker, and blue cord. He doesn't know why they call it "cord," but that's what Gerhardt calls it, and Gerhardt has been his tailor at Van Boven's for fifteen years.

His two winter suits are gray. (Brown suits are for insurance salesmen, navy blue suits are for lawyers, and pinstripes are for gangsters.) When

I suggested he get a pinstripe suit to go with his bifocals, he said, "Your mother won't allow it."

He wears the same shoes all year: black leather with laces and holes punched in a heart shape over the toe. The holes do not let in the rain.

After he stirs the sugar in his coffee, he carries the cup and saucer to the breakfast table, looks out at the driveway, puts the coffee cup to his lips and blows on it, then takes a quick sip before he sits. Then he leans back, turns his chair sideways, crosses his legs, and lights a Viceroy.

I have cinnamon toast and juice. Mother has toast with chutney and a soft-boiled egg. He doesn't eat toast or eggs. After a few more sips of coffee, he reaches into his jacket for his blue diary and goes to the telephone in the pantry. He sits in the chair, lifts the receiver, and dials a number. Then he leans forward with his elbows on his knees and stares at his diary while he tells his secretary to "Call so-and-so and tell him such-and-such a time will be fine" or to "Call so-and-so back and say that we can meet at such-and-such a time next week, whatever is convenient." He sounds very polite. Then he hangs up the receiver. Sometimes, he takes a pencil out of the jar and erases his diary and returns the pencil to the jar. Then, he brushes the erasures off the page. Then, he slides the diary into his suit jacket, comes back to the table, and sits down. Then, he gulps more coffee.

If I have any homework, this is when he inspects for neatness. "Messy people do not get very far in life." "If you press too hard on the pencil, it makes it hard to erase. If you have to erase, erase completely." "If you can't do something right, don't do it at all. Keep your pencils sharpened."

Marky knows better than to follow him to the lavatory. There is a tight turn by the lavatory door, and once, we heard my father shouting, "Damn it! Go lie down!"

My father is a good shaver, but if he has a speck of toilet paper on his neck from a shaving cut, that speck is gone when he comes back from the lavatory. He double checks his bow tie in the mirror in the back hall. Then, he takes his suit jacket off the chair, folds it over his arm, and picks up his briefcase. His briefcase is brown and has his initials, in gold, under the handle. We bought it for him at Wilkinson's Luggage Shop on Main

Street. The briefcase is smaller than the Wilkinson's suitcase we bought him, but they are both brown. He doesn't use his suitcase because we never go on trips, but he uses his briefcase every day.

Then, he lifts his hat off the hook by the back door, tells Mother the names of a few towns, pats Marky, reminds me to fill Marky's water bowl, says "Have a nice day," and goes out the back door, walking alongside the garage which is covered in ivy. His right shoulder touches the ivy. Once a bird flew out.

Then, he opens the rear door of his black Buick, puts his briefcase, his jacket, and hat on the back seat, and closes the door. Then, he gets into the driver's seat. When he turns his head to back out of the driveway, you can see his bow tie one more time, and if I run to the living room, I can see the black Buick flickering behind the lilac hedge after he turns the corner.

I observe him four mornings in a row.

On Friday morning, when I watch him turn right at the corner, I freeze. He has been turning right all week, but now it occurs to me that downtown is *left*, not right. Where is he going? Where has he been going every day?

Mother is wiping off the breakfast table.

"Where is Daddy going?"

"To work."

"But he turned right at the corner."

"He'd better be turning right."

"I thought he worked downtown at Argus."

"Not anymore. Sadly, Argus was sold to Sylvania. He works for a printing company now. Evans-Winter-Hebb is in Detroit."

"Detroit is a long drive!"

"Forty-two miles. He gets reimbursed for gas."

All week, I watched his car turn right and never thought twice. Mother says that's the thing about a routine; you don't really question it. So, the idea of him going to Argus was wrong. We haven't gone to an Argus picnic in years. Now I feel sick.

Leo

The next morning, I show him my paper. Mother makes him read the words, not just inspect for neatness. He takes out his bifocals (they were on the floor of his car). He is not a fast reader. When he's done, he says, "I do all that?"

"Very observant," says Mother.

"So, what do you really *do*? My friends keep asking, and I don't know what to tell them."

"Now? I work for a printing company in Detroit."

"Not Argus?"

"Not anymore."

Mother sighs. "All those pictures of you and Marky with the Argus C3."

He uses his cigarette to push the ashes to the edge of the ashtray.

"What do you do all day at this printing company?"

"I bring in accounts."

"What's an account?"

"A job. A printing company needs something to *print!*" He gets up.

"Does your company print books?"

"We print manuals, and brochures, and annual reports."

"What do you do at your desk?"

"Not much."

"I thought those men were coming to your office."

"I go to *their* office."

"Don't you have a desk in your office?"

"My desk is upstairs in this house."

"But you only draw cartoons up there."

"Those are mock-ups."

He lifts his chin, pinches the loops of his brown bow tie.

"Aren't you going to the lavatory?"

No answer.

We have a little shelf under the mirror for his comb. I forgot to describe how he combs his side hair.

"What is a mock-up?"

"A mock-up is a pretend brochure. If the customer likes the pretend brochure, then they hire my company to print the real ones. Hopefully, a *lot* of real ones. In color!"

He puts his hand on Mother's shoulder. He doesn't usually do that.

"How come you don't make your mock-ups at your office in Detroit?"

"If I spend all day in my office, then I'm not on the road, am I?"

"So, you *want* to be on the road?"

"How else am I going to put eggs and toast on this table?"

I hate this. Not only does he not work in Ann Arbor, he doesn't really work in Detroit.

"You spend all day in your *car*?"

"Some days I do."

"What do I tell my friends? That you are a *driver*?"

"Just say I'm your father." He pats Mother's shoulder. "That's a big job."

"Sam. She's trying."

"Tell them I'm an Advertising Printing Salesman."

"Can I just say you are a salesman?"

"My briefcase is not full of encyclopedias."

"He means," says Mother, "that he doesn't go door-to-door selling cookies like the Girl Scouts."

He takes out his diary, turns to the back, and shows me a page with dates, and towns, and numbers.

"Here's my mileage," he says. "Last Tuesday, I drove over two hundred miles. My territory got expanded," he looks at Mother, "to include northern Ohio. I'll be crossing the state line now—twice a week."

"*Ohio*?! That's a different *state*."

He puts one shoe up on his chair and reties the laces.

"Let's say Ann Arbor has two Good Humor trucks. Truck A and Truck B both work on Ferdon Road. But those of us who live on Ferdon Road are probably not going to buy two ice creams a day. Truck A and Truck B can only sell so many ice creams, but if Truck A's territory is Ferdon and Truck B's territory is Cambridge . . ."

I can't follow any of this. While he ties the other shoe, he tells Mother he'll be going to Toledo and Southfield, making a stop in Milan.

"Do you *ever* go to your office?"

"No more questions," says Mother.

"Twice a week I drop off my mileage."

"I think you should spend more time at your company."

"If I spend more time at my company, I won't have a company to go to."

He grabs his suit jacket and briefcase and goes out to the back hall. The door slams, and a second later he steps off the back porch.

"Hot day today," he calls. "Don't forget Marky's water bowl."

He used to park under the kitchen window, but Mother complained she couldn't see the garden, so they made a new parking place under the pine trees with just enough tar poured out for one car. Mother gets to park her Chevy in the garage, but he parks his Buick under the pine trees. This is where the junk man parks, and the Sinclair Oil truck, and where the electrician parked yesterday. Now the sap drips on his windshield. My father is a workman. He parks where the workmen park.

The Buick backs down the driveway. My father looks like a chauffeur.

Mother is making my sandwich.

"Where did he say he was going?"

"Toledo, Southfield, then Milan."

"How many miles is that?"

"I have no idea. Did you feed Marky?"

Turning the can opener, I try to imagine my father on the highway, going to different towns, putting money in a parking meter, walking into a building—but what building? On what street? How can he get all dressed up and drive so many miles every day?

"Don't forget your assignment."

Lately, Mr. Leinbach is asking us to read our papers aloud. If he asks me to read mine aloud, I won't be able to. I don't like my father's morning ritual anymore. No wonder Mother gave him a compass for his birthday.

"Where does he have lunch?"

"I suppose he eats in a restaurant or a coffee shop."

"All by himself?"

"Let Marky out, please."

Marky sniffs the corner of the garage. Then he sniffs the mock orange, then he sniffs the bridal wreath. The backyard looks different. My father on his way to Detroit has changed everything. When I give Marky his Milk-Bone, he takes it to the dining room and lies down by the sideboard. We used to get medium Milk-Bones, but last week Mother said he could have large. At least I know where Marky will spend his day, right there by the sideboard on the green carpet.

The Seven Hills

The last place we should be right now is driving down this flat country road. We need to get off this road right now and find a basement or a ditch because that sky looks just like the picture in the weather book—*grayish-green, ominous, threatening.*

"Can we please turn around and go home?"

No answer.

"Please, Mother."

"What did I tell you about crying wolf?"

Crying wolf means you talk about the same thing so much that nobody hears you anymore, and then, when you truly need them to listen, they are worn out.

"You want your father's birthday cake to have *fresh* eggs, don't you?"

If you have a difficult question, it's best to ask Mother when she's driving.

"Mother, last year, Uncle Walter and Aunt Martha came to Daddy's birthday dinner? Can Uncle Walter—"

"Probably not."

"When can I come with you to see him?"

"We'll see."

She's avoiding me again. *We'll see. Not far.* That didn't work.

"Mother! The sky turns a sickly gray-green right before the funnel forms—like *that* sky over there. Look how dark it is!"

She takes her hankie out of her blouse pocket and wipes her forehead.

"And the air gets muggy, not a leaf moving. Don't you think the air is muggy?"

"June is always muggy."

"Do you see a leaf moving?"

"I see cornstalks."

"But the cornstalks aren't moving. Look."

She looks for one second.

"I don't see a ditch or sunken area. Do you?"

She looks in the rearview mirror and blows her hair off her forehead.

"The seven hills will protect us." She wipes the back of her neck.

"I don't see any hills. Where *are* the seven hills?"

"It isn't every day your father turns fifty-five. Have you been having your tornado dream again?"

No, but I will tonight. Why do we have to drive a thousand miles for eggs? Not a leaf moving and not a house in sight, not a ditch or sunken area on this flat-as-a-pancake country road. We are going to die out here.

"Have you made your birthday card?"

"Please, Mother. Look."

She does look, finally, then she steps on the accelerator.

The egg lady's house is white with a fallen down porch. Mother parks by the shed, opens her change purse, takes out two quarters, and says, "I'll be back in a minute."

Back in a minute? Before I can grab her arm, she is walking to the clothesline where the egg lady is taking down her laundry. Behind them is a flat field with black and white cows under the only tree, some cows standing, some lying down. Mr. Leinbach says you can't stop a cow from taking shelter under a shady tree on a hot day, and you can't stop lightning from striking the only tree in a flat field. In the weather book, there is a paragraph about a farm where eight cows standing under a tree were electrocuted.

Which way is south? Which way is west? The Chevy needs a compass. I look out the back window. No funnel. I look to both sides. No funnel. But a funnel can form in a second. If the funnel comes now, Mother will get sucked up with the egg lady. And I will get sucked up in the Chevy.

The egg lady picks up the clothes basket. Mother walks ahead to open the screen door. There is a flash of lightning, then a rumble. Does it sound like a train? Mother looks over at the Chevy, then she goes inside the house. That could be the last I see of Mother. The sky is getting darker and darker. A red hen comes around the side of the house and disappears under the porch. If Mother doesn't come out in five seconds, I'm running for the back door.

Lightning bolts over the field. One bushel of thunder. Two bushels of thunder. Mother is walking toward the car. Three bushels—she reaches for the door handle. Four bushels—thunderclap. Four divided by five. The lightning is .8 miles away.

She's back.

"Just an old-fashioned thunderstorm," she hands me the egg carton. "The Midwest in June," she smiles, turning the key in the ignition. The cows are still under the tree; no smoke.

We bump along the track and turn back onto the main road. Pea-sized hail bounces off the hood. Hail is not uncommon in tornado weather. Mr. Leinbach showed us a hail pad.

"Mother, roll up your window."

"It's too hot." She turns on the windshield wipers.

"In a lightning storm, you roll up your window."

"We're safe in the car."

"Not unless the windows are rolled up."

For once, she believes me. Then she turns on the headlights and sings "Hail Thee Festival Day," her favorite Easter hymn. The egg carton is smeared with mud, and bits of straw are stuck in the mud.

"Let's imagine these dry fields and how grateful all those thirsty roots are to get a nice cool drink."

The left windshield wiper is slower than the right. They don't swipe together. When we get to the stop sign, Mother opens her mouth a tiny bit, then closes it. Whatever she was going to say, she changed her mind.

Mr. Leinbach said animals don't like bad weather, but they learn to live with it. What choice do they have? Sheep tuck into the gorse. Lambs lie down beside their mothers. Mice hide in the hay loft. Rabbits burrow. Birds find a hedge. Turtles pull into their shells. Frogs leap into the pond. Hens go under the porch. Most small animals have a place to hide. It's the big animals—cows, sheep, horses—that suffer, but they don't feel the weather like we do. Their coats are oily, and their skin is thick, and they are used to the rain and snow from centuries of living outdoors.

Turning onto Ferdon, the silver maple by the garage is swaying, and the sky is not as dark. Leaves moving, normal sky color—all good signs. Now I need a plan.

We park in front of the garage. I can't believe I didn't figure this out before. I ask Mother which way is south. She points to Mrs. Wollner's house.

I let Marky out, then I go downstairs to the basement and turn on the light in the furnace room. Mrs. Wollner's house is that way—behind the furnace. The southwest corner is between the furnace and the fuse box.

I go back upstairs and let Marky inside. After he's had his drink, I give him a Milk Bone. He goes to the dining room, sighs, then lies down by the sideboard. I put two Milk Bones in my pocket.

I find an old bowl we don't use in the pantry and take it downstairs. I find a shoebox in the box room. The bowl fits in the shoebox. I put the two Milk Bones in the shoebox and put the shoebox in the corner by the fuse box. The northeast corner is where the clothes from the clothes chute land in the bin my father built. It would be tempting to get inside that bin. But, no. Marky wouldn't fit, and I have to remember which corner is safe and which one is dangerous. *Southwest* and *safe* both begin with the letter "s." The northeast corner is not safe. The *northeast* corner is the *nasty* corner.

I go back upstairs. I make sure Marky's leash is where I think it is. It is—on the hook nearest the back door. Good. My plan is: clip the leash on Marky's collar; very gently pull him down the basement stairs and around the corner to the furnace room; gently make him lie down in the southwest corner while I fill the water bowl in the laundry room; set his water bowl where he can reach it; sit down beside him, put my arm around him, kiss him on the nose, and give him a Milk Bone. Why didn't I figure this out before?

Tizzy's Milk Pan

Once a month, on the weekend, we go to Forest Hill Cemetery. When I ask Mother if she believes "when you're dead your dead," she says, "No, I do not. I believe death is a mystery."

We drive past the stooping angel.

"For that matter . . . life is a mystery, too."

"Where is Aunt Martha's grave?"

She points. "Farther north."

"Why didn't I go to her funeral?"

No answer. I should have gone because I'm their Goddaughter, but it's too late to fix that now.

Mother points to the big monument that says "DAY" on one side and "FERDON" on the other. My two streets—where I was born and where I live now. Mother says Farmer Ferdon's son must have married Farmer Day's daughter. Or maybe it was the other way around.

When we get to our plot, I fill the watering can at the spigot and water the bushes. I brush off dead leaves and sticks. I leave peanuts for the squirrels. Mother pulls weeds. Bapa is on the right. Nanny in the middle. Baby Catherine on the left.

"How old were you when Catherine died, Mother?"

"I was seven."

I brush off the stone lamb on Catherine's grave. The mold never comes off. Catherine's lamb looks like the stone lamb in our yard for family dogs. The lamb is over Heidi now. Before Heidi was Caesar.

When Mother stands up, we say the Lord's Prayer.

On the way home, I ask if she is obsessed about cemeteries.

"One is obsessed *with* not obsessed *about*," she says.

"Who is *one?*"

"*One* is anyone. Remember when you were obsessed with tornados? Thanks be to God, one grows out of things."

We pass the street we take to Uncle Walter and Aunt Martha's.

"You haven't had your tornado dream in a long time."

"Yes, I have."

"When?"

"The other night."

"When I have a bad dream," she says, "I heat milk in the milk pan Tizzy always used, the white one with the red rim. It's a comforting ritual. A little less chocolate might also be a good idea."

Red

Tonight, I don't have a brownie for dessert, but I have my tornado dream anyway. I am too old to wake up my father, although I don't think he would mind—he never complains and gets me a glass of hot milk, but perhaps, at my age, I should get my own hot milk. Then, I remember what Mother said about the milk pan with the red rim, which gets me out of bed and across the hall. I cover my eyes so I won't see the tornado outside the window on the landing and head downstairs. I trip over Marky who yelps. What is Marky doing on the landing?! He never sleeps on the landing. Why isn't he asleep in the green chair in my father's room? Maybe I should go back to bed; maybe the kitchen is too far in the dark.

I am about to turn around, but Marky heads down the stairs, bumping into the wall at the bottom because his cataracts are worse. He thinks he's getting a Milk-Bone. Mother's right. He is getting too many Milk-Bones.

Walking through the dining room, I feel better. Thinking about Marky has helped, and the kitchen isn't pitch dark because somebody forgot to turn off the light over the stove.

I give Marky a Milk-Bone, then I get the milk from the icebox and the glass from the cupboard. I turn on the stove and pour milk in Tizzy's white pan with the red rim. Rituals are comforting.

A few cars are coming down Washtenaw, their headlights flickering between the trees next door. The trees are swaying. It's a windy night. You can't see the color of the sky at night, but you can check leaf movement. Tornados form only when there is not a leaf moving.

I take Kate's potholder off the hook. She made it in second grade. My friends don't believe me when I tell them my sister and I don't fight. If Kate asks me to find her red cardigan, I look for it. I like doing things for her, and she always sewed my party dresses. Not fighting can't be wrong. I can't explain what it's like to live with someone so beautiful. I'm not jealous. I'm really not. My teeth are pushed out and I'm not pretty, but I don't care. That Kate is very beautiful is not her fault. She was born that way.

Marky barks, and a second later, there is a loud crash in the icebox room. Before I can scream, Marky stops barking because leaning against the icebox, his bow tie undone, having just jumped down off the counter, is my rumpled father. He kicks Marky's water bowl and comes out to the kitchen. He doesn't see me or Marky; he just turns toward the back hall, says a few swear words, unhooks the chain on the back door, says a few more swear words, and goes up the back stairs.

The clock on the stove says 2:25. Did my father just climb through the window in the icebox room? Did he just jump off the counter? Where has he been? And why was the chain on the back door? We never use that chain. The milk boils over.

Teo

In the morning, when I come downstairs, there is my father in his white shirt and bow tie stirring sugar into his coffee. He cut his chin shaving. His gray suit jacket is over the back of the chair, white hand-kerchief poking out of the pocket. Marky's water bowl is full, no spills on the floor. Mother is standing at the sink where the milk pan is soaking, no questions asked about the mess I made on the stove. My father walks over to the breakfast room with his coffee and sits down. Who fed Marky?

The clock on the stove says 7:45, but it's summer; I don't have to go to school. We are having a late morning.

I sit in my chair. My father nods as if I just said something we agreed on. Mother sets my orange juice on the tablecloth. Then she puts cinnamon toast on my plate and places another plate with plain buttered toast on the table. She doesn't bring the chutney, so who is having all this toast?

Mother sits, sips her coffee, looks out the window. My father eats two pieces of toast, one after the other. He never has toast. Then he gulps down his coffee, makes a face because he burned his tongue, and walks to the pantry. While he calls his secretary, Mother watches him. Then he hangs up the phone, pushes the swinging door into the dining room, and Mother offers me the last piece of toast. I don't want it. She gives it to Marky. She's never done that before.

When my father comes back from the lavatory, the speck of toilet paper on his jaw is gone, a tiny red dot where the blood dried. Then, he grabs his suit jacket, picks up his briefcase, says something I don't hear, and goes out the back door—no towns mentioned, no "Have a nice day." He doesn't even turn the light off in the back hall which must have been on all night.

Mother clears the table, then scrubs Tizzy's milk pan and puts it in the dish rack. When she comes back to get the other plates, she forgets to turn off the water running in the sink. All these things he is so strict about—not leaving lights on, not letting the water run, not giving Marky scraps—totally ignored.

"Let Marky out."

I let Marky out. I look at the mint bed under the window—crushed. My father must have stood there to climb inside. The icebox room is the only room without a storm window. Now I know why.

I walk past the pricker bush where Charlie was shot by Tizzy. The day Mother told that story, I thought she was exaggerating, but now Tizzy shooting Charlie doesn't seem exaggerated. Sometimes a person has just had enough.

Honey

In my family, you do not stand in the doorway listening to someone else's conversation. You do not read letters on someone else's desk. If you pick up the telephone and you hear someone talking, you don't wait for the end of their sentence, you interrupt immediately, and say "excuse me for interrupting," then hang up, which is what I have every intention of doing, but in the second it takes to realize I am interrupting, I hear my father say "Honey" and a woman with a deep voice say "Love." I don't hear what they say next because I have, for the first time in my life, broken the rule about eavesdropping, and am burning with shame, and hang up without saying excuse me.

My father calls Mother "your mother" or sometimes "Lois." He calls Kate "Sweetheart," and he calls me "Toots" or, sometimes, "Tough Cookie." He calls Marky "Pooch." You don't call a friend "Honey." And he doesn't have a sister.

This morning, when Mother asked if I wanted to go to the Farmer's Market, I said I felt like helping my father in the basement, but when I got to his workroom, he wasn't building anything, just puttering, so I came up to my room to find the notice about the ping-pong tournament at the park. When I couldn't find it, I walked down the hall to call Milly because I saw her put a notice in her pocket. When I picked up the hall phone, how was I to know my father would be speaking on the kitchen phone? I thought he was in the basement because it's

Saturday. He said "Honey," then she said "Love," then I think I heard a door shut. And where would that door be? In the woman's house? What house would that be? What woman?

He was happy last weekend when we took down the storms and put up the screens. I stand inside and shout out the numbers on each window while he finds the matching storm or screen. Last year, I read a "6" when it should have been a "9," and he had to carry that window all the way back down the ladder, but this year, I didn't make any mistakes. Mother's job is to wash the screens or storm windows with the hose and dry them with a clean rag. We all did our jobs.

The telephone receiver looks sweaty when I walk into the pantry. He is standing at the sink, his folding ruler sticking out of his hip pocket, sawdust in his hair, a cigarette on the windowsill, the long ash about to fall off. You would think it was a normal Saturday and he had just come up from the basement. You would think all he had on his mind was the new fireplace project.

He talked about the fireplace project this morning at breakfast. We can still have fires, he said, but he is covering up the old mantel with paneling. The fire box will not be in the center anymore, but over to the left, and the Renoir will hang on the right. This is the modern look—off-center, not symmetrical. He says he is going to replace the ornate gold frame around the Renoir with a thin, varnished birch strip.

The folding ruler in his pocket means he is going back to the living room to take more measurements, which means he will have to walk by me standing here in the doorway. I can either go back upstairs, or I can stand here wondering if that long ash is ever going to fall off his cigarette?

"What do you need?" he says, turning off the faucet hard because it always drips.

He's right. Usually, I need something, or I have a question. What is my question now? Did he hear me put the receiver down? That is my question. Did he hear the little click? And who was he talking to?

He's still looking at me straight, like every other day we ever lived. He has always looked at me straight. And he has always talked straight. Now he looks straight, but he isn't straight inside. He has crossed the line. It might be a figure of speech, but I know what Mother means now. You step over, and you can't step back.

He dries his hands on the dish towel then he tucks the towel into the handle on the drawer.

"Okay," he says, picking up his cigarette—the ash still not falling, not falling, amazing—until he flicks it in the sink and turns toward the back hall just as Mother's car pulls up the driveway. By the time she comes through the back door, he is halfway down the basement stairs, and I have turned around because she will take one look at my face and start asking questions.

Marky is not in front of the sideboard. He is in the living room by the window seat. He used to climb onto the window seat, but he is too old for that now. I sit beside him on the floor. His brown eyes are cloudy and sad; I think he knows. So many things are wrong now. I don't know where to go or what to do. I thought my father was all ours.

As long as I can remember, the Renoir has hung over our fireplace. Now, it's leaning against the sofa. The new fireplace project has disrupted everything. When the painting was on the wall, I couldn't study it. Now I can: three fancy people sitting at a table. The man in a black suit is lighting his cigarette, his hand cupped around the flame. A red-haired woman sits across the table. She has a clump of violets on her white dress and another on her white hat. She has a ring on her left hand. The other woman wears a black dress, and black hat, and black gloves, and a white bow at her neck. The woman in the black dress is standing. There is no chair at the table for her. No plate or teacup for her.

"Grilled cheese?"

Mother always finds me.

"Dear?"

Mother is tall. She has wavy gray hair, dark circles under her eyes, and a pointy nose. She's wearing the same brown sweater she wears all the time. Maybe he is sick of that sweater.

"And tomato soup?"

Her voice is not low like the woman on the phone.

"Has Marky been out?"

Marky thumps his tail.

I always thought they slept in different rooms because he snored or she snored. Then, I figured out nobody snores, so I thought it was because Mother eats toast in bed while she reads. Now, I don't know what to think.

"Let's take Marky for a ride."

"But you just got home."

"You're right," she smiles. "I just got home."

What is going on?

"Marky? Want to go out?"

We leave the living room. It doesn't feel like our living room anymore.

Mother pushes the door to the pantry a little harder than usual. I let Marky out the back door. Marky stands on the step for a second. Sometimes his legs just won't work. Then he goes over to the pricker bush. He can't lift his leg anymore. He spreads both legs and pees like a girl.

Mother turns on the faucet, rinses my father's cigarette ashes down the drain. Then, she holds her hands under the water and just stands there. She went to see Uncle Walter. Maybe that's why she looks sad. She turns off the faucet. She doesn't notice it's dripping, and she doesn't dry her hands. She pushes her hair behind her ear and turns to the back hall, water running down her arm. I think she is going to call for Marky to come back in, but she keeps right on going down the basement stairs.

Once, when Marky went out and didn't come home, Mother said he was out in his Jaguar seeing his lady friends. I thought she was making up the Jaguar, but then she knew exactly what it looked like—a dark green convertible. I can't believe I fell for that.

"I don't know what's gotten into everybody," says Mother coming up the basement stairs. "Your father's not hungry, you're staring into space. Give Marky two Milk-Bones when he comes in. He's the only creature in this family I recognize today."

She puts the pan on the stove, turns the dial under the burner, and cranks the can opener around the soup can. She is making our lunch. And she will make our dinner. She bought beets at the Farmer's Market. My father loves beets. So, what is she doing wrong?

Borgie

Jim and Eleanor Robertson used to be our neighbors on Day Street, but after Nanny died, we moved into her house on Ferdon Road, and the Robertsons moved to Glacier Way on the other side of the Huron River. On our way home tonight, crossing the bridge, my father doesn't ask the hobo if he's caught any carp, and Mother doesn't sing "Over the River and Through the Woods."

"Jim's a doctor for Christ's sake!" says my father. "Doctors are supposed to be smart. But who had to hook up his new goddamned stereo?"

"You," says Mother in her soothing voice.

"And when he got those damned show dogs—who poured the cement in their kennel? Tonight, he couldn't even figure out how to operate a Polaroid! A Polaroid for Christ's sake!"

My father is right. He did all those things for Uncle Jim. Uncle Jim took a Polaroid of us on the sofa.

"Not everybody has your skills or generosity, Sam," Mother sighs.

"Now he wants to turn that closet in their sky parlor into a *sound booth*."

"A sound booth? Good Lord," says Mother.

"Says he's going to hire a disc jockey."

"A disc jockey?!"

"To sit in his soundproof booth and change the records and talk into a microphone."

"Whatever for?" Mother laughs.

"How should I know?"

"It's that Arthur Murray class they're taking."

"Then he said he wants me to take a look at his Porsche engine. Well, I'll be goddamned if I'm going to become his goddamned shade tree mechanic! I'm sick of his goddamned toys!"

We drive up Geddes toward the Arboretum.

"You have toys," says Mother in her gentle voice.

"I do?" He looks sideways at her. "What are my toys?"

"I don't know," she laughs, "you tell me."

"I would not call my twenty-year-old Speed Graphic four-by-five camera a toy. Nor my Argus C3. And I would not call this behemoth of a Buick, which is falling apart, a toy."

"What would you call it?"

"The family car," he says, opening the ashtray drawer. After he crushes his cigarette, he says, "If I ever get a sports car, it will *not* be a Porsche."

"What will it be?"

"A Borgward."

Mother turns her head. "Borgward? Funny name."

"Gene had one last week."

"Who is Gene?"

"My man at Buick."

"What a strange name for a car."

"They're imported."

"Imported?"

"From abroad. From Bremen, Germany."

Abroad, Germany, and *imported* are the magic words. My father's grandparents were born in Germany, and Mother approves of anything from abroad. I don't think my father ever thought he would own his own sports car, but after that night at the Robertsons', he trades in the Buick and before we know it, there is a small blue-gray sports car parked under the pine trees. To stop me from asking questions, my father hands me the manual. I love the drawings.

At dinner, my father announces he is calling his new car "Borgie." Then he says we are going out to the Robertsons' so he can take Jim for a spin. I squeeze into the back seat. I can fit if I sit sideways with my knees up. Mother squeezes in front. I can't imagine Uncle Jim, who is taller than Mother, will fit into Borgie, but my father says "He fits in his Porsche, doesn't he?"

My father takes Uncle Jim for a spin, and, at dinner, my father tells a long joke about the pope, the president, and the prime minister. He is having so much fun.

Red

Borgie's horn is not loud enough, so Gene orders a custom horn from Germany. Once Gene installs it, my father goes down to the Standard Oil station on South U. and asks Herb to check the oil. When Herb lifts the hood, my father hits the horn and Herb jumps ten feet in the air. Now, when Herb sees Borgie coming, he covers his ears and does a little dance, or he sends the other attendant Billy out to change the oil, then Herb and my father both have a good laugh when Billy jumps ten feet in the air. Eventually, everybody learns about Borgie's horn, and if the oil needs to be checked, Herb makes my father get out of the car and stand by the fuel pump. Everybody loves Borgie.

The buttons under the radio have symbols etched in the plastic. The buttons are explained in the manual. I quiz my father, then he quizzes me—choke, dash lighting, headlamps, side and taillights, fog lamp, windshield wiper, heater and parking light.

The manual says Borgwards should be stored in a dry, well-ventilated garage. When I read this out loud, I doubt Mother will move her Chevy, but the next day, she parks her Chevy under the pine trees and says it's fine if Borgie sleeps in the garage. Driving the old Buick, my father looked like a chauffeur. In Borgie, he looks like a jockey. He says drivers on the road to Detroit honk at Borgie, and he honks back. He says Borgie is becoming well known. Borgie is the color of my father's eyes and seems like the sort of car a bow-tie man should drive. My father says he doesn't know about that, but he agrees Borgie is a gem. When Mother calls Borgie a *bijou,* my father says Borgie doesn't understand French. Has she forgotten Borgie is German?

Uncle Jim's Polaroid

What's Mine Is Yours

Milly and I are playing Canasta on the dining room table when, out of the blue, Milly announces she wants the beaded belt back. When I remind her she never cared for it, which is why I always played Indian and she played Cowboy, she reminds me the belt belongs to her sister, and I remind her that her sister outgrew it, and I am the only person who appreciates the beaded belt. Then, because she doesn't know what to say to that, I take it one step further: "Pretend you're this belt, then you want to be worn by the person who enjoys you—not stuck at the back of a dark drawer. Well, I enjoy this belt! The belt is happy on me."

"My sister wants it back," says Milly, throwing her Canasta cards across the dining room table just as my father comes around the corner carrying a long board.

"What's going on?" he says.

"That's my belt," Milly points, "and I want it back."

"Because she's losing at Canasta."

"Whose belt is it?" My father leans his board against the wall.

"Mine," says Milly.

"No. It's her sister's."

"You know the rule," says my father. "Give the belt back, Toots."

"But she doesn't think it's beautiful, and I do."

"You know the rule."

I stare at his whiskers. He doesn't shave on Saturday.

"One bushel of thunder. Two bushels of thunder. Three bushels . . ."

That's how he learned to count at Hope Farm where he grew up.

"Five bushels of thunder. Six bushels . . ."

Marky is lying by the sideboard, chin on the carpet, eyes closed. He can't hear anymore.

"You know the bottom line. Seven bushels of thunder . . ."

The bottom line is you can't keep what isn't yours. The bottom line means the absolutely most final rule.

"Give the belt back to Milly. *Now.*"

Marky heard that.

"It's just because I'm winning at Canasta."

We don't hit in our family, but if we did, I think he might hit me now. He doesn't look mad, but when he takes me by the hand, I know I crossed the line. We walk through the front hall and into the study. He sits on the sofa. Does he know I know about the woman? Did he hear the receiver click when I hung up? He pats his knees. He's never spanked me or Kate. Never. We don't spank in our family.

"How else am I going to teach you this lesson?" he says.

What is happening to my family?

Milly has her arms crossed. Why can't we just play Canasta? Why can't my father be nice? On the weekends, he was always so nice. He let me help him on his projects, let me go with him to Fingerle's, and gave me a penny for the gumball machine. But this morning, I didn't go down to the basement. I can't look at him like I used to. Not since I heard the woman on the phone.

"What is going on?" Mother is in the doorway, holding her dust rag. Saturday is dusting day.

"She's getting a spanking," says Milly.

"Spanking?!" says Mother. "We don't spank in this family."

"We do today," he says.

"May I ask why?"

"Borrowing Milly's belt," he says, "and refusing to give it back."

Mother looks at me. We were talking about the beaded belt only yesterday, and about how we don't play Cowboys and Indians anymore, and how one can grow out of things. I said I'd outgrown the game, but not the belt. It fits perfectly. I always thought my father was the head of the household, but the way they both look now, she is the head of the household.

"Your father is right," she says.

I can't believe Mother took his side. They stare at each other. Nobody moves. I am in seventh grade. I am too old to lie across my father's lap. I stand up. I take off the belt. Milly grabs it, doesn't even say thank you, and leaves. The back door slams. Marky is under the front hall table when I run upstairs.

Marie Curie wore black all the time. She didn't care about beautiful clothes. She had her mind on higher things. I try to put my mind on higher things, but I don't know what a high thing is. God, maybe? But I can never picture God. Mr. Leinbach says nature is his God. I stare at the bumps in the bedspread. Inside the cotton are molecules. Inside the molecules are atoms. Inside the atoms are neutrons and electrons and protons. It doesn't work. I can't get high enough.

At dinner, Mother reminds my father the mailbox on the front porch is wobbling. He says he'll build a new mailbox, and when mother asks about his denture, he says it doesn't hurt anymore. Then Mother describes somebody's trellis on Vinewood. She would love a trellis, she says, over by the big porch, and what about an herb garden? I clear the table. Marky licks the roasting pan in the pantry. While I am tucking our napkins into our napkin rings, Mother comes out to the dining room. She puts the trivet in the top drawer of the sideboard and says we can look for a beaded belt when we next go to Goodyear's. Goodyear's doesn't have beaded belts, but there is no point in telling her this. That belt was old and worn out, not new, which is what I liked about it.

After dinner, I need to finish my poster for the ping-pong tournament, so I need to borrow my father's colored pencils, which are in his desk drawer in his bedroom. Last month, he took over my science project poster on mollusk shells and drew seaweed, and fish, and an octopus. Now, given what happened today and what happened yesterday, I don't want his help, but I need his colored pencils.

He is at his desk, drawing on brown paper—a sun shining, then a window frame, then a toaster on a counter, then toast popping out of the toaster. He knows right where to put the pencil point down and how to move it. He can draw anything—little black lines to show the toast really popping up high and yellow sunbeams hitting the toast in mid-air.

"Is that a mock-up?"

"Yes." Now he writes in black across the top: "Put the Sun in your Life with Sunbeam." Every letter is perfect, and they are all the same height. Below the toaster, he draws wavy blue lines which represent pretend words. The real words come later, in the final design. Now he sits back, puts the colored pencils back in the drawer, but doesn't close the drawer.

"Can I borrow your colored pencils?"

"What's mine is yours," he says, nodding to the open drawer.

He always says that.

Mother says he is generous by nature. He helps Uncle Jim; he got Mrs. Wollner's bats out of her attic; he climbed onto Uncle Walter and Aunt Martha's roof to fix their gutter. Giving is in his nature. Not giving goes against his grain. People have a grain, like wood. Mother says my grain is to ask questions. When I ask what is her grain, she says, "Oh, probably, looking after people."

I choose the colored pencils I need and close the drawer, but I can't leave. He doesn't say anything about the beaded belt, or the spanking, or Honey on the phone. He opens and closes his mock-up, pressing the crease, rubbing off little spills of rubber cement. I guess we are in a gray area.

The Old Brown Trout

Trumpet music on the record player after dinner means my father has gone out in Borgie and Mother is playing solitaire in the living room on the round coffee table, which she pulls up to the brown sofa. There is not enough room on that table to play solitaire, and drink, and smoke, but somehow her martini glass and ashtray never fall off.

Tonight, when I ask where my father went, she snaps down a red queen and says, "Your father has gone for a spin." When I ask where to, she snaps down a black three and says, "I'm the last to know." She doesn't notice when the record gets stuck. I go back upstairs.

Later, I can hear her putting pots and pans away in the kitchen. Then I hear a loud crash. When I get to the landing, Marky is running from the dining room into the hall, his tail between his legs just as a saucepan lands beside the sideboard. How could she throw a saucepan at Marky?! A big lid comes next. She knows Marky lies there! Milk pan. Roasting pan. Coffee pot. Last time she picked up the pots; this time she doesn't.

I call Marky, but he has crawled under the front hall table and won't come out. Then I hear two voices yelling in the kitchen. My father is home. It's not my fault I hear every word. I know I am breaking the rule about eavesdropping, but the squirrels in the attic can probably hear them screaming. Besides, I already broke the eavesdropping rule.

"I'd like to meet your mistress. Why don't you invite her for a drink?

"Don't be ridiculous. You're welcome to come. Sidney asked where you were."

"Really? I didn't receive an invitation. I wonder why that is?"

"Do all our friends have to be members of the goddamned faculty?"

"Doesn't Sidney Margolis teach in the medical school?'

"He does research and sees patients."

"Research on what?"

"Blood pressure."

"I wonder how *his* blood pressure is these days."

Eventually, I learn the woman's name. Whether it is the name Mother screams or I just figure it out, I don't know, but the woman I heard on the telephone was Mrs. Margolis—Gwen.

My father's regular doctor suggested my father see a cardiologist about his high blood pressure, which Mother mentioned to Pamela Norton, who suggested he make an appointment with the cardiologist who lives across their street, Dr. Sidney Margolis. So, my father went to Dr. Margolis, and it turned out, Dr. Margolis likes to fish. So, after a few check-ups, he invited my father to come fishing for the old brown trout on the Au Sable River up north somewhere. The idea was, fishing would relax my father and lower his blood pressure. Mother was invited, but she said she couldn't go; "have you forgotten, we have a twelve-year-old daughter at home?"

She always says people have different tastes and different hobbies. She likes to read and garden. My father likes to garden, but he doesn't read, and given a choice between gardening and fishing, it appears he would rather fish. Fishing is not a new hobby, he reminded her; he has been tying flies and casting in the backyard for years. He further reminded her one of his clients, Shakespeare & Co., is a fishing tackle company, and why shouldn't Mrs. Margolis go, too? "The fishing camp belongs to Gwen's father, for Christ's sake." So, one weekend, off he went with his rusty tackle box, and his fishing rod, and his suitcase from Wilkinson's.

When or how Gwen Margolis made her entrance—with a smile, a blouse, a remark, a gutted trout—I will never know, but the news is my father has a private life. Gwen Margolis is making him climb through windows.

Milly says I have it backward: he wasn't climbing through the window to get to Gwen, he was climbing through the window to get back to *us*. Milly is being literal. What does she know? Her father stays home at night reading French books. He is on the faculty. Besides, I told her, when my father jumped down off the counter, he was not glad to see Marky or me. He was not even ashamed. I remember it perfectly. He said a few swear words and turned toward the back hall, took the chain off the back door and climbed the back stairs. He used to say, "Houses don't need two sets of stairs," and Mother would say, "You need them if you have servants," to which he would say, "I have no intention of hiring servants who need back stairs." Well, he's been making good use of those back stairs lately.

Rock the Pans

Saturday mornings, my father and I go to Fingerle's. Sometimes, we buy small items; sometimes, we get lumber from the shed outside. This morning, at breakfast, he doesn't mention Fingerle's, so I go back up to my room and put away my laundry. When it gets to be eleven o'clock, I go back downstairs. He could be in one of three places: his workroom in the basement, his darkroom at the foot of the basement stairs, or out in the yard.

The basement door is closed, so I'm pretty sure he's in his darkroom. The rule is if the basement door is closed, knock on it hard; don't just open the door. Wait for him to shout that it's safe to come down. Today I bang hard three times. No answer.

"He's out in the yard," Mother calls from the kitchen. I looked in the yard. I didn't see him, but now I do. Over by the fence with his camera and his new Lawn-Boy.

"Are we going to Fingerle's?"

"In an hour."

His voice is soft. His voice was not soft yesterday when I forgot to knock on the basement door and he was in his darkroom.

Now, he wants me to sit on the Lawn-Boy, pretend I am changing gears; pretend I have just mowed the lawn. He wants to show his customers that a Lawn-Boy is so easy to operate, even a child can do it.

"I'm not a child."

"No. I need a teenager."

Marky, after his haircut, lying on the grass with an Argus Camera between his paws never got in any magazines. But when my father worked at Argus, Kate was in *The Saturday Evening Post* holding Mother's old leather doll. Back in the days when he worked in our town. Back in the days when . . .

"Red cap?" I ask.

"This'll be black and white. No pigtails. Keep your hair down."

When I get back, he's waiting.

"Lean forward. One hand on the gear shift."

He pushes in the film holder.

"Now look ahead."

I stare at the driveway.

He flips the film holder.

"Look at the gear shift."

I look down.

He takes out the film holder and pushes another one in.

"Pretend you operate the Lawn-Boy every day."

"But I am not allowed on the Lawn-Boy."

"I said *pretend*."

I stare at the gear shift. He clicks.

"That's it! Meet you in Borgie."

He usually gives me a penny for the gumball machine at Fingerle's, but given I leaked light downstairs yesterday, never mind everything else going on, I doubt I'll get a penny today.

I'm wrong. I get four pennies.

He buys sandpaper, and a tack cloth, and two large paintbrushes. On the way home, when we stop at Witham's for VO and gin, I get a Hershey bar which is the first time that has ever happened. On the way home, he says I can help in the darkroom which hasn't happened in months.

I rock the white enamel pans with the blue rim while the paper floats. I don't ask why there are three pans. I don't ask why he moves his hand under the lens and jiggles the little circle of cardboard on the wire. I don't ask how he knows how long to step on the pedal. I just rock the pans. Here comes our fence. Here comes Mother's delphinium, my head, my arm, the Lawn-Boy, our yard. The grays get darker, then they stop getting darker. I step aside. With his bare fingers—he doesn't use tongs and he doesn't wear gloves—he slides the picture across the edge of the first pan, holds it up, lets it drip, then drops it gently in the middle pan, rocks that pan, then slides the picture over the edge of the middle pan, holds it up, lets it drip, then drops it in the third pan, then he rocks the third pan.

"No questions?"

It wouldn't take much to start asking, but these days, it's better not to. Better to rock the pans. I don't need answers. I just need him.

801 Berkshire

Mother has been to see Uncle Walter ten times. I have not been once. She keeps putting me off. I think he may have lost his leg tumbling down the mountain in Greece. Then, out of the blue, she suggests I go with her to 801. I can hardly believe it. I run upstairs to change my clothes. Mother will prepare me in the car.

There is a bouquet of black-eyed Susans on the car seat next to some mint. We back out the driveway. I fold my hands. Mother says nothing. We cross Washtenaw and turn up Vinewood—no words. We turn left on Berkshire—no words. We drive past Aunty Douglas's house—no words. We turn into Uncle Walter and Aunt Martha's narrow driveway. We are not taking fresh vegetables from the Farmer's Market. We are not delivering a Monday Club book. I have never come on a sad mission. If Mother won't prepare me, I will prepare myself. Aunt Martha won't be in the kitchen; she won't be carrying the tea tray to the living room. Uncle Walter could have a wooden leg, or be using crutches, or have scars. He could look shaggy and rumpled. His hair could have fallen out from shock. I know the rules for this. Look Uncle Walter in the eye. Do not avoid his gaze. Smile softly. Don't ask a single question. One can convey kindness in many quiet ways. He never used to kiss or hug, so that won't happen.

She takes the flowers. We walk down the driveway. She knocks on the back door. The back hall is the same—long and dark. Where is he? She knocks again. Are we staying for tea? Will there be a jigsaw puzzle on the table in the corner of the living room? If there is no puzzle table, where will I sit? Mother knocks again.

What I know about Uncle Walter: he and Nanny played four-hand piano at the end of our living room; he speaks nine languages; he is a physicist; he and Aunt Martha also have an apartment in Washington, D.C. Topics we do not mention in his company: the atom bomb or the war. There is music in him. And science, which Mother says often go together. He has wiry, wavy hair, isn't very tall, moves like a bear, smokes, has a deep laugh, the laugh standing in for an answer.

Here he comes! No jacket, no vest. Pajamas? He opens the door, steps back, nods—no words, just a shy smile. He holds the door as we step into the back hall. He closes the door behind us. I know that sound. We walk ahead of him down the hallway. Mother says she saw someone at the Farmer's Market. They're talking like they've always talked.

When we get to the kitchen, Mother opens a cupboard, takes out a vase, and goes to the sink. He steps around me and sits at the little table by the window. I think he always shuffled. He is not wearing pajamas; he's wearing khaki trousers and a khaki shirt. He looks at me. He has a soft smile. I hope I have the right expression. I smile. I put the mint on the table in front of him. I know this tablecloth with the colorful Dutch women in wooden shoes around the border. His shirt is open at the neck. No tie. No scars. Canvas shoes, not leather shoes. Both legs. He looks like someone who doesn't work anymore. Will he go back to his job in Washington? I don't know what atomic energy is.

Mother boils water and sets a tray.

We go out to the hall and down two steps to the living room; Mother carries the tray, Uncle Walter shuffles behind her. His legs are working. Has the market puzzle been here all this while? They go down to their chairs by the fireplace. Mother puts the black-eyed Susans on the mantel next to the photograph taken after my baptism. She brings me the glass of milk. She nods to the puzzle table where I am to sit. She sits by the fireplace, pours tea. Uncle Walter hands her some letters. She unfolds one. He moves an ashtray, lights his cigarette. Nothing has changed, and everything has changed. She is sitting in Aunt Martha's chair.

I know this puzzle. An outdoor market in a foreign town. I recognize the piece shaped like an umbrella, the piece shaped like a top hat.

When I get tired of the puzzle, I watch Uncle Walter smoking, his head resting on the back of his chair, his knees crossed, his eyes closed while Mother reads someone's letter, slowly, aloud.

Uncle Walter and Aunt Martha

Four and a Half Minutes

Mother slips on her new gold sandal, bare toes wiggling, and says, "We're having drinks at the Margolises'—all of us—so put on something fresh. And wash your face."

That I accept the strangeness of this—walk out of her bedroom no questions asked—this is what it's like now. Anything to do with the Margolises—pretend they are friends.

"Don't keep your father waiting," she calls out, as if he's already in the car. He's not in the car; he's in his bedroom tying his bow tie.

We cross Washtenaw Avenue and turn up Vinewood. My father drives Borgie so slowly you would think he was watching for mating turtles who cross the road in June and get run over. But it's not June. It's July.

Usually, when we're driving to somebody's house, Mother talks about the people whose house we are going to. On our way to the Robertsons', she asks about show dogs, or badminton, or she will remind my father that Eleanor's sister is still visiting from Kansas City for reasons we are not to discuss. But what can she possibly ask about the Margolises? What will they talk about? Blood pressure? Fish?

At the next stop sign, the cigarette pack my father takes out of his jacket is—oh no—empty. He crumples it and throws it out the window. Litter Bug. He completely got away with that. Then, he opens the glove compartment, fumbles around—no cigarettes. Then, he sticks his hand down behind the seat cushion. Mother knows better than to offer him one of her Salems. He doesn't like menthol.

The next street sign says Birchwood. The Nortons moved to Birchwood from Day Street after we moved from Day Street to Ferdon and the Robertsons moved to Glacier Way. Three families left Day Street the same year. Now, my father's new heart doctor lives opposite the Nortons, which is another example of our upside-down life. Who would ever believe that a doctor would become a fishing buddy and the doctor's wife would become—I still don't know what to call her. When I asked Mother earlier, she said, "Dr. and Mrs. Margolis."

Whenever Mother refers to his "girlfriend" or his "mistress," he says she is no such thing and he only climbed through the window because Mother put the chain on the back door. When she asked him, "Doesn't Dr. Margolis have to get up early to go to the hospital?", he said yes. When she asked, "Don't the Margolises ever go to bed?", he told her she is welcome to join him and that I am old enough to be left alone for a few hours, which is true—I am. He sounds reasonable. But when they have this discussion, she always says the same thing at the end: "I wonder why I don't feel entirely welcome." As we turn into the Margolis driveway, she says, "How was this invitation made? Did Sidney call?"

He turns off the engine and says, "Let's not make a mountain out of a molehill," which is one of his favorite expressions, along with "come hell or high water" and "three sheets to the wind."

Mother's favorite expressions are "my sainted aunt," "fit to be tied," and "cast your bread upon the waters; it will come back buttered." When I asked how bread could ever come back buttered, she said it was a quote from the bible, sort of, and it means sometimes you just have to take a chance. I guess we are casting our bread upon the waters now.

"Who designed their house?" Mother asks, her hand on the car door handle.

I can't imagine he knows the answer to that question.

"Dick Osborne," he says.

She closes her door and lifts her head high.

Flat roof, windows that go all the way down to the ground, no bushes. I don't care for it.

"Sam!"

This must be Dr. Margolis coming out the side door, all smiles.

"Lois!"

Mother introduces me. Dr. Margolis pats me on the shoulder with a heavy hand. He is a big man, taller even than Mother, with big lips and even less hair than my father, who still has some on the sides and back.

The floor inside is like a patio, different flat stones arranged like a puzzle. No rugs and no doors; you just walk across the stones. The fireplace is raised above the floor with a ledge in front of it which is where a woman sits, fiddling with the chain curtain in front of the firebox. She can't get the right and left sides of the curtain to meet in the middle. When she does turn around, she has an enormous smile, her eyes far apart like a fish. I immediately think "her face is deformed." She is casually dressed in a short-sleeved, white blouse and tan slacks that button on the side, the blouse not tucked in. She has on those Japanese slippers with the toes divided.

Dr. Margolis puts Mother's shawl over a dining room chair. Then he points to an orange canvas chair with iron legs and says to me, "I think you are the only one limber enough to get in and out of that sling." Then he makes a joke about "butts wiping the floor." My father knows better than to laugh at "butt" in front of Mother, but Mother smiles as if "butt" is a word we use all the time. The orange canvas hangs on its black iron frame like a tripod. I sink right down to the stone floor.

My parents sit at either end of a long brown sofa facing the fireplace. Mrs. Margolis passes a glass dish with peanuts on one side and olives on the other. She gives everyone a yellow paper cocktail napkin. Mother takes an olive and a napkin. Dr. Margolis helps himself to a handful of peanuts. A few fall on the floor. He reaches down, groaning, to pick them up, then throws them all in his mouth. My father doesn't want

anything. Nor do I. Mrs. Margolis sets the glass dish on the coffee
table. When she smiles, you can see all her teeth.

Dr. Margolis brings me a ginger ale.

"What will you have, Madam?" he bows in front of Mother.

"Dry martini. Thank you."

"Olive?"

"Please."

Usually, when we come to someone's house, Mother finds something in the room to admire, but how can she admire this room? Dr.
Margolis's chair has metal arms, and all the paintings have bright
colors but no people, just splashes and mistakes. Listening to Dr.
Margolis describe the problem they're having up at the camp with
a rabid raccoon, Mother asks how he can tell if the raccoon is rabid.

"Raccoons are nocturnal," says Dr. Margolis, presenting her martini. "A raccoon wandering around in daylight is probably rabid. The
caretaker said he saw this raccoon twice up on the porch in the morning. I told him to shoot it."

Mother nods sympathetically, but I know she hates that idea. She
won't kill the centipedes when they crawl up the lavatory drain. She
carries them outside and sets them under the pricker bush.

"It's too bad Bud Norton never takes the family with him to Ar-
gentina," says Mother. Travel abroad is her favorite topic. Once, in the
middle of a fight with my father, I heard her say that by *well-traveled,*
she did not mean a weekend fishing trip up north; she meant the Hi-
malayas, and South America, and Europe, and Kenya. All places, my
father reminded her, that—because she had married a salesman—she
would never get to.

"Bud works too hard," says Dr. Margolis. "We've asked—"

Mrs. Margolis shrugs, "Ornithological research."

"We've asked him up to the camp several times."

Mrs. Margolis brings my father an ashtray. She does not hand it
to him. She puts it dead center on the coffee table. My father reaches
for the ashtray, touching it where she just touched it.

After Mrs. Margolis sits back down on the fireplace seat, Dr. Margolis says he has never adjusted to muggy Midwestern summers. I am expecting Mother to ask where he grew up, but she works her lips back and forth as if she just put on lipstick, smiles her church smile, and waits for someone else to speak. Then, she crosses her legs and says she heard Cynthia Norton was accepted at Holyoke. No answer to that. Mother graduated from the University of Michigan and studied English Literature. My father went to a two-year college and majored in athletics, which was all his benefactor would pay for. Dr. Margolis had to have studied hard to be a doctor, but he is not, I think, the sort of doctor who studied much else. There are no books in the living room, not even on the coffee table, and no books in the hallway. Mrs. Margolis lights her cigarette with a lighter. Hard to tell if she went to college. She just smiles that big smile and, every now and then, gets up to go to the kitchen.

My father touches the coffee table as if he is thinking he wants to build a table like that. Then he picks up *Life Magazine*, looks at the cover, then puts it back down. He puts the glass ashtray on the cushion so Mother can reach it, not afraid the ashtray will tip. This is not the first time he has balanced that ashtray on that sofa cushion.

Dr. Margolis says, "So what are you up to Sam? Got any new projects?"

"I'm designing a mural."

I look at Mother. What is he talking about?

"It's going to be an underwater biblical scene."

"Did you say *biblical*?" laughs Dr. Margolis.

My father throws his arm over the back of the sofa.

"Adam and Eve over the toilet and Jonah and the whale over the tub."

Dr. Margolis laughs. "Sounds ambitious."

"Jimmy Barker—old friend from Argus—gave me a lesson in mural painting."

I forgot my father met Jimmy Barker when he worked at Argus Camera.

"First, you make a sketch," he says, picking up the Life magazine, holding it sideways. "You draw a grid on the sketch: one, two, three, four and so forth across the top and A-B-C-D and so on down. Then, you draw the corresponding grid on the Masonite, which is cut to fit the wall. Eve's fin is in A2, A3, and A4, and Adam's leg is in C2, C3, and C4. Then you copy your sketch square by square onto the Masonite, and you nail the Masonite to the wall. Bingo."

"So . . . you don't paint *on* the wall?" says Mrs. Margolis leaning back against the stone fireplace.

"On the Masonite."

I know what Mother's thinking: that he's going to start painting murals all over the house. After she gave him the jigsaw so he could make a Dutch door, he cut all our doors in half. We now have five Dutch doors.

"Adam and Eve?" says Dr. Margolis.

My father drops *Life* on the coffee table.

"Adam is a deep-sea diver. Eve is a mermaid. Jonah is a businessman, swimming out of the mouth of the whale." My father leans back, one foot over the other knee so he can pull up his gray sock.

"Do you suppose she could watch TV? I think tonight is *Dragnet,*" says Mother, nodding at me.

Mrs. Margolis gets up. I struggle to get out of my chair.

"Take your ginger ale," says Mother, smiling.

I follow Mrs. Margolis across the stone floor. We walk past a plastic sideboard, then we turn down the hall. I can always hear Mother walking in her high heels, but Mrs. Margolis, in these Japanese slippers, makes no sound at all. Her brown hair is short and straight. Mother's hair is curly. Mother and Dr. Margolis are almost the same height. Mrs. Margolis and my father are the same height. The television is in Dr. Margolis's study at the end of the hall. He has a big desk and a black leather sofa. When Mrs. Margolis turns on the television, she smiles directly at me, but even with that movie star smile, her little feet, and those wide apart eyes, she is not—as far as I can tell from how she walks, or talks, or seems—nicer than Mother. All night, I have been trying to decide if her voice is the low voice I heard on the telephone. Now when she says, "What channel is *Dragnet*?" I'm sure of it.

The television flickers. She turns up the volume. The Friday Night Fights always advertise Gillette Blue Blades. Maybe Mrs. Margolis and my father sit on that leather sofa and watch the Friday Night Fights together.

"I don't think *Dragnet* is on. How about . . . baseball?"

I can't talk to her. Who does she think we are? Family friends? Acquaintances? Before shutting the door, she hits a switch, and a huge fish tank built into the wall over Dr. Margolis's desk lights up.

There are at least a dozen different fish in all sizes and colors. Striped, spotted, big fins, no fins, orange, yellow, silver, flecked. Real shells and coral, not plastic castles from the pet shop. I can name some of the shells—conch, cowrie, strombus, scallop, but there are no mollusks. And no coaster for my ginger ale. The shelves are full of magazines, not books, and there are photographs on the wall of unshaven men holding dead fish.

Leo

When the door opens, it's Mother. I tell her *Dragnet* wasn't on, just baseball. She asks, "Did you try the other channels?" It would never have occurred to me to touch the television or sit on the sofa. That I am standing when she opens the door, not sitting, has given her the idea that I was being nosy. There is no way to explain what it has been like walking around this room the whole time, looking at real fish and dead fish, and reading the titles of the heart magazines and the diplomas on the wall. Just holding my Ginger Ale, looking out the window at one pine tree in the backyard.

"Who's playing?"

"The Baltimore Orioles are beating the Tigers six to four in the eighth."

"Baltimore is winning," she says, as we come back to the living room.

Dr. Margolis drapes Mother's shawl around her shoulders, which is interesting, the way he does that. Cigarette smoke wafts above the coffee table. Where is Mrs. Margolis? I want to believe that when my father comes here in the evening after dinner, he and Dr. Margolis watch baseball or boxing while Mrs. Margolis does laundry and sweeps the patio. Or maybe she wears that orange bathrobe hanging on the hook in the bathroom. I noticed it because the door was open as we walked by. Now, she comes out of a doorway I didn't notice before and hands my father a small book, which he tucks in his pocket. Mother doesn't see any of this because she is walking out to the car.

In the driveway, Dr. Margolis takes a roll of LifeSavers from his pocket, flicks his thumb under the top one, and offers one to Mother who says, "No thank you." When he offers me one, I take it because I've never seen anybody do that before. I suppose a doctor learns these tricks so he doesn't spread germs. I suppose a doctor is a sort of life saver. We pull out of the driveway. I look at my watch.

Mother says, "I'm surprised a tall man like Sidney wears bow ties; he's a long-tie man."

"He didn't used to," my father says.

"Really? When did he start wearing bow ties?"

But that is the end of that conversation. Mother didn't see my father slip the book in the side pocket of the car door. But I saw him slide it down there: a small blue book with a pink title.

"How was *Dragnet?*" says my father.

"*Dragnet* wasn't on. The Orioles were beating the Tigers six to four in the eighth."

He doesn't ask who was pitching for the Tigers. We stop at the corner. Washtenaw is wider than Vinewood with more traffic. A turtle trying to cross Washtenaw wouldn't have a chance. When we pull in the driveway, I check my watch. Door to door: four and a half minutes.

Leo

I can't sleep. It's true; my father likes to fish. He can stand in the backyard casting flies all afternoon. He doesn't seem to mind that the hooks get caught in the mock orange and the bridal wreath. And he can spend hours in the basement tying flies and drawing cartoons for the company that makes flies. He says fly fishing is a game of wits. And he says there's nothing like standing in the middle of a cool river on a hot day in your waders. Before the Margolises invited him to their fishing camp up north, he went fishing only once, in Whitmore Lake. He didn't catch anything, not even carp. He prefers trout, he said, and you only find trout in the north. You would think he had fished his whole life, the way he talks now, but you can't fish in New York City, and I doubt they fished at the orphanage. So, when did he become a fisherman? We have never been camping. The only things we do outdoors as a family are rake leaves, put up the storm windows, and hang Christmas lights. Another thing: I don't think in the winter Mrs. Margolis usually sits that close to the fire, and if the leather chair is Dr. Margolis's chair and nobody else can get out of the chair I sat in, that leaves only one other place to sit—the sofa. And what if Dr. Margolis has an emergency and has to stay late at the hospital?

I can play this game all night. Imagine who sits where, and in what clothes? Who lights whose cigarette? With a lighter or a match? Where is the ashtray? On the coffee table or on the sofa cushion? And what if we have a late dinner, and my father goes over there after dessert, and she's already wearing that orange bathrobe and those black Japanese slippers looking like Halloween? If I keep this up, before you know it, I will break the rule about respecting every single human being no matter what.

Mother's bathrobe is blue and gray paisley Viyella. I'll never forget, she wore it the night we all woke up to people screaming on Washtenaw. When I looked out my window, there was Mother running barefoot in her Viyella bathrobe across the yard, holding a blanket. Mother, wearing her bathrobe, untied, outdoors, looked as dramatic as the news she shared when she came back. A convertible had crashed into the maple at the foot of the hill, and everybody seemed all right, but the couple couldn't find their baby—the baby wasn't in the car, not on the grass, or the sidewalk, or the street. Then they heard crying, Mother said, and everybody looked up and saw the baby snagged in the branches of the tree. I can see Mother now, tightening her bathrobe sash as she sat down on the hall chair, wet grass on her feet.

"What about the baby?" I asked.

"Thanks be to God, your father climbed the tree and got the baby down safely," she said, noticing a little blood on her hand. "The baby was fine. They're extremely lucky, that family."

"Where is our blanket?"

"I think we can do without that old blanket, don't you?"

"But where is the family?"

"They've gone with the police, and your father is waiting for the tow truck."

If that accident had happened on Birchwood Road, would Mrs. Margolis have run out at two in the morning, barefoot, in her orange bathrobe carrying a blanket? I doubt it. Dr. Margolis might have put a bandage on the person bleeding, but would he have climbed a tree to rescue the baby? I doubt it. In that neighborhood, all the trees are behind the houses. A baby flung out of its car on Birchwood would die.

Cool as a Cucumber

Mother usually comes down first to fix breakfast, followed by my father, then me. But lately, my father has been coming down last. If he does sit with us, it's only for a minute. He doesn't talk about his projects anymore or inspect my homework. He just says he's going to be late, forgets to tell us what towns he's going to, and walks out the back door. The other night, I heard him tell Mother that he'll be bringing home less money. You would think, if that's true, he would try to get to work earlier, not later.

When he didn't go up to the Margolises' fishing camp the second time, I thought that was the end of Gwen. Another few weeks went by, and he never went over there once. But a few nights ago, after dinner, while Mother was on the telephone talking to someone about selling Nanny's Danish jewelry, he went down to the basement and came back upstairs, stood in front of Mother, waved the mural sketch all rolled into a tube, then pointed to the driveway. I think she thought he was going over to Jimmy Barker's on Cambridge, which is a short walk. Then he pointed to the window to show her it was raining, which meant he was driving, not walking. But when my father got to the corner, he didn't turn left toward Cambridge; he drove straight across Washtenaw and up Vinewood.

The next morning, he was on time for breakfast. When Mother asked him how Jimmy was, he said they worked on Jonah. Mother said, "Given Jimmy is being so helpful with the mural, we should ask him to dinner." My father said, "Well, fine, the next time I go over to Jimmy's, I'll ask him to dinner." Then Mother said, "And when might that be?" And he said, "It will be the next time I get stumped." Mother lifted her eyebrow. She can lift one eyebrow at a time.

I think he comes down last for breakfast not because he oversleeps or has trouble tying his bow tie—I think he's calling Mrs. Margolis from the phone in the upstairs hall.

So, this morning, I don't get out of bed at my usual time. I hear him shaving in the bathroom, then I hear him go back to his room. When Mother calls up the stairs, I pretend to be asleep. A few minutes later, I hear her coming into my room to see if I'm sick, but when I open my eyes, it isn't Mother, it's him.

"Feeling okay, Toots?" he says, walking toward my bed.

I'm not used to him coming into my bedroom in the morning.

"Sleeping in?" he smiles.

Whenever I've stayed home sick, I wait all day for him to get home from work, listen for the back door slamming, then wait for him to climb the stairs and walk towards my bed, smelling like gasoline and cigarettes, a paper bag in his hand with the name of a store printed on it because in one of his towns, he bought me something. Now, he smells like the beginning of the day, not the end of the day.

He stands still next to my bedside table, that quiet look on his face as he leans over, puts his hand on my forehead, and says, "Cool as a cucumber."

Then he buttons his shirt cuffs—one side, then the other side.

"Tired?" he says, taking a step back, "or sleepy?"

Tired means you are worn out, fed up, and exhausted. Sleepy means you need a nap.

I say sleepy, but I mean tired.

Mother looks puzzled when I come down late and asks am I feeling all right. I tell her yes, but I mean no. I am telling lies right and left. He doesn't call his office. He doesn't say "Have a nice day." He doesn't talk about his projects at the breakfast table. Mother doesn't throw pots. When he goes out in the evening, she plays solitaire and says he's gone over to Uncle Jimmy's to work on the mural, which is a lie. She can look out the window as well as I can, and Borgie does not turn left at the corner. Then he stays home for a few nights. But then he starts going out again.

The Underwater Biblical Mural

After Christmas, my father says he will finish his underwater biblical mural. Sometimes, he says, you come up with an idea, then that idea has to lie fallow. Fallow means idle. He says the fallow period is when the germ grows inside you. You don't just have an idea—boom—and out pops the finished product. The germ has to marinate.

All fall, the mural has been marinating. Now, he spends every weekend in the basement painting on Masonite. The book Mrs. Margolis gave him with the pink title turns out to be a book about aquariums. At least she didn't write her name inside, so Mother probably thinks Jimmy Barker gave it to him. Adam in his silver deep sea diving costume is done. A hose connects his mask to an oxygen tank. Air bubbles rise to the surface. My father can't find any mermaid pictures to copy, but he says mermaids are pretty standard, so Eve has a swooped, scaly green tail and long, wavy blond hair, a green bathing suit with silver flecks, and a bright red apple balanced on one fin. Eve's wavy hair got him started on the seaweed. Now, there is wavy seaweed everywhere and lots of shells, coral, sea urchins, even a seahorse. He finds an old National Geographic with an article on whales. He says the trick with whales is where you put the eye. I think the proportions of Adam and Eve to the seaweed and the shells aren't right. When I tell my father I think the shells should be smaller, he says, "proportions are overrated." My father has a whole list of things he thinks are overrated:

even numbers, sod, thoroughbreds, Polaroid cameras, sherry, church, French cuffs, striped shirts.

I love the mural. But I hate Jonah's expression as he swims out of the whale's mouth, lungs bursting, cheeks red, gasping for breath. He is wearing a gray suit and long tie, and his black shoes are heavy, and if this is the ocean floor, then it is a long way to the surface. Jonah will never make it. My father says Jonah's bursting red cheeks provide tension. Life has tension. Art needs tension.

The day the mural is ready to be nailed to the bathroom walls, we invite Jimmy Barker for dinner. Kate is home for the weekend. She took the bus from college. She has joined a sorority, Kappa Kappa Gamma. Every sister in the sorority wears the same pin. A sorority sister cut her hair. I don't care for it. Otherwise, college hasn't changed Kate. She seems the same, maybe even prettier, except for her short hair. We set the dinner table together. She gets the silver out of the sideboard, and I put the silver pieces at each place. She asks about eighth grade. I tell her I'm going to be a cheerleader like she was. Big smile. We stop setting the table to do the Tappan cheer in the front hall. Marky runs under the sideboard. She says maybe I'll get her old uniform. I wish she could come home more often. I am her true sister. We don't need identical pins.

After dinner, Mother and Uncle Jimmy stay at the dinner table while Kate and I help carry the mural through the kitchen and the dining room and up the front stairs. Marky keeps getting in the way so my father has to yell at him, but once we get the mural into the bathroom, he says Marky can come in.

Mother and Uncle Jimmy join us. Mother brings coffee and ginger snaps on a tray. She sets the tray on the sink. Uncle Jimmy sits on the bench by the standing scale. He coughs something into his handkerchief. Maybe he has tuberculosis like Marie Curie's mother.

I sit on the end of the tub. Kate leans against the radiator. Mother puts a bath towel down the clothes chute then stands in the doorway with her coffee.

Adam and Eve will go above the toilet on the long wall. Jonah and the whale will go over the bathtub. My father has built a small ledge for the mural to rest on so we only have to keep it from falling forward while he puts the first screw in. He is afraid it won't fit because measuring is not his strong suit. When I ask if measuring is overrated, he says measuring is *under*rated.

We watch quietly while he puts in the rest of the screws. He keeps going back to tighten them even more. Then he goes down to the basement for some more paint and paints over the screws. The bathroom feels like an aquarium. Outside, it's snowing.

"What is your favorite part?" Mother asks Kate.

"Seahorse," says Kate.

"And you, dear?"

I can't look at Jonah. He will drown before he gets to the surface. I imagine Jonah swimming around the corner to take a breath from Adam's oxygen supply. I don't know what to say. Except for Jonah's bursting cheeks, I love all of it.

Uncle Jimmy says, "Top notch, Sambo."

Is my father disappointed nobody picked Eve or Adam or the whale or Jonah?

"Hand me that screwdriver," he says, putting everything back in his toolbox. I wish he would enjoy the mural after all his hard work, but he acts as if somebody else painted it. But then he is never proud of his cartoons or his mock-ups. He can't explain why he draws the way he draws or where his ideas come from. After he tightens the last screw one more time, all he says is, "Well, it's not going anywhere."

Mother, Uncle Jimmy, Kate, Marky, and I go down the front stairs. My father goes down the back stairs. I know that's the shortest way to the basement, and he has to return his toolbox, but we don't seem to be a family anymore. He seems off to one side.

Year-round

It is the first warm spring day. Usually, Mother cleans out the lilac hedge in the fall, but last fall, she never got around to it. She doesn't wear gloves, and she doesn't use tools. Just her bare hands. I used to play in these lilacs all the time—not here, where Mother is kneeling, but nearer the fence. I haven't played here in a long time. I have outgrown my lilac rooms.

"You are definitely a spring person," I say because I walked all the way out here and forgot what I was going to tell her. "Kate is a summer person, and I am a fall person."

"Why dear? Why fall?"

"I just am."

She stands up. I carry the basket full of wet leaves. I know what I came out to tell her—that I have finished practicing piano and am going down to the park—but now I don't feel like going to the park. I keep changing my mind.

Mother stops on the front porch and picks up the pruning shears she left after she cut forsythia for the Easter breakfast table. Forcing forsythia marks the official beginning of spring.

"Easter is early this year," she says.

"Why is Easter a different day every year?"

"It's a moveable feast," she says. "Something to do with the vernal equinox and the paschal moon. Your father might know."

"How do you spell that? Pas-cal moon?"

"P–a–s–c–h–a–l. Not like your scientist."

When we get to the garage, she says, "If Daddy would be the winter person, we could fill out the year."

He has been cleaning out the garage. He is wearing his new blue canvas shoes we bought at Moe's Sport Shop.

"What about winter, Toots?" he says.

"Mother is a spring person, Kate is a summer person, I am a fall person, so we were hoping you would be the winter person."

"All that snow to shovel? All those icy roads?"

"Then what season are you?" Mother asks.

"I'm year-round," he says, making sure the lid on the garbage can fits tightly. That is the best thing he could have said. I was going to ask about the vernal equinox, but I don't want to break the spell of year-round.

"Welcome Happy Morning"

We are going to be late for the Easter service because Mother can't find her nail brush. You don't wear gloves to communion, she says, and she can't go up to communion with dirty fingernails.

My father pins an Easter corsage on Kate's dress, then on mine—pink carnations. Mother gets a white rose. She says she found the nail brush in the little bathroom. She uses the big bathroom. He uses the little bathroom. He must have borrowed her nail brush.

Marky can't see as well, but he can tell we're all going out. His cataracts are worse. At night, when we go upstairs, I have to walk beside him so he doesn't bump into walls. He stands at the kitchen window while we walk down the driveway. I hate when he rests his chin on the windowsill. Mother hands my father the car keys. There are too many people for Borgie, so we take the Chevy.

They argue about where to park near St. Andrew's. He knows a good place behind the Farmer's Market; she wants to try the lot behind the choir loft so we don't lose our pew. He wins; it's her Chevy, but he's the driver.

Every year, Mother worries that somebody who comes to church only once a year will take our pew, but today, our pew is empty, the same old long brown cushion with the buttons. Mother pulls out the bench and kneels right away. My father doesn't kneel; he sits, and leans forward, and rests his head on his hand on the pew in front of us. This is the time for a short personal prayer. It doesn't have to include everybody.

I like to imagine what people pray for. Mother, thankful for the warm weather. My father, thankful for his parking place. Kate, thankful for her new boyfriend who loaned her his car. I am thankful for my corsage. There is a cleat on the stone pillar near our pew. My eyes follow the black wire up to the ceiling where a tiny oval window has been opened. I pray that the heavy iron chandelier right over our heads doesn't fall. Pray Marky's cataracts don't get worse. Pray my father never goes back to the Margolises'.

Mother is pleased by the hymns on the hymn board. "Hail Thee Festival Day," (her favorite) "The Strife is O'er," and "Welcome Happy Morning."

Red

Uncle Walter has gone back to Washington, so Jimmy Barker comes for Easter breakfast. Mother puts the picture from last Easter on the sideboard when her friend Mary White and my cousins from Grosse Pointe joined us after church—Mother, her brother Uncle Tom, Aunt Elizabeth, cousins Tommy and Anne, Kate, me, and Marky.

After breakfast, my father tells us to go out to the backyard where he officially presents Mother with the herb garden he dug yesterday over by the big porch. We stand to one side while he does a handstand, then starts walking on his hands around the herb garden, his skinny bare legs and gray socks showing. He doesn't quite make it all the way around because Marky is beside himself barking, so my father tumbles forward in a somersault and takes a bow. There is a big vein throbbing in the middle of his forehead. Mother kisses him on the cheek.

"Not as good as Tom Goodrich," he says.

He went to college with Tom Goodrich. Tom Goodrich was a gymnast. I expect he will tell the story about Tom Goodrich going up and down stairs on his hands, but he points to the wheelbarrow full of the grass he dug up to make the garden.

"Good sod," he says, a little breathless, "Now I can patch that bare spot under the study window."

I remind him, "You said sod was overrated."

"When you have to pay for it."

Kate leaves for Hillsdale in her boyfriend's car. Tim is coming to meet us in a few weeks. He went home to his parents for Easter, but he took the bus so Kate could borrow his car which impresses Mother. "How thoughtful," she says. "I like the sound of this one."

My father walks Jimmy Barker back to his apartment on Cambridge, and Mother and I do the dishes. She says not to put the Meissen in the china cupboard, "just leave it on the table." I think she wants to remember what a nice day we had.

Easter, 1958

Do As I Say

It is the Monday after Easter. When I come down for breakfast, Mother is standing at the sink pulling apart a brand-new SOS pad. My father is not standing next to the stove stirring sugar in his coffee. His gray suit jacket is on the back of his chair in the breakfast room, so maybe he's gone to the lavatory. Mother rinses the pink soap off her hands and says, "Your father is lying down in the living room. Sidney told him to lie down."

If she called Dr. Margolis, that means his heart. I don't want juice. I don't want toast.

Marky is standing in the front hall by the stairs. He turns his head, but he doesn't move. Sometimes he gets stuck. My father is not lying entirely on the sofa. Only one leg is on the sofa; the other leg is off the sofa, bent at the knee, his shoe on the carpet. His eyes are shut, his white shirt is unbuttoned at the neck, and his blue bow tie is undone. He is all sweaty.

"Shooting pains," he says, dragging his thumb across his chest, "from here all the way to here." He lets that arm flop off the side of the sofa like an oar off a rowboat. The other arm lies over his chest. He opens his eyes. "I thought you were Sidney." Shuts his eyes.

When we were both sick at the same time on Day Street, he rigged a pulley down the hall so we could send things back and forth in a basket: penicillin vial, sticky top from the cough syrup, cotton ball, book of matches, his cigarette. That was the only time he's been sick.

"Do you want a wet washcloth?"

"Go get your breakfast."

He does not say he will be all right. I can't move.

"Do as I say."

He has never said that before. Do as I say.

The Meissen is still waiting to be put back in the china cupboard, petals from the forsythia fallen on the plates. His handwriting on the place cards. He was fine on Easter, pouring champagne, telling jokes, doing handstands.

"Sidney's on his way," says Mother.

"When did you call him?"

"At 7:10."

Twenty minutes ago. It's a four-and-a-half-minute drive.

Mother drops quarters in my blazer pocket.

"For your lunch," she says.

No cheese sandwich. We look out the window. Milly is walking up the driveway, not Dr. Margolis. I can't imagine leaving, but, no, Mother says, I cannot stay home. No, I cannot wait for Dr. Margolis. She hands me a piece of toast, kisses my forehead, and opens the back door.

I stick the toast in the pricker bush. Let the birds have it. Milly notices the new herb garden, then we squeeze through the gap between our fence and Mrs. Wollner's fence. Usually, I duck under the wire brace, but today I grab it—a wire hanger I watched my father straighten, then wrap around one post and then the other before twisting the ends. The wire, once in his hand, now in my hand—for luck.

There is a phone outside the principal's office in the waiting area. You ask permission to use it, and the secretary tells you not to talk longer than one minute.

"Your mother's at the hospital," says Mrs. Wollner. She must be standing in our pantry. "Your daddy had a little heart attack this morning. Tell me what you're doing after school today. What are your after-school plans?"

"I'm coming home. Now."

"Well, no, Dear. Your mother wants you to stay at school. Do you have some sort of after-school activity?"

I hear Marky barking. He wants to go out.

"What are your after-school plans?"

"I am not going to the Party Planning Committee Meeting. I am going to skip my classes. I'm coming home *now.*"

"No!" she says. Her voice is strong. "Your mother specifically asked me to tell you to stay right where you are. Now where is that committee meeting? In what room?"

"The French room."

"Well, now . . . you go plan the party, and somebody will pick you up. Wait in the French room, please."

I don't like the way she says "please.'"

Leo

French verbs are at the top of the black board. *Etre. Avoir.* To be and to have. Below the verbs, somebody wrote the party subcommittees: Entertainment, Clean-Up, Refreshments, Decoration. I join Decoration. The theme is "Showboat." The Decoration sub-committee is gathered by the windows to decide how to design a river. Someone says the river should be Mississippi, and the Mississippi River is brown. So how do we make a brown river in the gym? My father would have lots of ideas.

Arms are waving out in the hallway. It's Kate and our cousin Suzy. Kate just drove back to Hillsdale last night, which is a two-hour drive. She must have driven all the way back today.

The paddlewheel, someone says, should be at least twelve feet high. I have to pick up my book bag and walk to the front of the room, walk past four rows of desks, and go out the door where I am certain I will hear, in the hallway at Tappan, that my father is dead, which means exactly the distance from this desk to the door is when he might still be alive, only because I do not yet have the news. How old am I? Thirteen.

When I get out to the hall, they aren't crying.

"He had a heart attack," says Kate, putting her arm around my shoulder.

"But he's alive," says Suzy. "We're going to the hospital."

He's alive.

Leo

St. Joe's Hospital is where I was born, and where I got stitches over my lip, and had my ears lanced, and my tonsils out, and where we visit elderly friends. St. Joe's has pale blue walls, nuns, and holy statues. When I tell Suzy she is going the wrong way, she says, "University Hospital." Mother always says only very sick people go there.

Suzy knows where to park, and Kate has a nickel for the parking meter. We walk down the steps into the lobby. They know where the elevator is. They know what colored stripe on the floor to follow. So, while I was in English, and Science, and Civics, they were here.

In the elevator, Kate says she got a call from Mother at the Kappa house. Suzy says she got a call from Mother, too. Suzy was in her apartment. Mother told Suzy to pick up Kate at the bus station, which means Mother must have spoken to Mrs. Wollner, who told her I was in the French room, and Mother sent Kate and Suzy to pick me up. Mother could have called Tappan and given a message to Mrs. Cranston at the front desk who would have sent a messenger to my class telling me which hospital to go to, and I could have run straight down Washtenaw.

There are signs everywhere, not crucifixes like at St. Joe's. Doctors with accents talking in the elevator, and people wearing different uniforms who have different jobs at the hospital. I have been to hospital rooms before. I know about the smell. The beds have railings on the side. Sick people wear gowns, and there is a one-armed table that swings over their bed.

But we don't go to his room; we go to a waiting room which turns out to be quite large, the furniture pushed back leaving space in the middle. Vinyl chairs and sofas in orange and green have iron legs and no arms. Mother's brown cardigan is on the back of an orange chair. The rack in the corner is for your coat, but the rack is empty. The magazines don't have covers. There is even a small kitchen where you can help yourself to coffee. People are smoking by the window. One woman holds the ashtray for all of them. They look like the family who sells vegetables at the Farmer's Market, outdoor people come indoors. We sit. We don't talk.

After a few minutes, Mother walks in, looking just like she looks in church which means that if there is to be conversation, she will be the first to speak. She is wearing what she had on this morning: her brown wool skirt and pale pink blouse with embroidery on the collar. She hands Suzy her pocketbook. Then she looks at me. Her mouth opens, but then she turns around suddenly because someone called her name. She crosses the room and stops in the doorway to talk to a black-haired doctor in a short white coat. The doctor talks. Mother listens, her hands at her sides, fingers moving. Then they leave. A few minutes later, she returns alone. She puts her hand on the edge of the counter as if it were her kitchen counter, her silver bracelet dangling. She is trying to remember something. Two doctors with short white coats are behind her, but she doesn't see them. Then she hears them, turns around. Her blouse has come untucked in back. While one doctor whispers, the other one looks at the floor. One is the black-haired doctor from before; the other is red-haired. They are joined by an older, shorter doctor. His white coat is longer, and his pockets are bulging with cards, and papers, and a stethoscope. They make room for him. The two doctors in the short coats tell him something. He nods. Then they all go back out to the hallway and disappear, and the older doctor puts his hand on Mother's elbow.

"Did Dr. Margolis bring him to the hospital?"

"Yes. In his car. The ventricular in his heart was *fibelating*," says Kate.

"No," says Suzy. "It was an *enfart*."

Kate says more words I don't understand.

I want a doctor to tell me exactly what each word means, and if there are words that mean the same thing, what are the duplicates? I need one sentence I can memorize. I need to understand every word in that sentence. Mother returns, looks at Suzy, and says "Stay with her."

Kate walks out with Mother. Where are they going? A minute later, they return. Mother whispers to Kate. Then Suzy walks out with Mother, leaving Mother's pocketbook on the chair. Kate is blinking her eyes, not talking.

"Did you see him?"

"No."

"Where did you go?"

"The hallway."

"Why?"

"No reason."

She lights her cigarette.

"What's in the hallway?"

No answer.

Where does everyone keep going? What's in the hallway? If this is a waiting room, why don't we just wait here quietly? The woman in the farm family tosses her paper cup in the wastebasket and goes out.

Suzy and Mother come back with Uncle Jim Robertson. He is a psychiatrist, not a heart doctor. I've never seen him in a white coat before. He has a folder in his hand and glasses around his neck on a strap. Now the short doctor comes back. He talks to Uncle Jim. Then he says something to Mother and goes out. I get up. When Mother sees me coming, she steps to the side, touching Uncle Jim's arm. They both look at me.

"Is it all over?" I have to know.

"Is what all over?" Uncle Jim is tall. He has to lean over to talk to me.

"The heart attack."

"We certainly hope so," says Uncle Jim.

"Where is he?"

"He's in the Intensive Care Unit, the ICU."

"Where is that?"

"Down the hall."

"This hall?"

"Yes."

"Which way?"

"Your father's very sick," says Uncle Jim, "and that's the best place he could possibly be. Only doctors and nurses are permitted at the moment."

"What exactly is a heart attack?"

Uncle Jim says he will explain it to me, but not right this minute.

"Have you seen him?"

"Yes," he says.

"Really?"

"Yes, really." He smiles.

"I need to have a few words privately with Uncle Jim," Mother says, not smiling.

"But where do you keep going?"

"Nobody is going anywhere."

Not true. Ever since I got here, everyone keeps going somewhere and coming back with different expressions. I want to go where they are going, which I now suspect is the ICU. Mother motions to Suzy. I can read her lips. "Take her home."

Leo

Suzy sits on the side of my bed. She says he had a heart attack in Dr. Margolis's front seat on the way to the hospital.

"Was Mrs. Margolis in the car?"

"I doubt it."

If Dr. Margolis told him to lie down on the sofa, he might have told him to lie down in his back seat, or maybe he pulled the lever to tilt the front seat back.

Suzy folds her hands. "His heart stopped for eight minutes."

"Did he slump over?"

"Probably."

"How do you know eight minutes?"

"Dr. Margolis told Aunty Lo."

Which means he looked at his watch. Or read the clock on the dashboard.

"When they got to Emergency, he was pronounced dead on arrival."

This is not the first time I have heard these words. Mrs. Wollner explained "DOA" at dinner.

"Then they performed a *cut down*."

"What is that?"

"Something about an *incision*, inserting a wire."

Suzy has talked to a doctor. She has all the words.

"Where did they insert the wire?"

"Into his heart."

"Who inserted it?"

"I don't know. A doctor."

"Was it an operation?"

"They did it outside the Emergency Room."

"Not in the hospital?"

"No. Outside. On the ground."

"How do you know?"

"Aunty Lo said they pulled him out of the car and laid him on the pavement."

"Why didn't they take him inside?"

"They didn't want to move him, or they couldn't find a stretcher, or there wasn't time, but whatever they did—his heart started to beat. Then they took him to the ICU."

"Have you seen him?"

"No."

"Has Kate?"

"No."

"But Mother has seen him."

"I don't think so."

"When are Mother and Kate coming home?"

"They're spending the night at the hospital."

"Why? If they can't see him?"

"So that someone from the family is always there."

"And I have to stay home?"

"I'm staying home, too."

Suzy tries to get Marky up on my bed, but he can't do that anymore. And he can't get into his green chair in my father's bedroom. Lately, he's been sleeping at the foot of my father's bed, but tonight Marky sleeps on the landing.

Red

When I come down in the morning, Suzy is making coffee, and the red plaid blanket we take to football games is on the kitchen counter. Suzy explains, "Aunty Lo asked me to bring it."

"She called?"

"Just a moment ago."

"How is he?"

"The same."

"Did she see him?"

"She said he's resting."

"Is the football blanket to put over him?"

"No. It's for us if we want to lie down in the waiting room. There's a sofa."

"You lie down in the waiting room?"

"We get tired waiting."

"Why can't I go to the waiting room?"

"Even if you did go, you couldn't see him. We just wait there."

The way she says "wait there," you would think it was boring. I can't think of anything I would rather do. I have to go to school, which is the last place I want to be.

Leo

Mrs. Wollner doesn't see why just the two of us should eat in the dining room, so we have supper in the study on TV trays. "The study is cozier," she says, as she snaps the metal tray onto the fold-out legs. I sit on the sofa. Mrs. Wollner sits in the armchair. Suddenly, Marky looks up because there, in the doorway, stands Mother holding her raincoat over her arm. She looks like a houseguest.

"I'm just going to grab a quick bath while Kate holds the fort," she says. "Doesn't that macaroni and cheese look good?"

"How is Sam?" says Mrs. Wollner, putting down her fork. We are desperate for news.

The way Mother turns around, not putting her hand on the door frame or touching the doorknob, which is what she would have done a week ago, she looks lost, as if this is not her house. She just holds her raincoat, and smiles her polite smile, and says to Mrs. Wollner, "He's holding his own. Thank you. Thank you, Louise, for everything."

I can tell Mrs. Wollner would like to talk privately with Mother. She starts to get up, but then she takes a swig of her drink and stays in her chair. She wants to know how he's doing, but she stays with me.

When Mother comes downstairs, I am waiting for her in the kitchen. She says a bath is just what she needed. And clean clothes. Then she goes over to the counter where we are putting the mail. She picks up one envelope, then drops it, picks up another, drops it. Then she goes over to the telephone. Maybe she will sit down in the telephone chair, but no, she stands over the telephone, reading the messages we have written for her on the pad, then she drops the pad on the counter. She can't hold onto anything. "Did you talk to Aunt Elizabeth?"

"Mrs. Wollner did."

"Jan Vreede called?"

"She made the macaroni and cheese."

"That was thoughtful. Who spoke to Mr. Ginzburg?"

"I did. Your jacket is ready."

She walks over to the sink.

"I filled the bird bath."

"That was nice, darling."

I wish she would sit down or at least pat Marky.

"Is everything all right at school?"

"If I go to the hospital, then Kate or Suzy could have a break."

"That's nice of you to offer."

"Have you seen him?"

"I haven't, no."

Not true. I know she has and that Suzy has, too. But if they admit this, they will have to tell me how he looks.

"Can't I go?"

"Maybe in a few days," she says. "We'll just have to see."

"See what?"

"When it would be appropriate. What Dr. Cairns—"

"Is he the short doctor?"

"Yes."

"What about Dr. Margolis?"

"Dr. Cairns is Daddy's specialist now."

"Aren't you going to take Daddy anything?"

"Not at the moment."

When we visited Mrs. Wollner at Mercywood, Mother took her mail, a book, flowers, and her robe.

Leo

"Good news," Suzy says the next day. "He's off the critical list."

"What's that?"

"They grade how sick the person is: Critical, Stable, Fair, Good."

"What is his grade now?"

"Stable. He doesn't remember having a heart attack, or Easter, or digging the new garden. You would expect with no heart beat for eight minutes he might have brain damage, but he can move both arms and legs. He just can't remember certain things. Dr. Cairns says that often happens. Dr. Cairns thinks digging that garden is what caused it."

Mother's Easter present.

Cornflakes

Kate is home to study for her final exams. Mother is home from the hospital. Suzy has mixed the martinis, and we are in the living room having cocktails. You would think everything was normal. You would think it was just another spring evening at home.

"It's all right," says Mother. "We needn't be there every minute. You can take that scowl off your face, dear."

"Does that mean he's better?"

"Well, it does, yes. He's a little better."

Kate needs the lighter so Mother hands it to her. Then Mother needs the lighter so Kate throws it to her. She actually throws it, and Mother actually catches it, like best friends. Kate has to go back Monday. I haven't had any time with her by myself yet.

"He pinched the nurse today," says Suzy, "and he said he didn't want any goddamn tea!"

"All good signs," says Mother, crossing her legs. "And they've taken out the catheter."

Catheter is another word for my list. Also *arrhythmia, fibrillating, and infarct.*

"But we're not out of the woods yet."

"How long will he be in the ICU?"

"A few more weeks. He sends you his love."

This is martini talk. He doesn't talk like that.

"When can I go?"

"Shortly."

It feels like the seven hills. There never was a hill, and I will never get to see him.

Ted

After Mother and Kate go to bed, I take a bath. Suzy comes into the bathroom. She puts down the toilet seat, sits, and sighs.

"Aunty Lo said something interesting."

From the way she says *interesting,* I think she knows about Mrs. Margolis.

"When Dr. Margolis arrived that morning—"

"What morning?"

"When he had his heart attack—there were cornflakes around his mouth."

"Cornflakes?"

"Aunty Lo made a joke about it."

If Dr. Margolis was eating cornflakes when Mother called him to say my father was in pain, and Dr. Margolis rushed out the door, not bothering to wipe his mouth, he would have arrived before I left for school. From the Margolises' to our house is four and a half minutes. That he did not arrive until after I left for school means Dr. Margolis did not rush out the door. So, when exactly—before or after the phone call—did the cornflakes get stuck to his lips? Maybe he was in his pajamas eating cornflakes, took the phone call, and ran back to the bedroom. But Dr. Margolis has big lips, and he would have seen cornflakes sticking to those lips in the bathroom mirror, or the toothbrush would have knocked them off, or they would have rubbed off on the towel after he brushed his teeth. It is unlikely the cornflakes stayed on his lips from before the phone call, through getting dressed in the bedroom, and through his passage through the house and out to the garage, which means it went like this: My father says he has shooting pains in his chest. Mother calls Dr. Margolis who says, "tell him to lie down on the sofa; I'll be right over." They hang up. My father lies down on the sofa in the living room. Meanwhile, Dr. Margolis hangs up the phone but does not reach for his car keys. Rather, he sits at the breakfast table and helps himself to another spoonful—not exactly rushing out the door. Not exactly a fishing buddy. Not exactly a life saver.

Red

Mother is right about the scowl on my forehead. I can see it in the mirror, and it won't go away. So, I put a note on Mother's bedside table and a note under Suzy's pillow. I beg to go to the ICU. Mother is not back from the hospital, but Suzy has read her note which is why she is coming down the hall.

"Move over," she says, creasing my note four ways. She takes a deep breath and sits on my bed. "The reason Aunty Lo hasn't let you come to the hospital is all the ICU equipment. Uncle Sam is attached to machines."

"What kind of machines?"

"A heart monitor, IV, EKG, some others."

They have all been going to the ICU for weeks now. At least Suzy admits it.

"Aunty Lo is afraid the machines will frighten you."

"What do they do?"

"Keep him alive."

Then how could she possibly think they would frighten me? If they are keeping him alive, I believe in them entirely.

"Dr. Margolis is taking all the credit."

"The credit for what?"

"For saving his life."

Suzy talks to me like my father does—straight.

Leo

The next day, when I get home from school, Suzy says we're going to the hospital. I can't believe it.

We go to the same waiting room. Suzy says he will probably be asleep, and to remember there are other people in the ICU, and not to touch the machines, and to be careful where I step because there are cords all over the floor. I don't understand why we have to wait here, but perhaps we are waiting for Mother who is in the bathroom. On top of the coat rack, neatly folded, is our plaid football blanket.

More minutes go by. I will explode if we don't get to the ICU. Finally, Mother comes in with fresh lipstick and a magazine. She was down in the gift shop, she says, and then she ran into Uncle Jim, and they had an ice cream in the cafeteria. She wasn't expecting us quite so soon. She walks right toward me, takes my hand, and we walk out to the hallway—very direct. I am old enough not to need my hand held, but if that's what it takes, fine.

We pass the door I thought was the ICU, then pass more doors until we get to a metal door at the very end of the hall that says Intensive Care Unit. She lets go of my hand to knock. There is a machine on a cart by the door. A tall orderly in a shower cap opens the door a crack.

"I'm sorry," he says, "A patient is having a procedure."

We step back. The door shuts. We go back to the waiting room. Doctors' names and "code something" on the loudspeaker. Mother says she needs to speak to one of the nurses. Suzy and I wait again. I can't believe it. When Mother returns, she looks completely different. How could her lipstick disappear in two minutes?

"Take her home," she says to Suzy.

I didn't think things could get any worse. But there is always a worse place. And a worse place after that place.

Leo

I hear Suzy coming down the hall. I move over. She sits on the side of my bed. That has become her spot.

"The code blue today in the ICU was Uncle Sam. He had another heart attack, but not like the first."

"DOA?"

"No!"

"While we were there?"

"Just before. He was right where he needed to be. They stabilized him."

I can spell stabilized.

"Where is Mother?"

"Spending the night."

"When can I go back?"

"I don't know," Suzy says. Not yes or no. "He's back on the critical list."

Better not to hope. No hope ever. Better to believe I will never see him until next year. Go where I am told to go, wait where I am told to wait, eat on the TV trays, be polite to Mrs. Wollner, hug Marky. There is no point in writing another note. They pretend to know how I feel, but they don't. They have never known or understood. Not once to see him. Not once in twenty-two days. Not since the morning when he lay on the sofa with one leg on the floor and one arm dangling. Marky has given up sleeping on the landing. He's gone back to my father's room and sleeps by the green chair.

The ICU

There are six beds—three on the left and three on the right—separated by curtains hooked to a rod attached to the ceiling. Some curtains are pulled around the beds for privacy, some are not. There are men and women, old and not that old.

Nobody has to tell me which bed he's in. I see him in the far-left corner, eyes closed, railings on both sides, his curtain partway open. A tall nurse stands on the far side of his bed in front of a window. She nods when she sees Mother and says, "Mr. Schneider? You have very special visitors."

He doesn't open his eyes.

"Mr. Schneider?" she says a little louder.

Nothing. His right arm is tied to the railing with strips of white cloth. On the back of his hand is a piece of tape over a clear plastic tube next to a bad bruise. The plastic tube goes over the bar and up to the plastic bag on the pole. The bag holds a clear liquid. A word I can't read is printed on the bag in orange. Suzy was right about the machines.

His gown is blue with a white neckband that ties in the back. One of the white ties has come undone and lays on his pillow. More pillows under his left ankle. A clip with sharp teeth is pinched to the sheet and is connected to a cord tangled up with all the other cords and cables. No place for cards, or flowers, or his glass of water, or his ashtray because the bedside table has only room for a machine with a TV screen. Numbers in boxes fill the screen.

The nurse puts two fingers on my father's wrist and stares at her wristwatch. Then she places his hand back on the sheet, pats it gently, and goes to the foot of the bed, takes the clipboard out of a plastic holder, writes, replaces the clipboard in the holder, and pokes her pen in her hip pocket. She has smooth black hair in a French twist. She moves around the machines without bumping into them or tripping. She pulls the curtain open wider, her white shoes squeaking on the linoleum. She tells Mother the wound doctor is coming later to have another look at his heel. She smiles at me, then goes out, head bowed.

A clear plastic hose in his nose is held in place by an elastic strap that goes across his cheeks, over the whiskers, and around his head. The hose is connected to a tank with a dial at the top. A tag wired to the nozzle says *Oxygen*. His blanket is white, loosely-woven cotton. It's cold in here. Why can't he have a warmer blanket? Our football blanket is just down the hall.

His left hand lies flat on his chest. That is no one else's hand. No one else's veins. I know those veins.

Mother moves her pocketbook to the other arm. She is thinking we shouldn't have come, that the machines are scaring me—too much equipment for a thirteen-year-old.

I step carefully over the cables. I put my hand on the rail. I watch the gown over his chest lift and drop, lift and drop—not much, but enough. He is not well; I can see that. But he is breathing. His gown is going up and down. His scar is still over his right eye. I wish he would open his eyes, see me, say something—but resting is important, and I have to learn how these machines work, what all the knobs and dials do. Learn where all the cords come out and where they plug in. I need to know the name of the nurse who just left and the name of the other nurse who just came in. What the liquid hanging in the bag is called and what it's for. Where they keep wool blankets.

Any minute now, Mother is going to say it's time for us to let Daddy rest. When she does, I will tell her to please wait for me in the waiting room. I will suggest she take a long nap under the football blanket. I wonder if the hospital has its own police force because that is what it's going to take to get me out of here.

Part II

Spring 1963–1966
1015 Ferdon Road and 1472 River Road

Sameul

Thirty-nine days after my father was pronounced Dead on Arrival, Mother takes two grocery bags to the University Hospital to bring him home.

"Looks like rain," she says, putting the bags in the back seat. I am trying to picture him riding in the front seat. He has never been a front seat passenger. When I suggest she take an umbrella, she says, "Have you forgotten? He hates umbrellas?" She is all dressed up in her yellow and green sundress and brown spectator pumps.

People keep calling to ask when he's coming home. She doesn't tell them which day; she just tells them "pray for a break in the beastly weather. I have never known it to get this hot in June." She is worried that his hospital room was so nice and cool and that the study, where he will be sleeping, is not at all cool because that side of the house gets the afternoon sun. The awning and Mrs. Wollner's fans will help, but will they help enough? Heatstroke is the last thing we need.

Watching her back the Chevy around the pricker bush, I notice the sky is approaching greenish-gray. For one second, a tornado seems entirely possible, then it seems absolutely not possible. Not today.

Jake Fried, our student who rents the third floor, cut the grass yesterday, and the new student whose name I haven't learned yet, has been helping, too. Yesterday, they brought the wicker furniture up from the basement to the screened porch. Then, they moved the sofa from the study out to the porch to make room for the rented hospital bed. Mother offered to lower their rent ten dollars for June, but they refused. I filled the ice cube trays and put the flag out. Our flag is famous; it comes from World War II when my father rescued it from the burning Chenango. The edges are singed, but in our family, you don't replace priceless things just because they are frail. If they are frail, you treasure them even more.

Mother borrowed a fan from someone in the Monday Club that needs to be returned, but we can keep the two fans Mrs. Wollner gave us. We put one across from my father's chair on the porch and the other one in the study where he will sleep now because he can't climb stairs. We may have to move the porch fan to the study when he goes to bed.

His New York City photographs, which Mother got framed, were over his desk upstairs. I moved them down to the study and hung them by the bookcase.

We have lilies of the valley on the dining room table, lilacs on the hall table, and azalea blooms on the mantel in the study. Kate comes home Saturday. She can bring Tim soon, Mother says, but not just yet. Suzy is coming for Sunday dinner.

I think he would like to know I washed Borgie and Jake drove Borgie around the block to oil the gears, but Mother says, "not one word about Borgie. He may not be driving Borgie right away." The thought of my father driving reminds me of Gwen Margolis. I have not thought about her in a long time. It feels like she stepped off a cliff. Dr. Margolis isn't his doctor anymore.

Marky knows something is happening, but he doesn't know what. When I let him out, he sniffs around the pricker bush, looks at me standing on the back steps, then walks over to the garden, looks at me again. Then, he sniffs around the birdbath, and comes back inside, and lies down by the sideboard. He has his nervous look. He doesn't close his eyes. Mother has been gone for half an hour. What is taking so long? Was there another code blue?

I make sure the flag doesn't fall out of the bracket. Marky thumps his tail when I walk by. I pet him on the head. I should sit beside him and comfort him, but I can't sit. I check the ice cube trays. I check all the flowers. Finally, I hear the Chevy.

Mother told me not to run outside, to take everything nice and easy. I look out the breakfast room window. Marky doesn't hear the car door slam. I see Mother, but I don't see my father. Oh no. But then I do see him. He takes a long time to get out of the car. Mother gets the brown paper grocery bags out of the back seat. He keeps his hand on the car as he walks around the hood, but the metal is hot, so he can't really hold on. His jaw is clamped shut, no smile. He doesn't look at the garden or the lawn; he just looks down. When he gets to the back steps, he puts his hand right into the grape ivy to feel the garage wall. A second later, he's in the back hall, and Marky is skidding around the corner, jumping all over him. Marky hasn't moved that fast in years. My father grabs the mitten box over the radiator. He shouts, *"Down!"* Marky runs back to the stove, then back to my father. He tucks his tail between his legs, but it keeps wagging and hitting the cabinets. Mother sets the grocery bags on the counter; the radio antenna is sticking out of one bag. My father grits his teeth, says he doesn't need any help. I grab Marky's collar, and pull him through the swinging door into the dining room, and make him lie down by the sideboard. A second later, the pantry door opens, my father takes one step, the pantry door bangs against his hip, and he grabs Mother's chair at the end of the table. Marky thumps his tail. I have him by the collar. My father holds onto the dining room table the whole way around, mumbling. Mother goes around the other way, carrying the poodle tray, and we all end up on the screened porch.

"What's the sofa doing out here?"

He's home. He's talking.

"Al doesn't want you climbing stairs for a little while, so we've made a bed up for you in the study." (We are not to mention it's a hospital bed because he might not notice.)

"I took a divine nap out here yesterday," Mother says, setting the poodle tray on the little table. She has everything ready—his VO on the rocks, salt-free crackers, cocktail napkins she ironed this morning, lemonade for me, martini for her, and a Milk-Bone for Marky.

"I don't need a divine nap," he mumbles. "What I need is this goddamned chair!"

At least he still swears, but not in the same way. When he says "goddamned chair," it is as if he can't wait to sit in it.

All week, Mother debated whether she should buy smaller khakis or just take his old paint-splattered khakis to the hospital. He wore the hospital gown for weeks, then they let him wear his pajamas, but he needs clothes to wear home. All week, she's been saying the old khakis won't fit, and she's right—they're way too big—but it's nice to see all the drips and strands of paint from his projects: green from the porch furniture, gold from Eve's fin, pink from the sea urchin, and blue from Jonah's tie. She was right: New trousers would be too big a change, and there's too much change as it is. She gives my father his drink and the Milk-Bone.

"Come here, Pooch," he says.

I let go of Marky's collar. Marky slinks over, tail between his legs.

"Sit," he shouts. He remembers Marky can't hear.

Marky sits.

He puts the Milk-Bone right by Marky's chin, the old trick.

"Staaaay," he says.

Marky remembers to stay. I am waiting for my father to move the biscuit over his nose and say, "Stay, stay, stay," but he skips this part and just says, "Release!" Marky's favorite command. Marky stares, confused.

"Take it! Good boy! Good boy!"

Marky opens his mouth, just barely enough to take the biscuit, then turns, bumps his head on the wicker stool, and lies down by the wall.

My father takes a sip of his drink, then he mumbles. He mumbled before in the dining room. Doesn't he know we're right here? Finally, he smiles. *Finally.* Then he winks at me. I forgot to learn how to wink while he was gone.

"I don't suppose there's a Viceroy anywhere?"

Mother had me search the house and all his jackets for any old packs. Now, she presses her lips together and shakes her head as if she has promised she will not say a word about smoking. Smoking and climbing stairs are the two things we must be strict about.

"Who moved the sofa?"

"Paul and Jake. Paul is our new student. Paul Harris."

I was there in the hospital when she told him about Paul, but he doesn't remember.

He turns around to look at the yard. If he sees things we did wrong, he doesn't say so. I am beginning to think he might not notice anyway. He hasn't noticed I hosed down the porch. He hasn't noticed Marky's green ribbon.

"Go get your science report," Mother says, adjusting the fan so it isn't right in his face.

For my Milky Way project, he designed a nice cover, but then he nearly ruined my mollusk shell report. It was during the mural period, and he wanted to draw seaweed everywhere. Now, when I hand him the notebook, I feel bad because it was so much easier without him interfering.

"Didn't she do a nice job?"

"*Marie Curie*," he reads. "Nicely centered."

I want to say, "Next year you'll help me," and I feel worse when the words don't come out.

"Very good," he smiles, "very professional." Then he looks at the hospital bracelet on his wrist and reaches for his back pocket.

"By the sink," Mother says, "points down!"

He doesn't want kitchen scissors. He wants his pocketknife, and I know where it is: the top drawer of his bureau that Paul and Jake brought down to the study.

I give him his pocketknife. When he slices through the hospital bracelet, Mother catches it before it hits the floor. He puts his pocketknife back in his pocket. Then she reads what it says on the bracelet and hands it back to him.

"They spelled your name wrong."

He doesn't want to look at it, so she hands it to me. I can barely read the faint purple letters under the plastic, but she's right; it says "Sameul." The doctor's name on the bracelet is Albert Cairns, not Sidney Margolis. It says his birthday—June 19, 1907. At least he will be home for his birthday.

Mother talks about Uncle Walter's trip to Copenhagen; that the Shoecrafts lost another elm; that Kate will be home tomorrow; that Mr. Knox took a load of junk on Monday; that for dinner we're having chicken salad, rolls, and lima beans. While she talks, he sips his drink and leans his head back.

Now, it's his turn to speak, but what can he possibly talk about? What he ate in the hospital? What color his pills are? I can't imagine what it was like sleeping thirty-nine nights in the hospital. Mother went every day, and I went three times, and friends went. I don't know if Mrs. Margolis ever went. "Look! There's Jake and Paul!" Mother points to the students walking across the backyard, which would have been strange before but isn't strange now that they're the ones mowing the grass.

"It should be open!" Mother shouts. We never use the porch door.

"Welcome home," says Jake, shaking my father's hand.

"Sir," says Paul, shaking his hand.

"Paul is from Baton Rouge, Louisiana," says Mother.

The boys sit on the sofa they carried out here. My father pulls out a hankie Mother must have put in his pocket. Then she passes the plate of crackers.

"Have you got enough fans upstairs?" Mother says.

"The heat doesn't bother him," Jake says.

Mother smiles. "How hot does it get in Louisiana, Paul?"

"Pretty hot."

Mother says she had a cousin who lived in St. Louis.

Paul is from Baton Rouge. Mother has the towns mixed up.

My father stares at his blue canvas shoes. He has hardly worn them since she brought them home from Moe's.

"The Tigers are playing the Bears tonight," Jake says, "double header." Then Jake nudges me because we often watch the games together—Jake, me, and my father. Jake can sit in Marky's green chair, which we moved downstairs, and I can sit on the end of the hospital bed.

Mother excuses herself and goes out to the kitchen. After a few minutes, I see her walking through the dining room carrying the radio he had at the hospital. A few minutes later, she goes back to the kitchen. When she comes back, the students leave by the porch door.

My father looks tired and doesn't argue when Mother suggests he lie down for a few minutes. You would think the last thing he would want to do is lie down. He hasn't even finished his drink. As Mother follows him, she explains that his pajamas are in the lavatory on the hook and his razor is on the shelf.

We moved his bureau and bedside table down to the study. She clamped the gooseneck lamp from his desk onto the bedside table where I put Life magazine. The lavatory is two steps down from the hall, but there is a little railing. Dr. Cairns okayed two steps, but no more than two.

When I come into the study to ask if he wants to watch the Tigers, the fan is rotating, and he is sitting on the side of the bed examining the switch that moves the bed up and down. He doesn't object to the hospital bed. Then he puts the switch down and starts fiddling with the radio, moving the antenna, and turning the dial until he finds the ball game. He doesn't invite me to stay. He hasn't mentioned the television in the corner. He hasn't watched television in forty days.

Mother is making the chicken salad when I get to the kitchen, her forehead sweaty.

"He doesn't want to watch the game."

"He got used to the radio in the hospital," she says. "He got used to spending time alone. When he wakes up, we'll have supper. Let Marky out."

Marky goes down the step and stands in the middle of the driveway. He doesn't go over to the pricker bush, but smells the corner of the garage, sticks his nose into the grape ivy, turns to the side, tinkles, and comes back in. When he wants to, he can still raise his leg a few inches.

"Chive, please?" Mother hands me the scissors.

Jake has a radio on the third floor, but the rule is if Jake comes down to see us, then I can ask if he wants to watch the Tigers on TV, but otherwise Jake and Paul are not to be disturbed. They pay rent and are entitled to privacy.

I hand Mother the chive and the scissors. She cuts tiny pieces into the chicken salad. Then she goes to check on my father and comes back with the news that he isn't coming to the table. She isn't even upset. She takes a tray out of the tray rack in the pantry. Then she goes to her purse. Takes out two bottles, goes into the dining room, comes back with the Meissen salt dish, dumps the salt down the sink, wipes the salt dish out with the dish towel, and opens the brown bottle. One pill goes in the salt dish. Round and white. What about the other bottle? That goes beside the sugar bowl. That is his breakfast pill.

"Can he have sugar?"

"Sugar, but not salt."

She goes back to the dining room, returns with the Meissen plate, napkin, and silverware. She spoons out chicken salad and lima beans. Glass of water, napkin, silverware.

"What about his napkin ring?"

"Not today."

Just when I expect her to pick up the tray, she takes everything off the tray, takes a blue placemat out of the drawer and arranges the tray again. Then she takes him his tray just as Marky comes through the pantry. He scoots behind the telephone chair. A few minutes later, Mother comes back with his food still on the tray.

"One bite," she says, putting the tray on the counter. "He's had a big day." Then she pulls out the bread board and drags the stool over next to it, pours a glass of milk, gives me his plate, a different fork, then goes to the icebox, takes out Vermouth, mixes a martini in the pantry, and goes straight to the porch.

The salt dish is empty. At least he took his pill. I can't eat. Marky gets it all.

Ted

When I go to say good night, it's only seven o'clock, but he's asleep. The curtains are closed. The radio is broadcasting the baseball game, the fan whirring, water glass on his table next to *Life Magazine*, dinner napkin on the floor. He has on his blue pajamas, the sheet pulled up to his waist. The light by his bed is off. Marky is asleep beside his green chair, and somebody just hit a fly ball to center.

His photograph we always called Old Woman in New York City

Astor Place

Nobody has to tell me the quieter things are the better. We walk quietly. We eat quietly in various locations. The days go by quietly. And the nights. Mother and I sleep upstairs. My father and Marky sleep downstairs.

There are so many restrictions. No salt. No cigarettes. No coffee. No driving a car. No fly fishing. No climbing stairs. No raising your arms above the shoulder, and, lest we forget, no more working to put food on the table.

Over and over, the story is told how his heart stopped for eight minutes, that he was pronounced Dead on Arrival at the University Hospital Emergency entrance only to be miraculously brought back to life. Dead one minute, alive the next. Someone says DOA means Date of Accident not Dead on Arrival. Well, DOA means both in our case. Eight minutes without a heartbeat. Dr. Margolis presented his case at the Department of Internal Medicine Grand Rounds. What a fine doctor to have done just the right procedure to bring this dead-as-a-doornail heart back to life after eight long, slumped over minutes in the back seat of the doctor's car that took twenty, maybe thirty, minutes to get to our house.

Saying goodbye at the back door, friends whisper how normal he looks. Mother smiles and says, "well, he did lose one thing." Then she says, "it's hard to explain, but he seems to have lost his tact! But then," she laughs, "he always did talk straight!"

His bow ties hang in his closet beside his white shirts, freshly pressed on the mangle. The cartons of paper from Evans-Winter-Hebb in the back seat of Borgie are put under his desk when he's taking a nap. We have plenty of scratch paper now. I can't believe he will never drive out the driveway again in his bow tie and white shirt. How will he earn a living? Nobody asks.

When my father is ready to come to the dinner table, Mother invites Uncle Jimmy. I get to set the table. The lilacs and daffodils are over, but the nasturtiums are blooming by the driveway. I put several in a small glass vase so we can see one another across the table. Mother loves flowers, but never tall ones in the center of the table. She says seeing one another is more important.

My father takes one pill with his dinner. The pill bottle is in the cupboard with the coffee so we don't mix it up with the pill bottle beside the sugar bowl. I put the evening pill in the Meissen salt dish. Our regular salt dish goes between Mother and Uncle Jimmy. We don't want to remind my father that he can't have salt.

I ask if Marky can sit at the table, given it's a special occasion. Mother says Marky sits at the table only for birthdays. Tonight, she wants everything to be as normal and relaxed as possible. We are having a chicken noodle casserole so he doesn't have to carve.

Mother wears her seahorse sundress. My father wears his new khakis and a plaid short-sleeved shirt from Van Boven's. Uncle Jimmy's white shirt has paint splashes. After my father serves the chicken casserole, Mother serves the vegetables and I pass the rolls.

"I saw Demaris Cash at the Farmer's Market," says Mother.

My father looks up. We don't know Demaris Cash. Uncle Jimmy doesn't either.

"She founded the Treasure Mart?"

Nobody remembers.

"Well, the Treasure Mart has a new president. Lima beans, Jimmy?"

"Just carrots," he clears his throat.

"Tell us about the ping-pong tournament, dear."

"I came in second."

My father isn't paying attention, but he's eating, and he's not slumped over.

The phone rings. Usually, if the phone rings during dinner, we let it ring, but Mother excuses herself saying, "Now, who can be calling at this hour?"

My father stabs another lima bean. He used to stab four at a time; now he stabs one at a time.

Mother comes back to the table, smooths her napkin across her lap and sighs.

"Well! Henry Lewis—he's our minister, Jimmy—thinks there may be a job at the University Hospital." Big smile.

A job for my father? No, a job for *her*—at the University Hospital where my father just spent thirty-nine days and nights. I thought we were through with that place.

"What has Henry Lewis got to do with the hospital?" says my father.

"He's the hospital chaplain."

Blank face.

"He came to see you every day."

Still blank.

"Henry retired from St. Andrew's two years ago, Sam. You took the photographs."

Blank again.

"Darling. Henry married us."

Still blank.

"Has Henry gone into the moat?"

This is her little joke when he can't remember something.

His denture drops down, he pushes it back up. He can't reach the rolls and leans forward. His chair tips forward and back. Marky looks up. He can't hear anymore, but he can feel vibrations.

"Henry called to tell me about a job," says Mother, and because none of us says anything because we are in shock at the idea of her going to work, she says, "Let's see," and starts counting on her fingers. "I was thirteen when Henry came to town, so that would be forty-one years ago." I know what's coming next. She will list all the ceremonies Henry Lewis has performed at Saint Andrew's for our family:

"First and *foremost*, he married me to Sam." (She leaves out the part about her parents disapproving until Henry Lewis said he was "a fine fellow.") "Then he buried Bapa, baptized and confirmed both girls, buried Nanny, buried Aunt Martha."

This is usually the end of Henry Lewis stories, but now she dips her napkin into her water glass and dabs the spot on the tablecloth where she spilled juice from the casserole, and says, "I told Henry to make it perfectly clear that I have no social work degree, so he said, when I have my interview, to describe what I did at The Henry Street Settlement House. Henry—the chaplain, Jimmy, there's no connection—also helped me get the job at the settlement house, through Grace Church. Of course, we have Grace Church to thank for many things," she smiles because we all know how she looked out the rectory window one day and saw a young man in the courtyard playing basketball. When she asked who was the fellow in white flannels, the rector said, "You should meet Sam."

Now, Mother is in such a good mood, I ask her to tell us about the newspaper on the subway, which is my favorite New York City story.

"Well! Your father and I had been to the theater, and the train was crowded, and we were holding onto the straps, and suddenly he looked down, and I looked down, and there, would you believe, around my ankles, were my undergarments. The elastic had broken. So, your gallant father," she bows her head, "dropped his newspaper, and as I stepped out of my undergarments, he bent over on that crowded train and scooped my undergarments into his newspaper, tucked the paper under his arm, and we got off at Astor Place. We walked east on 10th Street. When he said good night at my door, he said, 'You forgot your paper' and handed it to me. Well! I decided then and there that was the man for me. We were married the following December."

My father used to roll his eyes when she told this story, or say something funny about her "drawers," but tonight, he listens as if he's hearing it for the first time.

When Mother gets up to clear the table, I get up to help.

"Don't get up, dear. Tell Uncle Jimmy about your art class. Tell him what we bought at Overbeck's Bookstore."

Uncle Jimmy is having a coughing fit, and I don't feel like talking. Most of my friends have gone up north to their cottages. The O'Neills have gone to France. My sister is in summer school. I don't care for summer. The art class at the recreation department is boring. Mother just signed me up to get me out of the house. I can't earn money until I'm sixteen. Two more years.

Mother is still in the kitchen, and nobody feels like talking. Henry Lewis's phone call has transformed Mother. She is exiting our life, heading for—of all places—the University Hospital!

Mother, 1926

My father on
Broadway

Mother near
Grace Church,
NYC, 1934

My father, 1932

Their apartment on
East 10th Street, 1936

Lamb of Stone

Walking home from Burns Park after the tetherball tournament, I see our Chevy coming slowly down Ferdon Road. My father was fine this morning. The Chevy stops. I walk across the grass, step into the street, and get in. Mother looks in the rearview mirror. I know what I will do if she says my father just died. I've already planned it. I will get out of the car and run to the Arboretum all the way down to the Huron River.

"I took Marky to Dr. Hanawalt."

Not my father. Marky. Dr. Hanawalt is Marky's vet. Mother has prepared me. Marky living such a long life, fifteen times seven, which is a hundred and five dog years. Marky bumping into the wall at the foot of the stairs. Marky not able to climb onto his green chair. That when Marky gets too tired, Mother will take Marky to Dr. Hanawalt, who will give Marky a shot, and Marky will go to sleep, and never wake up. Now it has actually happened. He wasn't sick, but he was old, and deaf, and almost blind—sleeping by the sideboard when I left for the park.

"I didn't want you to walk in the door and—"

We are in front of the Spanish-looking house with the archway and the black iron railing. Marky and the Spanish house are now connected. I expect she will turn around, but she drives ahead. We are not going home; we are delivering a Monday Club book.

Nobody is home in the house on Norway so I leave the book in the mailbox.

We go to Jack's Market where we avoid the dog food aisle. I don't want to go home, but we have run out of errands.

As we walk in the back door, she says, "Naturally, your father is upset."

Marky's bowls are not on the floor in the icebox room, and the Milk-Bone box is not on the counter. Where has she put his things? Where was he last lying down? I look in the dining room at the green carpet in front of the sideboard—no dog hairs, just ridges from the vacuum wheels, not even a stray hair or a Milk-Bone crumb. I run for the stairs. Halfway up, I trip.

Mother sits on my bed and says all the things she has already said: that we didn't want Marky to suffer. That Marky lived a good, long life. That he had a wonderful family. That he had me.

"Why *today*?"

"When it was time to go out, he could hardly get up. Then, when I let him out, he tinkled on the back step, and his legs gave out. He collapsed."

"On the *step*?"

"So, I thought, 'it's time.'"

"How did he get in the car?"

"Mr. Knox carried him."

"*Mr. Knox?*"

"He was mowing the lawn."

Mr. Knox used to pick up our trash. Now he picks up our trash and mows our lawn and carries our dog.

"Where were Jake or Paul?"

"At college, darling."

"Where was Daddy?"

"Your father held the car door for Mr. Knox."

"Did Marky ride in the front seat?"

"The back seat. And Dr. Hanawalt came out and carried Marky inside. Then Marky just closed his eyes. He didn't feel a thing. He was tired."

"But in the car—where did he think he was going?"

"For a ride, I suppose."

"But we don't take Marky for rides anymore."

"I don't think he noticed."

"Did he look out his window?"

"No."

"Did he bark at Mr. Knox?"

"No. He was very well-behaved."

"Where is Marky now?"

"We'll get his ashes next week and bury them in the garden."

The word is *cremation*.

"But where is he *now*?"

"At Dr. Hanawalt's."

"Dr. Hanawalt cremates him?"

"No. He goes to a crematorium."

"Where is the crematorium?"

"I didn't ask."

She lowers her chin.

"Marky had a good life."

But I will never see him again.

Leo

Mother doesn't speak at dinner. Nobody speaks. After we have picked up our forks, Mother says she would like to say grace. We haven't said grace for a long time. She doesn't wait for us to bow our heads. She doesn't even put her fork down, but rests it, full of macaroni, on her plate and says, "Thank you, God, for our beloved Marky."

I can't eat. Everybody picks at their food. The children in China can starve.

Going upstairs, I remember how Marky's tail would go down when he climbed the stairs and how, when he turned on the landing, his nose would look pointy for just a second when he turned his head.

He had three favorite indoor places—in front of the sideboard so he could look into the kitchen, and the front hall, on the landing, so he could look down the stairs, and in the green chair until he was too old to climb into it; then he lay beside it. Outside, he didn't have a favorite spot. On the big porch, he liked to lie by the wall beside the French doors to the living room.

Leo

The next day, my father doesn't come for breakfast. When I go to the study to tell him I'm going down to the park, he says, "How you doing, Toots?"

He's still in bed, one arm beside him and the other arm over his head on the pillow, which is a new position. He is wearing the blue cotton pajamas with the red stripe we gave him last Father's Day. The green upholstery on Marky's chair is filthy. I never noticed how filthy before.

My father slides toward the wall and pats the mattress. I sit beside him.

He doesn't say anything, and before you know it, I blurt out, "Don't tell me Marky had a good life, or we gave him a good life, or he's in heaven!"

He blinks and stares at me hard, frowning.

"I can't fix it," he says in his gloomy voice.

When he's gloomy, he talks gloomy. He doesn't pretend.

"Going to the park?"

I nod. Where else is there to go?

"Close the door."

Walking by the car, I check the back seat, but there are no hairs or drool marks.

Leo

A few days later, Mother and I drive out Stadium to Dr. Hanawalt's house to pick up Marky's ashes. People sitting in the waiting room look down like they know why we've come. But their dogs are on their laps or on the floor. The nurse hands mother a brown paper bag with "Mark Schneider" written on the side. Mother lets me hold the bag in the car. I put it on my lap. I absolutely hate how small the bag is. We never called him Mark.

When we get home, Mother tells me to wait outside. Then she comes back with a bright red Maxwell House coffee can, the rim jagged from the can opener. We sit on the back step and pour the ashes into the coffee can. Some ashes get onto my shorts and Mother's skirt, and some fall on the step. I can't believe he tinkled right here. His tinkle has dried. The ashes could be fireplace ashes until I see a bone. There are quite a few small bones. Mother doesn't speak. She doesn't even tell me to be careful about the jagged metal edge. What do we do with the empty bag? There might be a few ashes in the bottom? Oh, well. I leave it on the back step.

"What about Daddy?"

"He's resting."

She goes to the garage and comes back with a trowel. As we walk toward the garden, ashes blow out of the can. Some land on my shoulder. At first, I don't want to lose any, but then I don't care—Marky all over me and all over the yard—what's wrong with that?

I choose a place by the bird bath so Marky has company. I thought about the pricker bush, but there is probably too much tinkle in that soil and blood is in there too. When Tizzy shot Charlie, that's where he was standing.

Mother kneels. She gives me the trowel. She doesn't offer to dig, and she doesn't go back to the kitchen when the phone rings, although I know she is expecting a call from Aunt Ginny.

It occurs to me, we could just pour the ashes into the hole, never mind the Maxwell House coffee can, but Mother has decided the coffee can is important. I'm not sure why. I set the coffee can in the hole and push in the dirt. I pat the ground. Mother pats, too. She doesn't have to tell me to go get the lamb.

All family dogs are buried in the garden. Caesar, Heidi, and now Marky. The rule is the most recent dead dog gets the sleeping stone lamb, which is now on Heidi's grave by the mock orange.

It's heavy, but Mother doesn't offer to carry it for me. I put the stone lamb on the dirt.

I think she's waiting for me to say a prayer. When I don't say anything, she says, "Dear Lord, please bless our beloved Marky."

"Let's say his full name."

"Marcus Aurelius Fortunatus Tidd Schneider."

I brush dirt off the lamb.

"It should be a sleeping *dog*."

"A lamb is fine."

Mother uses my shoulder to push herself up. She didn't used to have to do that.

She brushes the dirt off her hands.

"We all come from, and return to, the same kingdom."

Marcus Aurelius Fortunatis Tidd Schneider, age 16

The Grand Hotel

Mother announces at dessert that before she starts her new job at the University Hospital, we are taking a "frip." A frip is a fun trip.

"I took Kate to Chicago to get her a winter coat? Remember?"

I don't remember.

"A blue duffle coat from Marshall Field's? Well, I'm taking you to Mackinac Island before you start high school. We're staying at The Grand Hotel."

I look at my father. He hates hotels.

"And . . . your father is going fishing up north. What's the French river, Sam?"

"Au Sable."

"We'll collect Daddy on the way home. Hotels are not your father's cup of tea," she says, "and he'll be in good hands with his doctor."

I think of those photographs in Dr. Margolis's study of a log cabin and men holding up fish.

Leo

Saturday morning, Mother walks out the back door holding his rusty brown tackle box. She opens the trunk and puts the tackle box inside. Oh no. We forgot to close the garage door. Before I can tell her, she's gone back inside. The garage door is too high. I can't reach it. We don't want him to see Borgie, which will remind him he can't drive. She's back with his Wilkinson's suitcase, which also goes in the trunk. "Where is he?" She says, "the lavatory." I point to the garage door. She pulls it down just as he comes out the back door with his fishing rod, wearing his old khakis, and an old paint-splattered plaid shirt, and his blue canvas shoes from Moe's. He says he's going to catch the old brown trout come hell or high water. He knows which big rock he hides under. At least he's smiling. He gives me a quick kiss on the cheek and tells me to have a good time. He hasn't shaved. Mother tells me to finish packing, she'll be back in fifteen minutes. She is taking him to the Margolises' house.

I look at the sky which is getting cloudy. The air is humid. The leaves on the maple tree are moving a little, but not much. A tornado could come while we're driving to The Grand Hotel and my father is fishing up north. We could come home and find our house was sucked up in the funnel while we were gone. Given everything else that is going on, I am trying not to think about tornados all the time, but so many things are mixed up now.

Ted

It's hot in the Chevy. We drive and drive. When it's too bright to look outside, I study the white stitches on the red leather seat. Mother keeps pointing out all the places where we stopped on our way to Crystal Lake when I was six on our one-and-only family trip. All I remember is Marky ran away, and my father spent hours looking for him, and Marky came back on his own. Mother asks whether I remember that we stopped at the Doherty Hotel in Clare for lunch. I do. Marky was thirsty, and a waiter brought him a metal bowl that Marky drank from on a white tiled floor. And I used the bathroom, and I felt sick.

"Do you remember throwing up all over the front seat?"

Vaguely.

"Your father took us to a motel where we all took showers and changed our clothes?"

"Did we spend the night?"

"No. We just freshened up."

When we pass the exit for Otsego Lake, Mother starts talking about some childhood friend whose family had a cottage on Otsego Lake and who turned out to be a nudist.

"What's that?"

"Someone who enjoys being nude in public. She was fond of getting undressed in the Arboretum."

This casts a whole new light on the Arboretum.

More and more pine trees and more and more sand on the roadside, which I don't find all that interesting. What is extremely interesting, though, is the way Mother is talking to me about grown-up things. She even refers to the fishing camp a few times, and when we drive by the exit, which we will take on our way back, she tilts her head and says, "Let's hope for the best." When I ask if we really have to go to the camp, she says, "By all means. We are bringing your father *home*."

As we cross the Mackinac Bridge, she knows I don't like heights so tells me to look straight ahead. I have never been so high up or so far from home.

𝓡𝓮𝓭

"The Grand Hotel has the longest porch in the world," Mother says, "eight hundred and eighty feet. Fourteen presidents have stayed here."

It is a long white building with yellow and green awnings all the way around and a long, long porch, green rocking chairs and a horse and buggy pulled up to the front steps. It doesn't seem as hot up north. And there's a breeze.

"Didn't we go to The Plaza once?"

"I'm surprised you remember."

"How old was I?"

"Five. Right after Nanny died."

I don't remember much. A pigeon on our windowsill.

We cross the lobby to the front desk. Mother greets the clerk and slowly pronounces our name. We have a reservation. The clerk hands her a key. She asks what time dinner is served. From six to eight. Mother asks if we need a reservation for dinner. He says, "No Madam."

It's all new to me: how the man in the green uniform carries our bags onto the elevator, puts them down, presses the button, picks them up again. How we follow him down two long corridors until he turns his key in the lock on the door of our room and, with a bow, accepts Mother's quarter.

Our room has twin beds with a bedside table in between and a lamp with a flowery lampshade which matches the pink and yellow floral bedspreads. Mother hangs her bathrobe on the hook on the bathroom door. I take the bed by the window. It is not much of a view. Mother pulls the curtains closed.

"We'll freshen up and then have dinner."

There is a small, foil-wrapped square on my pillow and another one on Mother's pillow.

"Mints," says Mother.

"Who put them there?"

"Our maid."

I unfold the foil—chocolate. Mother unwraps hers, pops it in her mouth, smiling, lifting her eyebrows. She is being silly.

"Do all the guests get chocolate mints?"

"They do."

This treat on your pillow, placed there by some sophisticated tooth fairy hired by the hotel, is made even more exotic by Mother's matter-of-fact response.

Our room might look out onto the fire escape, but our table at dinner overlooks *the longest porch in the world.* There are silver branches woven in the green tablecloth, green plates and glasses sparkling, warm rolls piled in a basket, monogrammed butter squares. I order spaghetti and ginger ale. Mother orders salmon and a double martini. The dining room is enormous with green medallions evenly spaced across the pink wool carpet. There must be fifty tables. Waiters appear out of nowhere. And, out of nowhere, Mother speaks in her calmest voice ever. I'm not paying attention at first, then I hear "straight A's, in-state tuition, University of Michigan, Regents scholarship." Then a little paragraph about why she is telling me this now as I begin tenth grade, that "although you have always been a good student, getting good grades for the next three years is now a *necessity*." Then a few martini words: that my life is *in my own hands* and something about *consequences*. Then another new word—*powder room*—as she excuses herself.

The guests on the porch are rocking in identical green rocking chairs. The horse and buggy pulled up to the curb reminds me of the fringe on top song in *Oklahoma!* I used to move all the furniture in the living room to make space so I could dance to *Oklahoma!* I don't do that anymore.

By the time Mother returns, the table has been cleared, and two bowls of lemon sherbet have been placed before us. When the bill comes, Mother signs her name. We go out on the porch. I thought we would rock in the rocking chairs, but she forgot her sweater, so we go back inside. A different clerk is at the desk. He makes a little bow as we walk by.

Mother knows the way to our room. We take the elevator to the third floor, turn left, and left, and left. The corridors are long. "Why are there trays on the floor?" I ask. "Room service." "Why are men's shoes outside some doors?" "To be shined."

While we were having dinner, someone turned down our bedspreads and—unbelievably—placed two more chocolate mints on our pillows. "How do they know when we're having dinner?"

"The maid knocks."

"Well, our maid forgot," I say.

"Forgot what?" Mother calls from the bathroom.

"We already *had* our mints."

"Well, I guess we are entitled to two more," she says, coming back in her bathrobe.

"What on earth's the matter?"

My scowl.

"Darling?"

I can't explain. How can we afford this huge hotel? He isn't working anymore, and she isn't working yet. These extra mints are . . .

"Darling? What?"

I can't say the word I just found—*extravagant.*

Leo

The Margolis fishing camp is a log cabin with a porch surrounded by pine trees. The ground is sandy. There is a campfire outside and outdoor chairs. Mrs. Margolis looks ragged. Her hair is a little dirty, her face is sunburned, and she's wearing an apron over her blue jeans, but still has that big smile and wide-apart eyes. She says "the boys are fishing," then she shows Mother to the room where my father has been sleeping behind the kitchen. He didn't make his bed. It smells of Old Spice. My room is upstairs.

We go out to the porch. Mrs. Margolis brings a tray—root beer for me, cocktail for Mother. She remembered Mother likes an olive in her martini. Mother looks very relaxed. She tells Mrs. Margolis about The Grand Hotel, the horse and buggy ride, the long porch.

When my father gets back, he looks a little sweaty and sunburned. In his T-shirt and paint-splattered khakis, you would think it was a weekend at home and he had just come up from the basement. He kisses Mother on the cheek and then me on the cheek.

"I didn't catch the old brown trout," he says, "but I got a good look at him."

Dr. Margolis says, "The old brown trout is a figment of your imagination!"

"He damned well is not!"

Watching them all talking on the porch, having drinks, smoking and laughing, I wonder if I made up "Honey." Mother is the only person in a skirt, but she hasn't put on her lipstick, and her blouse is unbuttoned more than usual. She is starting to look like a camper. Dr. Margolis suggests I explore the woods, take that trail.

Pine needles are soft to walk on. The trail leads to an old shed. Somebody left the door open. There are cobwebs, a rocking chair, rusty tools, canoe paddles, and a trumpet hanging on a hook. Or maybe it's a cornet. We studied musical instruments at Tappan. Why would you leave a musical instrument in a shed?

Dr. Margolis says it was Roger's. Roger is their son who lives in Milwaukee. I ask if I can play it. He says, "You are welcome to play Roger's cornet." So, it is a cornet. Cornets aren't as long as trumpets. I go back to the shed, drag the rocking chair outside, and take the cornet off the nail. I brush off the cobwebs.

Eventually, I manage to get a few notes out. Playing the piano, you don't have to breathe. Just move your fingers and hands. I know the sections of the orchestra. Strings, woodwinds, brass, percussion. Cornets are in the brass section. The brass section is towards the back. Sometimes in the middle, sometimes off to one side. It feels important to be playing a musical instrument that is not a piano. Nanny was a concert pianist. So was Uncle Walter before he became a physicist. Nobody in our family played the cornet—or any other instrument, for that matter. I wonder if they have an orchestra at Ann Arbor High School, where I start in a few weeks. Maybe they have a marching band. Pressing on the buttons, the note changes. I wish I could play Taps. A squirrel is staring at me from a low branch. Have I scared him? No. He isn't running away. Just flicking his tail.

Catch What Comes

When I get home from Ulrich's, I drop my new books on the dining room table. Six heavy books were not easy to carry home. Mother runs in from the living room. She's actually running.

"You've been accepted at University High School!" she smiles. "*And,* my darling daughter, you've earned a fifty-dollar scholarship which will cover tuition."

"I didn't apply to University High School."

"I didn't tell you, in case you were declined. I didn't want you to be disappointed."

"But I just bought my books for Ann Arbor High School."

"I know, I know," she says, "They called while you were at Ulrich's!" She looks at the pile of books. "We'll just take these back."

I don't protest. Don't feel betrayed. Don't really care—that's what life is like now. Catch what comes at you, don't argue, and keep your mouth shut.

At dinner, Mother tells my father I can walk to U. High, and she won't have to pick me up or take me unless it's bad weather. She says Janet, Aunt Ginny and Uncle Tom's daughter, went to U. High. He keeps looking at me. I have a new facial expression: blank.

That night in bed, I watch the traffic lights on Washtenaw run around the walls of my room: rectangles that tilt at the corners, then keep going, then tilt at the next corner. I imagine walking to U.

High. Straight down Washtenaw, left at the rock, four or five blocks down Hill Street, turn right at East U. This house will be so quiet with Mother gone to work, me at U. High, Marky dead. I can't stand the thought of my father alone all day. No voices. No dog barking. Just baseball on television and the wham of the mailbox lid on the front porch.

Ted

Starting at a new school is not that hard. I just do what's in front of me. Don't look back. Don't miss things. Don't complain. Don't feel sorry for myself. Figure out the new rules and obey them.

My Civics teacher at U. High is Mr. Goodeve. He limps because one leg is shorter. He likes to read aloud *The Ann Arbor News*. Today, he reads the report of the March on Washington for civil rights. He writes the definitions for *civics* and *civil* on the black board. *Civics* is the study of the privileges and obligations of citizens. *Civil* relates to citizens. In America, Black people and white people are all citizens and entitled to the same privileges. We aim to live in a civil society. *Civilized* means having an advanced or humane culture or society. It can also mean polite and well-bred. Our homework lesson is to answer this question: "Are we living in a civilized society today?" Mr. Goodeve says the March on Washington was a civilized gathering.

My English teacher, Mr. Shafer, is short and strict. On our first day, we spend the entire class on the first page of the first scene of *Hamlet*. Bapa would be pleased. We never turn the page. By the end of that class, I understand *Stand and unfold yourself. Who goes there? Bernardo? He.* The next day, we turn the page. At dinner, when I tell my parents I understand Shakespeare, Mother says, "I told you, Sam!"

Every year, Mr. Shafer takes his English class and his 12th grade drama class to Stratford, Ontario. We will stay two nights and see three plays. I don't say what I'm thinking which is that we probably can't afford it. Mother seems to know what I'm thinking.

"And you shall go to Stratford!" she says, patting the dinner table.

U. High is a laboratory school for the School of Education at the University of Michigan. If you are studying to become a teacher, you practice on U. High students. There is also a University Elementary School. Some of my classmates have been going here their whole life. I do well on tests. Someone says public schools are better at teaching you how to prepare for exams. U. High is a little "loosey-goosey," whatever that means. My new friends are smart. Some don't seem to study at all, but they get A's. I get A's, but I have to study hard.

There is a phone in the front office at the end of the counter. You don't have to ask permission to use it. I hate when my father doesn't answer, but most of the time he does. He tells me to stop worrying. When my new friends ask where my father works, I say he used to work at Argus Camera, then a printing company in Detroit, then he got sick, and now he doesn't work anymore, but my mother works at the University Hospital. Nobody else's mother works.

I get busier and busier. Yearbook committee, choir practice, cheerleading, French club. If I don't have any meetings, I toss a football with my friends Victor and Mike. I am learning to throw a long, accurate spiral. And I can catch pretty well, too.

When I get home, my father is either on the big porch asleep on the old sofa or taking a nap on his hospital bed in the study. Somebody gave us their National Geographic magazines, and he looks through them. If my sister called, he reports what she said.

My father can't drive, so he can't go to Fingerle's, or Purchase Camera, or Witham's. He can't go anywhere. Maybe Mrs. Margolis visits him during the day, but I doubt it. I don't smell perfume. I don't see lipstick on any glasses in the sink. It's a good thing he takes naps because what else would he do all day? He can't sneak out in Borgie because Mother hid the key. His darkroom smells the same, nothing rearranged. The level of rubber cement in the bottle on his desk hasn't gone down, so it looks like he isn't climbing stairs in secret. When Mother gets home, she's tired. We never go anywhere. At least I go to school and Mother goes to work. My father never leaves the house. He is going to go berserk with boredom.

Becoming a Democrat

Every Friday, in English class, we write an impromptu essay about the quote Mr. Shafer has written on the blackboard. Today's quote is from John F. Kennedy and is about physical fitness. I write about my athletic father who had a heart attack anyway. When I look up, Mr. Shafer is not at his desk grading last week's papers. Maybe he had to go to the bathroom. I write about my father doing handstands. When I next look up, Mr. Shafer is standing by the blackboard looking very serious. I look at the clock. We have fifteen more minutes. Mr. Shafer takes off his glasses. He says, "Class: put your pens down." We put our pens down. Then he says, "Our president John Fitzgerald Kennedy was shot dead in Dallas an hour ago. Class is dismissed." Shot dead. We are not living in a civilized society anymore.

Leo

When I get home, I find my father sitting in Marky's green chair facing the television, a glass of VO in one hand, no ice cubes, tears on his cheeks, swearing at the television in a deep voice. Mother is in the kitchen. She left work early. Walter Cronkite's glasses are like my father's with big black frames. I have never seen Mother so quiet. When we go out to the kitchen, leaving my father swearing and crying, Mother says, "Your father met President Kennedy when he was a senator. They shook hands. He's taking this very personally."

I go back to the study. I ask about shaking Kennedy's hand. My father gets up, turns down the volume, and sits back down. With tears on his face, the story pours out in bits and pieces. I can hardly follow it but I want to remember it.

Tom Payne running for Congress. Tom Payne wanting his picture taken with Senator Kennedy who was coming to Ann Arbor. Kennedy's plane landing at Willow Run late at night, my father going out to Willow Run in Tom Payne's car. A crowd on the tarmac waving banners. Senator Kennedy coming out of the airplane, standing at the top of the staircase, buttoning his jacket, looking for the person supposed to greet him. Tom Payne waving. Kennedy not seeing Tom Payne. Tom Payne calling, "Senator! Over here. Senator!" Kennedy not hearing Tom Payne, not sure what to do.

"So I yelled '*Jack!*'" shouts my father in the study. "And he looked right at me."

Kennedy walking down the stairs toward my father, grabbing my father's hand. My father leading Kennedy through the crowd, holding Kennedy's hand tight, not letting go. Publicity shots in a hotel room. Then, my father running back out on the tarmac because he'd dropped his bifocals in the crowd, sure they'd been stepped on. Looking and looking. Finding them—not stepped on.

"My bifocals—not a scratch."

That's why his bifocals are famous.

"So that night I became a Democrat."

Mother chimes in from the doorway. "And, in the early morning hours, Kennedy announced the formation of The Peace Corps on the steps of the Michigan Union. Daddy photographed him there, too. And, the next day, down at the Depot, on the back of the Wolverine."

"Whistle Stop," says my father.

By now, he's crying and very drunk.

He stays drunk the whole weekend. Lyndon Johnson is now our president.

My father is seated on the left in profile. Photo by Eck Stanger, University of Michigan News and Information Services Photographs, Bentley Historical Library, University of Michigan

Realtor

After Christmas, my father goes to St. Joe's Hospital—not University Hospital which is for very sick people. My father is not very sick; he just needs to be observed. He seems the same to me, just crankier because they don't let him smoke. He stays a week, then he comes home. Now, he takes a third pill. All I can do is turn in neat papers and study hard. I have to get good grades because I need a scholarship to go to the University of Michigan. Mother made that clear.

Kate finally brings her boyfriend home to meet us at spring break. Tim is handsome and polite. So far, so good. Tim and my father talk about sports—even better. Tim sleeps in the guest room. Kate is as pretty as ever and is studying to be a teacher. I wish she would come home more often so our family is the right size. I enjoy her being home, coming down the stairs, walking through doorways, going back upstairs. Kate and Tim will graduate together next year, and it sounds like they might get married. Tim is Catholic. We are Episcopalian. Mother says she will talk to Henry Lewis. One step at a time.

Milly O'Neill is my one old friend from Tappan whom I still see. She lives around the corner on Baldwin. There are books in the O'Neills' bathrooms, leaning against the wall next to the toilet, with strips of toilet paper to mark pages. Books don't have to be in the bookcase; they can be on the stairs, on the windowsills, in the bathrooms, on the floor. Books about France and India, Greek gods, an explorer in Norway who froze in the snow, a Russian count, steam trains—I never know what book will be in their bathroom.

In the winter, Mr. O'Neill wears sandals and heavy socks, and Mrs. O'Neill wears trousers. Mr. O'Neill's hair is longer than Mrs. O'Neill's. They drink wine and take sabbaticals. The O'Neills drive an old car with an oval sticker on the back window from when they lived in France. I prefer our house, but I prefer their atmosphere. My grandfather taught English, so we are almost a faculty family, but my father is not a professor. Far from it, he says.

One day, Milly and I are carrying Mrs. O'Neill's groceries from her car to the kitchen when here comes Mother, walking up the driveway in her gray dress with the matching belt. This is the first time Mother has ever walked over to the O'Neills', but I can tell nothing bad has happened.

"So how is Sam?" says Mrs. O'Neill.

"Surviving," sighs Mother. "When I got back from the market just now, I found him working at his desk. A good sign!"

But his desk is upstairs!

Mother looks up at the O'Neills' house as if she's never seen it before. Milly and I carry more grocery bags inside. When we come out, Mother and Mrs. O'Neill are talking about somebody moving.

". . . bedrooms on the ground floor for Sam," Mother says, smiling at me.

"My sister is a realtor," says Mrs. O'Neill.

"Does she cover the west side?"

"I'll have her call you."

Mother touches Mrs. O'Neill on the arm as if they are old friends. They aren't old friends. They say hello at the choir concert once a year.

Mother and I walk down the driveway. If she thinks we are going to have a normal conversation after that conversation, she is mistaken. She tells me Aunt Ginny and Uncle Tom are coming to dinner. Fine. My other godparents. Fine.

Red

My father serves the meatloaf. Mother and Aunt Ginny discuss gardening. Uncle Tom says he is looking for a new medical secretary because Miss Peck is moving to Chicago. My father doesn't say much, but then he never talks at dinner. Hopefully, this is a bad dream and Mother did not ask Mrs. O'Neill for help finding a *realtor*. We own this house. Mother inherited it from her parents. This house is our ancestral home. And there is nothing *real* about any of this.

Mother made meringues and whipped the cream herself, and there is a bowl of strawberries. My father has two meringues, but no strawberries. The seeds get stuck under his denture. Then, Mother says, "Gin, I spoke to Bib O'Neill's sister. She's coming over tomorrow."

Normal voice. As if we have discussed this. As if this was the plan all along. As if this realtor lady is someone we know. As if we have meringues every night.

Aunt Ginny doesn't look surprised; it is not news to her. And it is not even news to my father who pushes back his chair so hard it falls over as he leaves the dining room without excusing himself. If Marky were alive, he would be crawling under the sideboard. The study door slams shut. I don't ask to be excused. I don't pick up the fallen chair. Mother can just think I am going to the lavatory. Actually, I don't care what she thinks.

He's in the study on his bed. He didn't close the door. I don't know which is worse: my father crying, or the fact that he knows I am watching from the doorway, or the fact that his crying is high-pitched. I have never thought about the way my father might cry. I never thought he would or could cry. Now he is crying harder than I cry. This is worse than the ICU. Much worse. I expect him to yell at me, but he just keeps crying. I close the door as quietly as I have ever closed a door in my life.

I stand outside the study door, by the door to the lavatory. I've never stood here before. There is dust between the spindles of the banister.

We don't have a cleaning lady anymore. I can hear Aunt Ginny's low voice in the dining room. Uncle Tom isn't saying anything. My father is still crying. Then chairs creak, and everybody gets up. I run upstairs.

Lying in bed fully dressed is horrible. This is a horrible night. The back door shuts. A car goes out the driveway. Headlights swing around the wall. After a while, I hear music. When I get to the foot of the stairs, the study door is still shut, no slit of light under the door. Mother is in the living room listening to some choir singing in some church. She is not playing solitaire. She is sitting in my father's chair by the grandfather clock. Not reading. Not knitting. No martini. Pocket doors open. She has moved the footstool and has put both her stocking feet on it. Shoes kicked off. Ankles crossed. Dark circles under her eyes. When she sees me, she says, "I saved your meringue."

Room by Blessed Room

A lot can happen in a day. One minute, you're going to Ann Arbor High School. The next minute, you're going to U. High. At breakfast, you own your house. By dinner, it belongs to a classics professor from Princeton. Say it a million times: Don Jones owns 1015 Ferdon Road. Mother says he doesn't own it until he pays the asking price on the listing, $42,500. Forty-two-five for an eight-bedroom, turn-of-the-century, English Cottage in the Arts and Crafts style, covered in grape ivy, with two chimneys and three fireplaces, and a one-car garage at the corner of Ferdon Road and Washtenaw Avenue, Lot # 63, Ann Arbor, Michigan, United States of America, The Earth, The Milky Way, The Universe.

Hate is corrosive, Mother says, but I have permission to hate Professor Jones for a few days. I don't care if I have her permission; I plan to hate Professor Jones for the rest of my life. I never thought about our house before. I just lived in it. I didn't think about it. I just went up and down the stairs, and sat in all the rooms, and enjoyed looking at certain things, but it never occurred to me I would one day not be able to look at them ever again. Well, that day has come. Mother suggests I make a list of what I want to take with me. I don't make that list. I make another list.

What Don Jones Gets

German tiles around the fireplace in the study: the lion's head, the candlestick, the fleurs-de-lis, and the shield

German tiles around the fireplace in the living room. They are behind the new paneling, but if Don Jones tears down the paneling, he will get the snake, the other lion, the rabbit, and the toad.

Frosted glass lampshades in the upstairs hall (4) and downstairs hall (2)

Copper sink in the pantry

Clothes chute

Canvas fire hoses with the brass nozzle bolted to the wall. One in the big bathroom and the other in the back hall by the pantry

Leaded windows on the landing (2) and beside the front door (2)

Newel posts (4)

All the glass doorknobs. Too many to count

The breeze on the sleeping porch

The lilac hedge, the dogwood and redbud trees, the forsythia, the herb garden, the mock orange and the bridal wreath, the lily of the valley and the silver maple in the front yard, and the elms down by the sidewalk, and the bag swing, and the cedar bush at the corner of the living room (not the Christmas lights that go in the bush), and all the flowers in Mother's garden

The bird bath with the copper bowl. No. We are taking it with us.

At least ten squirrels, two chipmunks, one rabbit, and all the swallows, blue jays, cardinals, the woodpecker, and the flicker, the four mourning doves, and two yellow finches.

Mother says that is not exactly true; he gets to enjoy these things and these creatures for as long as he owns the house but that he, like us, may one day move out. Move out, move in.

And what about Marky's ashes? Mother says we will take the stone lamb and the Maxwell House coffee can with us. Now I understand the coffee can. Mother knew all along we would be moving.

I keep expecting the house to shake or scream. Mother agrees a house is not an inanimate object, but "we shall rise to this occasion." I thought rising to the occasion meant having a good time. She says, "Darling, you have confused *rising* to the occasion with a sense *of* occasion. Rising to the occasion means coping as best you can with whatever life throws in your path." Who threw the heart attack?

One night, after dinner, my father goes back to his bed in the study to watch baseball. Something is going on, so I stay in the kitchen with Mother who keeps looking out the window. She says she is waiting for our student Jake to come back from the college. She needs his help with something, but she won't tell me what.

When she sees Jake coming up the driveway, she goes outside. I follow them into the garage. She points to the leaf burner and the wheelbarrow and asks Jake, "Could you please put the wheelbarrow in the driveway and set the leaf burner upside down on the wheelbarrow?" She shows him where she wants it. Jake says he'll just take his books upstairs and be down in a minute. Jake stops to get his mail out of the little mailbox my father built at the foot of the back stairs. I should add that to my list. The back stairs mailbox. Mother goes down to the basement. Jake comes down the back stairs, smiles his nice smile, and goes into the garage. He does what she asks. We stand in the driveway like good servants. The leaf burner is a big square aluminum bin. Jake lifts it onto the wheelbarrow, the wide end up, the smaller end, where the ashes come out, down.

Mother comes upstairs from the basement, her arms full. She dumps everything into the leaf burner—the needlepoint footstool with the broken foot, a torn striped awning, sofa pillows that never got mended. Then she takes a can of lighter fluid out of her skirt pocket and squirts it into the leaf burner, takes a match book out of her other pocket, lights it, and tosses the match. Kaboom!

She asks Jake to stand guard. She points to the window at the peak of the roof and says we'll be throwing things out that window.

Very quietly, we climb the back stairs to the third floor. I don't know why we have to be quiet—my father is watching the Red Sox play the Tigers with the door shut, but Mother has this quiet-as-a-mouse manner.

When we get to the third floor, she opens the little window at the top of the stairs as far as it will go. Then we open the door to the cubby hole. Dusty heat floats out. She pulls the chain on the light and starts handing me things. The game is: throw everything out the window, aim for the leaf burner. Don't hit Jake.

Jake waves. I throw Nanny's chameleon cage, a hatbox, a Parcheesi board, a black hat with a veil, a sewing basket with a velvet lid. Mother hands me shoeboxes full of postcards—scenes of cathedrals, monuments, carriages, fountains, castles, dead composers. Squirrels have nibbled on the post cards. There is one entire box marked "Leipzig," which is where Bapa went to university. "Those, too," she says. All the boxes land in the leaf burner, but the one from Leipzig splits apart midair, and all the little brown and black scenes with the beautiful handwriting and foreign stamps land in the gutter, on the garage roof, on the driveway. Some tilt into the bridal wreath, and the pricker bush, and the mint bed. One lands on Jake's sleeve. He looks up. Smoke is coming in the window. We are all coughing.

When I ask Mother, "will Jake and Paul have to move too?", she says "Don Jones can use the income." Another bad word—*income.*

When I look down, Jake is poking the fire with a broom he must have gotten, without asking, from the garage which, I suppose, he is permitted to do now that he is going to live here, and we are not.

"That's enough for one day," Mother says, pulling the chain. The light goes out. She closes the cubbyhole door, pulls down the little window, takes a deep breath, and heads down the stairs.

"You have to start somewhere," she says, which I've noticed is how she talks to me now—more like a friend. She talked like that to Kate when he was in the hospital. I don't want to be her friend. I prefer daughter.

When we get to the second floor, it suddenly occurs to me that this entire house has to be emptied. I can't imagine how we are going to do it. Later, I hear her tell someone on the phone who must have wondered, too, "room by blessed room."

1015 Ferdon Road

Another Old Part of Town

Today at the Farmer's Market, Mother buys lima beans, tomatoes, a dozen eggs, and red roses. Why roses? She always says gardeners don't *buy* flowers. Uncle Walter is not sick. Then she stops at the same table where she stopped a week ago and picks up the same pink and black crocheted potholder. A week ago, she looked at that potholder, then she put it down and thanked the woman. Today, she buys the potholder. Something is going on.

On the way home, we stop at Jack's Market. She tells me to stay in the car, then forgets to take her shopping list. It says: *FM, macaroni, anchovy paste, call Nan.* FM is Farmer's Market, but who is Nan?

She returns with two grocery bags. She bought a lot more than macaroni and anchovy paste; she bought meat from the butcher, milk, graham crackers, toilet paper, detergent. Before I can ask who Nan is, she says,

"That phone call this morning was Nan Bishop."

"Who is Nan?"

"Our realtor, Mrs. O'Neill's sister. I made an offer on a house. And that offer, apparently, has been accepted."

Both eyebrows are as high as they go.

"Which means," she pulls ahead, "on the first of August, we will be moving to 1472 River Road."

We come to the stop sign at Wells Street. She looks at me. I look at the rusted screws holding the stop sign to the metal post. We go up the hill to Ferdon, turn left on Ferdon. We drive past the Spanish house.

"I thought I would have to make a counteroffer, but the seller accepted my very first bid. Perhaps they have to leave in a hurry." She looks dreamy for a moment. "Like us."

She knows all the words.

When we turn in the driveway, she doesn't park under the pine trees. She drives right up to the kitchen window, blocking the view of the garden. She takes the marketing basket and gets out, opens the back door, takes out the bags from Jack's. That's it? That's all she's going to say?

Nobody's in the kitchen, but then who would be in the kitchen? Not Marky, not my father. She puts everything down on the counter, runs water over her hands. She arranges the roses in the big glass vase. She's not even going to tell me about the new house. Where it is. What it looks like.

"I think I hear baseball."

She's definitely not going to talk about it. She's going to check on my father. Going to stay busy. Going to put the roses in the dining room.

When I get to the study, she is standing a few steps inside the door, pretending to be interested in the baseball game.

"Second inning," she tells me. "Two and two."

"Double header," he says, nodding to Marky's green chair, which we moved to face the television. Last week, I sat there when the Tigers beat the White Sox. Watching baseball from the green chair is exactly what I want to do. I don't want to think about houses.

Mother touches my shoulder. "Aren't you babysitting this evening?"

"No. Tomorrow noon."

He is watching television. She is watching me. The White Sox are changing pitchers. Dixie Howell is relieving Turk Lown.

She taps my shoulder. "Isn't the tournament today?"

"Tomorrow."

Dixie Howell is walking to the mound. This could be a good game.

"Dear?"

I get it! Mother wants me out.

"Not watching the game, Toots?"

There are more feelings on his face now.

"I've got a tetherball tournament."

I am turning into a born liar.

Red

Mother calls our neighborhood around Burns Park and Angell School the old faculty neighborhood. Beyond that, there is the campus with the university buildings. Then there's the area around the Farmer's Market, which is close to our church and not far from the railroad station. Then there is South U. near U. High and where the Standard Oil station is, and Witham's liquor store, and Purchase Camera. Handicraft is somewhere in the middle. Wilkinson's and Goodyear's are on Main Street. Muehlig's is by the library. Fingerle's lumber yard and the hardware store are not far from the football stadium, which is near Ann Arbor High School. There is the area overlooking the river where the hospital and the cemetery are. There is the area out by the stables and the Huron River and the hobos on the bridge. There are all those newer houses out past the football stadium on the way to the mental hospital. But where is River Road?

Red

My father comes to dinner wearing only his undershirt; it is the first time that has happened. One good thing about my father: If he feels sick, he looks sick. If he feels like being quiet, he stays quiet. If he's sad, he looks sad. If he's angry, his mouth goes into a slit. If he's worried, he bites down hard and you can see the muscles of his jaw and the dent at his temple go in and out. Tonight, he is all these things.

At least Mother doesn't try to make polite conversation. She has told him about the new house. What more is there to say? We barely eat. As she picks up my plate to take it to the kitchen, he looks at her, his face red, and he stares at her with a look I have never seen before. Not mad, not sad. Lost, I think. Then he pushes back his chair slowly and leans toward the candle. It takes him three puffs to blow it out. I expect he will walk around the table to blow out the other candle, but he goes back to the study, then a few minutes later, walks out to the porch. His walking is better. He doesn't have to hold onto things.

While I'm putting the dishes in the dishwasher, I overhear Mother tell someone on the telephone that the River Road house is in one of Ann Arbor's "original" neighborhoods in "another old part of town" on the west side and that it was on the market a long time so she was able to get it "for a song."

When I get out to the porch, I can't quite see my father, but he's in his chair in the corner.

"What side of town do we live on?"

"Now?"

"Yes."

"Southeast," he says. Ever since Mother got him a compass for Borgie, he knows exactly where everything is.

"Is the train depot west?"

"North."

"Where are the Robertsons?"

"North."

Nobody we know is west.

Last Saturday, when we went to the Robertsons', Mother drove the Chevy. He wore a white shirt and his blue seersucker jacket, which was the most dressed up I have seen him in a long time. It was too hot for a bow tie. All those bow ties with the little pickaxe at 15 ½ are hanging in his closet. So many things he doesn't do anymore. Every day, he wears fewer clothes, eats less, talks less, weighs less, carves less meat, makes fewer decisions, climbs fewer stairs or no stairs. Today's subtraction is the shirt buttoned at the neck at the dinner table. Today's addition is River Road.

No Words

My father never asks about our new house, so Mother must have taken him to see it. Why didn't they include me? Then, one Saturday morning, when I come into the kitchen, Mother casually says, "We'll drop off a Monday Club book, then meet the telephone man." As if we have a standing appointment, like a hair appointment, with the telephone man.

Afraid to break the spell, I go straight out to the car. A few minutes later, she gets in, puts the book club book on the car seat alongside a spiral notebook from Overbeck's bookstore. She has written "1472 River Road" on the cover and underlined it twice.

My father used to fold brown paper covers for the Monday Club books.

"No cover?"

"He didn't feel like making one."

"You would think he could fold some brown paper."

"You would think," she says.

We go up Vinewood. When I deliver Monday Club books, I look for a dry place, behind the screened door or in the mailbox or the milk box. This house doesn't have a milk box or a mailbox and there is no screened door, so I lean the book on the windowsill beside the front door. I try not to break the cobweb. We don't kill spiders in our family.

Next, we go toward Main Street, then turn right. A few blocks the other way is the jailhouse where Tizzy ate her chicken salad sandwiches.

"There are several ways to get to the new house," says Mother. "This isn't the only way."

I came to the west side when Tappan played Slauson. Cheerleaders got to ride with the football team on the bus. The thought of living near Slauson is beginning to occur to me. We turn left onto Miller Avenue, go down a hill, bump over a railroad track, climb up a hill. Near the top, there is a green street sign: "River Rd." At the corner is a small cinder block store painted brown with a neon "Budweiser" sign in the window and a barrel outside for trash. We turn right onto River Road, which turns out to be a long straight street. There are a few young trees and not much shade. If this is going to be our new neighborhood, I had better find something I can enjoy looking at.

Suddenly, the sidewalks end and we go up a short, steep hill. Now, the lawns go all the way out to the curb. We turn right into a cracked cement driveway. There is a big pine tree with droopy branches in the middle of the yard. The house is—what? There are no words for what it is or isn't. No words. There is practically no house; it is that plain and that small.

Mother takes her spiral notebook. We walk across a narrow cement walk in front of scraggly bushes under a picture window. We step onto a cement porch. The pillar on the corner of the porch supports a small roof. Mother puts a key in the lock, looks through the diamond-shaped window in the middle of the door, and turns the key. I'm glad she is ignoring me. I have no words.

Mother has all the words. When we get inside, she opens her notebook. As we go from room to room she tells me her plans.

"Extend the rear wall to make a proper dining room which will be two steps down. Jay will build china cupboards either side of the wide doorway. No changes to the kitchen."

I guess there are no changes to what she calls "the back hall" either, which is just a small square hallway with doors leading to a bedroom, a bathroom, another bedroom, and the living room.

"We'll need shuttered saloon doors across the door to the living room; otherwise," she smiles, "if someone doesn't close the bathroom door, you could be sitting in the living room staring at the person on the toilet!" Eyebrows up!

She opens another door. We go downstairs to the basement. More linoleum.

"I've got to find out why the basement is damp and over there," she says pointing to the corner where there is a door to the back yard. "And we'll need bookcases because the living room bookcases aren't big enough."

We go back upstairs. She doesn't take me into the bedrooms or the bathroom. They're small and square. We go back to the living room, past the bookcases, around the corner—lots of going round and round in this house.

Mother opens another door. A door to what? Linoleum stairs! This railing is going to fall off. At the top of the stairs, there's more linoleum, a short hallway, and two bedrooms. The ceiling is slanted. I have to duck my head to get into the bathroom which has a toilet, small corner sink, a shower, and bathtub.

"Why don't you take the larger room?" Mother says.

That's right. Kate won't be moving home after college because she's getting married next summer, so the smaller room, I guess, will be a guest room. Kate's not ever coming home. She will never live with us again. Why—here, in this hot cramped hallway—does this occur to me for the first time?

"Where is the telephone man?" I ask.

"And where is the Clorox?" she scowls. "Didn't we put it in the car?"

No, we forgot.

"Not to worry," she smiles as we go back downstairs, "I'll just run down to that little market on the corner. Isn't that convenient? A market on the corner? Clorox will discourage the mold in the basement. If the telephone man comes, just tell him where we want the phone."

"Where do we want the phone?"

She walks back to the kitchen.

"Here, on this counter by the spice rack."

The way she says *by the spice rack,* as if we have always put our spices in that little rack on the wall, is the worst moment so far. At home, we have Tizzy's cupboard in the icebox room for spices, and food coloring, and flour, and sugar.

There are seven cupboards in this kitchen. At 1015 we have—I count again—eighteen cupboards, and that's not counting the pantry and the icebox room. I had better stop counting. What does it matter what this house has or doesn't have? We are going to live here.

When Mother returns with a bottle of Clorox, she says the owner of the market fought in the Korean War. She is waiting for me to say something about the new house. But what is there to say? I didn't look around while she was gone; I just stood by the sink. I didn't even turn on the water. She lied. She said we were moving to one of Ann Arbor's "original neighborhoods, in another *old* part of town"—not true. River Road is not a cobblestone street by the train tracks; we are not going to be listening to the whistle of the Wolverine, which would have been exciting. We will not be living near old wooden houses. We are going to be living at the top of a hill on a long street with not very many trees, where people live in small, uninteresting houses built not that long ago.

Across the Tracks

Mother's biggest regret is that all this upheaval is happening just as I start my junior year, but I'm not thinking about my junior year. On the one hand, packing is the last thing I want to do, but if you take things out of the cupboard, you get to enjoy the cupboard a little longer. And the three big drawers at the back of my closet? I haven't opened them in years. I am on the moving-across-town train, which is a fast-moving train.

Our neighbors across Ferdon buy the old sideboard so it gets to stay on Ferdon. Nanny's brown Steinway is going to Uncle George in Grosse Pointe. We will keep the black Steinway, though where it will fit in the new house, Mother has no idea, "probably the basement," she sighs, "because there is an outside staircase."

Nanny's ornate German furniture has been in our basement in the coal room covered in sheets since Nanny died, and Mother says it will be going to Maude Okelberg's basement on Sunset until Mother can take it to the Treasure Mart. It was Maude Okelberg, who lives around the corner from our new house, who apparently suggested Mother look at this little house for sale on River Road.

All the projects on River Road are Mother's projects. My father has no projects, and he will not discuss Jay, the carpenter Mother hired.

Moving day is scheduled. Mayflower is the moving company.

Leo

Marky and I have peed all over this yard. I used to tinkle by the bridal's wreath and sometimes here in the lilac hedge and sometimes behind the spirea. I say peeing now, not tinkling. Tinkling is for children. I peed a moment ago and wiped myself with a lilac leaf.

I've been here most of the day. I thought Mother might call for me, but she has her mind on getting through the list I saw on the counter. I did offer to sweep all the rooms once the movers are gone (the house has to be left in broom clean condition), but she's hired the Gray boy to do that tomorrow. I didn't even ask who the Gray boy is.

I watched her put paper cups and a box of Oreos on the poodle tray. Then she carried the tray outside and put it on the low wall near the outdoor spigot. "On such a hot day, the movers need to drink plenty of water."

"Then they will need to use the lavatory."

"Of course they will use the lavatory" she smiled her rising to the occasion smile. Then, the big yellow truck with the green ship on the side pulled in the driveway, and I walked straight back to the lilac hedge.

I used to play here all the time. I made different rooms in different areas. The way the trees grow in bunches here-and-there makes space for all sorts of things. Over here, I had a kitchen with a campfire, and a little further that way, I had a bedroom with a pile of leaves for a pillow. The leaves have blown away long ago, but I lie down there anyway.

Leo

When I wake up it doesn't seem as hot.

I could hide here forever, pee here, eat here, sleep here. Stay here, not move. Not drive across town. Not live on River Road.

I hear a big metal whamming noise which could be the back doors of the truck slamming shut. Maybe the movers are done.

When I get to the driveway, a man with a clipboard is standing by Mother on the back porch. He hands her the poodle tray, then turns his clipboard around, taps his finger at the bottom, and hands mother his ballpoint pen. Mother signs where he tapped and hands the pen back. Then he walks right by me, head down, too tired to be polite, walks over to the truck, and grabs a handle to hoist himself up. The truck engine is loud.

Mother walks past the garage and stands where she stands when family is leaving, wiggling her fingers beside her eyes, which is a family tradition. The family in the car wiggles their fingers back. We call it Hoot Owl. There is no Hoot Owl today. Mayflower movers are not family.

My father wasn't in his room when I came downstairs this morning, and he wasn't in the kitchen. He wasn't anywhere, which scared me. Mother said in her normal, everyday voice that he'd gone out for breakfast with Uncle Jim, as if this happens all the time. Uncle Jim and my father have never had breakfast. Cocktails yes, but not breakfast. I can't imagine my father and Uncle Jim sitting in a booth at Howard Johnson's to save my life. Then, she said Uncle Jim will drive my father over to River Road at dinnertime which gives us time to make up his bed.

I follow her inside. She doesn't ask where I've been all day, so it feels like the right time to explain what I need to do. She says fine, she will wait for me in the car. She says I can take my time, which is amazing given movers are paid by the hour.

It takes much longer than I imagined it would because I cannot exclude one room or one closet or hallway, not the coal room, the sleeping porch, the big porch, the cubbyholes in the attic, the back stairs or the areaways, the paint room, screen room, coal room, dark room, fruit cellar, box room. I never realized until I kiss the walls how many different surfaces a house has—wallpaper, paint, wood, cement, brick. Some are cooler or hotter or smoother or rougher than others. Some smell. It never occurred to me before how many different materials it takes to make a house.

After I finish in the garage, I am tempted to start on the trees, especially since Mother sitting in the Chevy isn't watching. I don't think she even noticed me going into the garage. She is leaning back, her head on the car seat, staring at the garden.

Spoiled Rotten

Mother unpacks plates, and glasses, and pots and pans. I organize baking ingredients in the broom closet on the shelf above the liquor bottles. I suggest we get a more *substantial* spice rack, then, having found the word *substantial*, I list what else is not substantial in this house: the railing that goes upstairs to my bedroom, all the moldings, the faucets, the clothes chute. Mother slams a plate on the counter.

"Look at me," she says in her deep voice.

Look at me is not the same as *listen to me.*

She tilts her head. I glare at her brown eyes.

"If you're any good, you can live any*where*."

"Then, I am no good!" I say in my deep voice and leave the kitchen.

I don't usually sit on the sofa in the middle of the day, but I need to do something I don't usually do. I don't expect Mother will follow me, but she does; she sits beside me and folds her hands. Now we are getting serious.

"Why don't you make a list of what you don't like about this house, and maybe Jay can fix some of those things."

I have a clever mother. She knows I like to make lists. I go up to my room.

Things I Don't Like About 1472 River Road

The windowsill next to my bed is covered in grubby fingerprints and globs of silly putty.

My bedroom closet is six inches above the floor. Why? There is no way to fix this, but I would like to know why.

I tried to screw a wire hook into my closet door for my nighty, but the hook won't stick. A door can be hollow. I didn't know that. I would like a solid door.

The pole in my bedroom closet where I hang my clothes keeps falling down. Somebody measured wrong. I am trying not to remember my old closet with three deep drawers at the back, and brass hooks on the wall and on the back of the door for my nighty, and the light with the lampshade and a dangling chain to pull with a key attached to the chain so I could find it in the dark.

There is no clothes chute on the second floor. There might as well not be one on the first floor because you can fit a pillowcase down it, but not a bedsheet; a washcloth but not a towel; socks but not blue jeans.

The cedar bushes under the front living room window overhang the path. These bushes need to be trimmed.

Outside my father's bedroom is a dead bush. Replace it with a mock orange bush.

The new china cupboards are not deep enough to hold the Meissen which has already gone down to the basement. I'd better get used to the rooster plates.

The moldings around the doors and windows are two-inch pine. The baseboard moldings are three-inch pine. I absolutely hate them.

Jay is nice enough and he says he can use the money, but he makes my father so uncomfortable and is a daily reminder of my father's heart attack. The coffee pot on the stove is for Jay, another reminder my father cannot drink coffee. We need to politely get rid of Jay as soon as we can.

The End.

The next morning, Mother says she read my list carefully, and my closet pole is a priority. She says the soil needs to be tested before we plant a mock orange, and she says Jay will not be here much longer. Then, she wants me to go down with her to the basement. When we get to the foot of the stairs, she says she's going to turn this room into a cozy study. Jay has finished the bookcases, so now all we need is a carpet and some furniture. I can't believe it. Has she forgotten my father can't climb stairs? We don't need a cozy study my father can't enjoy. We need an elevator. In fact, forget all the other projects and put all the money into an elevator because if he is never going to be able to go down to his workroom, he will die of boredom. What will he do all day without a job and without projects? Chew Gelusil tablets? Drink VO? Watch television? Eat a banana? Sneak cigarettes?

On the back of my bathroom door upstairs, in ballpoint pen, somebody wrote the heights of some children named Daphne and Tom. We bought the house from the Cartwrights, so I suppose these are the heights of Daphne and Tom Cartwright, or maybe children before the Cartwrights. Given the sailboat wallpaper in my room, my room was probably Tom's room. In this house, a boy and a girl I never met got taller. The idea of families moving into each other's houses, their clothes hanging in the same closet, their bottoms on the same toilet seats feels creepy. Mother says when you sit in a movie theater, you never know how many people sat in the seat you are sitting in. In church, we may have our own pew, but we can't forbid other people from sitting in it. In school, other students have sat at the desks—years and years' worth of students. What is the problem? Home is different. To be living in a house somebody else lived in is a new feeling. How do I know what went on in my bedroom? What if the children were mean? Nobody ever lived at 1015 but our family, I remind Mother.

"That's true," she says. "We were spoiled rotten."

Dislocation

I overhear Mother telling someone on the phone that I am dislocated. I suppose I am dislocated. Last week, when I registered for
typing class, standing at the counter in the front office at Ann Arbor
High School, I didn't know what to write on the line next to "Date."
I looked for a calendar. What month was it? What year? What day?
I was wearing a sleeveless blouse, so all I could think was "it must
be summer." There was a girl registering next to me, so I copied her
date: June 15, 1964.

Mother is not dislocated. She has adapted. She knows where the
light switches are. She moves around as if she has always lived here.
I keep bumping into the bookcase that sticks out in the living room,
and now I have a bruise on my thigh; I saw Mother getting out of
the bathtub the other day, and she has no bruises. Coming through
doorways, I turn too early, or too late, and bang my shoulder against
the door frame. Mother says if I would stop staring at the moldings, I
would have fewer bruises. I have always stared at things other people
don't find interesting, and out here there are lots more new things to
stare at.

Actually, I've noticed Mother is dislocated now and then. She has
not adapted to the mailman putting the mail in the postbox out by the
curb. The other day she said "a mailman in a car is a big loss" because
she always enjoyed greeting our mailman on the porch. Today, she

scolded herself for being thoughtless. She said, "the west side mailmen must be more comfortable in their cars; after all, they don't have to lug their heavy mail bag in the hot weather or worry about dog bites." When I asked if our old mailman really made the needlepoint seats on our dining room chairs (it seems like a dream, but why would I dream *that*?), she said, "Dear Norm. He did, indeed."

"What do you call our new house? What architecture?"

"Supposedly, a clapboard salt box, but actually," she says, scrubbing the casserole dish, "we have, if truth be told," she bites her lip, "*aluminum* siding."

Except for the new storm windows—which just slide up and down so we can go from winter to summer in thirty minutes—Mother hates aluminum. She won't even buy aluminum foil.

"Don't believe me?" she says. "Go outside and knock on this house. Go on."

I go outside. I knock. She's right. Sound of a saucepan. When I come inside, she says, "That real estate listing was misleading. We are not a proper salt box. There is no central chimney. No pitch to the roof."

"What are we, then?"

"A mishmash."

At least Mother has her own list. She is not all that good.

New Neighbors

I've noticed when Mother goes out to get the mail, she lingers at the mailbox. Today, coming in the front door, she says she just caught a glimpse of our new neighbors. I am folding laundry on the sofa.

"A Black gentleman downhill and a matron uphill," she says, then she sits by the window overlooking the driveway near the door to the kitchen. She likes sitting there with her feet on the footstool. She drops today's mail in her lap, unopened.

"There I stood at our mailbox and there they stood at their mailboxes, and nobody waved."

"Maybe they're shy."

"If anybody has the right to be shy, it's *us*."

She slaps her hand on the table. She never did that before. I am thrilled.

"I hope we didn't ignore newcomers to Ferdon."

There! That bewildered expression. I've been trying to figure it out ever since we moved. I have never seen Mother look unsure of herself until now.

"*Did* we ignore them?" she wondered.

"There was the family with the two Scotty dogs."

"Did I call on them? Did I send a note?" She looks out the window. "No, I did not. At least we bought Girl Scout cookies from their daughter."

"That was the girl in the Spanish house."

"You're sure?"

I am sure. I never liked that girl.

The biggest sigh yet. "Well, shame on me for neglecting newcomers. It serves me right."

Ted

I want to make two signs for our new house: "Doorbell Not Working. Please Knock HARD," in case our neighbors come over, and "Do NOT Discard" in case the new junk man thinks the underwater biblical mural in the garage is garbage. For my signs, I need to borrow my father's colored pencils.

I knock. When he shouts "What?", I go in.

He is lying in bed, watching baseball. His big toe is poking through a hole in his sock. I ask if I can borrow some colored pencils. He nods. Colored pencils are still in the left drawer, but they need to be sharpened, and the pencil sharpener is not on his desk. We had to unscrew it for the movers.

"Where did they put the pencil sharpener?"

No answer.

"Did the movers unscrew it?"

"Middle drawer."

I can't find it.

"In the back."

It is behind the rubber cement and the bottles of India ink. The movers didn't unscrew the pencil sharpener; he did. I feel around for the screws. Not there. He didn't even tape them to the base. He won't look at me. His mouth shut in a slit, his jaw clenched. I close the drawer. His desk is bare, except for the clean gray socks I put on the corner this morning, and next to the gray socks, the old screw holes.

"Do you want ice cream?"

"Negative."

"These socks don't have holes."

No answer. I close the door quietly.

I want to screw the pencil sharpener back to his desk, but Mother suggests the counter by the telephone in the kitchen; that way he won't be interrupted if we need to use it. I don't like this idea, but I go down to the basement. Mr. Cartwright left a small workbench in the laundry room. On the workbench are my father's fishing tackle box, shoe boxes we filled with his tools, and, saddest of all, the big box with all the jars of his nuts, and bolts, and screws, and washers. I find a screwdriver and two screws that look the right size.

"Leave it for Jay," says Mother.

No! Jay is not touching this pencil sharpener. There is a trick to doing this. *What is the trick?* I remember! Make a hole with a nail first, then the screw will go in the hole. I go back down to the basement for a nail.

I hold the pencil sharpener firmly and make pencil marks where the screws will go. I pound two holes with the nail. I line up the sharpener, and put the screws in the holes, and tighten the screws. Hooray! I never noticed the word *Giant* on the pencil sharpener before. I turn the crank, then I twist off the canister, and dump the shavings into the wastebasket. Seeing the little curls and bits of wood with yellow, black, brown, red, green waxy edges I have that sinking, bad luck feeling. The old shavings were from his mock-ups. I have done two wrong things: installing the pencil sharpener in the kitchen and throwing out the old shavings from his mock-ups. I should have saved them.

Mother is staring at me, shaking her head.

"What?"

"You and that pencil sharpener."

Bearings

Mother has her bearings. She knows the name of the owner of the market at the corner of River Road; she knows the name of the plants by the garage—hostas—and she knows trash day is Monday. She even knows the first and last names of the mailman and the paperboy. This morning, Mother got another bearing. She said, "See the morning sun? East is *that* way."

I don't really care which way is east. Or do I? Wait a minute! I'd better care. I'd better figure out where the southwest corner is. I forgot all about that. I go down to the basement. The northeast corner is over by the paned door that goes out to the back yard. When the debris goes flying, that door will get broken.

The southwest corner is . . . I go into the laundry room . . . furnace is to the right, so the southwest corner is behind the furnace—just like at 1015. I wonder if house builders know about tornados and put the furnace near the southwest corner. There is some firewood over there. Well, we can crouch in that corner easily enough.

During dinner that night, Mother reports, "Our uphill neighbor is Deborah Bacon, former Dean of Women at the University. Our downhill neighbors are Michael and Jane Abrams. They have a baby boy.

I invited them all to dinner. The Abramses," she nods one way "on Friday night, and Miss Bacon," she nods the other way, "on Sunday. Then Uncle Walter the next Sunday."

"Bull by the horns," says my father, eyes rolling.

When the Abramses come to dinner, we eat in the new dining room. The Abramses have to squeeze past the wall to fit into their chairs. I can tell my father wants to say something critical about Jay's measuring, but Mother keeps up a steady conversation. Jane Abrams holds baby Jason on her lap and feeds him pieces of soft bread, which she brought with her. Jason is a quiet baby. Mother asks how old he is, if he sleeps through the night, if he has any teeth.

Michael is tall and soft-spoken. He teaches science at Slauson Junior High School where Jane used to be a math teacher. Michael can walk to work, he says, and come home for lunch. Luckily, Michael likes baseball, so he and my father can talk about the Tigers and the bad call at home plate during last night's game. Maybe Michael will come over and watch baseball with my father. After they leave, I expect my father will say something about the dining room being too small, but he just goes to his room and shuts the door.

While we do the dishes, Mother says, "Cat got your tongue?"

I don't dare tell Mother that looking at Michael Abrams's hands reminds me of Vee Vee. We are not supposed to talk about Black people's skin. I don't know why. We've always talked about all sorts of things we care about—the flowers, the fireplace tiles, the leaded windows, Christmas lights.

"Where did Vee Vee go after Nanny died?"

"You've forgotten?"

I have forgotten. All I have now is a sinking feeling that I may never see Vee Vee again.

"Vee Vee went to live with Aunt Helen Van Tyne on Cambridge.

We visited once. You played in Vee Vee's room after she fixed our tea. Remember? You enjoyed her goldfish."

How could I forget this? Up the backstairs. Vee Vee's room with a bay window. Her goldfish, which used to be Nanny's goldfish, in a bowl on the windowsill, her bureau with three mirrors and a bench pulled up to it. She let me sit on the bench and open all the jars. Vee Vee showed me how she puts jelly on her hair. She put some on my hair, and all that day and night, I smelled like Vee Vee, and it helped me sleep.

"You loved your Vee Vee."

Mother is staring at me because I'm crying. Nanny would not let me climb up on her sofa. She would not let me crawl on the window seat, so I would run to Vee Vee who was happy to see me, and picked me up and put me on the counter, and let me lick the frosting bowl. When the straps on her apron fell down, she let me put them back on her shoulder. She let me tie the sash on her apron. She kissed me. She wanted my company.

"Why didn't Vee Vee stay with us?"

"We couldn't afford her. And Aunt Helen had just lost Jocelyn. It was a good arrangement. Vee Vee got a substantial raise."

On the side of Vee Vee's hands, the pink skin of her palm met the brown skin on the back of her hands. When she picked up the frosting—

"Darling? Come back to me."

I hate when she says that.

"Is Vee Vee still at Mrs. Van Tyne's?"

"When Mrs. Van Tyne died, Vee Vee went to Birmingham. Don't you remember taking her to the train?"

No. Why don't I?

"If she was Tizabel's cousin, why didn't she go back to Ypsilanti with her family?"

"Vee Vee had twin daughters in Birmingham, and she wanted to live with them. Last year, Vee Vee's Christmas card said she was singing in her old church choir. She sang in her choir in Ann Arbor, too.

"Where was her church?"

"Second Baptist."

"Why *Second* Baptist?"

Mother sighs.

"Second Baptist is a Black church. First Baptist—"

Why can't the Baptist's have one church for everyone? Mother's expression says she hates segregation, too.

"We got a Christmas card from Vee Vee last year?"

"We did, indeed."

"Is her address in your address book?

Mother smiles. "Of course."

Red

When Miss Bacon comes for dinner, Mother explains that my father is not feeling well and will have a tray in his room. When I take him his dinner tray, he is watching baseball, the volume turned up higher than usual.

"She isn't that bad," I tell him, "Maybe a little bossy."

"Your mother can handle her."

"Who's playing?"

"White Sox, third inning, two to one Tigers, one out, man on third. Donovan pitching."

I put his tray on his desk. If only he would ask for something, I would get it for him, but he has never asked for things, even when he's not sick.

"Would you like a cat?"

"Don't like cats," he says.

"You're a dog man, and a handyman, and a bow-tie man."

Why did I say that?

He reaches for his Gelusil.

"Not anymore, Toots."

Red

When I get back to the dining room, Mother and Miss Bacon are just sitting down at the table, and Miss Bacon is describing her recent trip to Stratford-upon-Avon—not in Canada, but in England. She says she saw *Macbeth* and *Twelfth Night*. We learn she is no longer the Dean of Women, but rather an assistant professor in the English Department. I am waiting for Mother to tell her Bapa taught Shakespeare, but she lets Miss Bacon talk about the actor who played Malvolio.

I think if Miss Bacon is teaching English, she would enjoy hearing about Bapa and Robert Frost, so when Mother goes out to the kitchen for more peas, I tell her Robert Frost used to come to our old house on Ferdon Road for dinner. I forget what years, but Miss Bacon says she heard Frost was here in the early 1920s. That sounds right. When Mother returns, she glares at me, but I keep going because Miss Bacon seems interested. I tell how Bapa would walk Robert Frost home after dinner, but when they got to Robert Frost's house, which we think was on Washtenaw opposite the Presbyterian Church, Robert Frost wasn't ready to go home, so he would walk Bapa back up Washtenaw to Ferdon, and this would go on all night until finally Robert Frost was ready to go into his house. Then—I love this part—I describe how my grandmother got fed up with Bapa coming back so late that she said, "Morris Tilley! Please! Pick a tree halfway!" When I'm done, Miss Bacon is laughing.

Red

After Miss Bacon has left and we are cleaning up, I ask why Mother didn't tell Miss Bacon about Bapa and Shakespeare and Robert Frost herself.

"I didn't want to steal her thunder," she says.

Oh dear.

"Did I steal her thunder?"

"No, darling. She enjoyed your story."

"Where was their tree?"

"Whose tree?"

"Where Bapa and Robert Frost went their separate ways."

"We never knew."

I go to my father's room to get his dinner tray. He's still watching baseball.

"Tell your mother I don't want dessert."

I return to the kitchen.

"That's all he ate? Go ask him if he wants coffee."

"He doesn't want coffee."

I have turned into a messenger.

Leo

When Uncle Walter comes to dinner, I don't miss Aunt Martha, which is not a good feeling, but then, Aunt Martha never came to this house. She never sat in this dining room. Uncle Walter has on a white shirt and a tie, and he sits across from me like he always has. How can such an enormous thing happen, and yet nothing seems different? We don't mention Aunt Martha, nor does he. They talk about his apartment in Washington, where he will be spending more time, renting his house on Berkshire Road. I want to ask what he does at the Atomic Energy Commission, but Mother says there are private rooms in a person's life and that is one of Uncle Walter's private rooms.

Suki and Opie

Suki is a small, four-year-old, brown mutt. Suki belonged to one of Uncle Jim Robertson's patients who had to move to Florida. Uncle Jim assured my father that Suki is sweet-natured, not too active, and will be good company. I suppose she is sweet-natured, but I don't find her good company. Does anybody care if she obeys? Nobody cares. My father won't pet her or teach her tricks. He used to throw his leather wallet to the end of the living room, and tell Marky to "Stay, stay." Then, he would say "Release," and Marky would get the wallet and bring it back to him, wagging his tail. Mother is the only one who pets Suki. I don't care for Suki. She is too docile and obedient, as if she'd been beaten. She has no personality. I prefer big dogs.

After dinner, I take Suki for a walk. When we get past Mixtwood, I take her off the leash, half hoping she will run away, but she just sniffs the curb. She isn't interested in bushes or car tires or freedom. She just walks along the grass next to the curb and never runs into the street.

At least our walks after dinner give me a chance to observe our new neighborhood; it may not have children, or flowers, or sidewalks, but it does have its own unique sound—a combination of Lawn-Boy motors, pruning shears, baseball on television, the flap of the halyard on the flagpole, and the faint click of the outdoor lights when they come on at dusk. Mother says one-story homes are called ranches because they are modeled after houses out west, which makes sense given this is the west side of the city. Ranches have big picture windows and a *breezeway* connecting the house to the garage. The roofs are not very steep. Mother says most of the men out here are retired which is why they wear slip-on shoes. Mother says my father is retired for medical reasons, not because of his age and certainly not by choice, and he refuses to wear loafers or slip-ons. Retired people plan ahead for the day when they will not be able to climb stairs which is why they live in ranches and prefer bushes to flowers. The only flowers at the ranches are in pots on the porch or around the post holding the mailbox, or sometimes in a hanging plant on the breezeway. Mother says maybe the owners once had big gardens in their former homes and have decided, now that they are retired, to just enjoy a nice green lawn, which requires some, but not too much, upkeep. One night, I see a woman through the picture window of her living room putting playing cards back in the playing card box; then she dusts the box.

When we get back, Suki goes straight to the kitchen for a drink, then comes back to the living room, jumps on the sofa, turns a circle, then settles down, with a sigh, on the far-right cushion. Maybe I am getting my bearings: this is our living room sofa, and this is our new dog.

Leo

Mother buys a small, red used car called an Opel from a retired man. She calls our new car Opie. She says Opie will be taking me to typing class and her to the hospital. We now drive *in* because we live so far *out*. Close to the egg lady?

"No," Mother says, "we are nowhere near the egg lady. We are 3.5 miles from The Ann Arbor Bank."

How did I not notice that the Chevy and Borgie disappeared? I don't seem to notice when important things happen anymore.

My father offers to teach me how to operate Opie's stick shift. I'm afraid he will want to drive the car, but he gets in the passenger seat and is more patient than my Driver's Ed teacher. When the car lurches ahead, he doesn't grab the dashboard, and he doesn't even swear. His mouth doesn't go into a slit. We practice parallel parking in the Slauson Junior High parking lot. The rules are: Turn off the headlights, don't ride the clutch, and watch your gauges. He says, "Women never watch their gauges." What *women* does he mean? I had forgotten about Mrs. Margolis until he said *women*. In fact, now that he no longer goes to the Margolises' and my father has a new heart doctor, nobody ever mentions the name Margolis, and he hasn't been invited to go fishing. Is that why we moved all the way to the west side?

Words Per Minute

Mother drives me to Ann Arbor High School for my typing class on her way to work at the hospital. This will be our morning routine for three weeks, after which, hopefully, I will get a summer typing job now that I am sixteen.

As I get out of the car, I feel for the quarter in the pocket of my shorts. "Take the number nine bus," Mother says, as if we collect bus numbers and the number nine bus is the last bus we need for our collection. I never thought about how I was going to get home. But Mother had. She points to the bus stop on the other side of Stadium Boulevard and says, "The number nine bus stops there at twelve-fifteen. It will take you to River and Miller. There's potato salad in the icebox. See if you can get him to eat something when you get home."

Class starts at 9:00 a.m., so I have forty-five minutes to roam the dark halls. I keep waiting for a janitor to turn on the lights. That my sister went here doesn't help. I was supposed to come here, but I went to U. High. The other day, I heard Mother say she felt U. High would be more attentive. Attentive to what? None of it matters. I don't quite know what *does* matter. When it comes to where I should go or what I should do, I am a good servant.

So far, I have seen only two students and one janitor in these dark halls. I thought the janitor might be hurrying to turn on more lights, but he was in no hurry. Maybe it is the wrong day. I check my registration slip. It is the right day. Turning down another long corridor, it feels typical of my new life—I am taking a typing class I never thought I would take but am, in the high school I always thought I would go to but did not. I am looking in the dark for a door marked A321, which I will never find in this dim light, and I am soon to ride a bus across the west side. Mother used to complain that we didn't travel as a family. That isn't true anymore. Every day feels like a trip.

The sun is so bright when I come outside, I can't see the bus stop. I stand by the brick wall, waiting for my eyes to adjust. We are in a heat wave, and it's noon. No one from summer school rides the bus. They are all getting rides. I am the only student walking across the grass to the bus stop where elderly people wait, their shadows on the lawn behind them. A woman fans her face with a folded newspaper. I stand beside her. Another woman looks at my typing book and smiles. The bus doesn't come. Sweat drips down everybody's faces. I can see the football stadium. From this direction, it looks different. I don't know this part of town. I cross Stadium Boulevard. I am not a bus person. I am a car person and, given there is no car coming to get me, I am going to walk. From now on, I am a sidewalk person.

One side of Seventh Street is shady, but after two blocks, I am sweating all over my typing book. There is no place to get a drink unless I knock on somebody's door. The houses are small with short yards in front, a driveway, bushes under the front windows, and maybe a railing or a bird feeder.

I cross Pauline Boulevard, Liberty, Washington, and Huron streets. I pass a park with a band shell I didn't see this morning. Maybe I am not on the right street? No, I am sure Mother drove across Seventh Street. The number nine bus passes me, the patient people who waited are sitting comfortably inside, out of the sun. I am still not a bus person.

By the time I get to River and Miller, my head is pounding, sweat is running down my back, and arms, and eyelids, and the Budweiser clock in the window of the Miller Market says 12:30. I have been walking for an hour and a quarter. Mr. Rawlings gives me one paper napkin for my Popsicle. I am too tired to ask for a second napkin.

Ted

That evening, Mother asks about my typing class. I tell her all those years of piano have paid off; I memorized the keys like a piece of music. (What I don't say is that unpleasant things will be over the sooner I can master them.) Instead, I describe the teacher who has a big mustache and dirty fingernails, but otherwise seems all right. All ten students each have a typewriter and a spiral notebook on a metal stand. You go over, and over, and over the sentences. At the end of the hour, there is a speed test. I don't tell them the teacher thinks I am talented. I don't tell them I just want to be good enough to get a job and earn some money.

When Mother asks how the bus was, I tell her I walked and bought a Popsicle with the quarter. No reaction. The next day, I notice a dish of quarters on the front hall table. As we go out the front door, Mother says, "Take one. It may rain." A Popsicle at the Miller Market becomes my goal in life. I don't care what flavor. Without that Popsicle to look forward to, I don't think I could make it home.

By the second week, Mr. Rawlings gives me two paper napkins for my popsicle which is all I need, and I have the houses on River Road memorized. I tell Mother, while I set the table in the dining room, that she may be the authority on east side houses, but I am the authority on west side houses.

When we sit down to dinner, she asks me to describe the west side houses, which is when I realize that nobody is going to talk about the real news—which is that we have moved to a poorer neighborhood where lots of Black people live.

I begin:

"Behind the Miller Market is a shack."

Mother winces.

"*Shack* implies deep poverty," she says, "and a run-down situation. Be careful what words you choose to describe people and their homes."

She suggests I look up *shack* in my dictionary, so I ask to be excused, go get my dictionary, and bring it back to the table.

"Webster's says a *shack* is *a hut, shanty.*"

"Look up shanty," she says.

I look up *shanty.*

"*Shanty* is *a small, mean dwelling, a hut.*"

I look up *mean.* There are lots of definitions for *mean: common, humble, destitute of distinction, of little value, unkind.* It goes on and on. This could take all night, so I say,

"I am sticking to shack."

Mother smiles and says, "To be continued . . ."

Ted

The next day, I see a Black man working on a car by the shack. Car parts are in the grass. His clothes are clean, and he has a toolbox. The small house next to the shack has a faded red and black cardboard "For Sale" sign with a handwritten telephone number in the front window. The numbers are barely readable from the sidewalk. I think the shack is on the same property. The window curtains don't look very fresh, but the house is not run down. The porch is swept and the yard is tidier than our yard.

That night at the dinner table I report that the Black man working on the car probably lives in the house with the "For Sale" sign.

"What did I tell you about presuming?" she says.

"Don't be nosy," says my father. "That's the bottom line."

"She's not being nosy," Mother replies. "She is taking an interest in her surroundings. She's being observant."

"She should be a detective," he says. "Earn a living being nosy."

"Or a journalist," says Mother, "now that she can type."

Leo

The popsicle and the idea of working for a newspaper is what gets me across Seventh Street in the unbearable heat. Every day, I study a different house on River Road and then give my report at the dinner table.

"At the corner of Hiscock is a two-story red brick apartment house with a white metal railing on the second story. There are eight apartments with reflective, stick-on numbers on the doors, and there is a large flowerpot on the ground level where you put out your cigarette in the sand."

"Very good," says Mother.

"But these apartments are only temporary housing until the people can find a better place."

"What did I tell you?" Mother says. "For all you know, those people lived somewhere worse before and those apartments are a step up."

I never thought of that.

The next morning, I point to the house with the huge oak tree in the front yard.

"The oak tree isn't the scary part."

"Scary?" says Mother, turning her head to look. "Why scary?"

We are past the house now, so I have to describe what I mean.

"The garage is connected to the house. Two families live there."

"How do you know that?"

"There is one mailbox on the front porch and another mailbox next to the door beside the garage door. That door, I think, leads to the room over the garage where the yellow curtains are never pulled shut and a beer can has been on the windowsill for over a week."

"That's not scary."

"On the garage door is a padlock that somebody, not the garage manufacturer, put on. And there are dents in the aluminum door on the apartment next to the garage as if somebody was locked out and was determined to get back in."

"You don't know the whole story," Mother warns, which is true, but the next day when Mother looks at the house as we drive by, she says, "I see what you mean."

I don't dare point out the house I wish we had bought on the corner: gray stucco with a vine climbing over the porch with a rocking chair, a big chimney, real windows upstairs, and a vegetable garden with bean poles in the side yard.

But the most fascinating house is the run-down gray shingled house. Not deep poverty, perhaps, but close. Toys are left out overnight on the dirt yard (no grass). A window is broken on the second floor. Christmas lights along the gutter were never taken down. One day, two new aluminum lawn chairs are out in the yard, and the empty pink toy box on the porch is filled with the toys that had been left out in the yard, and the broken doll's arm in the mud by the sidewalk is gone. I am excited by their clean-up efforts and wonder what they will clean up next. But the next day, the straps of one of the aluminum chair seats have come loose, the toys have drifted back to the yard, there is a muddy sneaker by the mailbox, and a wire running up the side of the house to the television aerial looks like it has come loose. I feel bad for this family. Their tidying efforts are never sustained from one day to the next—a little excitement, then everything goes back to the way it was, only to be redeemed by yet another effort, like a wind chime on the porch.

Leo

Walking Suki one night, I realize Mother was right when she said never presume. Who knows what is really going on inside these west side houses—or inside the east side houses, or, for that matter, inside any house, anywhere in the world. The perfectly tidy ranch, the flowerpot on the front porch blooming, the shiny car newly washed in the driveway, the flag taken off the flagpole at dusk, the lawn newly mown, and the weeds pulled from around the bushes under the windows—all good, but what about the people who live there? For all I know, they could be crying their eyes out inside. That woman who dusted off her playing card box could have just learned her best friend died. The man I sometimes see putting his golf clubs into the trunk of his immaculate car could have lung cancer, but doesn't know it yet. You would never know from looking at our house that the man in the front bedroom had been DOA. You would never know his wife has had to go to work. You would never know the sweaty daughter you see walking across the front yard every afternoon holding a Popsicle stick is confused. That I am finding someone who is poorer than I am unpleasant—well, not them but their house. That I am finding their house unpleasant: That can't be right. Does it follow that the people who live in the unpleasant house are unpleasant?

Leo

Driving to typing class is no longer the best time to ask Mother questions. She has her mind on the sick patients, but I have to ask: "Does the rule about respecting absolutely every person also apply to their houses?"

"I beg your pardon?"

"Should I respect every house no matter what? Can a person respect the people, but not respect the houses the people live in?"

"Absolutely," she says without missing a beat. She doesn't even have to think about it.

But I still don't know what to do about the fact that when I look at the moldings in our house, I feel sad. I keep waiting for them to look nicer, but they never do.

"That house, for instance." I point to a small brick house with a metal awning. "I like the house, but I don't like the metal awning."

"Nor do I."

"Is that all right?"

"You are developing your own preferences—your own taste."

"What is 'taste'?"

"People have different tastes. A person's taste is their preferences. That person likes their aluminum awning. We prefer canvas."

"Why do we?"

"I'm not sure. It's softer. I suppose, more colorful."

"Aluminum is stronger."

"Awnings have traditionally been canvas. You could say we like older things."

"Daddy likes modern."

"Yes, he does."

"Does he like aluminum awnings?"

"Ask him."

The Ann Street Boarding House

Mother never bought a car before, so she didn't notice that one side of Opie's back seat sags, and that where the rearview mirror is bolted to the ceiling, there is a screw missing, and somebody spilled what looks like Elmer's glue in the glove compartment. Then, one rainy morning when Opie won't start, my father says, "I knew it. Too good to be true."

Mother and I are standing around the car when Michael Abrams comes over with a machine to test the car battery. He says he might be able to help. My father does not come out to the driveway, but I see him looking through the venetian blinds.

Michael says it's not the battery. It's the damp weather, maybe a loose wire. When we go back inside to tell my father, he is on the phone talking to someone who doesn't seem to know him. When he hangs up, he says, "Herb's no longer at Standard Oil." He is disappointed, but I am happy he tried to help. Michael, who Mother has invited inside, suggests we go back out to the car. He seems to have another idea. My father goes into his room.

Michael puts the gearshift in neutral, then we push the car out into the street. Michael quickly jumps in and pulls up the emergency brake. He gets out and tells me to get in the driver's side while he gets in the passenger side. He tells me to "Keep your foot on the brake and your other foot on the clutch; then put the gearshift in first gear and let go of the emergency brake and the brake pedal. Halfway down the hill, release the clutch and the engine should start . . ."

It worked! Off we go!

The hill comes to the rescue. Michael has a name for this maneuver: *popping the clutch.* We can't thank him enough. We can get to work, after all.

When we drive by the emergency room, I look at the entrance where Dr. Margolis must have stopped his car and my father, with no heartbeat, was lifted out. I have it in my mind that it was not through the automatic doors, and not in the corridor inside the doors, and not even in a curtained-off room, but rather outside under the overhang that says EMERGENCY in red neon. It was there where they laid him on the ground, his head not on a pillow, the surfaces around him hard but with lots of space—the space important—for the doctors who came running to spread out their equipment.

Driving by the Emergency entrance every morning, I squeeze the steering wheel in thanks to those people. We may be three years later, but he came back from his eight minutes as a dead person, *right there.* I know he's not very happy, but he's with us.

Leo

I begin my summer job after I finish my typing class at the end of June. I am a clerk-typist in the University Hospital Personnel office. It was Mother's idea; we can drive into work together. I have my own desk in front of a woman named Audrey. I have my own green IBM Selectric II. I am learning all the departments.

Mother works in the Social Work Department. She is assigned to Pediatrics. There are five social workers and two caseworkers. Mother is a caseworker. In order to be a social worker, you have to have an MSW degree and, at the age of sixty-one, Mother says she is not going back to school.

In the 1930s, when Mother lived on E. 10th Street in New York

City, she worked at the Henry Street Settlement House and Bellevue Hospital. She says there was no such thing as a hospital handbook at Bellevue, and she wasn't called a caseworker. She didn't even have an office. Mother was called Miss Tilley. "Nobody had a title," she says, "and best of all, there were no forms to fill out. You just did what you thought would be comforting."

The MSW's in Social Work are young and well dressed. They eat lunch at the same table in the cafeteria. They might have their MSW degrees, but they don't yet have what Mother has—eight years' experience in New York City, white hair, her own children, a finely scratched gold wedding ring, and a little fingernail dirt from gardening, which the farming mothers can relate to. I never see the MSW's carrying a suitcase up the front porch steps of the Ann Street Boarding House, where the parents of the sick children stay overnight. Mother says the MSW's prefer to hand out maps with the sidewalks highlighted. True, the Ann Street Boarding House is only a block away from the hospital, but Mother says that's a long block if you just learned your child has leukemia.

Mother keeps rolls of dimes in her desk drawer. She tells the mothers of the sick children to put their overnight bags under her desk and come back to her office any time after five o'clock, that she'll drive them over to the Ann Street Boarding House and get them settled. I ride in back with their overnight bags which are pitifully small (sometimes just a grocery sack). In the car, she explains to the mothers that there is a pay phone in the basement for outgoing calls.

Mother says the hardest part of her day is when the parents of a dying child come into her office at four-thirty. In addition to the child's mother, there is usually an aunt or grandmother or a good friend of the family. Fathers can't face it, I've noticed. Mother says it's not that they can't face it—she has seen many courageous fathers—but somebody has to earn a living. That's the sort of thing she says now that she is that person.

Mother looks very professional in her new green dress, and dark blue stockings, and blue pumps with clip-on bows. She now wears a Timex watch. I rat her hair, and put Erase under her eyes to cover the dark circles, and add a little rouge and lipstick. She's put on weight since we moved, but she can still reach all the hooks at the back of her girdle. The final touch is the white coat with "Social Work Department" embroidered in blue on the pocket.

I thought she would act bossy in her white coat, but she is the opposite. Sometimes, when I wait for her after five o'clock, if her door is not quite closed and she's talking to a family member, I look in. I notice her shoulders droop, and her hands remain in her lap, and her head tips to one side, and she goes limp. When I first saw it, I thought she was asleep; now I realize she's just listening. She says, "there is listening and there is *caring*."

The patients' mothers who dress in colorful, comfortable, easy-to-clean clothes have usually been around the hospital awhile; they can fall asleep in chairs and dress brightly for their children. One day, there is one woman in Mother's waiting room who looks dressed for church in a plaid sleeveless dress and flats. She holds the ashtray in one hand. The ashtray is one Mother brought from home—the long brass leaf. You would think the woman would notice such an unusual ashtray in a hospital waiting room, but she doesn't seem to. After she smokes her last cigarette, she crumples the pack and holds it in her fist.

Mother finally comes out of her office. The nervous new mother puts the ashtray on the side table and leans over and stares at the floor. At this point, Mother usually introduces me, but now she just says, "I'm sorry I kept you waiting, Louise. We'll go now to the boarding house."

Louise stands. She doesn't pick up her overnight bag, so I pick it up. In the elevator, Mother feels inside her pocket.

"Here, Louise. Some dimes for the pay phone at the boarding house."

Louise puts the dimes in her dress pocket. Mother's never done that before. Usually, the mothers are in her office when she hands out dimes.

I thought Louise might want cigarettes from the vending machine in the lobby, but she walks right past it, still holding onto the empty, crumpled pack. Mother says nothing all the way to the parking structure which is when she usually recites the Ann Street Boarding House rules. I tell her "I started Opie during my lunch hour so hopefully she will start now." Opie starts. At least we don't have to ask this poor mother to help us push Opie over to the top of the ramp. That has happened a few times. Louise's overnight bag is green and purple flowered canvas with a brown plastic handle, no tag or initials.

Mother always tries to get the mothers to talk about their hometown on the way to Ann Street, but tonight she doesn't try. When we get to the boarding house, Louise doesn't move. This is what always happens; the mothers don't want to leave the car. So, Mother says in her soft voice, "Here we are," and gets out, opens the back door. I hand her the overnight bag, which she carries to the porch and rings the bell. Louise follows.

The Ann Street Boarding House is a white frame house with a porch and a white railing. There is a sign on a post in the yard with a hook for adding "NO" in front of "Vacancy," a swing on the porch, and, in the living room window, a huge geranium with leaves flat against the glass. Cora, the manager, takes forever to come to the door. Mother lets Louise go in first. While Mother sorts things out with Cora, I usually move to the driver's seat, but today, Mother seems so much in command, I sit where Louise sat. Mother returns to the car. This is when she usually tells me what disease the child has, but today she says, "That geranium needs water."

"Did you tell Cora?"

"I will do no such thing."

We turn right on Division and go down the hill to Depot Street. It never works to mention my father when Mother has something else on her mind, so I abandon my plan to ask her if there isn't some job he could do from home. Then she mumbles something about Mrs. Bradley and Kalamazoo. When I ask who Mrs. Bradley is, she gives me a sharp look.

"Louise Bradley whom we just took to Cora's?"

She called her Louise earlier, not Mrs. Bradley, but I let that go.

"What's wrong with the Bradley child?"

"Chris Bradley, age four, has Wilms tumor," she says. "Cancer of the kidney."

She parks by the train depot, gets out, and goes into the station. We have never stopped at the depot before. There are old luggage carts on the platform and a black taxi parked at the curb.

Mother comes back holding a train schedule. Her high heel catches on the cobblestones, but she puts her hand out on the bumper of the car just in time. She is not athletic like my father, but she is graceful. Once, when I was visiting my father in the hospital, he heard footsteps in the corridor and said, "I'd know that walk anywhere" just as Mother came through the door.

"We're in luck," she says. "There's a Wolverine at ten a.m. tomorrow, which means Louise can see Chris in the morning and won't have to take the bus. I'll drive her to the depot at nine-thirty, and there is an evening train that she can take that gets her back here at five-thirty. We can meet that train and get her back to the hospital in time to have dinner with Chris." She lights her cigarette. I pull open the ashtray drawer.

"Why does she have to go home?"

"Farm inspection."

As we drive across Summit Street, she slaps the steering wheel.

"Damn. I forgot to mention the pay phone."

"You gave her dimes."

"But I didn't tell her where the pay phone is. She probably thinks I meant a pay phone on the sidewalk corner." She bites her lip.

It took months for Mother to convince Cora that parents need some place private to talk to their relatives. "Hospital pay phones aren't private," she said, "not even the ones with folding doors. You can overhear the conversation on the phone beside you." Mother offered to make all the arrangements with the phone company, so Cora finally gave in, and a pay phone was installed in the laundry room in the basement. Mother bought an armchair, a side table, and a standing lamp at the Treasure Mart. Then she took one of our extra phone books, and a pad of paper, and a pencil to put on the side table. The laundry room was ideal: clean, and private, and warm from the furnace in the winter, cool in the summer.

"Won't Cora tell her?"

"Cora is forgetful. She still has the "NO" in front of "Vacancy," and those sheets have been on the laundry line for two days, not to mention the geranium."

Mother bends her cigarette into the ashtray. "Hell's bells."

"I'm sure Mrs. Bradley will find the pay phone."

"Would you go snooping into somebody's basement? I hope you would not."

We drive up the hill.

"You'd think, being a farmer's wife, Louise would be bold, but she's not—not in the city, anyway. She has a sister in Kalamazoo who could do her a world of good to talk to tonight."

Leo

My father isn't usually in the living room when we get home, but there he sits, in his chair by the fireplace, with a pad of paper in his lap and not very sharp colored pencils in his fist. It is one of the pads Mother bought him for his cartoons. He is drawing a ship, an island, and the sea.

Mother can't stop talking about Louise Bradley and the pay phone in the basement. When I suggest she call Cora and have Cora knock on Mrs. Bradley's door, she says, "Good idea," and actually goes out to the kitchen and dials the number. Then she comes back out to tell us Cora has apparently gone to bed.

My father draws a palm tree on his island. Mother stands in the doorway to the kitchen.

"I'm going back to Ann Street," she says. "If the light is on in her room and if the porch door isn't locked, I'll go upstairs and tell her about the pay phone. What they really need is a sign."

"Do you know which room she's in?"

"The room over the geranium," Mother says. She looks at my father. "Sam?"

"I had lunch. I feel fine."

He draws fish in the sea. I am so excited he's drawing.

"What if the porch door is locked?" I ask.

"I'll throw a stone at the window," she says, going out the door.

A stone at the window? Like Cyrano. Like Romeo.

My father has a fresh VO on the side table, but he isn't drunk. If I tell him how wonderful it is that he's drawing, he might stop, so I tell him about the problem at Cora's and the pay phone in the basement. I look out the window, glad Opie starts. She's backing out the driveway. But what if Opie doesn't start on Ann Street? Will she just leave it running?

"Find some cardboard," he says. "We'll make a sign."

He drops his pad of paper on the floor. He used to have cardboard in his filing cabinet, which is in the basement. I run downstairs. Some is still in the top drawer, moldy smelling. He wrinkles his nose when I hand it to him. His pencils could use a good sharpening, but I don't say a word. I don't want to break the spell.

First, he draws a black chair and the walls of a room. Then, he draws a woman in a blue dress with brown hair sitting in the chair. Next, he draws a black phone on the wall, the phone cord spiraling down to the woman's hand. Then he takes a sip of VO, draws a standing lamp with a brown lampshade and a cone of yellow light. Then he draws a staircase and a door at the top of the stairs. Then he draws a basket filled with clothes off to one side, sleeves flopping out, then a black string hanging down from the yellow bulb in the ceiling. Then, in big blue letters across the top, he writes, *There is a phone in the cellar for your*—"How do you spell convenience?"

I spell it.

At the bottom, he writes, in black, *Ann Street Boarding House, Management.*

"There," he hands me the cardboard.

"Cora will love this."

Actually, I'm not sure what Cora will think, but I love it. If Cora doesn't want it, I'll put it in my room.

He picks up his pad of paper and his drink and says, "I'm going to hit the sack, Toots."

I am tempted to get a few more colored pencils from his desk so I can add a red towel to the laundry basket or a red rug, but he shuts the door.

When Mother gets home, she says all the lights were out so she didn't disturb anyone and no, she didn't throw any stones. She has those dark circles under her eyes. When I show her the sign, she smiles and shakes her head side to side like a doll with a loose head.

Bill Knapp's

Every morning, I take tea to my father in bed. He takes a sip, then he sits up straight, turns on the gooseneck lamp, pulls out his bedside table drawer, and feels inside, rummaging and swearing. Then, he slams the drawer shut and tells me to go see what the hell Mother wants in the kitchen. Then, Mother sends me back to ask him if he wants toast and eggs, and he says "Since when do I eat toast and eggs," snapping his mouth shut like a turtle.

Today, while I watch him rummaging in the drawer, I ask what he's looking for and he says "A goddamned Viceroy," which makes no sense. If there was no cigarette in that drawer yesterday, why does he think there will be one there today? Viceroys don't grow in drawers overnight.

He keeps rummaging. Is he losing his mind? Eight minutes was a long time not to have a heartbeat. More rummaging. He knows there is a cigarette in there. If there is, then who is bringing him cigarettes? Mrs. Margolis walking in those black Japanese slippers suddenly lands in my head like a jagged knife. I thought that was all over, but maybe she comes out here to see him when we're at work, and he persuades her to give him a cigarette. Maybe he smokes one and asks her to leave one in the drawer. He did that sort of thing all the time with people who visited in the hospital. *One cigarette is not going to kill me. What's one more nail in my coffin?*

"Go see what your mother wants," he snarls, then slams the drawer shut, leans back, clasps his arms over his chest, and stares at the ceiling. I stare at the bedside table. There is no ashtray. When I empty his waste-basket, there are never cigarette butts or ashes in it. But he could flush the cigarette butts down the toilet, rinse an ashtray in the bathroom sink, and hide everything under the mattress. I stare at the smudge on the side of the mattress where he wipes his finger after he picks his nose. He doesn't pick his nose in public, but he does in bed. Maybe that's why Mother has her own bedroom. She can't stand nose pickers.

"I said, '*Go!*'"

Later, he goes out to the terrace to yell at the blue jays. I go back to his room and feel under his mattress—nothing. I open the bedside table drawer—pencil stub, nail clippers, TV Guide, a match book from a restaurant, but no cigarettes and no ashtray. I close the drawer. Wait. I open the drawer—a green and white matchbook from Bill Knapp's Restaurant. We don't go to Bill Knapp's Restaurant. Who has been to Bill Knapp's? Maybe Mrs. Margolis takes my father to Bill Knapp's which, actually, might not be such a bad idea—to get him out of this house for a change. I suddenly have the tiniest warm feeling for Gwen.

I feel around inside the drawer. A nitroglycerin tablet is stuck in the corner. He is supposed to keep them loose in the drawer in case of emergency. He is supposed to have several in the drawer, not one. I scrape out the pill with the Bill Knapp's matchbook lid. We have to do something about this.

Mother is washing garden dirt off her hands in the kitchen. She has been transplanting the mint she brought over from 1015 to the steep bank outside the kitchen door. We've noticed that when it rains, the soil on the slope is washing down into the stairwell, collecting outside the basement door, blocking the drain. The roots of the mint are meant to prevent this erosion.

When I tell her we need a better arrangement for his nitroglycerin, she looks at the bottle on his pill tray on the counter, then turns off the faucet.

"I mean the ones in his bedside table drawer."

"What about his bedside table drawer?"

I explain about the pills getting pushed to the back corners and how hard it will be to find if he needs one.

"That's why I gave him the pillbox."

"He doesn't use that pillbox."

She is not paying attention.

"Have you made his bed?"

"Not yet."

She dries her hands on an old dish towel.

"Are you coming with me to the Farmer's Market?"

She is writing her list on the back of an envelope.

"Zucchini, tomatoes, potatoes, onions . . ."

"Not today."

She looks up. I always go with her. Opie is starting now; I don't have to.

After she backs out of the driveway, I put six more nitroglycerin pills in his bedside table drawer. It doesn't solve the problem of them getting into the corners, but at least there are six, not one. I pull up his sheets and plump the pillows, then I straighten the blue striped bedspread that matches the curtains. If Mrs. Margolis parks her car in the driveway, then Miss Bacon and the Abramses must know he has a visitor. And now I know. The only person who doesn't know is Mother. Or maybe she does know, which is why she rarely comes into his room. I am the one who vacuums and dusts. I put away his clean clothes and change his sheets.

He's on the terrace sanding a wooden chair that used to be on the porch at 1015. Yesterday, he saw it in the garage and said he wanted to paint it, so I got his paints, and brushes, and turpentine from the basement. We decided all the paints should go in the garage in case he feels like painting other things. As long as he doesn't reach above the shoulder, he can paint all he wants. He glued the legs back on years ago. Now he is sanding the spokes between the legs.

"What color will you paint it?"

"Gray and white," he says.

"Two-tone?"

He doesn't answer. The side of his neck is sunburned because he fell asleep in his lawn chair yesterday.

Suki is scratching on the back door. I let her out, and she goes straight for her hollow spot under the pussy willow tree. I sit in the wicker chair. My father wipes the sawdust off the spoke. I don't recognize that rag. Now he needs a screwdriver to open the paint cans. There is one in the kitchen drawer.

"While you're up, bring me a beer."

He prefers beer to VO on a hot day. He takes a swig, sets it down. I hand him the screwdriver. He pries open the lid. Air hisses. He needs to stir the paint. "Don't move," he says, reaching for a stick on the grass. The greasy gold liquid on the top swirls into the white.

After Mrs. Margolis brings him back from Bill Knapp's, where do they sit? Out here? Will she sit in that chair once he paints it? Does she sit in Mother's chair? Do they have a beer together? I sit in the old blue deck chair for the first time since we moved here. The air is so still. I check the thermometer outside the kitchen window—eighty-eight degrees, no leaves moving, and I think the sky is getting greener. I sit back in the deck chair. I watch my father painting his chair. I look at the steps going down to the basement door. Is that door locked? I feel a slight breeze. I go back inside. I go down to the basement. The door to the backyard is locked. I unlock it in case we need to get to the basement in a hurry. I go back upstairs and out to the front porch. It's humid, and the air is very still. If I hear a siren, I will take my father down to the southwest corner. We will go down the outside stairs.

I look at the sky; it's not really greenish, but it is a dark grey. I say a silent prayer. Then I say it out loud, "Dear God, do not let a tornado form today, please. Please."

Leo

A few days later, when Mother and I get home, my father is out on the terrace painting. He has found the can of dark green paint left over from the mural. He has painted the railing around the patio. He has painted the bird bath, the deck chairs, the base of the hibachi, and the dining room windowsill. He has even painted the trunk of the pussy willow tree up to the first limb where, mercifully, the paint ran out. When Mother asks why he painted the pussy willow, he says "why not?" He has a point. What else is he supposed to do all day bored out of his mind? Watch the Tigers lose to the Red Sox? Yell at the blue jays? Convince Mrs. Margolis to bring him a Viceroy? Everybody knows how frustrated he is, but nobody, including Mother, has found a way for him to put food on the table. It is a given that everything he has ever done, he will never do again.

Ted

A few days later, I find him at his desk in his bedroom. It is so exciting to see him there. His colored pencils are scattered all over. He is sketching on a piece of Evans Winter Hebb stationery. He's drawing the same men he used to draw in his mock-ups. I stand beside him, watching. I am so excited. He says, "Your Mother has gone down to Overbeck's to get some paper."

Before I know it, Mother is home with a fancy pad of artist's paper. She went to the art department on the second floor. I love going up there.

The next day, he has his rapidograph out on his desk. He's making a sentence in a special font. The man ducking under the tree is talking to a squirrel? No, the squirrel is talking to the man who just hit his head. It's a cartoon! I don't get the joke. He's sending it to *The New Yorker* magazine. For the next few days, he does nothing but draw cartoons, one after another. Mother puts them in envelopes with cardboard and mails them to *The New Yorker*. This is the best thing to have happened in a long time.

Grass

Mother hoped we would eat in the new dining room every night, but it's easier to eat on TV trays in the living room. We use paper napkins, and half the time, my father eats in his room alone. Tonight, because it's cool, we eat on the terrace, which is just a rectangle of cement someone once painted dark red. Now, the red paint is flaking off. Sitting in a saggy wicker chair with a tray on your lap, no centerpiece and no candles, there is no sense of occasion. Last night, Mother put a candle on the railing which helped, but the candle wouldn't stay lit.

All through dinner tonight, Mother talks about her plans for the yard and where she should make a garden. My father has no interest in the yard or the garden. He hasn't even noticed how long the grass is. I was hoping Jay would cut the grass before he left, but he didn't. When the phone rings, Mother goes in to answer it. A few minutes later, she comes back with a sly look.

"Well!" she sits down and takes a sip of her martini.

"That was Professor Jones from 1015."

As if we didn't know where Professor Jones lives.

"He called to inform me there are squirrels in the attic."

My father looks disgusted.

"I told him the squirrels have been reliable tenants since 1907, as have the mice, and the bats, and the centipedes."

My father looks more disgusted.

"But I said I would sign on the dotted line there are no *flies*."

"You are not signing on any more dotted lines."

Mother winks at me.

"I'm just a poor little mouse, ma'am,
Who lives in the walls of your house, ma'am
With just a few peas,
And a small piece of cheese,
I was having a little carouse, ma'am."

I knew she would recite that poem. My father clicks his tongue. If he had a Viceroy in his pocket, now would be the time to light a fresh one. My father stares at the garage. I stare at the yard I know I should mow. I have to ask,

"Will Professor Jones put out poison?"

"No."

"Set traps?"

"No, no."

She is just saying that. We don't know what they're doing over there.

Miss Bacon shouts for Pooh-Bah next door. All her cats are named for Gilbert and Sullivan characters.

Ted

After Sunday breakfast, when I announce that I will mow the lawn, my father goes straight out the back door. I was thinking of doing it later, but cast your bread upon the water—you have to start somewhere.

When I get to the garage, he's pushing our old lawn mower down the driveway because we sold the Lawn Boy to a family on Baldwin. He enjoys pushing it, and at least, there is something to hold on to. Where is the gas can? I don't know this garage at all. We have not hung one thing on a nail, and these plastic rakes aren't ours.

Way at the back of the garage is my father's underwater mural with my "Do NOT Discard" sign. I still can't look at Jonah's face, his bursting cheeks, his tie swept over his shoulder; he won't make it to the surface.

The gas can is in the wheelbarrow.

My father demonstrates how to fill the gas tank on the lawn mower without splashing gas. It makes sense while I watch him, but the minute he sets the gas can down, I don't remember what he did. I was looking at the veins on his hand. He shakes the can.

"Still a little gas in the can. When you're finished, empty what's left into the tank, then put the can in the car and take it down to Herb. Have Herb fill the can."

He doesn't remember Herb no longer works there. Besides, we get gas on Main Street now.

While he fiddles with the choke, telling me how it works, I see the stone lamb on the shelf next to the red Maxwell House Coffee can that holds Marky's ashes. Some ashes have spilled onto the shelf. Mother said I could choose the location for Marky's grave. I can't believe I forgot to do that. What is *wrong* with me?

"Pay attention. The trick is to overlap the previous row about two inches. Pay attention. This is forward. This is idle. And if you get into trouble, just turn it off—here."

He hands me his pocketknife.

"When you're done, scrape the grass off the blades."

He reaches for the starter cord, stands back, and pulls hard. Oh no. He is not supposed to exert himself. He pulls again, hard. Too hard. The motor starts. His breathing is normal. My breathing is not. But the smile on his face is worth it. He is walking fine as he heads to the back door. He has never given me his pocketknife. It goes in my back pocket.

Vacuuming the living room, you learn about furniture legs, scuff marks on the molding, and carpet spills. Mopping the kitchen, you learn where grease collects under the stove, where Suki's muddy tail swished against the cupboards, and where the linoleum tiles don't perfectly meet. Mowing, I guess I will learn this yard.

I start by the terrace. It isn't that difficult to control the mower once I get used to the bump-along feeling and the noise. After two rows, my shirt is stuck to my back, and my head is pounding, and I am looking forward to a cold drink and a nap in the cool basement. This yard is much bigger than it looks. It goes way over to the left near Miss Bacon's and much farther back than I realized. I see what he means about the overlap. The grass changes all the time. Lush grass under the fruit trees, and sparse grass under the maple tree, and beyond the fruit trees, crabgrass and dandelions.

I am looking forward to the shade under the maple tree, but this is spoiled by the low branch I have to duck under which reminds me of the cartoon of the man and the squirrel. There are big roots protruding above the ground, which I try, but fail, to avoid.

Around the fruit trees, the grass is lush and thick. I should rake the cut grass into a pile, pick it up with my hands, put it in the wheelbarrow, and dump it somewhere, but I can't imagine touching this grass. This yard feels like a public playground where strange animals have peed.

I turn the mower to idle when I get to the high grass at the back of the yard. Hidden in the grass is a broken fence covered in vines with hard, green grapes. I can't possibly cut this high grass. Looking for some sign of a boundary, I step on something pink and sodden—a small flannel blanket. I am not touching that blanket. I turn off the lawn mower. I don't know where our yard ends. I can hardly see the house behind us. It's low and brown and . . . ?

I decide the pink blanket is not on our property. This high grass and fallen down fence don't belong to us. They belong to the low, brown house.

The grass in the front yard is sparse over by the mailbox and around the corner of the house. I begin my overlapping rows. I mow on the other side of the driveway up to Miss Bacon's forsythia. On the Abramses' side, there is no hedge or fence, so I am not sure where our property ends. By this time, the heat is so intense I turn off the mower and come inside. Blinded by the sun, I feel my way to the kitchen.

About the Abramses' boundary, Mother says, "Just estimate" and hands me a glass of water. If I rest now, I'll never finish, so I swallow two glasses of water and go right back out to the furnace. I push in the choke, pull it out, pull the starter cord—the motor starts. I mentally draw a line between our yard and the Abramses', and mow to the line and turn back.

My father's bedroom is at the corner of the house, the venetian blinds drawn. Is he watching baseball? Given the grass is so sparse around his room, I could easily not mow outside his bedroom, but that feels like bad luck, so I push the mower right up to the side of the house under his window. Dirt spits out. A stone hits the aluminum siding. Did he hear that?

Pushing the mower down the cracked cement driveway, I expected I would have a feeling of accomplishment, but I don't. I did not play in this yard; I did not help my father on any projects in this yard. Mother has no garden and no flowers for me to pick.

I park the lawn mower in the garage next to the trash cans, pour the last of the gas from the can into the tank, put the gas can in the car, and walk around to the back door. I want to take my ice water down to the cool basement. I don't want to see my father, but there he is in the doorway.

"Did you scrape the blades?"

"Yes."

This is my first bold-faced lie. I couldn't scrape the grass off the blades because there might still be 1015 grass stuck to the blades, and I am too tired to decide what to do about that.

"Did you put the gas can in the car?"

"Yes." I did do that. I hand him his knife. He opens it.

"I wiped it off." Two lies.

"Good job." He goes back to his room.

It is my job now. My worst new job.

Ted

After dinner, I go back outside. The yard actually looks nice. I can smell the cut grass, and there aren't too many places where I missed. I spent time. I got sweaty. The yard looks better because of me. Is this how farmers feel?

I vow to find a place for Marky's ashes and not let him spend one more night in the garage, but looking at the yard, I don't know where to put Marky. He never spent one second in this yard.

I finally choose a place in front of the trashy high grass because I can't find any place that feels right, and I am tired of carrying the stone lamb. The edger cuts through the grass nicely and the earth is soft and dark. It's easy to dig a deep hole, so much easier than the ground at 1015, which was root bound. I put the grass I just scraped from the lawn mower blades in the grave, then the Maxwell House can. I like the green grass, red can, dark earth. Then I fill the hole and pack the dirt around the can and on top of it and place the stone lamb on top. There's always been a bright green stain in the lamb's ears and black streaks under the neck.

Burying Marky at 1015 we said a prayer. It felt important. Digging him up was also important, but burying him out here feels like a chore. I walk back to the house, ducking under the low branch of the maple tree. One of the protruding roots has a bright gouge where I nicked it with the lawn mower. I lean the edger against the garage wall and put the trowel on the shelf.

When I come inside, Suki is lying on the end of the sofa. Maybe that will be her spot. I wash the few remaining blades of grass off my hands—no way to know which yard they came from.

Mother is opening the mail. The editors at *The New Yorker* have responded! My father is leaning on the counter while she reads aloud. "They want you to use only black and white," she says. "They don't print color cartoons." Then she reads specifications required—larger margins which means much bigger paper and another trip to Overbeck's.

"To hell with cartoons," he says, not even mad. "Just get me a map of the world."

He walks back to his bedroom and shuts the door quietly.

Leo

When she gets home with a rolled-up map, he asks me to go down to the basement and look for a piece of Masonite left over from the mural.

I find it. He puts the Masonite on the dining room table and unrolls the map. It is a Mercator map of the world, He has to trim the edges of the map to make it fit on the Masonite. Then, he asks me to get his rubber cement. I am so excited he's going to use his rubber cement and he's going to let me help him. I bring him his bottle of India ink and his fountain pen. Then, without using a ruler, he draws perfectly straight black lines in India ink: from San Francisco across the Pacific Ocean to Guadalcanal, from Guadalcanal to Okinawa, from Okinawa through the Panama Canal over the equator across the Pacific Ocean to North Africa, from North Africa to Sicily, and from Sicily across the Atlantic Ocean to Long Island, through Long Island Sound down to Brooklyn. Straight lines. No ruler. Eight minutes without a heartbeat did not take away his steady hand.

After the ink has dried, he writes the dates above the lines and the name of the aircraft carriers below the lines—Hornet, Enterprise, Chenango, Ancon, Spelvin. Then he writes his name at the bottom of the map: Lt. Cmdr. Samuel F. Schneider, United States Naval Reserve. His handwriting hasn't changed either.

He might not work for Evans-Winter-Hebb anymore, and *The New Yorker* might not want his cartoons, but look where he went in World War II—all over the world!

The next day, Mother and I hold the Masonite while he pounds in the nails. Nobody tells him not to raise his arms above the shoulder. He just does it, and now, from his bed, he can stare at the Map of the World. Somewhere in this house are his Navy photographs.

Mother's smile is the best part. When we go back to the kitchen, she says, "There are good days, too."

Water Level

"No wonder I got this house for a song," says Mother. We are staring at a big pool of water in the corner of the basement over by the door to the backyard. The northeast corner in this house is going to be nasty. I check behind the furnace in the southwest corner—it's dry.

"Not mentioning squirrels in the attic is one thing. Not mentioning this basement floods is quite another. Not a word to your father."

She pulls out Bapa's books from the lowest bookshelf and hands them to me. They're wet on one edge. Jay should have built the bottom shelf higher from the floor. Bapa's Dictionary of Elizabethan Proverbs is upstairs, thank heavens. When I suggest she complain to the Cartwrights, she says the Cartwrights could care less in Alaska. The Cartwrights moved to Alabama, but I don't correct her. I tell her I'll check the stairwell off the terrace. It's been raining. Maybe the drain is clogged.

We put Bapa's damp books on the living room sofa. Where is Suki? Mother sits down by the window that looks out on the driveway; it is becoming her thoughtful place. I take my father's green raincoat off the nail at the top of the stairs. Organ music is coming from his bedroom. Shouldn't we check on him? She says "not yet." I wonder who's playing the Tigers?

She sits down by the window and looks out at the driveway. "You're barefoot," she sighs. She doesn't tell me what to do or not do anymore. She just announces her observations. I walk out the back door.

Cement steps to the basement door are off the terrace. Five steps down, then a right turn, then five more steps to the bottom. Outside the basement door, there's water in the stairwell. The drain is clogged. The retaining walls on either side are meant to hold back the dirt, but dirty water is trickling down the retaining walls.

If there wasn't a door to the basement, the water would just keep rising, but there is a door, and that door doesn't close tightly, so the rain, sensing there is a lower place to go on the other side of the door, seeps under the door and trickles over the sill to the basement floor. Because the basement floor isn't level, the water collects in the north-east corner.

I remember coming home from the Robertsons' one rainy night. My father was driving, so it was before his heart attack. Police were preventing people from crossing the Huron River and directed us to take the Broadway Bridge down by the train station. As we drove over the Broadway Bridge, I asked if the bridge we normally take was going to collapse? My father said he'd seen storms at sea during the war. "Nothing you can do," he said. "Water has a mind of its own. It seeks its own level."

We studied that rule at U. High last year. The scientist who discovered it was Blaise Pascal. I have not become a scientist, have I? I have become a typist. And a handyman. Well, our water has found its own level.

I find a plastic pail in the garage and go back to the stairwell full of water. I can feel the drain with my bare toes. It's clogged. I pull out soggy leaves, a Juicy Fruit gum wrapper, cigarette butts, grass, little sticks, more grass. I put them in the pail. When the water seems to be receding a little, I go back up the steps, and dump the muck behind the garage, and go back inside.

"How's it going?"

"The drain was clogged,"

I need a broom. His door is still shut. I take the broom from the broom closet, which is also the baking ingredients closet and the liquor cabinet.

"Precisely why I planted the mint," she sips her martini. "I guess it hasn't rooted yet."

No, it hasn't.

"Your father is asleep. Suki is with him."

I go back down to the basement. I sweep the rainwater towards the laundry room where there is a floor drain. The light brown linoleum turns dark, but the water wants to go back to the corner. Whoever laid this floor didn't use a level. From the northeast corner to the drain in the laundry room is uphill. And—aha—the drain in the floor of the laundry room is clogged with dryer lint. I pull out the lint.

For every water molecule I manage to get down the drain, more water molecules flow back to the northeast corner. But there isn't as much rain trickling inside from outside. It takes an hour. Before I go to bed, I clear the outside drain again. My new job: checking drains.

Ted

The next day, *The Ann Arbor News* reports we are having the wettest August in sixty-five years. The total rainfall accumulation on Sunday was 2.98 inches. The total accumulation for the week was 5.10 inches.

Mother buys a dehumidifier. The rules are: Don't let my father know about the flooded basement. When you go down to the basement for any reason—to find a book, or do laundry, or play the piano—empty the dehumidifier in the laundry tub, and when you mow the lawn, remember to turn the lawn mower around so the cut grass blows away from the stairwell. Don't leave the pail by the back door where my father might see it and ask why it's there.

Short Cut

We have been here more than a month, and I still don't know where our backyard boundary is, and Mother won't look for the deed. She thinks we go as far back as the sumac. Well, the sumac is behind the long grass, and I am not mowing that high grass around the soggy pink blanket. When I come in for a drink of water, Mother says, "We need to imitate Aunty Douglas and just let things go." Then she tells how one day, Aunty Douglas just stopped weeding, stopped planting annuals, stopped picking up fallen branches, stopped mowing and raking, and let her whole front yard on Berkshire grow wild. Mother says when she looks at the back of our yard, she thinks of Aunty Douglas. But I don't want to let things go. We have let a lot of things go and it will upset my father if the yard goes, too.

I take the kitchen scissors off the hook by the sink and go back out to the Aunty Douglas section. I mow up to the trashy grass, then leave the lawn mower puttering on "idle" while I trim the grass around the stone lamb. When I look up to wipe the sweat off my forehead, there are two Black children walking toward me. They must live in the low, brown house behind us. The boy looks about ten, the girl younger. They each have a rolled-up white towel tucked under one arm. I turn off the lawn mower. They are walking right toward me, stepping confidently through the grass, as if we regularly meet here.

"Hi," says the boy. He doesn't stop to talk; he just keeps walking toward our house. He is neither impolite, nor particularly bold. He just walks like he has walked through our yard every day of his life. This must be his shortcut.

I catch up to them, dragging the lawn mower behind me. Their names are Reynard and Jean. We walk by the maple tree where they duck naturally under the low branch.

When we get to the terrace, they head straight for the opening between the garage and the house. Reynard says, "We're going to the free swim at Northside School." I say "Good luck" and stand there on the terrace in the bright sun, stunned. I look back at the yard. Neighbor children just cut through our yard. This is the best thing to happen since we moved out here.

I put the lawn mower back in the garage, then use the scissors to scrape the grass off the blades. When I look down the driveway, I see two specks of white on Mixtwood—their swim towels.

The next day, I am clearing the dining room table when I see Reynard and Jean in the yard again. When I get to the back door, they are approaching the terrace. Reynard waves, so I wave. Do they attend Northside School? Will they be cutting through the yard every day? Will my father get to know them?

"Who was that?"

Mother is watching from the kitchen window.

"They go to the free swim at Northside School. Reynard and Jean."

"Reynard?" Mother says. "What a nice name."

Red

When Suki runs away the following weekend, I drive around the neighborhood, thinking she would be better off somewhere else. I see Reynard getting off the bus at the corner of Summit Street, so I pull the car over to the curb. I know where the bus stops; I know Reynard —I am getting my bearings. When I ask if he's seen a small brown dog, he says, pointing up the street, "Check the McLemores'. I saw a dog in their pool the other day."

"In their *pool*?"

"The McLemores don't mind."

"Where is the pool?"

He points.

I've been tired all morning—tired of having this dog, tired of popping the clutch, tired of my job, tired of driving in this neighborhood, every house new, every person a stranger. But now, recognizing Reynard, our easy conversation, this exotic detail of a swimming pool on Summit Street, the owners not minding if our dog swims in it—I feel better. I drive up to the McLemores'. There is a pool in the side yard, but no dog. When I get home, Suki is soaking wet, lying on the front porch. She is getting her bearings.

Ted

Mother plants more mint from 1015. I thought she had dug up all there was, but she says she gave some to Aunt Ginny, and when Aunt Ginny heard about the flood in our basement, she dug hers up and brought it out here. Mother thinks nothing of transplanting living things from one place to another. These poor mint plants wilting in the sun have been dug up twice. She sits back on her heels, trowel in one hand. She looks about ten years old with a ribbon in her hair.

"I was thinking we *could* move Marky's ashes and put him under the pussy willow tree," she says. "Nice and shady and not so far away?"

I won't do it. This digging up and moving around has got to stop.

Wedding

Kate and Tim are to be married on August 28. St. Thomas, St. Francis, and St. Mary's Chapel are the three Catholic churches in town, but since we are not Catholic, and Tim is from Flint, how does the bride pick a church? Mother makes a lot of phone calls, and, in the end, St. Mary's is where the wedding will take place, on East William, opposite the pizza restaurant, Cottage Inn.

The priest at St. Mary's won't allow Henry Lewis to be part of the wedding ceremony, which is a disappointment to Mother, but what can she do? She hoped Henry Lewis could at least assist the Catholic priest, but that is not allowed. It appears Catholics have the final word.

The reception will be in our backyard. A big white tent arrives and folding chairs, and long tables for the food that is being catered by D'Agostino's, which is where we are having the rehearsal dinner. I am the maid of honor. Cousins Suzy and Anne are also bridesmaids, as is Meredith, Kate's best friend from Hillsdale. Kate does not want to wear the Victorian wedding gown worn by Nanny, Mother, and Aunt Elizabeth. She chooses a plain white linen dress with a scoop neck and a long linen train from Jacobson's. Bridesmaids dresses are also from Jacobson's—pale blue linen, sleeveless with a scoop neck and empire waist.

All these plans go on for months, but I can't stop worrying *will my father be able to walk my sister down the aisle?* He says yes—come hell or high water.

Tim comes from a big Irish family in Flint. We meet them at the rehearsal dinner, and they seem very nice. My father and his father get along. They are both short men and can draw. Tim's father was not just in charge of the paint shop at General Motors in Flint, he painted the fancy stripes on the cars by hand. Looking at Kate and Tim, I can't believe how handsome they are. Kate is more beautiful than she has ever been. Everybody gets drunk, but oh well.

When we wake up Saturday morning, it's pouring rain. We can't have the reception in the backyard. Mother is on the phone all morning. Bridesmaids all go to a beauty parlor on South U. I hate my hair. When I get home, I take a shower and start over. I am not wearing my hair in a puffy French twist. Mother doesn't care. She is too worried about moving the reception.

When we get to the church, Uncle Tom has printed notices that he hands out at the door notifying the guests that the reception will be at Mother's old sorority house—the Sorosis House on Washtenaw. I guess someone figured out how to move the food and set things up. I keep a very close eye on my father who waits quietly in his chair at the back of the church. He is very nervous, I can tell, but he looks wonderful in his old gray suit, white shirt, leather shoes, and a green-and-blue-striped bow tie. The bridesmaids go first. I go next, then comes Kate and our father. His mouth is in a slit, but his back is straight, and he lets Kate take Tim's arm, and then he sits. Later, at the reception, he sits the whole time in a comfortable chair, enjoying all the friends who come over to talk to him. I bring him cake. Mother brings him a cocktail. When I check on him, there are several adults I don't recognize sitting near him. A woman I don't know is talking about the Voting Rights

Act and President Johnson. I need to read *The Ann Arbor News* more. A lot is going on, and I'm not well informed.

When it's time for photographs to be taken of the bridal party, I get a nosebleed. Mother rushes off and brings me a small white towel. I don't drip on my dress, at least. We stand on the staircase in various arrangements. Watching my father watch Sam Sturgis take pictures is not a good feeling. My father had to be told that he was not photographing the wedding, that Kate wanted the Sturgis studio.

When we pass out the rice to throw at the bride and groom as they are getting into Tim's car, I can't describe what I'm feeling. The rice throwing goes all right, but seeing Tim's car backing out onto Washtenaw and disappearing, I realize Kate will never live with us again. This is not like camp when she came back. Not like college when she came back. Now she is moving to Akron. They have rented an apartment. I run back indoors. My father is still sitting in the same armchair. He couldn't face it either. Mother stays outside with the guests; I sit with my father. We don't speak. Kate is his firstborn daughter.

Morning Glories

I make a quick call home at noon from my desk at work. My father sounds grumpy. I don't ask if the basement is flooded because he is not to know about that, so why does he say, "I see the goddamned rain," and hangs up. He's never done that before—just hang up.

Opie starts in the parking structure, which is a relief. Mother looks especially tired. When I ask how her day was, she says Petey McDonald died this morning. His parents were with him. Petey was eight years old. He had leukemia.

We cross the railroad tracks and go up Summit. Cars are slowly making their way through deep puddles. Our piano could be floating by the time we get home.

Mother also called my father in case he had, for some reason, gone down to the basement, seen all the water, and was having a fit about it. She reports he did not go down to the basement, and was not having a fit, but he did sound crabby.

"At least he's swearing," she says. "Always a good sign."

I don't blame him for being crabby. Home alone all day in the rain.

"Lucky we live at the top of the hill," she says as we turn right onto River Road. "These poor souls down at the bottom will get the worst of it. Remember what Daddy always said? Water seeks its own level."

He did say that.

Usually, we use the back door. Not tonight. Mother probably

doesn't want to see the stairwell flooded, so we take the front walk. The paperboy put *The Ann Arbor News* behind the storm door. This is what rainy days will be like out here: worry about the basement flooding, worry that my father will discover the flood in the basement, the newspaper behind the storm door, and a puddle by the front porch because the path to the porch tilts to one side.

Suki greets us, wagging her tail, then she jumps back on the sofa, rests her chin on the arm.

"We made it!" calls Mother, taking off her rain hat, shaking the drops off the plastic. Then, she stops. There is a brown suitcase beside the front hall table.

"Sam?"

Are we expecting a guest?

"Sam?"

She isn't moving. The suitcase is the Samsonite suitcase we bought him years ago at Wilkinson's. Mother drops *The Ann Arbor News* on the front hall table. Martin Luther King Jr. is on the front page.

My father comes around the corner from the kitchen, wearing his trench coat, seersucker shirt, gray trousers, lace-up shoes. He walks in a hurry to the front window and looks out.

"I called a taxi."

He doesn't look sick. We don't take his suitcase to the hospital; we take the green tote bag. He puts something in his coat pocket.

"I'm going away for a little while."

Mother walks behind him to her chair by the window that overlooks the driveway, sits, raincoat on, pocketbook on her lap. I want to go upstairs so she can bring him to his senses, but the look on her face says *don't move one inch.*

My father leans over the sofa to look out the window. It's still raining, but we made it around the big puddle at the bottom of the hill, and we made it up the hill, and so will the taxi. He walks past me, turns on the porch light, walks back to the front window. The grandfather clock strikes. Mother squints, clasps her hands over her pocketbook. She does nothing and says nothing.

Finally, she gets up, drops her pocketbook on the chair by the door to the kitchen, which is the chair for newspapers, not the chair for pocketbooks. When he was in the hospital, she did the same thing— everything she picked up she dropped in a new location.

Suki thumps her tail. She is so stupid. Marky would have crawled under the house by now. My father nods toward the door to upstairs. "Look on the stairs."

Now what is Mother doing in the kitchen? Running water. How can she wash dishes when he is about to walk out the door with a suitcase and get in a taxi? There are black taxis with white telephone numbers parked outside the train station. One of these now pulls in the driveway and honks.

"About time." He hates when people are late.

My father has to walk behind me to get to the suitcase. His hat is on the front hall table. I didn't see it before. Now he tips it onto his head, grabs the suitcase handle, lifts it easily—not much in it—opens the front door, steps onto the porch, pulls the front door shut, and steps down, his sleeve brushing against the bushes. He hands his suitcase to the driver who swings it into the trunk. My father gets in the back seat. The driver shuts the door and goes around to the driver's seat. The taxi backs out the driveway, turns, headlights aimed downhill, my father in the back seat, leaving us.

Mother comes into the living room with her martini, still wearing her raincoat. The door closing a moment ago in the back hall was his bedroom door. She must have closed it. Now, she pulls the curtains across the front window and the two side windows then sits by the window overlooking the driveway, crossing her long legs.

"Where is he going?"

"Out. Apparently."

"Out where?"

She chews the olive.

"At least he remembered his nitroglycerin."

Mother is thinking fast; she checked the tray in the kitchen where we keep the bottle. I am not thinking fast. I am stuck in the moment when we came in the door, his Wilkinson's suitcase by the front hall table, his gold initials under the handle. The day we ordered the suitcase, the clerk at Wilkinson's wrote "SFS-gold" on the order slip.

"Could you bring up some wood? It's a chilly rain. We need something cozy."

I turn on the basement light. I have no idea where we keep wood in this house.

"Where is the wood?" I sound crabby shouting because I have just seen the northeast corner of the basement, and the puddle has gone all the way to the grand piano.

"Behind the furnace."

We keep firewood behind the furnace in this house. This is the southwest corner. Okay. The movers brought it from the garage at 1015. I didn't know wood could look familiar. I put three logs in my arms and turn off the light. I set the logs on the hearth. We have no kindling. Nobody collected any sticks. We've never had a fire in this house. All those Saturdays mowing the yard, and I never once picked up a stick. I take newspapers from the pile by her chair and start wadding them up and twisting them. This is our fireplace. This is our house.

"Can you please get the mail?"

His footprints are in the mud. I can't believe he called a taxi. Where did he tell the driver to take him?

I'm wet. The mail is wet. One letter and something from The Ann Arbor Bank. I hand her the letter.

"Dorothy Lind," she says, tucking the envelope beside her hip in the seat cushion. She has her glasses on. Reading the newspaper will help us feel normal.

I put the bank envelope next to the phone. Suki wants to go out. I open the front door. She sees the rain, then comes back inside. She jumps back on the sofa. Mother has taken off her raincoat and dropped it on the sofa.

"He'll be back," she says in her calmest voice, as if he often calls a taxi, packs a suitcase, and leaves. There wasn't much in his suitcase. I remember he said "look on the stairs." I open the door. There is a torn envelope on the stairs that came from the phone company. He wrote on the back, "Your Daddy loves you." He took the envelope out of a waste basket. He found a dull pencil and didn't sharpen it. The phone rings. We both walk to the kitchen.

"Hello?"

No expression.

". . . Yes, she's at Ann Street."

When she hangs up, she says, "I forgot to make a note in Cynthia's chart that her mother is staying at Ann Street." Then she looks at me directly, the first time all night.

"How bad is the basement?"

"Under the piano."

"Just let it go."

"Aunty Douglas?"

She smiles.

"But what about—?"

"Don't worry," she says. "For once, don't worry."

Worry is what I feel when he goes to the hospital. Worry is what I feel when he won't come out of his room. Worry is what I feel when we pull out of the driveway every morning, when I call him from work, and when we come home every night. Worry is not what I feel now. I feel sick. He looked strong. Nobody dragged him away. The ambulance didn't come. He packed his own suitcase, called a taxi, and walked out the front door.

"Are you calling the Margolises?"

"I will do no such thing."

"Where did he get money for the taxi?"

"I keep twenty dollars in Nanny's cabinet, in case of emergency.

Bottom drawer."

I see the gold scarf, but not the twenty dollars.

"It's not there."

"He won't get far on twenty dollars." She goes back to her chair by the window. "Let's have a fire."

Fine. A fire.

Mother, reading *The Ann Arbor News,* is rising to the occasion and I am, once again, sinking fast. His wallet is in his desk. If he took his wallet, he has identification. But if he didn't take his wallet—

Mother shakes her head when she sees me carrying his wallet. If his taxi has an accident, he won't have identification. Initials on a suitcase don't tell you anything. His suitcase doesn't have a luggage tag with his name and address. The police won't know how to reach us unless the taxi driver remembers our address, and what if the taxi driver is unconscious . . .

"He doesn't have identification on him."

"Put that back."

I love this wallet. We got it at Van Boven's. Mother chose the long size that opens like a book. I open it. A receipt from Fingerle's. A business card from King-Seeley. A business card from Evans-Winter-Hebb with another man's name. A business card from Argus. More business cards from companies. His driver's license, expired. Mother drops the newspaper in her lap and takes off her glasses. I am standing by the bookcase. Holding his wallet helps. I know the rule, but rules are being broken tonight all over the place.

In the middle of the night, I hear the front door shut. When I look out the window by my bed, headlights are swinging over Miss Bacon's hedge. I get up to look out. Not a taxi, a regular car. Whose car? I want to see him. No, I don't.

In the morning, when I come downstairs, Mother's raincoat is still on the sofa, and mine is on the wing back chair. Our raincoats never made it to the closet.

"Here," she says, handing me his breakfast tray with tea and buttered toast. "Be normal."

Normal? Last night my father left us.

I knock. No answer. I open the door. His eyes are closed. He could be asleep, or he could be pretending, or he could be dead. He is wearing a white T-shirt, not his pajama shirt. His suitcase is next to his desk. His raincoat and hat are on Marky's green chair. The blanket over his shoulder is lifting and dropping. I place the tray quietly on his desk, like a good maid.

"Is he asleep?"

"I can't tell. His eyes are closed. He's breathing."

"We'll deal with the basement tonight," she says, putting one hand into her blue kid glove. The nitroglycerin bottle is back on the tray. "Come along." Now, the other glove, calm as can be. "On the double. We'll be late." On the double is Navy talk. What if he calls another taxi?

Maybe something went wrong with his plan last night, but he will have all day to fix what went wrong, and tonight, when we get home, he might be gone for good.

Walking through the living room, I see *The Ann Arbor News* on the floor by her chair. I can't pay attention to the news. I know a lot is happening in the world, but too much is happening at home.

Ted

When Mother and I get home around five-thirty, my father is sitting on the terrace. The sun is out. He actually smiles when he sees us. No greetings, no explanation, as if he often leaves our house in a taxi. I still can't believe he did that. What is that on his arm, dried milk?

I go inside. When I look out the kitchen window, she is standing over him, shaking her head, feeling his wrist. He is shrugging and telling her something.

A minute later, she comes in the back door, gets a glass of water, and takes it back out to him. Did he forget his pills? There is white powder on the counter. Why was Mother holding his wrist?

"Is he all right?"

"He's fine. Would you mind stripping your bed?" she says.

It's Tuesday. I do laundry on Saturday.

"I'd like to get a head start on the laundry." She wipes off the counter.

What is going on?

When I get to the top of the stairs, there are white blotches on the linoleum floor and a chalky smell. My bed is a few inches away from the wall, and my lampshade is crooked, and my desk chair is by my bureau, and the walls are covered in the wallpaper Mother and I picked out before we moved—blue morning glories. Jay never got around to hanging the wallpaper, and we ran out of money to pay for another project, so the rolls of wallpaper ended up in the basement. How did he find them? While we were at work, he climbed stairs. He raised his arms above the shoulder. Now he is climbing more stairs. Mother's voice behind him. He isn't out of breath as he sits on my desk chair.

"Well darling? Doesn't it look nice?" says Mother.

It does look nice. But I cannot bear the thought of him lifting his arms above the shoulder and climbing stairs. Nobody says anything about all the rules he broke. Never mind that he left us last night.

"Thank you, Daddy."

He sits on my desk chair. She sits on my bed.

"No more sailboats," he smiles.

I had made peace with the Cartwright sailboats.

"More feminine," says Mother.

I don't know what else to say. I don't want to think about how he did this in the heat all by himself.

"How was work?" he asks. "What have they got you doing?"

"I type change of status forms."

I have never talked to my parents in this bedroom.

"She is the fastest typist in Personnel," says Mother.

Mother watches him all through dinner. He has two helpings of macaroni and cheese. He finishes his pie and has coffee. Then, he falls asleep in his armchair in the living room. When I go into his room to say good night, he is asleep with the light out. I don't see his suitcase. Standing in his room in the dark, I feel four years old, the tornado raging outside, worried that if I wake him, he might be furious because of all the other times I have woken him. But he was never furious. Never. Not once. He always opened his eyes slowly and asked me in his quiet voice what I needed. Now, I have a different terror. When he had his heart attack, he didn't have it the day he dug the garden and did handstands. He had it the next morning.

In the morning, he seems fine. Miss Bacon is in her garden when we go out the back door. Mother goes through the forsythia hedge to speak to her.

When she comes back, she says, getting in the car, "I asked Deborah to look in on your father."

"But she has never looked in on him."

"Well, I told her to make up some excuse."

If that doesn't give him a heart attack, I don't know what will.

A week later, he goes back to St. Joe's. Mother says it has nothing to do with hanging my wallpaper. He just needs to be checked out every now and then, and it's good for him to get out of the house. I don't remind her he got out of the house a week ago, but she's right; when he's at St. Joe's, he has company during the day and has stories to tell us when we visit him after work.

One day, he's laughing when we arrive, and out comes the story about Nurse Karen who collects his urinal every day in a plastic bottle with a handle. He hates peeing in the urinal, so he says he poured his tea (with milk) into it. Karen held up the urinal, stared at it and said, "Hm, looks a little cloudy today Mr. Schneider." So, he says, he grabbed the urinal and said, "Then let's put it through again," and drank it! I haven't seen him laugh this hard that in a long time.

He stays one week. The day he is being discharged, I pack his clothes. When I open the bedside table cabinet, I find a small bottle of VO.

He says he had it delivered.

Mother asks how he paid for it.

He reminds her she gave him a ten-dollar bill in case of emergency. "I had an emergency," he says. "and Witham's delivers."

Part III

———

1965–1968
1472 River Road

Senior Year

In October, Mr. Shafer takes our class to Stratford, Ontario on the bus. I enjoy it even more than our trips in 10th and 11th grade. When I walk from the lobby into the theater and look down at the stage, it seems I have been on that stage. I know where the entrances and exits are. I recognize some of the actors. When the trumpeters go out to the balcony to tell people to take their seats, I recognize this is a Stratford tradition. I plan to keep going to Stratford for the rest of my life. On the bus ride home, I am sad our trip is over, but I have more plays to look forward to because on Wednesday afternoons, Mr. Shafer takes us to see the APA-Phoenix Repertory Theatre at the Lydia Mendelssohn Theatre. I can now recognize a dozen of the actors in the company. I am keeping a list of all the plays I've seen.

I write my end of semester report for Mr. Shafer not on Shakespeare, but on E.E. Cummings. When Mr. Shafer passed out copies of "[rain or hail]" I was thrilled. It starts:

rail or hail
sam done
the best he kin
till they digged his hole

:sam was a man

He doesn't know my father's name is Sam which, I admit, is one reason I love the poem, but I love it for other reasons. "[rain or hail]" is unique. There are no capital letters, and punctuation rules don't apply, and it doesn't have a title, so people sometimes just call it "Sam Was a Man." E.E. Cummings reminds me of my father who doesn't obey rules and does things his own way.

I spend Saturdays at the Ann Arbor District Library. I thought I would focus on Cummings' choice of casual words and his plainsong vocabulary, but I don't get very far on that topic. Instead, I write about Sam Ward who was the caretaker for the Cummings' family in New England. Sam Ward died falling down steep stairs when he was going to feed the Cummings' pig who lived under the barn. Cummings wrote the poem as a eulogy for Sam Ward. I hate thinking about Sam Ward dying that way, and I hate thinking about the pig living in a dark basement, but that pig and Sam Ward are long dead.

I think I understand every stanza but this one:

gone into what
like all them kings
you read about
and on him sings

a whippoorwill;

I think "gone into what like" means Sam was a simple man, but he's gone to heaven where kings go. But I don't understand "*on* him sings a whippoorwill." Is the whippoorwill sitting *on* dead Sam Ward in that basement? Whippoorwills sit parallel to the branch they are perched on, so he would have to be perched on Sam Ward's finger.

When I ask Mother what she thinks, she says I'm being too literal again, and maybe she's right. Especially with poetry, one can't be literal.

I enjoy the library. I've found a quiet place on the second floor by the restroom and the drinking fountain to read and write. All is going well until I read that Iroquois Indians believe that if you hear a whippoorwill call *whip-poor-will* by a window or a door, it is an omen of death because whippoorwills can capture a departing soul, like a bug, and eat it. After I read that, I can't concentrate. I check out my books and catch the bus home.

On Monday, when I ask Mr. Shafer about that stanza, Mr. Shafer smiles.

"That's the thing about poetry," he says. "Sometimes you aren't sure what a line means, but you sense something beautiful and intriguing, anyway."

I decide I am not going to dwell on that line. Dwelling on scary things is an old habit of mine, and I need to get over it and yet—I am intrigued by whippoorwills. I don't like the shape of their eyes, though. The upper lid has a straight area which seems unnatural and mean. I decide, rather than think all the time about what I will do if I hear a whippoorwill, I will focus on these two words: "beautiful and intriguing."

We are having drinks by the fire one Friday night which seems like a good time to recite the poem and read my paper aloud. I am determined to get over my dread of this bird and enjoy what I've learned.

I stand by the fireplace. Mother is on the sofa and my father is in his chair.

First, I read the poem aloud, then I read my paper aloud. They both clap. My father is in a good mood. He's been more cheerful lately; I have no idea why. Mother looks tired because a little girl died this week from brain cancer, but she claps, too, and because she doesn't have to go to work tomorrow, she's having her third martini.

My father says, "I think I would have gotten along with Sam Ward."

Mother says, "I think whippoorwills have replaced moldings."

Leo

I sing alto in the choir to keep my music going, but singing is not the same feeling as playing the piano. The Steinway in the basement hasn't been played in I don't know how long. I suppose there is no point in having it tuned. Mother no longer asks me why I don't play anymore, and I can't explain why I don't, but I do know this: I would never have stopped playing if Mr. Weber had stayed in town. I didn't care for the lady teacher Mother found after Mr. Weber left who wanted me to practice four hours a day. She kept saying, "if you're going to be serious, you have to buckle down, young lady." I guess I couldn't buckle down, so I just stopped. At least Mother isn't pushing me anymore. What nobody understands is that the person I am disappointing most is me. I have let myself down, and I can't explain it. Nanny was a concert pianist and Uncle Walter studied piano in Germany. Nanny and Uncle Walter played four-hand piano in our living room, and when I hear a piano being played in someone's house, it sounds familiar and important. Piano music in a house is not the same as piano music in an auditorium.

Peд

Mother says there is no way I won't be accepted to the University of Michigan, given my grades and all my extracurricular activities. One night, she asks how I got so busy and popular? I don't really know. I annoy my physics teacher because I ask too many questions, but otherwise, my teachers tolerate me. I see my boyfriend on Friday nights when I'm not cheerleading. Danny and I make out by the Arboretum, and on Saturday nights, I go out with my intellectual friends. Holly plays guitar, and Jim has a Ouija board. Nobody has a crush on anybody else. Sometimes we go to Mr. Shafer's to play Risk.

Singing with new friends

Kate and me at Nanny's piano

"Sheep May Safely Graze"

Rescue

The last few months of my senior year are hectic. Prom. Year-book. Cheerleading. Committee meetings. Parties. Choir concert. Awards ceremony. Graduation. Our life has a routine. Mother drives me to school and picks me up at five-thirty. I call home at noon to check on my father. I call every day. I try not to worry if he doesn't answer the phone because he told me he sometimes goes out to the yard. When we get home, he's usually in his room behind the curtains, venetian blinds down, door shut. Sometimes, he's in the kitchen. I can't imagine what he does all day. He usually joins us for cocktails and dinner on the TV trays in the living room.

The Awards Ceremony is the week before graduation. Mother says of course my father is going. Then she leaves to get her hair done by Philip.

When she comes back from seeing Philip, my father is standing in the kitchen, and I am coming up from the basement. When he sees her, he quickly shuts the closet door. I saw him take a swig from the VO bottle, but Mother didn't. She doesn't look suspicious; she just wants us to react to her new hairdo.

"Well?" she says.

He mumbles.

"And you, Mademoiselle?"

"It's nice."

"I told Philip it has to last through the awards assembly today and graduation next Sunday."

"That'll last until Labor Day," says my father, going back to his bedroom.

"Too stiff?"

"No, no," I say.

Another bold-faced lie. It looks like a helmet.

Later, when I come into her bedroom to zip up her dress, she asks, "How long will the ceremony last?"

"The choir isn't singing, so we can leave after the award presentation."

"Then we'll wait until we get home for his afternoon pill. How far is the gymnasium?"

"Third floor. There's an elevator."

"He'll be fine," she says, stepping into her spectator pumps. "You look lovely."

I feel like a nurse in this white dress.

"Wait for us in the car? Roll down the windows, let some air in."

"What about his nitroglycerin?"

She opens her purse to show me the bottle.

My father, walking across the driveway in his blue cord suit, green-and-white-polka-dot bow tie, and white shirt is a wonderful shock. Mother mouths *be normal* as she gets in the car.

How can I be normal? He hasn't worn a bow tie since Kate's wedding. And that is my favorite suit. And we haven't gone anywhere, the three of us, in a long, long time.

"I've got a nice lunch prepared for when we get home—chicken salad, garlic bread, ice cream cake."

At first, he faces forward, jaw clenched, hands folded in his lap; then he stares out the side window. We have never ridden all three of us in Opie. Why is that? Why haven't we taken him anywhere before now?

Ever since he got home from the hospital and he was forbidden to drive, Mother has done all the driving, and he has stayed home. We could have driven him down to the river so he could talk to the hobos on the bridge. We could have taken him back to the Standard Oil Station so he could have a laugh with the mechanics. He has been a prisoner. Why didn't I realize this before?

Mother peers at me in the rearview mirror, then turns onto Hill Street. I can't bear it. Since he came home from the hospital, he went once to his doctor for a check-up, and a few times back to St. Joe's, and to Kate's wedding and reception, but I can't think of another time he has been out of the house, except for the taxi night. No trips anywhere! Unless Mrs. Margolis . . . What is the matter with us?

There is a sign on the sidewalk in front of school telling people to park in the Business School parking lot around the corner.

"I'll find you," says Mother, pulling over to the curb. My father gets out, slams the door hard. I get out. Mother drives ahead. He grabs the brass railing, walks right up the front steps. A boy I don't recognize holds the door for us. We walk past the front office where I call him every day at noon.

"Which way, Toots?"

He isn't sweaty or pale or drunk.

"Just go straight."

We pass the chem lab and the choir room. Mrs. Ransom, my eleventh-grade social studies teacher, walks by. A few tenth graders walk by. The elevator is next to the boys' bathroom. At home, he never walks as far as he will have to when he walks down this hall. But he doesn't reach for the lockers or for my hand.

"Turn right."

I don't have to tell him about the elevator. He hits the button. I point to the career day mural the senior art students painted, but he isn't interested.

The elevator doors open. He steps in, grabs the handrail. I push the button for the third floor. There is a coffee stain on his jacket. I wonder when he last wore it and why Mother didn't take it to the cleaners.

"Relax," he says.

I wish he would wink. His denture drops down. I point to the Otis plate on the floor. He doesn't understand. We get off the elevator. Turning right, around the corner, I see some friends who, when they see my father, wave, but don't come over. You can't blame them. Whenever they come to our house, he's in his bedroom with the door shut.

"Over there is the bathroom," I point to the door by the water fountain. "Are you thirsty?"

He isn't. He walks straight to the gymnasium.

"This is good," he says, taking a seat by the rear door.

I thought he would want to sit up front, but he sits right by the exit, crosses his knees, looks around the gym. He doesn't have much hair on top, but the hair around the back of his head looks tidy. Did it stop growing? His barber is Pete on State Street; why haven't we taken him to Pete?

"At Hope Farm, did you play basketball?"

He looks at me like I'm crazy. I am crazy. I know he didn't play basketball.

"Baseball," he says. "Short stop."

The woman in front of us turns around and smiles. My father ignores her, takes out his handkerchief, and unfolds it, the "SFS" monogram under his fingers as he wipes his forehead.

"Where did you learn to do handstands?"

"Suffolk Academy."

"Was that a college?"

"Two-year."

He tucks the handkerchief into his side pocket, folds his hands in his lap, veins bulging no more than usual. His gray socks don't match.

"Was that where you climbed the smokestack?"

"Tom Goodrich climbed the smokestack. I watched."

Tom Goodrich was his gymnast friend in college.

Mother comes through the far door, talking to some woman. Then she sees us and waves. Folded over her arm is the red plaid football blanket. Why do we need that blanket? It's June!!

"That was Marge Lassiter," she says, sitting beside him. "Aunt Helen's cousin's nephew is in your class. Josh Wilder?"

I wondered why that blanket was in the back seat. We usually keep it in the front hall closet.

"Where do you sit?" she asks me, putting the blanket on my father's lap and tucking it around his knees. He doesn't look cold, but he doesn't protest. He actually folds his hands over the red plaid wool. She knows he gets cold. Why don't I know that?

"Go join your friends," says Mother. "Go on!"

We sing the school song. The national anthem. There are speeches. Awards are presented, certificates handed out. Applause.

There is only one award that means anything to me: the Bausch & Lomb Science Award. I am shocked when my chemistry teacher, Dr. Conrey, who has been in the hospital for the past month, climbs the steps to the podium, his hand shaking horribly, his head bobbing. He has Parkinson's disease. He is a wonderful teacher. He calls my name. I can't believe he came. I walk to the podium, so glad to see him. He hands me the medal. His daughter is in my class. Her father is sicker than mine.

It's over. We can go home.

"Oh, Darling," says Mother, "we *are* proud. And your microscope was a Bausch and Lomb!"

My father kisses me. He can't stop smiling.

It's over. We can leave. Mother folds the plaid blanket and tucks it under her arm.

When we get off the elevator, she says, "Are any of these rooms your classrooms?"

She is trying to distract me so I don't see my father leaning on her arm.

"That's the chem lab, and that's the choir room."

I won't be going back to those rooms where all I had to do was study, and think, and pay attention.

"Where is your locker?" She walks slowly, head high.

"Seniors are on the second floor."

"Dr. Conrey is your science teacher?"

"Chemistry. He's been in the hospital."

She is making polite conversation. We pass the front office. The drinking fountain. The bench. I wish I had a class now to go to. School is so much easier than home.

Mr. Middleton, the football coach, holds the door for us, nodding to my parents, "Congratulations!"

We sit on the stone seat by the front steps so my father can rest while Mother gets the car. At least when people say hello, he doesn't say anything tactless. When a woman stopped by to ask directions to Sunset Street the other night, he told her she should lose weight. Mother was appalled, then she admitted tact was never his strong suit. When I asked what was his strong suit, she said, "telling the truth no matter what."

"Uncle Jimmy," he says, pointing to a dark brick apartment building across the street.

"He lived there?"

"Until they raised the rent and your mother got Mr. Ginzburg to rent out his third floor."

"How is Uncle Jimmy?"

"Emphysema."

Why don't I know this?

When our car pulls up to the curb, he stands up, then stumbles forward down the steps. Before anybody can help, he catches the railing—a beautiful save—half a second of perfect coordination when who he used to be rescues who he has become. It is my graduation present.

Leo

Mother has set the table in the dining room with the pink damask table-cloth and matching napkins. She found a few peonies somewhere. My father is arranging my awards on the bookcase, certificates on one shelf, plaques on another while Mother counts them like Christmas cards.

"Eleven!" she smiles.

"Plus the science medal," he says. "Twelve."

"Dear?"

It's all wrong.

"What? You think you don't deserve them?"

I deserve some of them.

"Valedictorian!"

"*Co*-valedictorian."

"And the DAR. And the athletic achievement."

The athletic award makes *no* sense. When Victor and I throw a football around, no teachers are present. Maybe someone told them I can throw a forty-yard spiral.

"What is the *matter*?"

I can't tell them the advisory committee called me into the administrator's office last week to tell me they were going to give me the Citizenship award until they suddenly realized, that morning, I was getting all the others. Since then, I have been dreading this day.

"What on earth are you upset about?"

"Humble pie, Toots?"

If they weren't so proud of the awards, I would bury them in the backyard.

"It isn't right," I say.

"Of course, it's right," she says. "Hard work is rewarded."

"Not always," says my father.

"She knows what I mean."

It has all been a mad dance, a trick—and I pulled it off.

"False modesty is not becoming," says Mother.

I am not being modest. And I am not humble. Running up the stairs, I am horrified when my father follows me and Mother doesn't stop him. I fall onto the guest room bed. Why the guest room, not my room, I have no idea. My father sits beside me. The bedspread is red and cream-colored wool, very old and heavy and hot. Someone told Mother it was valuable. I have my finger through one hole the size of a quarter—not that valuable. Mother found a place downtown that can "weave back," but the phone number tacked to the bulletin board is as far as she got.

His hand is on my back. Not a big hand, but a strong hand, resting. Downstairs, Mother has turned on the radio to her favorite classical station. The end of Mendelssohn's "A Midsummer Night's Dream." I did well in Music, too. I did well in English. I did well in everything, but he is not well.

"What's wrong, Toots?"

His right hand grips his knee, the wobbly veins criss-cross his finger bones, the cuff of his white shirt, his blue cord trouser, his knee shaking. She must have ironed that shirt. Who trimmed his nails? At least he's breathing normally. The Mendelssohn is over; now a heavy Bach organ fugue.

"Lunch is read-y!" Mother calls from downstairs.

"You worked hard," he says, patting my back. Then he stands up, waits for a second, then turns. He puts his hand on the bureau, then walks out to the hall. At least we have a strong banister now.

It's a Mozart symphony by the time I get downstairs. The martini pitcher is on the dining room table, and Mother's coming out of the kitchen in her apron holding the rooster platter piled with chicken salad.

Before Uncle George became a lawyer, he wanted to be a hobo, so he used to jump the Wolverine to Detroit. Jumping on the train, he said, was easy; jumping off, he said, was hard. And that's what I did all through high school. I got on a train I couldn't get off. I was so busy making things better in the only way I could, I didn't want to admit other things were still getting worse. My father hasn't been to the hospital lately, but he almost fell on the front steps at school. Awards will not heal my father. There was no other father with a blanket on his lap. When Mother put it over his knees, I thought he would kick it off, but he didn't. Time to talk straight. He is getting *cold.*

Dormez Bien

The University of Michigan in-state tuition will be affordable with the Regent's scholarship, so long as I get a part-time job during the school year and a full-time job over the summer. My aunt and uncle offer to pay sorority dues, but, to Mother's horror, I say "no thank you." Joining a sorority will only put me in a house full of girls who don't type ninety-two words per minute.

When I offer to live at home, Mother says absolutely not; living at home would not be *a true college experience*. The solution is simple: live where my friend Holly lives, a suite at Oxford Housing, where residents work on the premises to pay for their room and board. I've seen those modern buildings, a block from Forest Hill cemetery and almost across the street from Angell School.

❧

Tomorrow, I will move out. Coming back from Suki's walk, I think *this is my last night at home.* I hang Suki's leash in the closet and close the door. Mother is dozing in my father's chair, her stocking feet on the footstool, martini glass on the side table, newspaper spread across her lap. Suki jumps onto the sofa, turns her circle, and lies down. She looks at Mother, then she looks at me; she could be smarter than I realized. Mother yawns.

"Darling? Did you see the St. Bernard?"

"His name is Teddy. A man called to him from the porch."

All summer, I have wanted to know this dog's name and now, just as I am about to leave for college, I find out. Today has been full of signs like this. We also ran out of laundry detergent and the light bulb on my bureau lamp went out.

"Suki will miss you."

I don't ask who will walk Suki.

Mother looks at the shuttered doors behind which is the back hall and the closed door to my father's room. She knows I am worried about my father.

Rules for college: Do not worry about my father. Do not call him every day. Mother will call me only if my father goes to the hospital. Do not come home every weekend.

"I want you to find your own way; follow your own star."

This is martini talk.

The University of Michigan—3.1 miles away, where her father taught English, where she and her two brothers graduated, and where my three cousins are now—is not on the East Coast. She is pleased about my scholarship, but I know she is not pleased about my living at Oxford Housing, even though I can earn my room and board there. She would rather I not be a waitress. Besides, sororities don't look to the co-ops for pledges, she says, they look to the dormitories.

"You would make a lovely Chi Omega."

I am sick of this discussion. Kate is a Kappa Kappa Gamma; Nanny was an Alpha Phi; Mother was a Sorosis. But I am not a joiner. A co-op suits me. I can afford it, and my friend Holly will be sharing my suite. I need to finish packing.

"Holyoke, Radcliffe, Bryn Mawr, Smith, Vassar . . . how many is that?" she counts on her fingers. "Holyoke, Radcliffe, Bryn Mawr, Vassar, Smith . . . who am I missing? Holyoke, Radcliffe . . ." She gives up and stares at the fireplace, then she asks, "Do you remember Aunt Harriet across the street on Ferdon?"

"I thought she moved to Florida."

"She did, after she retired. Do you remember her sister?"

"Aunt Carolyn?"

"Do you remember going to play at their house?"

"They had a terrier named Jim."

"That's right, and you played on the sun porch."

I stare at her stocking feet, thinking of all those nights she asked me to tickle her toes.

"You wouldn't leave my side, wouldn't sleep over at anybody's house, wouldn't eat, and then there was that tornado business. When you were at Angell School, I used to get to the rock half an hour early in case they let you out from kindergarten early."

I remember the rock, at the corner.

"Why didn't you pick me up in the parking lot?"

"Parking lots are confusing, cars coming and going, but rocks don't move, and you needed stability."

That rock is still on the corner of South University and Oxford. I will be walking by that rock every day.

"I was just thinking, neither of the Shoecraft daughters married, but they both became fine doctors."

"Aunt Carolyn was a doctor?"

"A child psychologist."

"I went to a child psychologist?"

"She said you were troubled by something, maybe Nanny's death, but that you would get over it. I guess she was right. You're going off to college, aren't you?"

Ted

When I go downstairs to say good night, my father is in the kitchen pouring milk into a glass.

"Tell your Mother I'm out of Gelusils."

He puts the milk carton back in the icebox.

"Do you let Suki out during the day?" I ask.

"That dog goes out more than I do."

He turns to go back to his room. He has forgotten I'm leaving in the morning.

Mother is reading in bed. She tied the ribbon from Miss Bacon's gift in her hair like Greer Garson in *Mrs. Miniver*.

"He needs Gelusils."

She looks over her glasses.

"All packed?"

"Pretty much."

On her bedside table is a piece of buttered toast spread with anchovy paste. I thought I smelled toast in the kitchen. When we lived at 1015, she used to have tongue sandwiches at night. Since we moved out here, she's switched to anchovy paste.

"Bonne nuit," she smiles. "Thank the Lord you are well."

This is my *Madeleine* cue to say, "And so, good night said Miss Clavelle," but I can't. I just say good night and turn around.

Suki is asleep on the sofa. She has never slept in anybody's room, but then I doubt anybody ever invited her. My bags and boxes are by the front door. Hopefully, I will get the car packed before my father comes out of his room in the morning. If I were going to Radcliffe, how would I get to college? Has Mother thought of that?

Climbing the stairs, I am wide awake. On that step, my father left his goodbye note. On that step, I spilled hot cocoa. I don't like this house any more than I did two years ago, but the linoleum doesn't bother me anymore, and the closet seems big enough.

Oxford Co-op

Given how new Oxford Housing is, I thought Mother would not have any stories, but it turns out she does.

"All that land from Geddes down to Hill Street belonged to Fred Logan's family. His father was a landscape architect in the School of Architecture, and when he died, he left his property to the university without designating how the land should be used which, for an architect, was quite a remarkable gesture. He would turn in his grave if he knew it became student housing."

"Students have to live somewhere."

"I think Professor Hogan probably had in mind something quite different, but unless you specify . . . "

"You gave Bapa's letters from Robert Frost to the university."

"I did, indeed, but we have Xerox copies. In the bookcase next to the Chinese cabinet."

"Turn here. Keep going. I'm in Noble House."

She parks near the garbage containers. Getting out of the car, she asks, "And who did you say is the house mother?"

"Mrs. McCormick."

"McCormick. Scots or Scots Irish."

As we walk through the back door, she doesn't look into the kitchen or the lounge, but she perks up when I introduce her to Mrs. McCormick.

"I'm in room two-twelve."

I leave them to talk.

Holly is not here yet, but our other two suite-mates must have moved in. I like the layout—two bedrooms with bunk beds divided by four bureaus and four closets in the middle. It doesn't take long to unpack.

When Mother sees my room, she says, "More spacious than I imagined."

"It's a suite."

"Yes, I know. And who are your suite-mates?"

"You know Holly. I haven't met the others."

"And where is the bathroom?"

"Down the hall."

She smells the mattress. There is a chair, but she would rather stand by the window.

I explain that every house has a different color scheme. Noble is blue and purple. Goddard is red and orange. Each house has two tones. The chairs and sofas down in our lounge match our purple and blue curtains.

"I have this bureau and this closet."

"Which bed?"

"Top."

"You always wanted a bunk bed."

While I unpack, Mother looks out the window and tells me Mrs. McCormick comes from Pitlochry and attended the University of Edinburgh.

"Look! There is Dr. Burton's house at the corner of Hill Street," she says. "Dr. Burton taught in the School of Music."

Does she realize we are only five blocks from 1015?

"So that's your telephone?"

She writes down the number.

"Is there a switchboard?"

"Every suite has its own phone."

"Your father will approve."

She looks in the mirror over my bureau, fluffs her hair. I can tell she is going now. I wanted to show her the kitchen, and the laundry, and the lounge. I wanted to show her the other houses and walk on the gravel paths.

"There is a grand piano in the lounge."

"Did you bring your music?"

I didn't.

"Remember the rules: Plunge into college life, and do *not* worry about home."

We have never been very good at hugging or kissing.

I am starting to like modern architecture. With less details to look at, you have more time. Residents take turns in the kitchen, preparing, serving, and cleaning up after meals. Residents check the calendar on the bulletin board and find out what their meal duties are, and if they conflict with a class, then you trade your duty. The dietitian, Anne Doerr, plans the meals, orders the food and, for the first month, will explain the preparation. All food preps must wear hair nets. If you would like a birthday cake, let Anne Doerr know. Residents are allowed in the kitchen at all hours to make coffee or tea. If you see a light on in the kitchen at one in the morning, there is no cause for alarm. If there is ice cream left over from dinner and the carton is nearly finished, you can finish the carton. Put your dishes in the dishwasher. Don't leave bits of food in the sink. There are four washing machines and four dryers in the basement. Clean sheets are delivered every week; you pick up your sheets in the canvas laundry cart in the stairwell. You put your dirty sheets in the laundry cart in the basement. Fires are permitted in the fireplace after December fifteenth. The piano cannot be played after ten o'clock at night or before ten o'clock in the morning. If you have a complaint, see Mrs. McCormick. I have no complaints.

Leo

The telephone rule is Mother will only call me if my father goes to the hospital, but I can call home if I absolutely need to. I wait one week. When she hears it's me, she says, "Bonjour, ma chère."

I have been studying French since seventh grade; why is it now that she's trying to talk to me in French? I don't mean the old Miss Clavelle and "dormez bien" at bedtime. She really wants to have a conversation! Besides, it shouldn't have even been dormez, which is formal.

"Comment ça va?"

I say I'm fine and classes are fine. Everything is fine. I forget why I called.

"Tu dors bien?"

"Très bien."

Not true. I am not sleeping very well. What is going on? Maybe if we speak French, she can pretend I am at The Sorbonne?

"Mon père? Comment est-il?"

"Très bien. Merci. Dormez bien."

"Soyez tranquille."

We hang up. That was weird.

Mother wants me to see the world. Well, I have a Ukrainian roommate, Holly has an Indian boyfriend, and there is a Japanese boy in my chemistry lab.

Leo

I study in the janitor's lounge on the third floor of the Chemistry building. It's empty at night and the vending machine has hot chocolate. The janitors come in around ten o'clock to eat their sandwiches. They leave me alone, although once in a while, a janitor will look over. I know their names from reading their shirts when they use the coffee machine. The tall one is Giuseppe. The bald one is Pete, and the young one is Mike. The library closes at midnight, but I can stay as long as I like in the janitor's lounge.

Walking back to the co-op in the dark, I pretend I am Marie Curie returning from her laboratory to the Rue L'Homond. I stop at Dan's Coffee Shop, which is open all night. I don't remember ever seeing it before, but the neon sign outside is broken, so maybe that's why I never noticed it. You would think all those times Mother parked outside the Village Apothecary and went in for her gin, I would have looked across the street and seen the dirty windows and the faded red door and wondered what sort of place Dan's was, but the beauty of Dan's is you don't notice it.

I get a cup of coffee and a powdered doughnut and sit in the corner booth which is usually empty. The other customers are townspeople who look down on their luck. Not deep poverty, but almost. The woman who pours coffee is Polish. She always spills some coffee in the saucer so there we all sit, coffee puddles in our saucers. Mother would not approve of Dan's, but she would approve of how I feel at Dan's, which is very far away from home. This feeling continues as I walk all the way up South University past Purchase Camera, where my father used to buy his darkroom supplies, past the Standard Oil Station where he used to bring Borgie, past Witham's who delivered his VO to the hospital. Places I have known all my life do not seem familiar at all. I know their history, but I am alone now, and I'm walking, not a passenger in the family car.

Finally, I walk by Angell School where, in first grade, Alice Payne ran into me on the playground on her bike. The hand grip cut my lip, and ever since my accident, there has been a rule that you can't ride your bicycle on school property. I am part of the laws of this town. I have a scar to prove it. You can't get more hometown than that.

At the corner, I walk by the rock, which is not nearly as big as the rock on Hill Street. I don't remember being troubled. I don't remember the rock making me feel what Mother hoped I would feel—that it was a safe place to wait. But then, I never had to wait. Mother was always there. You don't have to go to a private college, out-of-state to feel far from home. Night will do it.

Le Cauchemar

My two worst dreams are Tornado and Basement. I still have the Tornado dream occasionally now, but I haven't had the Basement dream in years. Now, it's back.

I am trying to fall asleep. I am in an elevator, going down to a basement. The basement is where I need to get to because that is where I can sleep. But I never make it to the basement. I get stuck, one level above, in between awake and asleep. In between is dreadful, and painful, and some of the pain is because it's familiar. My brain is going to burst in this in-between place. I need to get all the way down to the basement or go all the way back up to the top, but I'm paralyzed. I need to try harder. I can't move. The pain in my head builds until it bursts, and I wake up. Relief! But then I'm back in the elevator, going down, down. Oh no! Stuck again! I keep starting over and getting stuck.

Holly is studying psychology. She says it is a classic anxiety dream. She suggests I sleep in the lower bunk, and while she is studying, she will keep an eye on me. She puts a pencil in my hand. I roll over on my right side and put my hand against the wall. When I feel I can't wake up, I am to write on the wall. If she sees me writing, she'll wake me up. I find a pencil. It needs to be sharpened, but it still writes. Holly goes back to her reading, looks over, looks back at her book. I close my eyes. Sure enough, in a few minutes, I don't make it to the basement.

Stuck, paralyzed, I dig my pencil into the wall. At least I can do that. I dig harder. Holly doesn't wake me. Perhaps she isn't watching. I press harder. I am going to break the pencil. The pain is worse than before. I wake up on the floor. I'd thrown myself out of bed. I look at the wall. No pencil marks. No pencil lead either, just dirty white plaster and Holly in the corner flirting on the phone with her boyfriend.

"You weren't moving," she says. "There's your pencil on the pillow."

I go back to the top bunk. If I am on the top bunk, I might be less likely to throw myself out of bed. I don't throw myself out, but the dream repeats four times before I finally fall deeply asleep. The next night it repeats two times.

After a week of this, I call home. Mother and I have been stumbling through phone calls in French, but thankfully, she doesn't speak French this time. She sounds a little drunk. She tells me she found a neighbor boy to rake our leaves. Suki barked and barked at the man delivering the oil. I don't know why I called. I don't know what to say. When she asks how I'm doing, I say fine. "That's good," she says. "Well, your father is asleep, I don't want to wake him." Then she says what she has said every night of my life: "dormez bien." Little does she know je ne dors rien. What is French for nightmare?

One night, trying not to fall asleep, afraid I will throw myself on the floor which would be a five-foot drop, it occurs to me that part of a true college experience is occasionally going home. Mira goes home to Detroit on Friday night. Cindy gets a ride with someone who also lives in Jackson. Holly, who lives on Pontiac Trail, could get a ride home with her father who teaches Latin, but she chooses to spend her weekends with her new boyfriend. Mother has never invited me home or even hinted that she would like me to come home, but if everybody else who doesn't have a boyfriend and lives within an hour or so of campus goes home on the weekend, going home must be a true college experience, and maybe I will sleep better.

Mrs. McCormick has a map of the bus route. It looks like the crosstown bus stops at the corner of Division and Catherine which is a few blocks from my French class that gets out on Friday at 4:45 p.m. The bus then goes down Division, past St. Andrew's, and across Summit where it stops at the corner of River Road. This was our route to the hospital.

Thursday night, I call Mother to ask if I can come out on Friday. I don't say home. I say out. She doesn't say I can't, but she doesn't ask how am I getting home, and she doesn't offer to pick me up. Part of a true college experience is learning to be independent, apparently, but then, just before I hang up, she says, "I presume you are getting a ride with someone?" When I tell her I am taking the crosstown bus, she says, "Oh my."

Leo

The bus door opens at the corner of River and Summit. River Road feels entirely different without the summer heat. Leaves have blown up against the porches and steps. The houses I used to stare at have not changed that much. Nobody is out in their yard or on their porch. It takes less effort to climb the hill in cool weather, but walking at an angle across the front yard is the same; letting myself in the front door, also the same. Mother is in the kitchen. She notices my longer hair which I now wear up. "You look like Nanny," she kisses me on the cheek. "Go see your father." Not a word about the bus.

My father is watching Walter Cronkite. I get a big smile. He used to grin when he told his jokes, but he didn't smile, not like this. It is a nice smile, not just his mouth smiling, but his eyes, too. He puts his cigarette in the ashtray, pushes the ashtray towards the back of the bedside table.

"How's my girl? How's college?"

I kiss his stubbly cheek. I can't believe she is letting him smoke. Is she buying him cigarettes?

"Like your teachers?"

I sit on the side of his bed.

"For the first anthropology lecture on hunters and gatherers, Dr. Kollars held a long spear all through his lecture, then, at the end of the lecture, he threw the spear, and it stuck in the proscenium."

"That's something," he says, looking at his cigarette, but not reaching for it. Suki is under his desk.

"Does Suki sleep in here?"

"Guess so."

Mother comes to the doorway.

"Doesn't she look well?" she says.

He nods, approvingly. "Different."

"It's her hair—up like Nanny."

Ted

There is a fire in the fireplace when Suki and I get back from our walk. The TV trays are set up in the living room. My father is in his chair wearing new, stiff, brown corduroy trousers with a crease and his old Viyella shirt, a full pack of cigarettes in the breast pocket. Suki jumps on the couch, turns her circle, and lies down with a sigh. This is our home.

"Tell us about your classes," says Mother, unfolding her paper napkin.

"My conversational French teacher has short bangs and wears short black skirts, black stockings, black high heels."

"Très chic," says Mother, taking a bite of her baked potato.

I repeat the story about Dr. Kollars throwing the spear. I tell them a little about my chemistry lab and my English class which mother presumes is still being taught in Angell Hall where Bapa had his office. I don't tell her my English class is in a new building. I know better than to describe how I serve eight girls at a round dining table. I do tell them how the dough boys at Domino's Pizza spin the pizza crust. I don't tell them Professor Goode gives me a hamburger when I baby-sit at his house on Church Street two nights a week. I do tell them that

Domino's and Professor Goode pay me cash. Mother says she hopes, with all my commitments, I still have time to study at the library. I let her think I study at the library. I don't describe the janitor's lounge which is not my mother's sort of place. It is, however, my father's sort of place. It is my father, I realize, who taught me to go my own way and to get to know all sorts of people. I have been noticing that I am most comfortable around people who are not like me.

After supper, my father goes back to his room, but he doesn't turn on the television. Mother and I do the dishes.

"Did he watch the playoffs?"

"I don't think so."

I can't believe he didn't watch the World Series.

"You know he's smoking."

No comment. Mother puts a plate in the cupboard.

𝓟𝓮𝓭

When I go into his room to say goodnight, he's in his pajamas, the light on, sitting on the side of the bed, not smoking, or reading a magazine, or watching TV.

"Going back?"

"I have to listen to the French tapes in the library."

"So how did you get out here?"

"Crosstown bus."

"Tough cookie," he smiles.

I want to suggest he could take the bus some time, but I can't picture my father on the bus. I want to sit beside him. Why don't I? Mother comes in with a glass of water and the Meissen salt dish. Two pills are in the salt dish, which he takes, one after another. She never used to come into his room. Now she walks right over to the bed. There was a time when he forgot to take his pills. When he hung wallpaper, said inappropriate things, painted the pussy willow tree, hid a bottle of VO under his bed, when he swore, and felt rotten. Now, he thanks Mother politely and tells me to come back soon. Mother seems happier, but I don't like him like this. He is half of his old self.

Nobody is waiting at the bus stop. I read the sign. The crosstown bus doesn't run after eight o'clock. I walk back home. Mother will have to drive me back to the co-op and that drive, I realize as we go down the hill, is going to be one long reminder that I am not going to a seventh sister. We drive by St. Andrew's. We drive by my dentist's office. We drive by Forest Hill Cemetery where Nanny, and Bapa, and Catherine are buried. We drive by Angell School. We drive by the rock. She has been getting quieter and quieter the closer we get to Oxford Housing. She knows where to turn into the driveway. When I lean over to kiss her goodnight, she looks straight ahead. She is thinking I could have avoided these modern buildings and pledged a sorority if only I had said thank you to Uncle Tom. I say good night and shut the door. Actually, I slam it.

Marge, from Detroit, is in the kitchen when I come in. She didn't go home for the weekend. She has a history paper due Monday, she says, and she hasn't even started it. Marge burns her toast, so we talk while she waits for two more slices and I get ice cream out of the freezer. There is no one in my suite. Holly is probably out with her boyfriend. Mira is in Detroit, and Cindy went home for her mother's birthday. I take my books down to the lounge to study. I have never tried this, but maybe with people coming and going, I can fall asleep in the chair. Lying in bed doesn't work, so maybe this will work. It doesn't. I go back up to bed around three o'clock and lie there until five-thirty. When I fall asleep in French Class, Mademoiselle taps me with her pencil. The French word for nightmare is *cauchemar*.

The following Monday, my father is admitted to St. Joes to be monitored. Dr. Cairns wants to observe him, Mother says, maybe change his pills. I walk over to the hospital after Chem lab. He is in good spirits, kidding the nurses and his favorite nuns. He looks all right. There are cigarette butts in his bedside table drawer. Mother has totally given up on the no smoking rule. He says he hasn't pulled any pranks. He tells me he is trying to convince Sister Cecelia and Sister Mary to leave the church, get married, and have lots of Catholic babies. He says Al Cairns is as close-mouthed as ever. He calls him "the mother hen," and he calls his medical students "Al's chickens." At least he doesn't mind the hospital. He has more company, and he never complains about the food which is probably like the food at Hope Farm.

Ted

When he comes home a few days later, Mother invites me and my three cousins out for supper. She even picks me up at Noble House after work. It snowed all day—our first snow—but the roads have been sanded. Suzy, she says, is bringing Anne and Tom in her Jeep. Mother is in a good mood. Her supervisor in the Department of Social Work has asked her to contribute to an article to be published in a medical journal. When we get home, the driveway has been plowed. The man who sold her Opie has a plowing business.

When my cousins arrive, Tom puts on a Kingston Trio record and builds a fire in the fireplace. Suzy mixes martinis. Anne puts cheese and Triscuits on a wooden plate. My father sits in his chair. We let him smoke because nobody wants to ruin a cozy family gathering.

I go out to the kitchen for more crackers, and when I come back with the plate, I don't go back to the sofa where I was sitting next to Tom. I hand Suzy the plate and stand next to my father's chair. Nobody says anything, but I have never done this before—stand guard.

When he gets up to say good night, I sit in his chair, the cushion still warm. He leans over to give everyone a goodnight kiss, his new corduroy trousers hanging off his hips because he forgot his belt. He shuffles through the shuttered doors, having made a joke, which I didn't hear. A few minutes later, he's back in his blue pajamas and bedroom slippers holding a hairbrush. He goes to Suzy and gives her the hairbrush, making a little bow. She says, "Thank you, Uncle Sam."

He shuffles through the shuttered doors.

"Good night Uncle Sam! Now go to bed!"

"I will, I will." He's back, holding his old bathrobe. I haven't seen that bathrobe in years, red plaid Pendleton because that year Van Boven's was out of Viyella. He gives the bathrobe to Anne. Roars of laughter. He gives Tom the little square leather box with his Navy medals. Mother gets his shoehorn. They actually kiss. And for me? I get his back scratcher.

"Very funny! Now go to bed, Sam. And stay there!"

"All right, all right."

While I was out in the kitchen, he told a joke. He has become a comedian. He makes everyone laugh. Mother tells me to tiptoe into his bedroom in a little while and put everything back, then she puts a record on the record player. Suzy pours from the martini pitcher. Soon everyone is singing along with the trumpet music. "Bum, bum bum. Ba bum ba bum ba bum bum." How can my father sleep with such loud music? He is not well. He just got home from the hospital. I go up to my room. My bed is made, my desk closed, a few clothes in the closet. Dust on my bureau. Dust on my jewelry box. I find my old nightgown and crawl in bed. My room is lifeless, maybe that will help. A few minutes later, the flashing yellow light of the sand truck blinks on the morning glory wallpaper, and there's snow outdoors on the windowsill. Where the window doesn't quite close, I feel a draft. I imagine snowflakes landing on my cheek. I hear the sand spraying off the sand truck and I feel the elevator going down, down.

Christmas in the Basement?

Kate and Tim are expecting a baby in February. When Tim has National Guard duty in October, Mother insists Kate come home to be with Daddy. Keep him company. I was always the daughter at home and Kate was always away, but not anymore. When I hear this news on the telephone, I can't quite picture it. "Oh yes," Mother says, "she's staying in the guest room. She's fixing things up around here. Her maternal instincts are in full bloom."

Kate will work three days a week at Artisan's Gift Shop where she worked in high school. The other two days, she is home with my father. They have a Christmas project, Mother says. They're making little wooden trays. Old postcards glued onto Masonite. They glue the cards to the Masonite, then varnish, then nail a strip of trim around all four sides. I thought all the postcards burned in the leaf burner. Apparently not.

"Where did they get the trim? Who cut the Masonite? Who varnished?"

Mother doesn't know. When I come out for the weekend, the little trays are spread out on the dining room table, ready to be wrapped. My father has not made anything in so long, but I can tell he didn't entirely make these. My sister has her own way of doing things, and these trays look more like her than him. He says, "Take one." I choose a Renoir with two girls at the piano. They made ten trays. One for each of us, one for Tim's Mother, one for Aunt Ginny, Deborah Bacon, the

Abramses, the Robertsons, and one for Sister Cecelia at the hospital. Mother also made sugared nuts, and Kate and my father are going to deliver them in the paper bowls Mother found at The Caravan Shop. Kate has been addressing the Christmas cards which she bought at Artisan's with her employee discount. She even found time to paint the upstairs bathroom blue and the guest room peach. She polished Mother's silver, rearranged the china cupboard, and she makes my father lunch every day when she's home. They watch *As the World Turns* together. I'm happy and slightly jealous. Mother says, "This is a special time, with the baby due." Mother brings out cookies on our Christmas plate. I haven't seen the Christmas plate in a long time. My father is shorter than mother, but he drew them the same height. He used to draw on everyone's Christmas boxes.

I no longer expect I will sleep better at home. I don't sleep anywhere. Now that I sit at a different table in the janitor's lounge, over by the radiators, sometimes I can sleep there, my head in my arms. One night, it is too rainy to walk down to the janitor's lounge, so I climb into the empty laundry cart in the stairwell at the co-op with my geography book and fall sound asleep there, which is exciting, but when I climb in the next night, I can't sleep. If I get the corner booth at Dan's coffee shop, sometimes I can sleep there. The trick seems to be finding a new place. Mira lets me try her bed, but beds are hopeless. When Mother picks me up three days before Christmas, she says, "You must be studying too hard."

Kate's three months at home has done everyone a lot of good. Mother looks less tired and says they already trimmed the tree, but that I can arrange the German figures on the mantelpiece. When I walk in the living room, there is no tree. Maybe I'm so tired I can't see the tree?

"It's in the basement. Thanks to the Treasure Mart!"

We go down to the basement. In addition to the hide-a-bed, there is an armchair, hooked rug, and a standing lamp. I always imagined the Ann Street Boarding House basement would look like this. I half expect to see the pay phone sign.

"Kate and Tim need privacy," says Mother, proud of the new arrangement.

The Christmas tree is in the corner, lights on, the tin star my father cut out of a soup can on top.

"I saved you some ornaments."

The box is on the Steinway. She saved me the cuckoo and the armadillo.

I understand making a private room for Kate and Tim, but why do we have to have the Christmas tree down here?

"Isn't it cozy?"

Not a word about my father climbing the stairs. Why, now, when he is getting weaker, are all the rules being broken?

"Kate drove back to Akron to pick up Tim. They're spending Christmas Eve with his parents in Flint, leaving their old car, and driving down here for Christmas Day in Tim's new car. They'll go back to Akron on Tuesday."

"What new car?"

"His father's Oldsmobile. A good family car."

I can't get excited about Christmas in the basement. No fire in the fireplace, no view of the snow on the trees and bushes.

When we get back to the living room, Mother takes a Christmas card off the bookcase. It is a manger scene, and it's from Vee Vee! Vee Vee thanks me for my note and says she's fine and her daughters are taking good care of her. She wrote her telephone number, which I asked for. I have never seen Vee Vee's handwriting before.

That night, I sleep in the guest room under the valuable, but hole-filled, red wool bedspread. Why I don't sleep in my own bed, I have no idea. At least I actually fall asleep.

Red

It snows Christmas morning. Kate calls to say they are getting a late start, and Tim promises to drive carefully. We spend Christmas morning in the living room, watching the snow blow around, listening to the radio and waiting for the phone to ring. We have burned cinnamon buns, and coffee, and orange juice.

My father sits by the fireplace in his red vest. A cord of wood was delivered and stacked in the garage. I keep putting more logs on the fire. Mother quietly makes a martini, but she doesn't offer him a VO, and he doesn't ask for one. When did he stop drinking? Suki has a few white whiskers. He blows a perfect smoke ring. It stays round for two seconds, wobbles under the lampshade, and comes out the top, not a ring anymore.

Mother doesn't think the man who plows the driveway will come on Christmas morning, so I shovel. Suki watches from the porch. She is turning out to be a loyal, if stupid, dog. By two o'clock, Mother wants to call the police, but my father says it's good they're taking their time.

At four-thirty, a big car pulls in the driveway. "Thanks be to God," says Mother clapping her hands, pretty drunk by now.

After we hear about the car accident outside Flint, and how many cars slid off the road, and Tim talks about his Oldsmobile, everybody fixes themselves a drink, and Mother puts crackers and cheese on a plate. She puts the baked potatoes in the oven, takes out the ham, and doesn't seem terribly interested in the carrots and peas. Kate says she feels fine. I touch her stomach. This baby is real.

By the time we go down to the basement, it's dark. It doesn't feel like Christmas. It feels more like a slumber party.

Mother sits on the new sofa, Kate hands out presents, Tim sits in the dining room chair, my father sits in the new armchair, knees crossed. He used to wear the red and black striped bow tie with the red vest, but a tie is too much to hope for. He doesn't seem the least bit excited to be in the basement. He doesn't even go into the laundry room or look at his work bench. I think he has been coming down here all along when we're not home. To do what, I can't imagine. You would think, the way nobody says a word about having Christmas in the basement, that we've always had Christmas in the basement. From where I sit on the stairs, I can hear the whoosh of the pilot light in the hot water heater. Mother writes on the back of the cards who gave what to whom and drops the cards in the silver bowl, her Christmas thank-you card ritual. I stare at the areaway window. Outside is the driveway. I can see the ice on the spigot where we attach the outdoor hose. After we open our presents, everybody goes back upstairs. I am behind my father who climbs slowly, holding onto the banister. If he falls backwards, I won't be able to catch him.

Tim rebuilds the fire in the fireplace, and everybody settles in the living room. My father sits in his chair. He has gotten himself a VO. Mother puts on her English Christmas carol record. She lights the candles on the mantle. Dinner is on TV trays.

Mother passes cookies on the Christmas plate. Someone we know saved my father's cartoon and had it printed on a plate. I can't imagine how. He hasn't drawn Christmas cartoons in a long time. And we haven't used cloth napkins in a long time. Oh well. I'm glad Kate and Tim are safe, and Tim is finished with guard duty, and they like the presents for the baby, but why was the Christmas tree in the basement? *Why?*

I want to call Vee Vee. Mother is a little startled—and so am I—by the thought of making this phone call. I haven't seen Vee Vee in so many years, I can't think how long. I find her Christmas card by the telephone in the kitchen where I put it. I close the door to the living room. I open the card, but I can't dial the number. I will fall apart if I hear her voice.

Leo

After dessert, Mother shows Tim how to work the heater she bought for the basement. My father takes off his red vest and leaves it on the back of his chair. I go back to my room upstairs and have the worst night I have ever had. I sink down and wake up more than ten times, and three times I throw myself out of bed onto the floor. In the morning, Mother says, "I think you're coming down with something."

A Patient's Prayer

It is a Wednesday afternoon in the middle of February when the phone rings in our suite. Mira answers because it is usually her mother calling from Detroit. Today, she holds the phone out to me.

"*Your* Mother" she says. Heads turn.

My Mother never calls. If my father died, would she tell me on the phone? No, she would come over. She would be waiting in the lobby when I came in from class. Or maybe not. Maybe she would find me at Dan's. No, she doesn't know about Dan's. In the time it takes me to think about this, I have walked across the room. When did I last see my father? A week ago; I took him a pork chop and Stouffer's creamed spinach on a tray at home.

"Hello hello! Toots?"

It's *him*. Not her.

"Congratulations, Aunty!"

I picture him standing in the kitchen by the spice rack, then I remember he went to the hospital because he was having some chest pains. He went two days ago, or was it three days ago? I can't keep track anymore which is not a good feeling. He must be talking on the phone beside his hospital bed.

"You have a nephew."

"Thomas Jeffrey!" Mother shouts in the background, then takes the phone from him, laughing. "Ten forty-eight this morning. Six pounds ten ounces. They're sending a picture. Thanks be to God everybody is *fine*! Come after five. We'll celebrate."

My father has never before called me on the phone. I have always called him.

𝒫ed

Crossing Huron Street, it occurs to me how different University and St. Joe's hospitals are, only a few blocks apart. St. Joe's is where we now visit my father who is fifty-nine years old. St. Joe's is not capable of handling a major heart attack or DOA, but perfectly capable, Mother says, of treating angina—*treating* the sort of word she uses now that she works in a hospital. Unlike the University Hospital, with doctors from all over the world, and colored stripes on the floors, and construction going on all the time, St. Joe's feels like a sleepy Italian convent. It has clean marble floors swept by the black habits of the nuns, evening prayers on the loudspeaker, statues of saints, crucifixes, and holy paintings too widely spaced on the pale blue walls. The only hospital room I ever went to at University Hospital was the ICU, but I've been to several rooms at St. Joe's. They all smell of vinyl, and lotion, and mashed potatoes and have crinkly Saltine wrappers on the floor.

Mother is sitting in the chair. An aide with a black ponytail is standing over my father's bed, holding the gray plastic lid over his dinner tray, inspecting what he didn't eat.

"Mashed potato and Salisbury steak looks pretty good to me," says the aide.

My father clamps his mouth.

The aide makes a note on a folded piece of paper, shoves it into her hip pocket, and places the plastic lid over the plate.

"Keep the Jello?"

Mother takes the Jello and sets it on the bedside table. Then the aide leaves the room.

"Aunty's here!" says Mother. "Now we can celebrate."

She unpacks her tote bag—jars filled with martini and VO, a can of ginger ale, Triscuits, Cracker Barrel cheese, the wooden plate. She takes the blue plastic cups from the bedside table, pours VO into one, Gin into the other, Ginger Ale into a third. The jars go back in the tote bag, but the Ginger Ale bottle stays on the bedside table. We each get a freshly ironed cocktail napkin, which is impressive; we don't iron cocktail napkins anymore. Last week, they were at the bottom of the heap in the laundry room. I sit on his bed. The plate of cheese and crackers tips beside his knee.

"To Thomas," says Mother, standing. If a nurse comes in now, we are drinking Ginger Ale. "I forgot to ask Kate are they spelling Jeffrey with a 'J' or a 'G.'"

"What difference does it make?" says my father, enjoying his drink.

"None whatsoever," Mother laughs. "They are already calling him Tommy," she says. "But then, we called Uncle Tom 'Tommy' until he was about twenty."

"Speaking of Tom . . ." says my father.

Here comes a Tom Goodrich story.

"Tom Goodrich dove off the high board and landed smack on his belly, swam to the side, and said, 'that's what makes you rugged.'"

"Tom who climbed the smokestack?"

"Did a one-hander when he got to the top."

"Tom who went upstairs on his hands!"

"Tom the Bomb. Good, but not rich."

My father hasn't told Tom Goodrich stories in a long time. His hand with the big veins lies flat over the blanket. Sitting up straight in bed, in his clean pajamas, with his glasses on, newspaper on the bedside table he looks good. Mother must have gone home for the cocktail treats and driven back here.

I am not terribly interested in the baby's length and weight and the minutes between contractions, although it is good to know Kate is all right. I need to study for a chemistry exam and must now figure out how to make up the hours spent here that I was meant to be studying.

While Mother tells us about Kate's birth in 1942 at French Hospital in New York City, I suddenly remember her saying last week, while my father was in the bathroom, that they might transfer him to the VA Hospital. Then my father came out of the bathroom, so nothing more was said, but now this terrible possibility begins to sink in. I don't want to think of my father at the VA Hospital—with the old men, and their urinals, and bedpans, and wheelchairs, where I wore my Candy Striper blue and white striped pinafore every Thursday night, and wrote postcards dictated by a thin man with no teeth. My father is not going to the VA Hospital.

"At least our Tommy was not a blue baby," Mother says with a deep sigh.

Blue? What is she talking about now?

"Some babies are literally born blue if they are without oxygen for so many minutes," she says. "Carol Bellamy was a blue baby."

Evening prayers come over the loudspeaker.

". . . *sustain me by your grace that my strength and courage may not fail; heal me according to your will; and help me always to believe that what happens to me here is of little account if you hold me in eternal life, my Lord and my God. Amen.*"

"*Amen,*" says Mother. "Your prayer was so much better!"

It was. After he got here, he wrote his own prayer and showed it to Sister Cecelia, and the next thing we know, "A Patient's Prayer" was being broadcast at the close of visiting hours. They broadcast it all week. My favorite part:

"*Dear Lord, keep this door from ever closing. We need our family and friends, and ever lean on those who watch over us. Our sick friends are all around us, above and beneath us, and just down the hall. They feel our pain as we feel theirs, and this is a comfort to us.*"

"They started that Catholic nonsense again yesterday," he shrugs.

Mother says "But your prayer is being printed in the St. Andrew's bulletin."

He shrugs again, but I can tell he is impressed. It is a good prayer, but ever since he wrote it, I am more miserable about leaving him. I used to think he was not miserable in the hospital because he got a lot of attention, but what he expressed in the prayer was how lonely and frightened a patient can be.

"Hasn't the week gone by quickly?" Mother says.

"No," he says. "It has not gone by quickly."

Are we going to call Kate? Apparently not.

Visiting hours are over. Mother rinses our cups in the bathroom and returns them to the bedside table. She wraps the crackers and cheese in paper towels and puts them in his bedside table drawer and slips the wooden plate back into the tote bag with our cocktail napkins. Saying good night, we call each other Grandpa, Grandma, and Aunty. I wish he could come home with us.

We don't ride the elevator in case somebody inspects the tote bag; we take the stairs. In the stairwell, she says, "I'll ask Dr. Cairns if I can go to Akron for a few days to help Kate get settled."

We pass the entrance to the third floor.

"They'll have to wait until I get back to transfer him."

"Transfer?"

She does not say to the VA Hospital. She says Dr. Cairns thinks he needs close monitoring which could go on for weeks, and we can't afford St. Joe's. We walk down the stairs in silence. When we get to the ground floor, I push open the heavy steel door.

"He can't go there!"

She hands me the tote bag because I am unlikely to be carrying anything suspicious. We walk by the chapel and the statue of Mary with the great marble folds in her skirt.

"The VA Hospital was smelly and dirty. And the patients were miserable!"

It is dark out.

"Let's not think about that now," she says as we slip on the icy sidewalk sprinkled with sand. "Nothing will happen until I get back."

We are parked in front of the old entrance. I was born in that dark brick building. I can't imagine Mother having a baby.

We are about to get into the car.

"Please don't let him go there. Please!"

She gets in, hands me the tote bag to hold on my lap.

"One day at a time," she says, looking straight ahead.

I better figure out how to keep my father out of the VA Hospital.

Dr. Cairns has said Mother can go to Akron, so we plan to meet at the hospital. I am keeping Opie, and Aunt Ginny is driving her to the airport.

I get to his room first, but she soon walks in wearing her gray suit. She's put on rouge, and lipstick, and eye shadow. My father is sitting up in bed wearing his bifocals, grinding his teeth.

"Well, well. Aren't you all painted up?" he says.

"Am I?" She sounds like a schoolgirl.

"Take that gunk off," he says. "I don't recognize you."

He's right. She doesn't usually wear makeup—New Year's Eve maybe, but not every day. She laughs and goes into his bathroom and wipes off her lipstick and rouge. I thought she would be upset, but she doesn't seem to be.

"Better?" she says.

"Much better."

I never saw them kiss here before.

Jonah

Parents visiting the U of M always want a souvenir snapshot. The favorite background, I've noticed, is the West Engineering arch. A blond girl is posing there now. Her red coat reminds me of the red baseball cap in my father's color photographs. It wasn't my cap or Kate's. It wasn't even my father's—nobody wore that cap—but there it is in a dozen pictures as if someone had casually tossed it on the grass, or the beach, or the back porch steps. This girl's father needn't worry about not having enough color. Her coat is red, the sky is blue, the snow is white. I think I have my father's eye for color and composition which is a comforting idea until I remember I have Opie. I drove to campus for my nine o'clock chemistry lecture, but where did I park? Did I put money in a meter? I could have a ticket by now. I completely forgot about Mother going to Akron, my nephew, my father at St. Joe's. It's twelve-thirty! He is probably wondering where I am. I promised to be there for lunch. I could walk; it's not that far, but what about the parking meter? I don't want to think about expired parking meters. I don't, actually, want to think about my sick father. What I want to do is study for my Music Lit exam tomorrow. I would like to go back to the co-op for lunch, then go to the janitor's lounge.

Now I remember; I parked across from the Chem building. Running, trying not to slip on the ice, I pray I don't get a ticket. What does a parking ticket cost?

I didn't get a ticket, but I have only two dimes for the meter. I get in the car.

The St. Joe's parking lot is full, so I drive around and around until I find a place—wouldn't you know it—in front of the Ann Street Boarding House. I put my two dimes in the parking meter. At least I'm on a hill in case I have to pop the clutch. I'll visit my father, then drive back to Oxford, leave Opie there, and walk to Music Lit. Today is a mess. My father in the hospital. Mother out of town. Icy sidewalks. The sooner I get rid of this car the better. What I really want is a nap. I found a good place to nap last week in the storage closet behind the Chem lab. I sleep like a rock on that floor—no pillow, nothing.

On the way up the hill, I pass Mr. Weber's house. His piano was on the other side of that front window. If Mr. Weber hadn't moved to California, I would have kept studying piano. When I asked Mother why he moved so far away, she said he was having a difficult time; he was a homosexual, and the landlords around town were not broadminded. Come to think of it, he moved about four times while he was here. This was his last house. Poor Mr. Weber. I haven't really played in years. "Waltzing Matilda" every now and then, some hymns, but that's about it. The last piece I studied with him was Chopin's "Raindrop Prelude."

My father has been in the hospital so many times since last fall, I can never remember which room he's in, although he's always on the fifth floor. I look in every room as I go down the hall.

I wish I'd come sooner. He doesn't look right. One side of his face droops. All the time I spent eating breakfast, standing under the engineering arch, driving around, he was lying here, alone, looking like this.

"Your Daddyth gonna leave you today."

Why is he lisping? I drop my book bag on the floor, put my coat on the armchair where Mother sat last night for our little party. I put my snowflake mittens in the coat pocket. I have lost two pairs of mittens this winter. Suzy knit these in a Norwegian design, red and white snowflakes with a pointy top. I pull the armchair closer to his bed.

His smile is crooked. He looks at the bedside table. What is he looking for—cigarettes? The door opens. I am expecting the nurse, but it's Dr. Cairns and his chickens. They usually come in the morning. Dr. Cairns walks to the side of my father's bed, both hands in his white coat pockets. The chickens stand around the foot of the bed. I never seem to be here when Dr. Cairns comes. This is a piece of luck.

"Sam!" he says in a loud voice.

My father squints.

"How are you today, Sam?"

"Tho-tho."

Did he bite his tongue?

"Just so-so?"

My father tries to laugh, but only one side of his mouth moves.

"Got any VO, Al?"

The chickens smile.

"Not today, Sam."

"Tomorrow?"

"Ask me tomorrow, Sam."

Dr. Cairns pulls the blanket down, takes his stethoscope out of his pocket, pokes the ear tips in both his ears, bends over, and places the silver disc on my father's hospital gown. He moves the disc around his chest, shuts his eyes, listens, then takes off the stethoscope, drapes it around his neck. He reaches under the blanket, pulls out my father's arm by the wrist, looks at his watch. The chickens are staring at my father who tries to wink. Then, Dr. Cairns lets go of my father's wrist, squeezes his hand. He moves to the foot of the bed. The chickens step back. He writes in the chart, pokes his ball point pen back in his pocket, puts the chart back in the holder, returns to the bedside, and says in a loud voice, "I'll get you a few blankets, Sam."

My father isn't deaf.

"Thigarette," says my father, "I'm all out."

It is a running gag. Then, before I can ask about his droopy face, they're gone. It has always been like this—a little show my father puts on for the chickens. I hurry to the door, but they are gone when I get out to the hall, and when I return to my father, his eyes are closed.

A few minutes later, a nurse's aide brings a white cotton blanket. We spread it over his arms and shoulders. Hospital blankets are never warm. They are woven too loosely. Our red plaid football blanket should be in the bureau. It is. I spread that over the cotton blanket. I reach under the covers to find his hand. It's cold. I tuck his hand under both blankets.

"Do you have hot water bottles?"

The aide smiles. "I'm afraid not."

Then she checks his water pitcher, which is full, then goes out, pulling the door quietly behind her. You would think a hospital would have a hot water bottle.

Nobody has said anything about his crooked face. Maybe I could shave him when he wakes up. I have never shaved him before, but Mother has. You take the plastic basin and fill it with soapy water. His razor is probably in the bathroom.

Staring at the paper towel dispenser, I realize this is the bathroom my father has been using for what—two weeks? How long has he been here? I can't remember. I've been so busy at school.

When I come out of the bathroom, there is a woman pushing the door open. Usually, nobody comes for the longest time.

"Sorry," she says, "a little mix-up in the kitchen." She puts his lunch tray on the bureau and goes out. Steam comes through the hole in the plastic lid over the plate. It smells like meatloaf. There's Jello, a pitcher of tea, more saltines. He is not supposed to eat saltines, so I take the package from the tray and two more packages from the bedside table drawer. I haven't had lunch.

I don't really feel like studying, and I don't feel like napping in the chair. Mother will probably call his room after she sees the baby so my father can talk to Kate and hear the baby cry. We can't call her, but she can call us. Should I wake him? He's breathing fine. He looks lopsided, but calm. And tired.

I would like to change my clothes. If he's going to rest, I might as well leave. It won't take me long, maybe half an hour. Besides, the meter might be running out. I whisper that I'll be back in about an hour, but he's sound asleep. I pick up my book bag and coat, and tiptoe out of the room. I tell the nurse at the station I'll be back in half an hour. She stares at me, waiting for me to say something else. I don't have anything else to say.

Empty hall. Empty elevator. My mittens are still in my pocket. Snow piled everywhere so bright I can hardly see. No parking ticket.

Driving back to the co-op, I realize I don't have any duties until tomorrow's dinner clean-up. I park, grab a few graham crackers from the kitchen and go up to my room. No one there. I change into my suede green jumper and light blue blouse, leave my book bag on my bed, go to the toilet. When I get back to my room and see the clothes I was wearing on the chair, I can't understand why I changed my clothes. Why did I leave his hospital room? What am I doing here? I should never have left him with his face like that. I run downstairs.

There is no place to park anywhere near the hospital. All the meters are taken, and the lot is full. I park in a loading zone. I shouldn't have left him. I should *never* have left him. I never even asked the nurse at the nursing station what was wrong with his face. Nobody is telling me anything, but I am not trying very hard to find out, am I? What is wrong with me?!

When I explain who I am at the nursing station and that I am wondering why my father's face is lopsided, she says, "Well, he had a little stroke last night," and then looks sympathetic. Why didn't anybody tell me this?! I know what a stroke is. Mrs. Van Tyne had a stroke and was paralyzed on one side.

When I get back to his room, he is breathing in little puffs of air, the football blanket just as it was. I hope he didn't wake up while I was gone. His lunch tray is still on the bureau. I take off my coat, jam my mittens deep into the pockets, pull the chair closer to the bed. Our football blanket is too small. I start braiding the wool fringe, but the strands are too short and too widely spaced. By the time you pull all three short strands together there is nothing to braid. I touch his hand under the blanket—still cold. No, colder.

The door opens. A tall Black man in a short gray jacket goes to the foot of the bed and pulls out my father's chart, then he walks back out to the hall. A second later he pushes a hand truck with a tall steel tank balanced on it over to the bed. It says "O2" on the side. Oxygen. He tips the hand truck forward very slowly. The tank hits the floor with a loud plunk. He hangs a rubber mask over the nozzle and leaves. The rubber mask is gray. White elastic straps. All that racket and my father doesn't wake up. A nurse I never saw before comes in. She pays no attention to the oxygen tank, reaches under the blanket, brings out my father's hand, holds his wrist, and squints at her dainty watch. Then she lets go of his hand, doesn't tuck it back under the blankets, and says, "To help him breathe a little easier." She writes in the chart and goes out. But he's breathing fine. He's sound asleep.

Sister Cecelia comes in. She is taller than Sister Mary. I've always liked her best, but I'm not sure why. She feels like a relative. There is a spill on her black habit from lunch. I know what Mother would say about that—Sister Cecelia has her mind on higher things. I expect her to whisper something polite, but she shakes my father's shoulders— hard. Why? Why can't he sleep? She puts her hand under his head. His eyes flutter open. She grabs the mask off the tank and slips the elastic around his head in back. She is not gentle. She is behaving like a Phys Ed teacher, not a nun. He doesn't want the mask. He wants to sleep! His face goes into an awful grimace. He wants to be left alone. Can't she see that? His hand flies up. She pulls the mask over his nose, pushes his hand away. What is going on?! Is she trying to smother him? He's scared. She turns the nozzle on the tank. He turns his head from side to side. *Why is she doing this?*

"Trust me, Sam. Sam! Relax. Try to relax."

"He doesn't want it."

"Sam! Listen to me! Take deep breaths."

I didn't know a nun could work hospital equipment. Or be so cruel. She used to call him Mr. Schneider. Her wedding band, mother said, represents her marriage to Christ.

Finally, he sinks back on his pillow and shuts his eyes, the mask over his nose and mouth. He's calm. He's breathing.

"Deeeeeep breaths," she says, staring at her watch.

My poor father, too scared and too weak to fight back. After so many seconds, she takes the mask off, stares at her watch, then puts the mask back on and this is the routine. He actually looks better—his forehead a little pinker. Oxygen for one minute, no oxygen for one minute. How long will this go on? I wish he would open his eyes. Every time she takes off the mask, she has to pull the elastic over his ears. Mother always said he had nice ears, close to the head. I can't get over how bossy Sister Cecelia was just now. She saw he was frightened, but she didn't give up. She won that little battle. Maybe she should stay in the church and not become a mother.

"I hear you have a nephew."

She's looking at me for the first time.

"Thomas Jeffrey."

"Thomas is a nice name," she smiles, taking off the mask, looking at her watch.

"Is Dr. Cairns coming back?"

She doesn't know.

"What about his crooked face?"

She stares at her watch.

"Droopy on one side?"

She looks at me like a teacher, as if I have just raised an interesting point.

"Is a nurse coming?"

She shakes her head no, as if she has asked for the privilege of doing this. She puts the mask back on, looks at her watch.

"How is your nephew doing?"

"I don't know."

"Where was he born?"

"Akron."

"Ah, Akron. I'm from Ohio," she looks at her watch. "I once sailed on Lake Erie."

She takes the mask off.

My father would love the idea of her sailing on Lake Erie. I can hear him: "So, when was that, Cecelia? Before you become a nun?"

Wait! What just happened? He's sitting up. Yanks off the mask. Opens his mouth wide, but no words come out. Wider. No words. He can't speak. He looks up at the ceiling, falls back on his pillow.

He needs oxygen!

He sits up again, face contorted. Tries to scream. Mouth wide open, open wider. No scream. No sound. Eyes open. Mouth open. Falls back. No sound. Mouth still open. I need to stand up. I can't stand up. I can't move.

Sister Cecelia turns her head towards me as if she is trying to move me out of the room with the tip of her chin, as if we have talked before about this moment, and this is the time to do what we talked about, as if all along we were expecting precisely this to happen.

What is going on?! What just happened?

She hangs the mask on the oxygen tank, turns off the valve. Puts her left hand over his face. When her hand pulls away, his eyelids are closed. She holds his wrist. Then she closes her eyes, clasps her hands. Is she praying? Then she opens her eyes and says,

"I'm sorry. You'd better wait in the hall."

What just happened? His mouth is still open.

I leave my coat on the floor. I walk around the foot of his bed past the lunch tray on the bureau.

The hall is empty. I turn left, lean against the wall, press my back into the wall. I try to be Jackie Kennedy in that pink suit. I compose my face, lift my head. I pretend people are watching me. Nobody is watching me. There is nobody out here. I press my back into the wall.

Here comes Doctor Cairns and two chickens. Their white coats are flapping. Dr. Cairns is the shortest doctor in the longest coat. They slow down at his room, Room 522. It is still his room. One of the chickens looks at me. They go inside. The door shuts. Mother was right about Dr. Cairns. He is *profoundly unhandsome.*

A few days ago, they were joking.

"When am I going to get outta here, Al?"

"Oh, we'll know in a few days."

"When, Al?"

"Give it another day or two, Sam."

"Talk to me straight, Al."

"Sam, I'm giving you a straight answer."

"I want a day of the week."

"Okay, Sam. Friday."

Today is Monday.

Two chickens come out, whispering. They walk down the hall. Dr. Cairns comes out. He touches my elbow. It is time to come away from the wall and walk with him, I can't imagine where. All the way down the hall, he holds my elbow. I am not a chicken. I am a daughter.

Opposite the nursing station, where the corridor turns at an angle, is a room I've seen the nurses go in and out of, and this is where we go. It is a small room with a poster about a fire drill and four chairs around a Formica table. There is a phone on a corner table by the window. Not a hospital phone, a normal phone on a small wooden table, not hospital furniture. Maybe it came from the Treasure Mart.

"Do you know your sister's telephone number?"

"No. They have a new apartment."

"It'll be in his chart. Excuse me."

Wadded up wax paper and brown paper in the wastebasket, cigarette butts, a white paper wrapping from a straw. The nurses have their lunch here. Someone needs to wipe off this table.

Dr. Cairns returns, holding a scrap of paper. He dials. Is he calling Mother? He says something, listens, says something else then hands me the phone and steps away.

It's Mother saying she's going to call Aunt Ginny. Aunt Ginny will pick me up at the Emergency entrance in about fifteen minutes. There are scratches on this old table. Mother says she is getting a flight home as soon as she can, this evening. Tim will arrange it. We hang up.

"She said Mrs. McEachern will pick you up?"

"My Godmother."

"You can wait here."

"No, she said to wait in Emergency."

Two nurses at the counter look at me. We walk to the elevator. Dr. Cairns presses the down button. At the second floor, a woman steps into the elevator wearing a winter coat. When did I put my coat on? How did I get my coat? It fell on the floor. Dr. Reichert must have brought my coat and my bookbag. When was that? No, a nurse brought it. Where are my mittens? Still in my pocket. Dr. Cairns touches my elbow again. We turn left through double doors to Emergency. I am afraid a trolley will come rushing through the door, but nothing seems to be happening. Nobody is anywhere. Outside, there is an ambulance without a driver, dirty snowbanks. I don't know what color Aunt Ginny's car is. When I turn around, Dr. Cairns has left. Did I say good-bye?

A green car pulls around the parked ambulance. I don't recognize it, but that is Aunt Ginny in the front seat. I recognize her thick gray hair piled up on her head. I get in. She says mother's plane arrives at nine thirty-five. I am waiting for her to ask me *What happened? What was he like today? Did he say anything? What did Dr. Cairns say? What did the nurses do?* But she stares straight ahead and keeps checking the rearview mirror. We pull out onto Ann Street. We pass the Ann Street Boarding House. Maybe, when somebody dies, the polite thing is not to ask a lot of questions. Mother never prepared me.

We go up the steep hill. The metal letters on the building spell *Alice Lloyd*. Our family knew Alice Lloyd. When the Lloyd house was torn down on Washtenaw, my father and I went over with a wheelbarrow and collected wood from the paneling in the front hall and banister

rails. I can't think about that now. We pass the observatory where
Aunt Elizabeth studied the stars. There is the University Hospital main
entrance where I used to work. Where Mother still works. There is the
cemetery and the dormitories where my cousin Suzy lived. There is
Strickland's Market. We go up Geddes past the Arboretum. We turn
left on Harvard Place. Aunt Ginny and Uncle Tom live at the foot of
Harvard Place. Mother has known Aunt Ginny her whole life, and
Uncle Tom is my pediatrician. Aunt Ginny grew up in the big house
behind the stone wall across from 1015. Uncle Tom asked Mother
to marry him first, but she chose my father, so he married her best
friend. Aunt Ginny's gray hair used to be red which is why they called
her Ginger, although her real name is Virginia. Her mother's maiden
name was Angell, like Angell Hall and Angell School with two Ls.

I have visited their house a hundred times. All these familiar places
and connections are meant to be reassuring, but as we drive down
the hill, very slowly because it is steep, there is no point in reassuring
me. Everybody who came into his room today knew he was dying—
the nurse, Dr. Cairns, the chickens, the oxygen delivery man, Sister
Cecelia—and nobody warned me. Nobody said what might happen.
Here's who prepared me: my father. He said he was going to leave me
today. He always talked straight.

Pots on the stove, butter on the counter. Aunt Ginny puts on her
apron. Uncle Tom will be home soon from the office, she says, and
after dinner, we will pick up Mother at Willow Run. Hearing this, I
realize there have been several phone calls made on the black phone
at the end of the counter. While I was standing by the scratched-up
table in the nurses' lunchroom, arrangements were being made.

I ask if I can play the piano. When she smiles and turns back to
her stove, I remember Aunt Ginny, a long time ago, had a nervous
breakdown.

Their living room is five steps down from the front hall. There is a
fireplace and a window seat that looks out on Aunt Ginny's garden and
the Arboretum. Everything in this room is grayish green—curtains,

carpet, cushions, walls. It's soothing. Chopin Preludes are on the music rack. Their grand piano is brown. Ours is black. Janet, their daughter, took lessons from Mr. Weber, too—another connection. Janet is three years older than me and also went to U. High.

I turn on the music light. I learned five Chopin Preludes. I find No. 20 which I almost know by heart. I recognize Mr. Weber's pencil marks on the music staff. Mr. Weber had clean fingernails and dark hairs on his knuckles. I wonder how he is. This is the prelude with all the heavy chords. I play it well. I play it again.

I find my favorite —No. 15. It doesn't say "Raindrop Prelude," but that's what Mr. Weber called No. 15. Five flats. I play slowly. Maybe too slowly.

I haven't played Chopin in years, but I can still read ahead, anticipate, so that by the time the note should be played, I am ready to play it, my finger in the right place. I pretend I have an audience in this gray-green room. Jackie Kennedy performing at the White House. I even manage the stormy middle section. The best part is the end when you turn back and start all over. Janet must have gotten further than I did before Mr. Weber moved to California because I see the notation for pedal—the squiggle that always looks like a spaniel dog—underlined by Mr. Weber. Janet learned to pedal. If Mr. Weber hadn't moved to California, I might have learned to pedal, too. I start again. I could play all night. I belong with this music. I hear Aunt Ginny's voice. She is at the top of the stairs. She's been calling, and I didn't hear her.

Dinner is on the table. Uncle Tom is home. He reminds me of Mr. Weber, tall and quiet, except he has white hair slicked down, not brown hair sticking up. He has been my doctor my whole life. I sit facing the back yard which looks out on the Arboretum. Macaroni and cheese, and ham, and peas. He bows his head.

"Bless O Lord this food to our use and us to Thy service. And please remember, especially tonight, the Schneiders and the newest member of their family, Thomas. Amen.'

I wish he'd said all our names.

Aunt Ginny passes a basket of rolls. Uncle Tom says some boy has measles and there are too many toys in the waiting room. Aunt Ginny says she will clean up the waiting room. Uncle Tom looks at me every few minutes. I am waiting for him to ask about my father, but he doesn't. Nor does Aunt Ginny. Why is nobody curious? My father just died. Are we not supposed to talk about dead people? Who would have thought my father would die, and Mother would be out of town, and I would be eating here, and going to the airport to get her? Who would have thought Willow Run would be part of this horrible day? It is like the Spanish house when Marky died. You never know what unfamiliar place will be associated with something terrible.

When we get to the gate at Willow Run, Aunt Ginny says Mother should be on the plane that just landed. I can't see the passengers, just the small oval windows lit in the dark. In a few minutes, Mother will be walking towards us. Aunt Ginny opens a heavy door. We are standing on the tarmac. It's cold. Is this where my father held Kennedy's hand? It's dark except for the runway lights and the lights on the plane. I have never been on a plane. What is taking so long?

Finally, two men roll a metal staircase out to the plane. Then, the airplane door swings open. A stewardess appears, wearing a coat. Passengers start coming down the staircase. Not Mother. Not Mother. Where is she? Maybe she is on the next plane. No, there she is! Stepping out of the plane onto the staircase—tall, head tilted, coat, hat, pocketbook, gloves. A man behind her is in a hurry to get off, so Mother steps to the side of the staircase—don't fall off!—her hand touching the outside of the plane, which terrifies me, her glove touching the metal that moments ago was high in the sky. The man is in a hurry and runs down the metal staircase. Then, Mother steps down slowly, her gloved hand on the railing, her other hand keeping her hat on her head, the hat with the ribbons looped on one side, her pocketbook in the crook of her elbow. She looks down until the last step when she lifts her head, looks across the tarmac, confident we are waiting, somewhere, in the dark. Do we walk out? Meet halfway?

Aunt Ginny is paralyzed like me. Mother walks forward. She sees us. Here she comes. I will collapse if she hugs me. She doesn't hug me or Aunt Ginny. She isn't crying. How will I ever thank her for that? She thanks Aunt Ginny for coming to get her and smiles a gentle smile as we turn around. No arm around my shoulder or kiss on the cheek. I am so grateful.

It is a short walk back to the airport and down the hallway to where passengers pick up their luggage. Mother walks like a queen, head high, long legs. No wonder my father said, "I would know that walk anywhere."

Aunt Ginny asks about the new baby whose name I have already forgotten.

"Oh, he's lovely," says Mother. "Thomas Jeffrey has a full head of black hair. They are spelling Jeffrey with a J."

"And how is Kate?"

"Holding her own. I spoke to Tom and G."

Her brothers, Tom and George, who live in Detroit. Aunt Ginny knows them because they all grew up together.

At the end of the hallway, there is a short staircase. At the foot of the stairs, Mother drinks from the water fountain. When she straightens, water on her chin, she says, "I was lucky to get a seat."

We stand beside a pillar, waiting for her suitcase to come down the chute. Everything is normal—other passengers, their suitcases, the loudspeaker announcing the arrival of a flight from Pittsburgh, the sign for Al Green's Restaurant. We ate there once so my father could enjoy the roquefort dressing.

"I left messages for Suzy and Anne. I spoke to Tommy," says Aunt Ginny.

How did she get my cousins' telephone numbers?

"Tom met Henry at the hospital. They've spoken to Muehlig's."

"Bless him," says Mother.

There are too many Tom's: Daddy's friend Tom Goodrich, Uncle Tom my Godfather, Uncle Tom Mother's brother, Tommy my cousin, and now Tommy my nephew.

But I get it. Uncle Tom who is a doctor and Henry Lewis our minister drove to St. Joe's while I was playing the piano. When Uncle Tom sat down at the dinner table, he had not come from seeing sick children in his office; he had come from seeing my dead father. Now, Mother turns to me for the first time, specifically, and says, "Your cousins might all be there when we get home." Preparing me.

I lift her suitcase off the conveyor belt. The handle is the color of the suitcase, almost the color of Aunt Ginny and Uncle Tom's living room décor. Her initials, L.T.S., in gold, are still under the handle.

We walk outside to the parking lot. It's cold but not snowing. I put the suitcase in Aunt Ginny's trunk. I get in the back seat, behind Aunt Ginny, so mother and Aunt Ginny can talk up front. I prefer to be alone in the dark.

Mother gets in the back with me. Mother and I have never ridden together in the back seat of anybody's car ever. She folds her gloved hands in her lap although, occasionally, she leans forward, her kid glove on the back of the front seat, to listen to Aunt Ginny. There is about an inch between us on the back seat. I could use two inches.

"I called on Aunt Helen," says Aunt Ginny.

This is how they always talk. Two old friends gossiping about people in our town. Mother sounds genuinely interested. I can't believe Aunt Ginny can laugh her throaty laugh.

"Handicraft installed the electric chair lift."

"It's about time."

They talk about their friends. Aunty Douglas. Mrs. Pillsbury. Miss Peck, Uncle Tom's secretary. When we are alone, at home, Mother will want to know what happened because Dr. Cairns wasn't in the room when my father died, so he couldn't have told her how he died.

She must be wondering how and why. When she said good-bye on Sunday, she expected to see him again.

We pass the Ford plant opposite the lake. We pass the farm with two silos. There are no hills out here, either.

"Henry said for you to call any time."

At the mention of our minister, Mother turns to look out the window. It is Monday, February 20th. The year is 1967. I am eighteen.

Leo

Our house is all lit up, Suzy's Jeep in the driveway, the porch light on.

"Thank you, Gin."

"Good night, Lo."

This is what Godparents do—show up at times like this.

I take Mother's suitcase out of the trunk. I close the trunk.

"Where is our car?"

I don't know.

"Where is Opie?"

"At the hospital."

"In the lot?"

"I can't remember."

"Never mind," Mother says, stepping onto the porch. "We'll find it."

Someone shoveled the front walk. The shovel is on the porch. As Mother opens the storm door, she takes a deep breath. I hold the storm door while she opens the front door.

Cousin Tom's girlfriend Shelley is kneeling by the sofa, petting Suki, who is in her usual spot. My other cousins are curled into chairs, their feet tucked underneath them, like amputees. A fire in the fireplace, cigarette smoke curling, shoes kicked off on the floor. It could be Thanksgiving or Easter. Suddenly, I remember Opie is in a loading zone. Suki jumps down. The cousins stare at us. Nobody moves or speaks. Then, Mother becomes the person we all desperately need her to be.

"Tom darling," she commands, "get Uncle Sam's portrait. Time to hang it over the mantel."

He wouldn't allow his portrait to be hung while he was alive. "Over my dead body," were his actual words, but nobody dares remember that out loud.

I carry Mother's suitcase to her bedroom. The sooner I get away from everybody staring at me the better. I put the bag on her bed. Why did I change my clothes in the middle of the day? I never do that. I am wearing what I wore for my high school yearbook picture. When I return to the living room, the cousins are all talking.

"He said we could hang it up when he died."

"He did. He did say that."

All these things he said in the past which, from now on, is the only place he will ever be.

Mother remembers we kept his portrait at 1015 in the cubbyhole on the third floor, but where is it in this house? She looks at me. This house is so small, how lost could it be? While everyone goes looking for it, Mother walks over to the mantel, still in her coat, pushes the candlesticks to either side, lifts the Renoir off the nail. Cobwebs cling to the back as she leans it against the sofa. So many years of the man lighting his cigarette, squinting; so many years of the woman in white and the woman in black. I've always loved how the man's hand is cupped around the burning match, exactly how my father lit his cigarettes, even when he was indoors. He said he got into the habit when he was in the Navy on the aircraft carriers.

Tom found the portrait behind the furnace wrapped in a blanket. Suzy tosses the blanket onto the couch. The portrait is bigger than I remember. Suzy leans it on the seat of his chair where he won't ever sit again. Shelley hands Suzy a wet cloth to wash off the glass. Anne takes Mother's coat to the closet, then she takes my coat; the warm expression on her face is the nicest expression I have seen all day. Anne has joined a sorority, although I think I remember hearing she was going to move out. We don't see each other very often, I realize. And, given her nice expression, I wonder why that is. She seems to be the only person struggling besides me.

Tom is appointed to hang Uncle Sam's portrait. A cobweb on the wall is brushed away. Tom lifts the portrait as if it were suddenly twice as heavy. He can't get the wire over the nail. He tries two or three times. Finally, it snags. Tom becomes a perfectionist, tilting the frame right and left until he's satisfied. I've never seen that side of him before. I always thought of him as a handsome, soccer-playing frat boy.

"Too high," says Mother, "but leave it for now."

She pushes the candlesticks closer to the gold frame which is not ornate. Mother lights the candles. Everyone stands back to stare at the serious, long-faced young man with scarce, sandy hair swept back, high forehead, mustache, shirt lapel, long tie. The gray-green shadow behind one shoulder is the color of Aunt Ginny and Uncle Tom's living room. The shape of his head is wrong. The long tie is wrong. It looks nothing like him.

"How old was he, Aunty Lo, in 1937?"

Suzy counts back. "Twenty-nine? Thirty?"

Then someone says his age now, fifty-nine, which is how long he lived.

Tom squints at the signature of the artist.

"Ziggy? Was that the painter's *name*?"

Ziggy with a huge "Z" painted on a diagonal not in black but red. That red is perfect—like the baseball cap.

Tom's girlfriend Shelley is crying uncontrollably. Mother says she's going to change her clothes. Tom and Shelley go into the kitchen. Suzy whispers that Tom took Shelley to the hospital, but when they got to Uncle Sam's room, the light was off. When a nurse came in, Tom apologized for going into the wrong room. He said he was looking for Mr. Schneider. The nurse told him he was in the right room and Mr. Schneider had died at four o'clock. Shelley became hysterical. Finally, what happened—that he died—is mentioned. But nobody looks at me or asks me anything. Maybe they don't know I watched him die.

Mother knows and Aunt Ginny knows, but did Aunt Ginny tell the cousins when she called them? I can hear Shelley crying in the kitchen. I hardly know her, but I love her now. She started dating Tom after her father died. She and my father liked each other.

When a person dies, a nurse puts their clothes in a plastic bag and gives the bag to a family member which must have been my cousin Tom. How else did this blue plastic bag smelling of the hospital get into my father's bedroom? I suppose Tom didn't know where to put the bag, and nobody wanted to touch it, so Suzy or Anne said just put it in Uncle Sam's bedroom. I can see the bag over by his bureau, the reflection on the plastic bag is from the floodlight in the Abrams back yard.

I never minded the smell when I was in his hospital room, but I do now: lotion, vinyl curtains, steam from the food trays, rubber lids over the plates, sweet tea. His bedroom at home now smells like his hospital room. I lie down on his bed anyway. I changed these sheets when he went to the hospital. If I go to my bedroom, everyone will see me open the door in the living room and I want to be alone.

Somebody put the trumpet music on the record player. They're drinking, putting logs on the fire. Mother has probably made a martini and is making phone calls. The smell is getting worse. I don't think I can stay here.

The door opens. I expect Suzy, but it's Mother. I want her to put the plastic bag in the closet, but she sits on the bed. She can't see the bag in the dark, and the smell doesn't mean anything to her.

"Can we promise one another?" she says, not too drunk, but a little. "I won't be angry with myself that I wasn't with Daddy, if you won't be angry I was with Kate."

"I'm not angry."

It never occurred to me.

"Give me your hand."

She whispers the magic words, "Dish Come Bubble."

She always said that when we were sick, opening Nanny's cabinet and taking out the gold scarf. But I'm not sick. The words make no sense without the gold scarf. I am embarrassed for her.

What I have, my father's final hours, she can never have, nor can I give them to her. No one has those hours but me. What she wants to give me, comfort, I don't want. I can't hold another thing. Tom and Shelley saw his face in the dark, but I have his face with the light on. I have his bedside table with the saltine crumbs. I have Dr. Cairns and the chickens joking. I have the short fringe on the football blanket and the "O2" painted on the side of the heavy tank. I have the stain on Sister Cecilia's habit. I have my father's cold hand and his horrible silent scream. I have that scream twice.

He hated this picture

He loved this picture

Per • il *noun*

1. exposure to injury, loss, or destruction; grave risk; jeopardy
2. something that causes or may cause injury, loss, or destruction

When I get back from the co-op, there is a car in our driveway. Coming out the front door is Henry Lewis. I can see his clerical collar under his winter coat. I am used to seeing him at St. Andrew's, giving a sermon or walking down the aisle behind the choir. In 1936, he married my parents, then he baptized and confirmed Kate and me, and he buried everybody who died in our family. I have never seen him where we live. There's Mother on the porch, waving. I need to move the car so Henry Lewis can back out the driveway.

Mother is sitting on the sofa when I come inside, not in her chair. She pats the sofa. I put down my suitcase, hang my coat in the closet, and sit beside her.

"Daddy's funeral will be Saturday at four o'clock. Henry will officiate with Gordon."

Nothing I can say to that. Gordon Jones is the rector now. Henry Lewis has retired.

"We'll have 'Sheep May Safely Graze' as a prelude, 'Oh God Our Help in Ages Past,' 'The Strife is O'er,' and 'The Navy Hymn.'"

I know those hymns.

"Uncle Grover is coming," she smiles, then she sighs. "Kate and Tim can't bring a newborn baby so they will not be coming, but they will, of course, be at the internment, probably sometime in May."

I hadn't thought of any of these things. That Uncle Grover is coming is the best news of all. That Kate is not coming is horrible.

"Darling? Did you see your professor?"

I report that Dr. Kollars will let me take my Geography exam in his office when I'm ready, and I found someone to take over my co-op duties. We haven't talked about how long I will stay home. If the funeral is Saturday, then I can go back to the co-op next Monday.

"Maybe Kate and Tim would like Suki," says Mother.

Mother is moving fast.

The phone rings. We go to the kitchen. She tells whoever is on the phone that Henry Lewis just left. She has turned the little counter by the spice rack into her desk. Her address book is beside a notepad with names on it. That phone is going to ring all day and all night.

I make two cheese sandwiches. I put hers by the pencil sharpener, and I carry my sandwich and my suitcase upstairs. Today is Tuesday. I am missing Music Lit, and Chem Lab, and French Comp. I take my toothbrush and my hairbrush to the bathroom. When I go back downstairs, Mother is still on the phone. I go down to the basement. The hymn book is on the piano. "The Navy Hymn" is 512. My father cried when they sang it at Kennedy's Funeral. My father was a Lieutenant Commander in the Navy. He can have that hymn. *Eternal Father Strong to Save.* I pull out the piano bench. I play it over and over, verse after verse. My favorite line is *for those in peril on the sea.* Finally, the word I need—*Peril.* Mother is calling. When I get to the kitchen, she says, "That was lovely! Just lovely."

She is still sitting at the counter. One bite out of her cheese sandwich.

"I'm going to Muehlig's in an hour. Do you want to come with me?"

"What for?"

Blank face.

"To see your father . . . and to make arrangements . . ."

Muehlig's has his body. That makes sense. I have never been to Muehlig's, but I know where it is—a block from the library before you get to the Beer Depot.

"I thought you might want to see him."

"I saw him."

Blank face.

"Of course, you did."

Mother is rarely embarrassed, but she looks embarrassed now. Then she picks up the phone to dial a number and says, "I'll be leaving at quarter to three if you change your mind."

Driving to Muehlig's, she might ask me what happened when he died. No. She won't. We have passed that point. She has moved on to planning. And I haven't asked her about her grandson, Tommy, have I? Or what it was like to get that phone call from Dr. Cairns. Tim probably answered the phone. And what about Kate hearing the news? I haven't thought about Kate, have I? And Mother's flight home alone. It could have been horrible in Akron.

Mother probably thinks he closed his eyes and just didn't open them, and that when his nurse came in to check on him, she couldn't wake him, so she took her stethoscope out of her pocket, and listened to his chest, and then shook her head, and looked sad. Mother probably imagines I was holding his hand, and that I kissed his forehead, and whispered I love you, and quietly walked out with my head held high. Well, none of that happened. I touched his cold hand, but I didn't hold it, and I didn't kiss his forehead. I didn't even whisper good-bye. Or I love you, or thank you. I just left.

Becoming

The funeral this morning was a blur. Mother said his coffin would be down front, so I pictured it parallel to the communion rail but it was in the middle of the aisle just to the left of our pew. The American flag draped over it looked brand new. I wish we had thought to bring out own flag from the burning Chenango.

I didn't cry except for the Navy Hymn "for those in peril on the sea," and I lost my hankie, but Mother had an extra, which I dropped as we walked out, and I left my purse in the pew. Someone I didn't recognize handed my purse to Mother in the parking lot. And now I've made it through the reception back here, and everyone is gone, and I want to go to bed, but the minute I reach for the door knob to go upstairs, Mother calls from the kitchen.

"Darling! Kate! Kate is on the phone! Come! Come!"

I didn't think about my sister all day.

"Please!!! It's Kate!"

Dishes in the sink, counters are stacked with platters of half-eaten food, wastebasket overflowing with bottles, and Mother handing me the phone and pulling out the chair. I haven't talked to my sister since before she had a baby. We don't talk on the phone. We never talked on the phone.

"Katie?"

"I had to hear your voice," she says.

Now I will cry.

"You there?"

"How's Tommy?"

"Tommy's asleep, finally! He's such a fussy baby. Very determined."

"That's nice."

"Well, not always nice," she yawns.

Mother is standing by the broom closet staring at me hard. This is the first moment we've had all day—just us in our house—and I don't want to keep her company. I want to be alone in my room. I want to lie down.

"Mother said the church was full."

"I didn't turn around."

"Meredith was going to come. And Linda. Did you see them?"

Her old friends.

"I didn't look. Henry Lewis read aloud his Patient's Prayer."

"Oh, that was nice."

"Everybody talked about that afterwards."

Mother takes the phone.

"Now, get some sleep. Give Tommy a kiss from Grandma. The internment will be in early May when the ground is warm . . . "

I leave them talking.

This is our living room. That's where Uncle Grover stood by the Grandfather clock. I wish he could have stayed another night, but he had to get back to Aunt Emma. If I could pick one thing I want to remember, it's sitting beside Uncle Grover in the pew, his hands in his lap, when it seemed the Schneiders were a real family.

When I hugged him goodbye, he said, "My brother must have been so proud of you," which was the nicest thing anybody said all day. They look a lot alike, but then, in certain ways, they don't at all. Grover has a high waist; my father has a low waist. They both have bald heads. Uncle Grover's eyes are more deep set and brown not blue. I couldn't tell which one was damaged in the elevator shaft. Both brothers are the same height, and their hands are identical, although Uncle Grover wears a wedding ring, and his New York accent is stronger, and he's three years older. I have to find out when his birthday is.

Climbing the stairs to my room, I think at least I never cried or sobbed in my father's hospital room, not outside his room in the hallway, not in the nurses' lunchroom, not at Aunt Ginny and Uncle Tom's house, not in the car with Mother coming home from Willow Run, not with the cousins in the living room, and not in his bed alone that night, and only once today during "The Navy Hymn." Crying is overrated.

Backfire

Mother likes to list the phases of grief. I don't recognize these phases. I can't imagine moving on to anything after this. How can life possibly get different or easier? It's so hard now, and the only thing that made it easy is gone. After I blurt that out, Mother arranges for me to see a psychologist. She says Dr. Feller can see me on Saturday mornings so I won't miss classes. She hands me a piece of paper with his address on Berkshire Road. She says it is at the intersection of Day Street.

Curious to know what a psychologist does, I dress up a little and decide to go. I find the house and ring the bell. Dr. Feller knows my name, touches my shoulder, walks ahead of me down a carpeted hallway into a room with bookcases. He points to a long brown sofa. I sit like Suki, at the end. Then, he turns on a small tape recorder already placed on the coffee table in front of me and goes to his heavy desk under the modern windows. "Go ahead," he says, pointing to the tape recorder. "Whatever comes to mind." Then, he sits in his desk chair that tips back and folds his hands.

After three of those silent appointments, I tell Mother I'm not going back, and Dr. Feller tells Mother when I have something to say, I can call him anytime. I don't tell Mother what I'm actually thinking: that I have a lot to say, but I'm not saying it to him. I don't know who I'm saying it to. The right person hasn't shown up.

Dr. Feller is probably expensive, so Mother doesn't argue, and whether he told her I never said a single word, I will never know. Apparently—big news—my father went to Dr. Feller and sat on the brown sofa for a few months one winter when we lived on Day Street. Why? Because he got anxious after he learned about his high blood pressure, and our friend Uncle Jim, who is also a psychologist, suggested Gerry Feller because he was within walking distance.

I hate hearing this. I never saw my father anxious. I saw him stern about homework, and thank you notes, and returning other people's belongings. I'm not sure what anxious looks like. I saw him tying his bow tie, and working hard, and drawing cartoons, and doing handstands, and going to work to put toast and eggs on our breakfast table. I saw him puttering, and building things, and asking me about school, and petting Marky, and drinking VOs, and driving Borgie. I saw him working hard to make a living. Okay, there was Gwen. But we were his family, and he never really had his own childhood family. We were important in his life, and I never felt we weren't. And yet, apparently—all that time—he was *anxious*?

Frightened means you are afraid and scared. I can imagine my father occasionally frightened. Anxious means you are full of mental distress or uneasiness because of fear of danger or misfortune. You are greatly worried and apprehensive. Anxious is so much worse. It means you are living with dread.

Mother meant well when she sent me to Dr. Feller, but it turned into more bad news—that my father was living with dread. Talk about a backfire.

Help

I'm starting to sleep better in my bed at the co-op. One evening, I'm cleaning up the dishes in the kitchen when one of the girls on my floor touches my shoulder. She says my mother is in the hallway. I can't believe it! Mother has not come to Noble House since the day I moved in. I dry my hands. She's standing by the back door. I'm so frightened something has happened, but she's smiling. She doesn't say anything, she just hands me a small envelope. Inside is a single ticket to Hill Auditorium to hear Louis Armstrong on April 1st.

Even from the balcony, I can hear every note. I know what it feels like to blow on a brass instrument, but Louis Armstrong doesn't work at it like I had to. His cheeks puff out, and his eyes are closed, but he's not struggling. He's relaxed, and he plays like he's never done anything else in his life, and he's been holding that trumpet in his right hand every single day and maybe through the night. And when he sings, his voice is like no other voice I've ever heard. He isn't a bass, or a baritone, or a tenor. He is just himself. I think that might be the lesson. Just be yourself.

My father was himself. He could draw and paint, but he wasn't famous. He could do handstands in the backyard, but not on top of a smokestack like Tom Goodrich. He worked hard, but he wasn't rich. He fixed broken things around the house, mowed the lawn, went to work, watched his gauges, made cartoons and murals, worried about the electricity bill and the oil bill, put food on the table, trained Marky, watched Tigers baseball and the Friday Night Fights. He also watched The Lawrence Welk Show, Ed Sullivan, and Walter Cronkite. He shoveled snow, raked leaves, helped Mrs. Wollner, tied his bow ties, made a mistake with a woman, got anxious and sick, and died young. But analyzing his life doesn't help. Dr. Feller didn't help. Taking my textbooks to the Arboretum to study under the pine trees doesn't help. Sitting closer to the janitors doesn't help. Even a doughnut at Dan's in the corner booth doesn't help. Actually, I like the fact that nothing helps. I don't want help. Help is overrated. Here's what helps: music.

The Cardboard Box

I did not want to wear my Goodyear's funeral suit to the internment, but Mother said "it's forty-five degrees, and it's so becoming." Becoming to whom? I can't wait to push this suit all the way to the back of my closet. Talk straight: What I wear doesn't matter. Not much does matter except getting through this day.

All morning, Mother has been looking for signs of life. Leaving the house on our way to the cemetery, she made us admire the buds on Miss Bacon's forsythia. She had Tim slow down his car so she could point to the one and only crocus on River Road.

I am getting to know Tim a little. He looks smart in his black suit. Mother is wearing her gray suit, black kid gloves, and pearls. Kate is wearing a loose, black crepe dress with white buttons down the front. She is more beautiful than ever with her long hair. Tommy is her first child, but she seems to know just what to do, and how to hold the baby, and when to pat his back.

I sit in the back seat beside Kate. I am holding the not-quite flowering quince and plum branches, which I try to keep away from the baby's eyes. That's all we need—the poked-out eye of the newborn grandson. When I ask why we are taking the long way, Mother says, "They can hardly begin without us." Then she turns a little so we can see her face.

"Daddy will be buried behind Nanny and Bapa and to the left of the Bellamys."

Preparing us. Kate rolls her eyes. I love when she does that.

Whenever we go to the cemetery, Mother mentions the Bellamys whose family plot is next to ours. There is probably a Bellamy story we haven't heard yet.

"I have yet to see Henry Lewis wear a coat to an internment," Mother adds. "When I called the church yesterday, Betty said Henry just got over pneumonia, so I wouldn't be surprised if he does wear a coat today. I so hoped it would be warmer. Oh, well." She faces front again. "Have you got your coats?"

She has been talking about coats all morning. Whether or not we need coats. Take them. Don't take them. "Take them," she finally said, "but leave them in the car."

"They're in the trunk," says Kate. "Can someone turn up the heat?"

Tim knows which knob.

When we get to the railroad tracks, the bar is down and the lights are blinking. We have never seen a train at this crossing. I wish Uncle Grover was here.

"Relax. We're not in a hurry. How is Tommy?"

"Asleep."

We could back up and go another way, but Mother is content to wait.

"Here comes the train. Have you got the song sheets?"

I typed seven copies of "Now the Day Is Over," all six verses, without carbon paper. This day is far from over.

Finally, the bar swings up.

"Timmy, at the next light, turn left. Girls? Don't be surprised by the gravediggers. They are told to park their truck a respectful distance away, but they never do."

I roll my eyes. "Don't be surprised when the wafer sticks to the roof of your mouth." "When you pass Aunt Helen her tea, don't be surprised if her hands shake; she has Parkinson's." "Don't be surprised by the flag draped over the coffin."

We rumble past the railroad station, over the cobblestones, up the hill where the cobblestones run out at the Catholic Church, then turn left on Huron. We drive past the power plant, the tennis courts, the back of the Natural History Museum. No bears in the bear house. We turn left on Geddes. We drive past Strickland's Market.

There are two entrance gates to the cemetery.

"That one," Mother points. "Go around the Randolph's, then up that hill past the winged angel."

A woman kneeling by a grave doesn't look up as we drive by. Behind her is a heap of dirty snow in the shade. It may be May, but it's still cold. Mother is so calm. Kate has the baby to distract her. Tim is steady, but I am not steady, or calm, or distracted.

"There! See all the cars. Park anywhere. Oh my. There's Louise."

"Mrs. Wollner?"

Everybody crowds around Kate to see the baby, smiling and congratulating, tucking the blue blanket around his little booties. Behind everyone, next to a small pile of dirt—is a cardboard box nobody paying any attention to it, nobody guarding it. It looks like a package going to the post office. Mother did not prepare me. She did not say, "Don't be surprised by the size of the box."

Henry Lewis has a gray wool scarf and no coat. Everybody else is wearing a coat. We are not wearing coats.

Aunt Ginny and Uncle Tom, Uncle Tom and Aunt Elizabeth, Aunt Bobby and Uncle George, Tucker, Jeff, Mrs. Wollner, Tom and Shelley, Suzy, and Anne are all here. I thought the Robertson's might be here, but Mother said family only. No close friends, no doctors, no doctors' wives. I'm glad Mrs. Wollner came anyways.

Anne offers to pass out the song sheets. I mean to let go of them, but she has to tug them loose from my hand. I am carrying too many things—the flowering branches, and the song sheets, and Mother's hankie. My heels are sinking into the ground. It isn't like church. There is no place to sit.

The box is light brown cardboard. Marky's ashes filled a Maxwell House coffee can. Do my father's ashes fill that box? I can't believe he is in that box next to a deep hole.

Henry Lewis walks around the mound of dirt and turns just before he might have kicked the box. He is used to these boxes. He gestures for everybody to come closer. Kate stands next to Mother. Tim stands next to Kate who pulls the blanket around Tommy's head. I stand next to Mother on the other side. Nobody looks at the box, or if they do, they don't look for long. I can't take my eyes off it.

How could I have possibly thought these branches were important? When I cut them from the backyard—some plum, some quince—I was so pleased to have thought to bring them. It wasn't Mother's idea. It was mine. But I can't stop them from shaking.

Henry Lewis opens his prayer book, takes a white card marking the place, and slides it between other pages.

Man that is born of woman hath but a short time to live and is full of misery.

Aunt Ginny looks so calm she could be waiting in line at the bank. Uncle Tom holds his hat in front of him. Aunt Bobby is wearing a brown coat, brown hat, brown shoes.

He cometh up and is cut down, like a flower; he fleeth as it were a shadow.

Mother stares at baby Tommy. She should be looking at Henry Lewis.

Kate said the trick to not crying is to stare at something until you have drilled a hole in it. I stare at the spigot.

Yet, O Lord God most holy, O Lord most mighty, O holy and most merciful Savior, deliver us not into the bitter pains of eternal death.

Mother spent a half hour getting her hair poofed just right. Now, she ignores the wind blowing it the wrong way. My song sheets flutter. My branches are shaking. Mother lifts her chin, perfectly calm. She may be rising to the occasion, but I am sinking fast.

O holy and most merciful Savior, thou most worthy Judge eternal, suffer us not, at our last hour, for any pains of death, to fall from thee.

Henry Lewis puts his prayer book on the grass, lifts the box—not heavy—and puts it in the grave, then he picks up his prayer book and steps back. Mother steps forward, bends over, grabs a handful of dirt. When did she take off her gloves? Clods hit the cardboard. Suzy drops her dirt. So does Tom, and then Tim, then Anne. Shelley takes two handfuls. Where is Mrs. Wollner? Aunt Ginny dribbles her dirt slowly. Tim holds Tommy. Kate takes her dirt, drops it into the hole. A pebble hits the box. Mother looks at me. It's my turn. I can't.

Unto Almighty God we commend the soul of our brother Sam departed, and we commit his body to the ground; earth to earth, ashes to ashes, dust to dust, in sure and certain hope of the Resurrection unto eternal life, through our Lord Jesus Christ—

A squirrel leaps onto a branch.

Let us Pray. Our Father, who art in Heaven, Hallowed be thy Name. Thy kingdom come, Thy will be done. On Earth as it is in Heaven. Give us this day our daily bread. And lead us not into temptation, but deliver us from evil. For Thine is the kingdom, the power and the glory. For ever and ever, Amen.

Henry Lewis closes the prayer book. His voice is so familiar.

Bless, O Lord, the members of this family, that, guided by Thy love, they may walk bravely and calmly amidst the changes of this life, knowing that Thou are with them here and with those they love in the life to come.

Mother squints at her song sheet. I stare at the white and pink petals hopelessly jiggling; I should not have cut them, now they will die. Why, on this day, of all days, didn't I think of that? Uncle Tom leads the singing. I know all the verses, but I can't sing.

Now the day is over,
Night is drawing nigh,
Shadows of the evening
Steal across the sky.

Sunday school was a waste of time. Now, when I could use some help, I don't feel God.

Grant to little children
Visions bright of thee;

Guard the sailors tossing
On the deep blue sea.

I see the gravedigger's truck. The gravedigger is leaning against the bumper, smoking.

When the morning wakens
Then may I arise
Pure, and fresh, and sinless
In thy holy eyes.

Mother turns to me. Eyebrows up. I walk over to the hole and look down: dirt on the cardboard box, the box sealed with brown tape. Ulrich's sells that wide brown tape. I don't want my branches snapped into smaller pieces so they will fit in the hole. Poor branches have had enough for one day. They are miles from their tree where they have lived their whole life. What was I thinking?

I place them beside the grave on the grass, and when I turn around, everyone is admiring the baby who has more status now than he did before. Thomas Jeffrey has power. He always will have power, given that my father knew he was born, and given Mother left to go see him, leaving my father alone to die and me alone to watch how he looked when he did.

Uncle George is standing by Nanny and Bapa's grave. Anne is collecting the song sheets. Mrs. Wollner has stepped through all the Bellamys and is walking to her car. She was not invited, but she came anyway. I love her for that. But nobody spoke to her. That's not right.

Tim has gone back to his car, the sort of thing my father would do—warm up the car. Where is the gravedigger? His blue truck is still there, but he isn't. Yes, he is. He's sitting inside. When he sees me coming, he flicks his cigarette out the window. He has a bushy mustache. I ask him to please leave the flowering branches on the ground beside the grave, not move them. He says, "I understand" which is just right.

Mother tells everyone the reason she postponed the internment until May was to give Kate time to recover and for the hard frozen ground to thaw, but people are buried in the dead of winter all the time. How many mornings, on my way down Geddes to my nine o'clock French class, have I seen the big yellow digger at the cemetery?

No, I think the real reason we waited until May was to prevent the Margolises from coming to the burial; if they came to the funeral, Mother couldn't stop them from joining the procession. Mother would never admit that, but I'm sure about it. You can't control who joins a funeral procession, I learned that when Mr. Ginzburg died. You wave to the Muehlig's attendant who gives you a flag to stick on your car. Anybody with a flag on their car can go to the cemetery, and you don't have to stop at red lights.

And, lest we forget, Mother wanted signs of life—the grandson, buds on the trees, renewal. I wish she would stop looking for life in everything. I know life goes on, but death goes on, too. Has my father showed up? Do you hear organ music from the ballpark coming from his bedroom? Has the level of VO gone down in the bottle in the broom closet? The tray we used for his dinner never comes out of that slot next to the icebox, does it? He did die.

Another thing: she never prepared me for what sort of container the ashes would be in, or what size the container would be. If I thought about Marky, I might have figured it out, but I just got out of Tim's car, walked onto the grass, and there was my father in a cardboard box waiting to be mailed. When his heart stopped for eight minutes and he was pronounced DOA, he came back. Not this time. Mother keeps saying "time heals." No, it doesn't. He said it best: "When you're dead you're dead." You stop showing up. You never show up anywhere ever again. All that's left are photographs.

Mrs. Wollner

I am home for the summer when, late one Sunday afternoon, there is a knock on the front door. Mother is in the bathroom, so I open the door and there stands Mrs. Wollner. She says she took a cab. It is so good to see her. I introduce her to Suki because I know she likes dogs. Mother fixes martinis. We sit on the terrace. Mrs. Wollner says she went to the Art Fair on South U. this afternoon in spite of the heat. We have been in a horrible heat wave, but Mrs. Wollner says that didn't keep the artists away. I forgot all about the Art Fair. We just go to work and come home. We don't drive near South U. anymore. Mother talks about Bruce Henry who owns Artisan's where Kate worked. I didn't know Bruce Henry started the Art Fair.

Mrs. Wollner says the Jones' at 1015 have fenced in an outdoor area by the screened porch for their fox terrier. I try to picture a little dog in our back yard which reminds me that Suki needs her walk, so I excuse myself. Mrs. Wollner asks if she can walk Suki with me. She hasn't finished her martini, but okay, fine. With Mrs. Wollner, Mother says, one must expect the unexpected.

We go out to the street. I can't tell if she likes Suki or not. Maybe she would like to have Suki.

"When I was growing up," she says, "we had a dog named Rex."

Then, she tells me Rex was a border collie. Border collies herd sheep. They round them up and bring them to the corner of the field, but there were no farms or sheep in Plymouth where she grew up, so Rex was bored. While she talks, I remember visiting her in the mental hospital. We sat outside on bouncy green aluminum chairs. We turn onto Vesper.

"I loved Marky," she says, which is so nice. "I watched him from my kitchen window . . . over by the pricker bushes. I miss Marky. And I miss your father."

I can't believe she said that. Nobody has said that. Not like she did. But then, more and more, I realize, when Mother reads letters aloud, all sorts of people say they miss him.

"Your father made an impression."

Impression is the perfect word.

"Have you heard from him?" asks Mrs. Wollner.

"Who?"

"Your father," she says. "I used to have visits from my father."

I point to the front window of the brick house.

"Sometimes there's a Dalmatian on that sofa looking out."

The Dalmatian isn't there.

"Your father was a patient man," she says. "Patient with me."

"I'm afraid he'll show up."

I can't believe I just said that.

We turn right on a street I never take and don't know the name of. Mrs. Wollner walks ahead, looking down. I let her walk alone for a few steps. At least it's a short street. We turn left on Robin Road. Then, she waits for me to catch up.

"What will you do if he does . . . show up?"

I was expecting her to say dead people don't show up.

"Think about it," she says, "so, when he does, you'll be prepared."

Leo

That night, I see my father standing in the middle of a basement room. He says, "Doin' okay?" and I say, "I'm okay. Are you okay?" and he says, "Don't worry about me."

I have this dream a few times. It doesn't frighten me. And it varies. Sometimes he starts burning, and he burns all the way and sometimes he only burns half-way.

Maybe he's burning up in front of me because I know he was cremated, or maybe it's because we've been watching the evening news with live pictures of the horrible fires and the race riots in Detroit—all these burning buildings and Black people fighting with the police. We don't usually watch the news at dinner time, but when Mother saw the article in *The Ann Arbor News*, she said, "we've got to watch—history is being made."

And every night since, we've been watching the news. We sit on my father's bed together. Mother's birthday is July 25, but we watch TV on that night, too, because the riot is still going on. She says it's much more important than her silly birthday.

I can't believe this is happening so close to us. Detroit is about an hour away by car. My father drove to Detroit every day for years. I wonder what he would have to say about these riots? My cousins live in Grosse Pointe, a white neighborhood in Detroit. The riots are downtown and in neighborhoods where Black people live, not Grosse Pointe. I have never had a Black person as a close friend. Schoolmates, yes. Neighbors, yes. Football players to cheer for, yes. And Tizzy and Vee Vee who weren't family, but felt like family.

Black people have had enough. I'm glad they're not taking it anymore.

The Northeast Corner

When Mother started working at the University Hospital, she was issued three white coats with "Social Work" embroidered in blue on the breast pocket. Now, she is down to one coat. I thought the hospital laundry lost the other two coats, but she said she hasn't the faintest idea how she misplaced them. She'll be issued two replacement coats once the new fiscal year starts in a week. I am well aware of that date now that I'm working again in the personnel office.

Last night, at dinner, she realized she forgot to bring home her one-and-only white coat to wash it, so, she said we need to leave by 8:00 a.m. tomorrow, which will give her time to go up to her office, get that white coat, wash the stains out in the bathroom sink, and get down to the Probst Auditorium on the ground level by 8:55 a.m. for the monthly Social Work Departmental Meeting.

It is now 8:25 a.m. and given it takes fifteen minutes to drive in, and the elevators are crowded in the morning, Mother has probably decided to skip the white coat and go straight to the meeting. Even if she is a few minutes late, all she has to do is walk in with her mind-on-higher-things expression, and they'll think she was handling a crisis, which would not be a lie. She is handling a crisis—it's just not on the sixth floor of the hospital. I can't get out of bed.

She looked horrible standing in the doorway a moment ago.

"Will you be getting up?" she said, not pushy, not ironic, lipstick smeared, too much rouge, hair lopsided. Every day, I rat her hair, spray it, and put makeup on her face, but today, I missed our beauty parlor session in front of her bureau.

Will you be getting up?

What do I say to that? *I don't see the point in getting up, and I don't see the point in telling you I don't see the point.*

I say nothing, so she disappears. I don't know where she is now.

I wonder if my father hated this ceiling as much as I do. Twelve acoustical tiles by twelve acoustical tiles, which is 144 tiles, plus six more tiles by the door, which makes a total of 150 tiles—three out of four digits of our old address. The design in each tile is meant to look like stepped-on cigarette butts, but if you look closely, the same cluster of eight is repeated four times per tile, a cheap manufacturing trick. My father would hate that. No wonder his mouth was always in a slit when he stared at this ceiling. Did he also stare at the window? Watch the daylight withheld first by the horizontal slats of the Venetian blinds, then by the vertical stripes in the curtains from 1015, a nice polarizing effect—where we used to live and where we live now at ninety degrees.

I hear the sound of water running in the bathroom; she's washing hair spray off her hands. The sound of electric can opener; she's feeding Suki. Ah well, if she walks into the meeting a few minutes late, she will not lose her job. I saw her personnel file. She got all tens on her evaluation. Besides, she's already reached the top of her salary range, which is $7,350, and it's not as if she has a merit raise pending; without a Master's degree in social work, she can't earn another penny.

"Will you be going into work?"

She's back. I wish she would just tell me to *get the hell out of bed*. But ever since my father died, she treats me like a china doll.

She has her plastic rain hat in one hand, her other hand buttoning her raincoat, dark blue stockings, and new navy pumps with clip-on bows. Mentally, I drive us down River Road, over the railroad tracks, past the purple house, the train station, the cobblestones, the Catholic church, the parking structure. Then we walk by the flower bed in front of the hospital, the colored stripes across the lobby floor which some man would have by now made brighter with his mop. I only have to get out of this bed, and the day will carry on with me inside it: waiting for the fan on Audrey's desk to revolve in my direction while I type the digits in the boxes on the new Change-of-Status forms. I typed Mother's form yesterday. I only had to make two changes: add her cost of living raise and change her marital status.

"Are you tired?"

I stare at the ceiling.

"Sleepy, then?"

She unfolds the plastic rain hat, ducks under it, ties the plastic straps. Is it raining? No, just incredibly humid. Humidity ruins her hair.

"I'll be in the car."

She could always call a black-and-white cab.

When I get out to the car, she is wiping the inside of the windshield with the pink washcloth I keep under the seat. Crack the window, don't crack it, open the air vent, run the defroster—no matter what I do, Opie fogs up.

When Mother sees me, she puts the washcloth on the dashboard, gets out, shuts the door quietly, and walks to the curb. I throw my bag in the back seat, slam the door, open the driver's door, grab the door frame, and push with one hand, steer with the other. Once I get Opie out in the street, I turn the wheel sharply, jump in, step on the brake pedal, pull up the emergency brake, check the rearview mirror, and pray no cars are coming over the top of the hill.

Mother gets in, pulls the door shut, puts her pocketbook on the floor, and folds her hands in her lap. Teamwork. I release the foot pedal then the emergency brake, step on the clutch, put the gear shift in second. Mother looks straight ahead. Not going to say anything. Not going to look at her watch. She has complete confidence in my timing with the clutch. Halfway down the hill, when I release the clutch and step on the gas, she grabs the dashboard as the car lurches forward.

When we cross the railroad tracks, she grabs the pink washcloth and wipes the windshield. Sweat dribbles down the inside of my arms. The back of my blouse is soaked. No black-and-white cabs at the train station. No nuns outside the Catholic church. When I pull around the flower bed in front of the main entrance, it's seven past nine. She puts the washcloth under the seat. She is going to be late because of me. I am going to be late because of me.

"See you at five-fifteen," she says.

"Where is the Probst Auditorium?"

"Not far," she says, closing the door.

Like the seven hills.

She lifts one hand to hold the rain hat in place and walks down the steps to the front door. My steady Mother. You would think it was a crisp, fall, kindergarten day, and she was waiting at the rock. Not feeling sorry for herself, not in a hurry, not rising to the occasion, or sinking, really. She was like this the night he packed his suitcase and left in a cab—absolutely level.

Hospital talk in the elevator revives me. *Multi-focal, not localized; Four thousand cc's, they canceled tumor board.* Doctors from foreign countries in their white coats with stuffed pockets and hard-to-pronounce names on their name tags, an electrician holding an orange cable—everybody trying to help someone sick or get some piece of equipment to work. I will never work in a gift shop again.

When I get to my desk, Audrey smiles, her long fingers curled around the telephone receiver.

Typing gives me something to worry about that I can do well. The way I see it, if I don't worry about fitting the correct digits and letters precisely inside the box, then, before you know it, typing the correct salary won't matter, and before long, nothing will matter. I am having a hard time getting anything to matter; but typing forms perfectly—I can do that, especially, with these new forms which have carbon painted sheets attached at the top with a tiny rubber seam. Usually, I can fit the employee name in the box if I use ten-point Prestige Elite, but for a few neurosurgeons, I have to switch to the smaller twelve-point Courier.

On my lunch hour, I go down to the laundry in the sub-basement to see when Mother's two white coats will be ready. The standing fans in every corner are doing no good at all. A short woman in a mop cap, her face glistening, says, "Next Wednesday." I take the back way to the elevator so I can pass by the morgue. Audrey told me it was around the corner from the carpentry shop. She said the bodies are brought down in a special elevator after ten o'clock at night. There are dents in the metal doors where the trolleys bump the door on their way in. My father did not die in this hospital. He did not get rolled down to this morgue. St. Joe's has its own morgue. The funeral parlor collects the bodies from the morgue.

Hospital basements are a kingdom all their own. They have their own carpentry shop, electrical shop, plumbing shop, their own store, and an enormous furnace room. People don't understand why I like hospitals. They think because my father died in a hospital, I should hate hospitals, but they're dead wrong. If he'd spent weeks in a sewer pipe, I would love sewer pipes.

By five o'clock, I have completed General Surgery and Otorhyno-laryngology. Tomorrow will be Infectious Disease, Ophthalmology, and Food Services. I want to ask Audrey about the morgue, but she's on the phone when I leave. Last week, she got a call from Muehlig's. Audrey used to be a beautician and hairdresser. Muehlig's hires her when a Black family wants an open casket. What I want to know is *do bodies go to the crematorium naked?*

Ted

When I get up to Mother's office at five-fifteen, she is filling out papers.

"Everybody wants to be discharged on Friday," she says, putting the form in a brown interoffice envelope. While she winds the string around the button, she doesn't smile or ask about my day, but she doesn't look annoyed, either. This is not the first time I have benefited from her life-and-death job. I don't think she remembers being late for her morning meeting. She takes off her white coat and folds it to fit in our striped tote bag. I tell her I stopped by the laundry and her replacement coats will be ready next Wednesday.

"That was thoughtful," she says, locking her office door.

"All day long," she says, referring to the rain outside the window in the waiting room. Another thing about hospitals; you completely blot out the rest of the world. The Personnel office has no windows; I didn't even know it was raining.

The dark circles under Mother's eyes look darker than ever in the elevator. No matter how much Erase she puts under her eyes in the morning, it's completely gone by the end of the day. In the overhead light, her hair looks crusty where she held the hair spray too close. There is a candy striper in the elevator in her pink and white uniform. My uniform was blue and white when I worked at the VA hospital. At least my father never went there.

We take the underground tunnel to the parking structure. Given the rain, I worry Opie won't start, but she does start. She knows we need a break.

"Thanks be to God," says Mother, reaching for the pink washcloth. She wipes dutifully. The streets are wet with leaves, small branches. The windshield wipers only work on high, but at least they work. We pass St. Joe's. There is a new sign with brighter neon letters over the main entrance. I ask why St. Joe's is a *Mercy* hospital.

"When you become a nun, you join an order. An order is like a sorority. The nuns at St. Joe's are Sisters of Mercy. Did I tell you Sister Cecelia wrote?"

She did not.

"She got married and moved to Grand Rapids. Now she can have all those Catholic children your father told her she ought to be having."

We drive past Mr. Weber's house.

"Did Mr. Weber have a car?"

"I beg your pardon?"

"Did Mr. Weber drive?"

"He must have. How else did he get to the high school?"

"High school?"

"Where you had your recitals."

"He could have taken a cab."

"True." Mother looks at me.

"How long did I study with Mr. Weber?"

"Six and a half years."

I remember my last recital. I played a Clementi Sonatina.

"What was his first name?"

"John."

We drive by Goodyear's. The rain is heavy, but no thunder or lightning. On the next corner is a Shell gas station. Mother doesn't say anything when I pull up to the gas pump. The mechanic runs over, pulling up the hood of his raincoat.

"Fill her up?"

"No, thank you. I have to pop the clutch every morning. Otherwise, she won't start."

He has a chip off his front tooth.

"Bring her tomorrow morning and I'll take a look. Give you a loaner for the weekend."

That was easy.

"And the right blinker is broken. And the windshield wipers only work on high."

"We open at ten."

He ducks back into the station. I can only make so many left turns. Mother looks at me again. We got paid yesterday. We can afford to have our car fixed.

I usually park at the end of the driveway to shorten the push to the street in the morning, but it's raining, and Mother has on new shoes, so I drive her up to the front path. She tightens her rain hat and makes a dash for the front porch, splashing through the puddles. I reverse to the end of the drive. With this much rain, I am going to be popping the clutch tomorrow; hopefully, for the last time.

I put the damp mail and *The Ann Arbor News* on the inlaid table by the window overlooking the driveway. My father made this table out of the mahogany he salvaged from Alice Lloyd's front hall before the Lloyd house was torn down. We took a wheelbarrow across Washtenaw. The table legs are the banisters from the Lloyd staircase. He let me work on it with him in his workroom in the basement. I put some of those pieces in their places.

Mother has turned the Alice Lloyd table into her desk with the scrapbook from Muehlig's beside her address book. He died six months ago, but she still gets occasional condolence letters. Condolence letters, flower arrangement cards, and telegrams all go in the basket. After she answers them, they go in the Moe's shoe box. She even kept my letter, which I wrote her the day after he died. I can see it now in the basket, the little ruffled, torn edge where I ripped it out of the notebook. I can't believe I wrote it in French. Her new shoes stuffed with newspaper are on the kitchen floor.

"Any mail?" she says putting pizza rolls in a baking pan.

"Two letters."

She puts the pan in the oven, takes our TV dinners out of the freezer, stabs the tinfoil with a fork, and sets them on top of the stove.

"Suki won't go out," she says.

This dog doesn't pee anymore, not even in the house. I looked around the basement last week—no pee. Mother thinks Suki is depressed. When I put her food down, she comes over to her bowl, sniffs, then turns away.

"Wine?"

When my cousins come for dinner, I have wine. Mother holds up a half-full bottle of Blue Nun. Fine. She pulls out the cork, pours me a glass, mixes a pitcher of martinis. We don't usually have pizza rolls, but why not; yesterday was payday.

I change into shorts and a t-shirt. I used to make my bed every morning, but I've let that go. My clothes are in a heap on the green chair. I am turning into Aunty Douglas. Mother changes into her blue swirl dress.

We sit by the window. Mother reaches for the silver letter opener, slices through a damp envelope. Several people have sent the cartoons my father drew on their Christmas boxes. My favorite is the one with Marky as the puppeteer holding the four of us on strings. Dr. Cairns's handwriting was so small, Mother had to get the magnifying glass. Dr. Margolis didn't send a letter, but he signed the condolence book "Dr. Sidney Margolis." She signed, "Mrs. Gwen Margolis, friend."

"Mary Campbell." Mother writes the name in the condolence book. "Old Monday Club." Then she picks up a blue airmail envelope.

"My sainted aunt! John Mason Brown in London! How on earth did *he* hear about your father?"

"Who is John Mason Brown?"

"Drama critic," she says, casually.

She reads the letter, looks at the return address again, then points to the bookcase.

"Second shelf at this end, see if you can find *To All Hands*."

I find it.

"*For Sambo*," she reads aloud, "*Whose book this really is and whose devoted friend is—Scoglitti! - John Mason Brown.*"

"Scoglitti?"

"The beach in Sicily where the Husky invasion went ashore."

She turns the pages until she finds what she's looking for.

"Listen. . . *The indefatigable Lieutenant Samuel F. Schneider* (he became Lieutenant Commander later) *and his crew of Navy photographers have managed to say superlatively well with their cameras . . .*"

Martini sip.

"John Mason Brown spoke over a public address system onboard the ship, giving news to the sailors so they knew what was happening elsewhere in the war."

I never knew about this book, or this man. Old newspaper clippings fall onto her lap. She unfolds one.

"Oh my. January 15, 1955. John Mason Brown came here to give a lecture in the Journalism program—*Brown Says World Crisis Harms Modern Writing*. After the lecture, your father presented him with a woodcarving."

I never knew this. I was seven. We were living at 1015.

"Daddy carved a bust of George Bernard Shaw and presented it to him. I always wondered why Shaw?"

I know. "Because John Mason Brown and George Bernard Shaw each have three names."

"That could be it."

I love her smile.

She hands me the clipping. There is a photograph of my father and John Mason Brown.

"Daddy wore a vest?"

"Vests didn't last."

"John Mason Brown looks bewildered."

"Because this tactless reporter had just said the woodcarving didn't look like Shaw, to which your father replied, 'How the hell should I know what Shaw looks like? That's how I *imagined* he looked,' to which John Mason Brown said, 'Sambo through-and-through,' and patted him on the back. He mentions that in his letter—here."

The letter is typed. Not one mistake. "*Everything he made was unmistakably his.*"

"Isn't that nice?" says Mother, putting the letter in her lap.

I love *indefatigable* and *unmistakable*.

There is a flash of lightning. One bushel of thunder. Two bushels of thunder. Three bushels of thunder. Sharp clap of thunder. The lightning is less than a mile away. She hands me the book, then re-reads

John Mason Brown's letter.

All through the book are candid photographs of sailors relaxing around the ship. One picture has sailors seated on benches on the ship's deck, their heads bowed, facing away from the camera.

I study their backs with the magnifier—tall, short, stocky, thin— there he is! Most of the sailors are wearing khaki shirts. My father is wearing a khaki jacket with epaulets, his head bowed.

"I found him!"

I give Mother the magnifier.

"Good for you."

We know his back and the shape of his head.

"I've been thinking . . . " she says, putting her stockinged feet on the footstool. "Would you like to organize his 4x5 negatives? They're in the basement. Make a list—you like lists."

Last week, she started giving his belongings away. Henry Lewis got his oil paints. She sent Uncle Grover his Viyella shirts. Cousin Suzy got his overcoat. Cousin Anne got his fishing hat. Kate got his wood-carving of the African chief. Tim got his Christmas vest and socks. I got his colored pencils, pencil sharpener, bow ties, and pocket knife.

"Are you giving away his 4x5 negatives?"

"Of course not. But they should be organized, don't you think?"

I picture the yellow Kodak boxes with his handwriting on the lid. It is just my sort of project.

"Where are the boxes?"

"I don't know."

Lightning flashes over Miss Bacon's house.

"Check his desk," she says.

They are not in his desk. Then I remember—the filing cabinet in the basement. I turn on the light. This railing is loose, too. What is it about the railings in this house? I turn the corner at the bottom of the stairs. Oh no! There is a huge puddle in the northeast corner spreading halfway across the room. I run back upstairs.

"When did Greg mow the lawn?"

"Tuesday. Did you find the boxes?"

"Flood."

"Oh dear. Should we check the drain?" She bites into a pizza roll. I don't expect her to help. She was forty-two when I was born. So was he. I pull off my sandals, grab my father's raincoat. There is a matchbook from the Standard Oil Gas Station in the pocket.

Greg, our paperboy, mows our lawn now, but I never showed him the trick about pulling the lawn mower backwards to blow the mown grass away from the stairwell. The grass he mowed Tuesday is probably clogging the storm drain again. I grab the pail by the back door.

The stairwell has about six inches of water. I reach down, pull out fistfuls of muck, leaves, and soggy grass. Where are these little sticks coming from? I put them in the pail, climb the steps, and dump the sludge over by the garage. Why is the pussy willow tree dropping leaves this early? I go back, put my hand over the drain, and feel the suction. Thank God the drain is working, but there are more leaves, and bits of sticks, and grass floating in the standing water. It will take a long time for the mint roots to do what Mother hopes they will do. This is a perfect example of erosion. I marvel that, after all these years, there is any dirt left on the bank at all. An hour's rain would be fine, but five hours is too much.

"How is it?"

I drape the raincoat over the sink.

"Do you need anything?"

She slits another envelope.

"Dinner won't be ready for forty-five minutes."

My father used to say *come hell or high water*. Well, this is hell *and* high water. It's 6:15 p.m. Dinner at 7:00 p.m. I go back down to the basement. Last summer, the rain came in under the stairwell door a few times, but never like this.

The bottom shelf of the bookcase is submerged. At least we got Bapa's books off that shelf. I move the armchair and the hooked rug. I find the broom in the laundry room. Either this foundation was never laid properly, or the house is sinking, or both. The rainwater spreads out with each sweep and wants to go right back where it thinks it belongs. I examine the laundry room drain, pull off the grate, pull out the bits of dryer lint, and put them in the bucket under the washtub.

I sweep the rainwater past the piano, through the doorway, and halfway across the laundry room floor, which is cement. Water moves faster on linoleum. For once, I am grateful for linoleum. Sweeping water has to be the most unsatisfying job on earth. Maybe a snow shovel would be more efficient. I could push the water further along. But Mother threw out our old shovel. We will need a new one next winter. Maybe Greg wants that job, too. We don't have a sidewalk, but we have a driveway and paths to the front and back doors.

By 6:25 p.m., the water is no longer trickling under the door and over the sill, and I've swept most of it down the drain in the laundry room. The rest will have to evaporate. If I keep unblocking the outdoor storm drain, maybe I can get ahead of it.

The raincoat has dripped all over the kitchen floor. Mother has set up the folding trays by our chairs next to the Alice Lloyd table, a paper napkin on each tray under a fork. I eat a cold pizza roll. She looks up from reading a long letter. Thunder booms. We look out the window. No lightning, just far away thunder and vertical rain. I eat another pizza roll. She flexes her feet. The toes of her stockings are stained blue from her new shoes. I go back outside.

"No coat?"

Muddy water is still coming over the retaining wall, but not collecting as much in the stairwell. I pull out a few more sticks and leaves and put them in the pail. The drain will probably clog again, but it hasn't yet. I empty the pail behind the pussy willow tree and turn it upside down on the retaining wall.

Mother is settled in for the night. She has her martini pitcher, letters to read and re-read and record in the condolence book, *The Ann Arbor News'* obituaries, and half a dozen pizza rolls, which should hold her for at least an hour.

Back down to the basement. Nothing trickling under the door. No puddle. I take a hand towel out of the clothes chute and wipe my face and arms and hands. My evening will be sweeping water. I rather like the physics of it. Nature demonstrating Herself. The condensation in the sky and all the conditions coming together to produce the rain. Gravity pulling the water down the bank, the size of the debris versus the size of the holes in the drain, the engineering of the drain and sewer system (which I know nothing about), our uneven floor, water which can't help seeking its own level. I feel peaceful. While the water accumulates in the stairwell, I will sort my father's black-and-white 4x5 negatives. It could be worse. I could be watching Mother get incrementally morbid upstairs.

My father's filing cabinet used to be in his bedroom. I never looked inside the filing cabinet because his colored pencils were always in his desk. When we moved out here, the movers put his filing cabinet in the basement, not in his room. That's sad. What if he needed what was inside? If the Kodak boxes aren't in here, I don't know where else they could be. He wouldn't have thrown them out. I know he wouldn't.

Top drawer: no yellow Kodak boxes—just brochures, and fly-fishing catalogs, and band books—band books! I haven't seen his band book in such a long time! *Fundamentals of the Michigan Marching Band.* He photographed the Michigan Marching Band practicing, in uniform, holding their instruments. What was his name, the conductor? My father had the book printed, then he built a plywood cart, painted the cart blue with a yellow "M," and attached two wheels. Revelli! That was the conductor's name. One Saturday, we pushed the cart to the stadium and wheeled it around at half time. When we got home, Mother said it had been too far for me to walk, but we had such a good time. He only sold a few band books at the stadium, but he didn't give up. I remember checks coming in envelopes from high schools in other states for a dollar or two dollars.

Second drawer: manila file folders. I love seeing his handwriting— he always wrote in pencil—Libby Owens Ford, General Motors, Kellogg's, Argus Camera, King-Seeley. These folders are empty. Why did he keep them? No, one folder has a typed label: GOOD IDEAS. Inside, are letters on stationery from companies in New York, N.Y., addressed to Samuel F. Schneider on Ferdon Road.

I pull off the rusty paper clip. How did he get the addresses for these New York companies? He must have gone downtown to the Ann Arbor Library. Too bad he didn't make carbon copies of what he wrote.

President Horton has asked me to reply to your letter of March 12, 1961, describing your dandy idea . . . Dandy is just the word my father would have used. *Although we realize that your idea has merit, we do not feel that at this time . . .* All these letters were written not by the president, but by someone the president tasked with replying politely to Mr. Schneider in Ann Arbor. *I question whether a book as expensive as the one you propose could be justified.* These are so depressing. *Next time you're in the area again.* As if he drove Borgie to New York City every day!

The last person to touch this paper clip was him. I put it back on the letters and put the folder in front of the other folders. He didn't call this folder REJECTIONS. He called it GOOD IDEAS. He believed in himself. I wish I had his mock-up of the toast flying out of the Sunbeam toaster.

Thunder. More rain.

Water is trickling under the door again. I return the folders to the file drawer and go back upstairs and outside.

This time, I pull out cigarette butts (my father's?), a Snickers candy wrapper (Greg's?), more sticks, and grass. Down by the plum tree, it's starting to look like a lake. When I go back inside, Mother has moved on to the classifieds.

"You're soaking wet."

She doesn't mention the mud I am tracking all over the floor.

"Would you check the oven?"

What is there to check? TV dinners are covered in foil.

I look inside anyway. Yup, covered in foil.

"Shall I turn it off?"

No answer.

"What happened to the dehumidifier?"

"It broke."

I turn off the oven, go back downstairs.

Not nearly as much water as before, but this is going to be a long night. It's almost eight o'clock. No wonder we got this house for a song. I get very little water down the drain this time. I just increase the surface area so it will evaporate more quickly. Every fifteen minutes, I will have to check the storm drain outside.

Back to the file cabinet.

In the third drawer are big manila envelopes with photographs of planes landing on aircraft carriers, sailors staring at the sea, aerial shots of islands with palm trees. This time, he used the orange wax pencil to write on the envelopes USNR Chenango, USNR Hornet, USNR Enterprise.

In the bottom drawer, I finally find his Kodak film boxes—his handwriting in India ink on the bright yellow cardboard. I take the boxes over to the sofa and position the standing lamp. Mother was right; this is just my sort of job. I run back upstairs, find a legal pad and pencil on his desk, sharpen the pencil, grab the magnifier from the Alice Lloyd table, and run back down.

He wrote on every film box in India ink, identifying the negatives inside using our initials.

"Children playing on floor"

"K with lamb"

"K with ball"

"Day Street"

"M haircut"

"C in diaper"

"C & K on swing"

"K with brades" He never could spell.

There is a box marked "Christmas Cards," and a box marked "JFK

AA," and a box marked "Advertising" with negatives from all those times we posed for his mock-ups. I hold the negatives up to the standing lamp. It takes a minute to get used to reading them in reverse: me in a sleeveless blouse holding a box of Rice Krispies, wearing the red cap sideways for a jaunty look. I suppose he took a color slide of that one so the red cap could do its job. Marky on the grass with the Argus C3 camera next to his paws, my friend Emmy and me spinning the gyro in the driveway. Me, older, on the Lawn-Boy; Kate looking exhausted, her suspenders falling down, holding Mother's old leather doll. These were all taken when he worked at Argus Camera. One of Kate with the leather doll was published in the *Saturday Evening Post* with the caption: "What would you give for a picture like this? Give <u>Argus</u>."

Mother has put on the trumpet music.

The box marked "Henry Lewis" has pictures of his retirement party at St. Andrew's taken in the parish hall. The box marked "Shakespeare" has pictures of a tackle box, fishing rods, reels, flies, a woman sitting on a bed. What? What woman? What bed?

I hold the negative up to the light. I grab the magnifier. Striped curtains, gooseneck lamp, window next to the bed, venetian blinds— his bed in his bedroom in this house. The woman sitting on the bed has wide apart eyes, big mouth. Gwen. I drop the negative. I pick up the next one. Different pose, legs crossed, head tilted, skirt and blouse. I drop that negative. I pick up the next one. Now she's leaning back, legs uncrossed, barefoot. Drop that negative. Pick up another. My hand is shaking. When I saw the Bill Knapp's matchbook in his bedside table drawer, I thought she might be coming over to take him to lunch, but I talked myself out of believing it. I let it get hazy. Well, it's not hazy anymore. Gwen drove out to this house. She went into his bedroom. She sat on his bed. She took off her shoes. He stood by the doorway with his Speed Graphic Camera, which is still in the basement, which means he went down to the basement to get the Speed Graphic and climbed back up the stairs. Then he put his Speed Graphic back in the basement.

I put down the negative. I go into the laundry room. Over by the furnace is a small closet. We put his darkroom trays in there, his Speed Graphic, and his enlarger, and some boxes, I think. He never set up his darkroom here—or did he?

I open the door to the closet. I feel around for the overhead string, pull it. The white enamel, blue-rimmed trays are on one shelf. There is an old mop leaning in the corner, a flowerpot on the floor filled with dry dirt, a dusty Monopoly game on the top shelf, an old rag with rust stains hanging on a nail. And, in the corner, something covered with dish towels. I pull off the dish towels to reveal his 4x5 Speed Graphic, the strap on one side where he slid his hand through. Next to it are some film holders. He never set this closet up as a darkroom, and his enlarger, I just remembered, is in the attic, in the cubby hole off my bedroom. So, he came down to get his camera when she was coming over. Maybe she bought film for him at Purchase Camera on her way across town. I turn out the light and close the door.

I am surprised he would hide these negatives in a Kodak box marked "Shakespeare," which my Mother could relate to and might have opened. But in my father's world, Shakespeare was a fishing tackle company and fishing at the Margolises' fishing camp was how he got to know Gwen. I put the lid on the Shakespeare box and slide it under the sofa cushion. I need to get rid of that box. Maybe Gwen drove him in her car so he could go into Purchase Camera and place the order, then, a week later, after they picked up the prints, they came back here to look at the prints in his bedroom, to lie down together. Was his heart racing? Is that why I could find only one nitroglycerin tablet in his drawer? When he didn't answer the phone, I thought he was asleep or out in the yard.

I walk up the stairs, tiptoe through the kitchen and out the back door, rain pouring down. I stand in the stairwell. The water is level with the bottom of the door. I lean against the retaining wall and stare at the mud and rain flowing over the edge. It's getting dark. There is a light on at Miss Bacon's house.

With the exception of our last Christmas card, taken in 1961 when he was drunk, and those pictures of Kennedy and Tom Payne he took the night he lost his bifocals on the tarmac, his negatives were always sharp as a pin. Those bedroom negatives were in focus. He knew exactly what he was doing, nothing drunken or hasty about it.

"Are you out there in that rain? What's going on?"

The terrace light comes on. She can't see me.

"Is the drain still blocked?"

Mother peers around the screened door. Handel's "Water Music" in the background. Perfect.

"Where are you?"

"Clearing the drain."

"Take a nice warm shower when you come in."

She steps away from the door. A few seconds later the music stops. Then it resumes. She turned the record over. Purcell's "Voluntary."

Maybe Gwen took him for drives along the river. Maybe he talked to his hobos. That would explain why he never asked to go anywhere. He wasn't a prisoner; he was getting out all the time. They could have stopped for a pack of cigarettes along the way, stopped at Purchase Camera, had lunch at Bill Knapp's. When he left with his suitcase, maybe it was Gwen who brought him back. When Kate was living here, Gwen would have had to stay away until Kate went to work.

Water is rising. I pull out more grass and leaves and sticks, sling them in the pail. There was talk about building a new retaining wall, talk of replacing the outside basement door and pouring a new basement floor, but after Jay left and I moved out, Mother gave up. Her solution: Remember what somebody said about pianos needing humidity so you don't need to waste money on another dehumidifier that will only burn itself out. Concentrate on sick children, find solace in writing and receiving letters, reading obituaries, and sipping gin. Mother is like this water; she is finding her own level.

A dead mouse washes over the retaining wall. I dip the rim of the pail next to the little pink feet until the mouse floats into the pail. I go back up the steps, empty the pail behind the garage. There was a time when I would have buried that mouse and said a prayer.

When I check the drain again, nothing is blocking it—but the water is not receding. I feel with my feet. No suction. The storm sewer can't take any more water. I've seen that at intersections—water bubbling up.

The kitchen floor is covered in muddy footprints. Mother won't mind. Being late for work, the car not starting, flooded basement, muddy kitchen floor—very little bothers her anymore. What does bother her? "A badly written obituary," she said last night.

"Now come dry off," she calls.

How did she get like this? A widow who reads obituaries, wears makeup, works nine to five, comforts the families of sick children, drinks martinis, eats TV dinners, saves the washed-out tin trays for the hospital playroom?

She rests her elbow on the arm of the chair, rests her head on her hand, and closes her eyes. She hasn't asked about Bapa's books getting wet, or the Steinway, or the Meissen under the basement stairs in dish cartons which, if they get wet, I suddenly realize, will start to collapse.

I run downstairs to check the dish cartons. At least someone, probably Jay, thought to put several boards underneath them. And the water hasn't reached the closet yet.

The water has, however, made it all the way to the back leg of the piano. I try sweeping at different speeds, from different angles. It makes no difference. The last time the basement flooded, I squirted food coloring to see if I could determine the direction the water was going in, which was fun, but a waste of time. The water was only going in one direction—towards the northeast corner.

Clap of thunder. I sweep more. By the time I get to the laundry room, there isn't much water ahead of the broom; it has all spread out or receded.

I splash back to the puddle in the northeast corner, which is now rising fast. What if it gets as high as the light socket on the baseboard molding? Where is the fuse box? I resume sweeping. It's 8:50 p.m. At some point, this rain has to stop. Will the drain in the laundry room back up, too? Where does the water in all the drains all over the city end up? I have no idea, but this water knows exactly where it's meant to be. All those water molecules outside in the stairwell know that on the other side of the rotting door, it's lower, and lower is better. Lower is the destination. They don't mind that there is a door. A door stops burglars. It does not stop water.

Big strokes. Long strokes. Did Gwen come in the back door or the front door? No wonder my father was rude to our neighbors. I wonder if Mother's choice of a west-side neighborhood was to get him away from Gwen. Well, that backfired. Nobody out here would recognize Gwen's car. What about the morning he had his heart attack? Was Gwen watching while Dr. Margolis swallowed more cornflakes? And when my father was in the hospital week after week, she must have felt like I felt—frantic to see him—but with Mother keeping vigil, how could she visit? How did she feel signing *friend* in the funeral book? Driving across town to see my father even when he was getting older, and sicker, and thinner, and wasn't handsome anymore—maybe she loved him.

I can't believe I just thought that, but the word *love* is sinking in, and it doesn't feel wrong. It feels like how life sometimes turns out.

I turn the broom around and try pulling the water instead of pushing—no improvement. Maybe I'm pushing too hard. Maybe the clue is to push very slowly. Molecules don't ask questions. They just succumb to the uneven floor. Did he call her Gwen? I know he called her Honey.

"How's it going?"

Mother comes down a few steps and leans around the railing.

"It's not going."

"I turned off the oven."

No, I did.

She goes back upstairs. The gravy around the Salisbury steak will have a skin on it, and the peas will be wrinkled, the blueberry muffin scorched.

The water is now pouring onto the floor from under the door. The storm drains are definitely backed up. Maybe I should get Mother down here to help. Maybe I should unpack the Meissen and set the plates on the piano.

I put down the broom. I lift the lid on the keyboard. I turn on the lamp which has been on the piano my whole life, the pewter base decorated with pewter ginkgo leaves. I play a C-major chord. It sounds fine. I should write a letter to the Steinway company, recommending they stand their pianos in three inches of Midwestern rainwater.

"The Shepherd Boy" is on the music rack. Bapa learned to play it for my grandparents' fiftieth wedding anniversary—the oversized music sheets with the flaky edges and the drawing of the shepherd and his flock. I should be able to manage this simple piece. The sound of the shepherd's pipe in the right hand going up and down the scale, then the variation that repeats, then back to the melody. Do I remember the chords? I do—amazing—then a lazy, uphill climb to the final G.

Somewhere at the back of the Fireside Songbook is "Waltzing Matilda" with the picture of the swagman dancing with the kangaroo. The third verse is my favorite, about the stockman riding on his thoroughbred, *down came the troopers, one, two, three.* There is even a little glossary at the bottom of the page. Swagman means hobo. I didn't know that.

Can she hear me? Probably gone back to her chair. Do advertising-printing-salesmen have obituaries? I don't remember seeing one in the paper. Yes, I do. There was a small paragraph written by Muehlig's.

I open the *Scott Joplin Songbook.* Those slow, dreamy first few stanzas of "Solace," not too shabby. I'm better at going slow now, and the syncopation feels natural.

Chopin "Preludes." I played "the Raindrop" in Aunt Ginny's living room the night he died, all those gray greens around me. I feel like "Raindrop" now—No. 15. Two of the digits of our old house. I am getting cornier and cornier. Do I care? What do I care about? I care about music. I care about Mr. Weber. I recognize his handwriting, a big penciled "C" under the opening *crescendos*. The *Ped* still looks like a little spaniel, but what does the tiny snowflake mean after the *Ped*? I never learned to pedal because Mr. Weber moved to California.

My left hand is weak, little finger on the A-flat getting tired, but I can do the eighth notes. Typing has paid off. The theme returning at the bottom of the page was always a relief, but I still dread the storm on the next page, all those bass notes for the left hand below the staff—amazing, I can still read them. The key change to four sharps, but a G-sharp now instead of an A-flat repeating and then those big right-hand octaves. The melody is weak in the left hand—too bad. I try to lighten the right hand, but the left hand is weak—too bad.

Now the storm, building slowly in the left hand leading to the double forte thunder burst. I never conquered this section. The same feeling of barely keeping up, not in control, stumbling through wrong notes and wrong tempo. But I manage the double *forte* bass octaves— no problem with those.

Now, another chance to get the thunderburst right—not great—but I love the chord changes afterwards. The left hand with more octaves again and those great chord changes, not easy, getting to the *piano* section.

Top of last page—I always loved this part—all the way across. Amazing. Not too many wrong notes—good for me. The next section with a lot of flats, sharps, naturals—not so good— but the octaves in the left hand are solid. A few more flats and sharps as I head home— not too bad—then the gorgeous *diminuendo*. Amazing, what the hand remembers.

Now, raindrops falling, ten sixteenth notes, which I used to play quickly, but *smorzando* means fading away, dying gradually. Oh yes, much better. So much better—*smorzando*.

Now, the final *forte* in the right hand all alone. Heavy, steady quarter notes coming down, storm over, drops heavier, hard to play softly, hard to give each note equal weight, steady, very steady, all the way to the double *pp pianissimo*.

Now the final six bars, and there's my spaniel—pedal down—and there's my snowflake, which must mean—I get it—*Release*. Release the pedal.

Release was one of Marky's commands. It meant he was free.

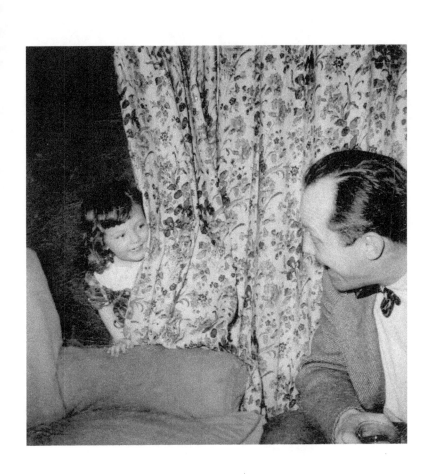

Acknowledgments

Thank you, Richard Shafer for introducing me to Shakespeare, theatre and language. Thank you, Robert Willis for insisting in 1984 that I take a writing class at The New School. Thank you, Richard Brickner for saying, "Now tell me what you've seen this week with those God-damned eyes of yours." Thank you, Alice Morris for saying the only thing you ever regretted was "When you went against your nature." Thank you to my parents for allowing me to bewilder you and for teaching me to cherish people, not things. Thank you, Daddy, for every moment we had together; I hope you understand that I'm talking straight. Thank you, Mother, for showing me how to cast my bread upon the waters and to respect every living thing. Thank you, Katie, not only for your beauty which I miss, but for never making sarcastic remarks when you had to change my address in your address book one more time. Thank you, Charles Clubb for making me "Stand behind my words" and thank you, Barry O'Donnell for your faith that I had something to offer. Thank you, Marky, Crispin, Tweed and Hal, for giving me so much joy.

Let me now thank the living. Dear John, thank you for giving me space to write, for being an honest, wise, faithful and loving sound-board. Thank you, Suzy Lincoln, Anne Arthur, Tom and Joanne Tilley, Peggy Hagen, Janet Macidull, Flora May Wuellner, Nina Hauser, Michael Pardy, Michael Cullen, Bronwen Crothers, Harriet and George Price, Denise Finn, Marcia Wood, Jennifer Harmon, Peter Goldmark and Susan Szeliga for your encouragement. Thank you, Erin Helmrich, Sonya Vann DeLoach and especially Emily Murphy at The Fifth Avenue Press.

Lastly, thank you reader.

Colby was born and raised in Ann Arbor, the inspiration for *The Northeast Corner*. After graduating from UM, she and her husband ran a photography business in the Nickels Arcade. Her passion for theatre took her to graduate acting school at Wayne State University's Hilberry Theatre, followed by further training at The Circle-in-the-Square Theatre School in New York City where she studied acting with Nikos Psacharopoulos, subsequently performing at his Williamstown Theatre Festival for several years. In 1979, she partnered with Charles Clubb at his Off-Off-Broadway The Theatre Exchange, a 50-seat loft theatre in Tribeca. After the death of Mr. Clubb in a tragic accident, Colby left the theatre and began writing. Several of her short stories have been published. Her as-yet unpublished *Bicycle Boy* involves the mysterious death of Mr. Clubb and the closing of The Theatre Exchange. Colby was based in New York City for 30 years. Over several periods of living and writing in Ireland and the UK, she developed lifelong friendships with an elderly farmer in Shropshire, the subject of her current book project *Fos-y-Rhiew*, and with a country doctor in North Wales, who inspired her as-yet-unpublished novel *Locum Tenens*. Since returning to Ann Arbor in 2006, she has been able to focus on her writing. Her one-act play *Somewhere Between Lost and Found* was performed in Ypsilanti, and her full-length play *Bird of Passage* premiered at The Bagaduce Theatre in Maine in 2019. Colby lives with her husband in Ann Arbor.

Printed in the USA
CPSIA information can be obtained
at www.ICGtesting.com
JSHW020745311024
72716JS00005B/6

9 781956 697377